ASPEN AND THE DEMON PRINCESS

ALEXANDER CHAU

E-Book ISBN: 979-8-9909557-1-4

Paperback Print ISBN: 979-8-9909557-0-7

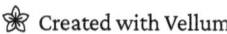 Created with Vellum

PART ONE

"It's my birthday. I can cry if I want to," Aspen says, softly wiping up his dried-up tears while still lying lazily on his bed. "Will I be alone again this year?" Although today was supposed to be his special day, it was a day he did not look forward to in the slightest. After all, there was no one he'd be celebrating it with.

"I just want mom's homemade stew for my birthday, it's not asking for a lot," Aspen wished aloud as he clasped his hands together. Oh, how he loved his mom's homemade stew: marinated beef, homegrown carrots, fresh potatoes, and a secret ingredient she would never reveal. Just thinking about it, he could almost taste it— how it was so hot it burned his mouth, how the carrots seemed to melt on his tongue, and the succulent smell that wafted in the air. But that wish would never be granted as his mother was dead.

Although, he was not completely alone. His father was still around. But *he* was just about useless, like the broken clock down-stairs in the living room, when it came to being a nurturing parent.

Aspen peered around his room. The clothes he wore yesterday were still scattered across the floor. His winter scarf still laid atop his desk. Everything was as it should be. Except it wasn't. He jumped out of his bed and opened the window, letting the sharp January winds strike his exposed face. The cold breeze felt good against the bags under his eyes. After taking one long deep breath, he closed the window.

His mother was gone, gone for years now. But there are times where he'd have dreams of her, dreams that seemed so real that it lulled him to a false sense of security. It made him feel like he wasn't alone, as if wrapped around the warm embrace of familiarity. Although those dreams terrified him, these were the only times when he was able to relive the happy memories of his mother and father and go back to a simpler, more blissful time. And every time, without fail, the sweet dream quickly turns sour, morphing into a nightmare, and ends with him back in reality, devastatingly abandoned.

Aspen slapped his face twice, "Stop thinking about it, there's no point anymore." He headed to the bathroom to wash his face and get ready for the day.

As he brushed his teeth, Aspen stared at the mirror and couldn't help but see his father in his reflection, from his messy black hair and awkward smile to the dimples on his face. One of the few things he hadn't inherited from his father were his eyes. His father's eyes were black while his eyes were blue, as blue as precious sapphires bathing in sunlight. *Those* he inherited from his mother.

"Aspen, you better get down here and eat your breakfast before school! Hurry up!" The sound of his father's sudden outburst made him drop his toothbrush. He'd better hurry or his father was going to scold him for the millionth time. Aspen rushed downstairs, almost tripping on the last step, but luckily caught himself at the last second. He sat down at the kitchen table, stared at his breakfast, and groaned. Burned toast and burned eggs, not that he wasn't thankful, but he'd basically eaten it for the hundredth time in a row. Oh, how he yearned for his mom's fresh, hot pancakes at this moment. Each bite would melt in his mouth, bursting into a sugary sweet flavor that made it hard to contain his squeals of delight. Instead, here he was, having to eat around the burnt bits of what is supposed to be breakfast.

He glanced at his dad; his hair and appearance was unkempt as usual, and the big scar that ran from his right lower eyelid to the bottom of his cheek was as visible as ever. His dad hadn't always had that scar (a result from the war). Ever since returning from the battlefield, and then losing his wife, he'd changed, both outwardly and inwardly. Sometimes his dad would appear in his dreams. Clean, scarless, and without the nasty scowl he normally wore, a far cry from reality. Sometimes he wished that version of his father was here with him now.

His dad sat across from him and opened up the newspaper. He typically read the newspaper before he started his day as Mayor Ben Chase of this quaint town, Grasalia; a role that surprisingly fit his character, even though his appearance may give a different impression.

Ever since his mom had passed, it had become difficult for Aspen to open up to his dad. Years ago he used to sit on top of his father's shoulders and they would explore the woods and talk for hours on end. Nowadays, every time he tried to speak to him it always ended with awkward silence or a cold, snappy remark. Though, it was his twelfth birthday, so he thought today might be different. Aspen took a bite of his burned toast, "Hey, Dad, you know—"

"Finish your breakfast and hurry on out to school," his father scolded, burying his face deeper into this morning's newspaper. Ben nonchalantly poured his flask into his coffee and took a sip.

He did as he was told. After consuming the last bite of eggs, Aspen licked his lips. "Dad, today—"

His dad shook the newspaper, almost ripping its sides. "Those no-good animals deserve to go away! Off with them! Just kill them all! The world's a better place without them red demons!"

When his dad got like this, there was no point in talking to him. Aspen slipped away, put his dishes in the sink, and headed out the door for school. He sighed to himself. *Well, it's not like it wasn't expected, right?* Ever since his mom passed away, his dad hadn't been the same. Always distant, always angry.

The winter chills sent shivers down his spine, and each step became slightly less bearable than the last. Aspen looked around; it was that time of year when all the leaves had fallen from the trees, no animals in sight. He figured that all of the animals were snuggled up with their families in their nice little warm homes. A part of him wanted to ditch school and grab a hot chocolate, but the thought of his dad finding out quickly made him rethink this plan. A gust of wind blew his way, and he clutched his badly knit white scarf even tighter, rewrapping it around his neck. It was his most prized possession—not only did it keep him warm, but it also was one of the last few things he had to remember his mother. From what Aspen could recall, she wasn't the greatest at sewing, which could explain some of the patchwork on the scarf and the comically large length of it (for a six year old at the time). But she did try her best, and that thought is what made him treasure it even more.

It had always been difficult for Aspen to talk about his mother's passing with others. She was sick and bedridden a few years ago, but still acted strong in front of him, so that he wouldn't worry. Still, even at the young age of eight, Aspen knew what was going on and worried about his mother's situation behind closed doors. His mother was a strong woman, but her illness had robbed her of that and left her with extreme weight loss and a fatigue so great she struggled to get out of bed. The doctors couldn't help, even they were stumped as to what to do when she started coughing up enough blood to fill several kitchen cups. And then there were the even more useless neighbors who would swing by and talk to her, consoling Aspen, telling him that, "She's a strong woman that one, she'll be up and running around the house in no time." Back then, Aspen was mad about how useless they were, being more of a nuisance than help, and, of course, he wasn't an exception. He felt completely helpless, knowing that whatever he did, he could never stop the impending doom that was to befall his dear mother— and this was the worst feeling he had ever known. The only person who had taken it worse than Aspen was his father.

It was around that time when a small war broke out between the humans and the demons. All the able-bodied men were sent over to the northern front around the town Cresnough, about a hundred miles north of Grasalia, to fight, with his father being no exception. Aspen couldn't remember much besides the fact that his father came back early near the end of the war, due to injuries. Though, by the time he came back, his mother had already lost her last fight. In her final moments she was gasping for air, fighting to cling onto life until her lungs had failed her. His father had always said if only he could have come home sooner, maybe things would have turned out better somehow This was probably the reason why he resented the demons so much.

As Aspen stepped into town, he could smell the scent of freshly baked bread and hear the droll conversations of fellow townspeople complaining about the weather. *Bong!* The clock tower rang loudly, almost deafening him. *Well, this means I have about fifteen minutes to get to class. Just in time.* He had just enough time to do his daily stroll around town, imagining all the other places he'd rather be than at school.

Aspen stared at the bakery window, gazing at the fresh loaves of bread and cakes decorated with his favorite fruits. At the very sight, his jaw lowered to the ground. *No, no,* he thought to himself— cakes were definitely not something he should be spending money on right now. Though reluctant, he briskly strolled past the shop. Around the corner, he could hear a few men rattle on loudly. Whatever it was about made everyone agitated, like a bunch of wild monkeys fighting over a banana. Curiosity got the best of him, and he leaned a little closer to listen in on their conversation.

"Those red demons are like animals themselves. Ya hear that they hunt other animals in the woods and just swallow 'em then and there?" exclaimed one of the men.

"You better watch out yourself, Kenny," chuckled the other man standing across from him. He wore a shirt two times his size, dotted with holes. Aspen couldn't understand how the man wasn't freezing over. "Those animals eat humans, too, especially little kids!" The man looked over in his direction and winked at Aspen, as if trying to scare him. Which, to be honest, worked a little bit.

"The world would be better off without them!" babbled another while precariously swinging a bottle of hard liquor. This man was notorious for being drunk before one would hear the birds sing in the morning. One look at him, and you could tell he'd reek of alcohol. Aspen had seen the group of men before in the mornings on his daily strolls, and without fail, he would usually see this particular person already drunk while on his way to school. "A good demon is a dead demon is what I always say, even them tiny ones! Back when we were warring with them, I swear I took out a hundred of 'em."

"Sure, Jeremy, you keep telling yourself that," someone said sarcastically. "So, if one was right in front of you right now, what would you do?"

"Why, I'd shoot them dead on the spot, of course! I'll kill any before they even get a chance to speak!" Jeremy shouted.

Jeremy stared into the distance and yelled, "Hey, Abe, come over here." A soldier across the street walked over to the group of men. He looked pretty young for his age, couldn't be five, maybe six years older than Aspen. The young man was wearing a brand new soldier uniform, albeit one size too large. "I'm getting too old to get them demons, you have to get them in my place! You hear?" Jeremy declared.

The soldier chuckled. "Of course. When I see one, I'll pop 'em in your honor, sir." He brandished his rifle with a wide smirk on his face as he spoke.

Aspen walked away from the group; he couldn't bear to listen to any more of their rambling nonsense. Maybe he was the odd one out. Everyone in town seemed to share the same sentiment as the group of men—all demons are bad, the world is better off without them. It's not like Aspen himself particularly cared for them, but he always pondered whether all of them were actually that bad. Where there were bad demons, there were bound to be good ones too, right?

If it came down to having to be in the same room as a demon versus being stuck in a room and having to hear Old Man Jeremy ramble on, there's no way I'd survive listening to his story, Aspen thought to himself. Then, with a little chuckle, *Yeah, the second option is definitely the worst of the two.* Aspen walked past a few more stores until he heard his name called out nearby.

"Hey, Aspen, come over here real quick."

Aspen turned around, this voice sounding familiar to him. He locked eyes with an older gentleman, the owner of the sweets and confectionery store. Most kids would drop by after school to satisfy their sweet tooth here, the store had it all—from gum drops to chocolate to sour things to gummies. Everyone called him Old Man Willey, and he was one of the nicest people you would ever meet in this town.

"Sorry, sir, I wasn't paying attention at all," Aspen apologized, putting on the most sarcastic but playfully apologetic face he could make.

"Sir?" Old Man Willey scoffed. "Only strangers call me *sir*, are we really strangers? Were we never friends?" he said in a joking manner and then went back to restocking the candies on the top of the shelves. The two of them could hear the group of men lamenting about how the world would be better off without the demons from inside the store. "Boy, I wish they would stop yapping on about that stuff. Half of them probably have never seen one with their own two eyes. They're probably just as bad as the monsters they hate for making us listen to their blabbing all morning."

"Yeah, that's true." Another thing that Aspen liked about Willey was that he was different from most of the townspeople, he always saw things differently.

"Oh, do you need any help with that?" Aspen asked, watching him slowly and carefully step up the ladder. Old Man Willey had a bad leg, some say it happened during the war, but no one knew exactly how.

"Oh, come on now, I ain't that old yet. Step inside, it's cold out," Willey said as he finished stuffing the top shelves with candies.

Aspen kicked all the snow off his shoes and walked in. Instantly, he was embraced by the warmth of the stoves that were running, melting away the numbness of his toes and fingertips. He closed his eyes and took a deep breath, smelling the alluring sweetness of the chocolate and freshly baked cookies in the air, and then proceeded to open them to stare down the rows of all sorts of chocolates and gummies one could imagine. His eyes darted from one corner of the store to the next, mesmerized by all the bright colors. It was hard to imagine that such a place belonged to his hometown filled with drunks, cold winters, and bleak skies.

"So, Aspen, give me the truth, Are you alright?" Willey asked with a stern look, resembling a concerned parent.

Aspen averted his eyes and gave a nervous chuckle. "What do you mean? Of course, I'm fine."

"I saw them bullies picking on you again...what was his name?" Willey scratched his head as if he was trying to dig out the answer. "Little Gerard!" he exclaimed. Willey leaned in closer. "Yes, if he's bothering you again, you come see me. I will talk to his parents for you and set that kid straight." He patted him on his shoulder—a gentle reminder that he'd be watching out for him.

"No, no, no, we're just kids you know, we're just playing around," Aspen explained nervously. *Hopefully, he doesn't realize that I'm lying,* he thought. Little Gerard, who was actually not so little, was a kid in his class. He and his goons were stereotypical bullies that relished making everyone's lives miserable. And unfortunately, Aspen had been his target for quite some time now, which started perhaps a few months after his mom had died. Aspen was always nervous when morning came because he knew who was waiting for him in the classroom. This partly contributed to why he had always taken the long way through town to school, trying to delay as much time as possible before he had to deal with Gerard's squirmy, displeasing face.

Involving the adults would only bring out more trouble for him. Everyone always sided with Gerard anyway. He could basically get away with anything because everyone was either afraid or tried to suck up to his father.

Willey looked unconvinced, but eventually gave in and took a deep breath. "Well, if he ever bothers you too much, just give him a good knock in the face," he said with a smile. "But just know, if you ever need some help, you just let me know."

Aspen smiled widely. "You betcha." He looked at the clock behind Willey and his happy grin quickly flipped upside down. "Sorry, Willey, I'm late for school. I'll come back and chat next time!" He made a dash for the door.

"Wait, one more thing!" Willey yelled before Aspen could run out.

Aspen turned around to Willey, who was holding out a large, gold tin-foiled chocolate bar. It sure looked good, and also looked expensive.

"Here you go, Aspen," Willey smiled as he forcibly gave him the chocolate bar, already knowing he wouldn't take it willingly. "It's your birthday, isn't it? Happy birthday!"

"T-thank you, I appreciate it a lot." Aspen put the chocolate bar in his backpack. His eyes were almost watering, but stopped midway. He hated how emotional he got. Why was he *this* happy that someone—Old Man Willey, no less—remembered his birthday?

"Now get on, get to school, don't want to be late," Willey said as he ushered him to the door.

Aspen thanked him once more and then ran straight to school, making it in time with just a minute to spare.

CHAPTER
ONE

"So, did the demons really come from beneath the ground and come to eat us?" Ingrid asked, a classmate of Aspen's who was gullible beyond belief.

"No, Ingrid, though we call them demons, that is actually a nickname. They are not actual demons that spawned in," Mr. Gallafo informed her. Today, Aspen's homeroom teacher was teaching a lesson about the Mogoniwai race, popularly known as demons. "Separated by a treacherous mountain terrain where the weather was just as vicious and unsafe, our two civilizations had never crossed paths. Neither side knew that there were others on the opposite side of each other. It wasn't until fifty years ago that Christoph Johannes went on an expedition with his team to journey beyond the mountain. That was when he made the shocking discovery of beings that look far different from our own.

"Now, can anyone tell me the defining features of a Mogoniwai?" Mr. Gallafo adjusted his glasses and surveyed the room to find a student to call on. Everyone in the class avoided eye contact and slumped lower into their seats, hoping they weren't his next target.

He sighed in annoyance, "Well, Gerard, how about you give it a shot?"

Gerard stood up from his seat, irritatingly smug as always. He was a lot burlier than most of the boys in the class and often used his size to his advantage. No one at school messed with Gerard, not only because of who his father was, but because he's the type of guy who always tries to physically intimidate everyone he meets. He was the toughest kid in school and wouldn't hesitate to fight you if you looked at him funny. Though, it was only a few years ago, back on a school field trip to the woods, that a wild boar charged Gerard who froze in fear in his newly soaked pants. Aspen, without thinking, had jumped in front of Gerard to protect him, only for the teacher to scare the boar off at the last second. He was probably quite embarrassed that day, as he punched and bullied anyone who dared mention that field trip. It had infamously become taboo to ever speak of it, or else they would suffer his wrath.

Gerard cleared his throat and answered, "Well, Mr. Gallafo, there's a perfect example sitting here in the classroom!" pointing to Aspen. His goon friends cackled in the back of the class as if it was the funniest thing they'd ever heard. Gerard had bullied Aspen for four years now, with no signs of stopping. Growing up, whenever he showed any sort of retaliation or defiance, it was met with a far worse punishment.

Aspen groaned in annoyance. *Wow, what a lame joke, very original.* He slumped lower into his seat, as if he could hide himself from the rest of the class.

Mr. Gallafo, unmoved by Gerard's words, carried on with his lesson, "Well, that is not correct, class. Since no one is capable of telling me the correct answer, the answer is that the distinguishing features of a Mogoniwai are the red pigmentations of their skin, the white color of their hair, and the horns growing on their head. We also know that they have slightly more pointed ears than us humans. They closely resemble demons in folklore, hence the nickname." He let out a big sigh, and continued on with the lesson with a dull expression on his face, "A few years ago, there was a war between the Mogoniwais and the humans. So, what started this war, class?" He didn't wait for anyone to attempt a response. "Well, it was all because of one unfortunate instance. At a town near our own, a few Mogoniwai traveling merchants were killed by off-duty soldiers who had acted out of defense. This, in turn, made the Mogoniwai head chief angry, and requested the heads of the soldiers." Mr. Gallafo's nose wrinkled as he shook his head from side to side. "Such savagery could have sadly been avoided. Any negotiations that happened fell through and thus The War of the Demons occurred." Mr. Gallafo paced around the classroom for a couple of seconds before continuing on with his lesson. "So, Annie, what makes the Mogoniwais so dangerous?" he asked without any warning.

Annie jumped from her seat, startled that she was singled out. She often tried to cover her face and hide herself in class with her voluminous brown frizzy hair, but it did not work this time around. "Well...uh...they, like, have dangerous powers, right? And the scary part is that they eat people," she answered meekly.

"Yes, you are correct," said Mr. Gallafo. "The Mogoniwais contain magical powers that let them do out-of-this-world feats, such as turning their bodies into a weapon or cause huge explosions. But despite their grand powers, we humans were able to fight them off with our intellect," he explained, pointing to his own head. "Hundreds of thousands of lives were lost on both sides, bloodshed was rampant everywhere. After years of fighting, the war ended not too long ago with the massacre of the Mogoniwais. No one knows now where the remaining tribes are, no one has seen one in years."

Gerard snorted and kicked up his feet on his desk. "Yeah, you guys have my dad to thank for that. Because he led the armies and won, you guys can sleep soundly in your pajammies at night." He always made sure to let everyone around him know who his father was. His father, General Ulger, led the humans in defeating the demons in what seemed like a never-ending war. Through his multiple strategic assaults at their bases, he inevitably forced the demons into surrendering. Because of this, adults would often turn a blind eye when he bullied countless classmates—that, or because Gerard was too good at acting innocent.

"Yes, we all know your father was the general," said Mr. Gallafo before returning to his original discussion. "Well, despite the peace treaty being in effect, I do still advise the class that when you are out in the woods or wherever in the world, to express caution as the Mogoniwais are all dangerous," he warned.

Aspen rested his chin on his palm and blankly stared at a distance, muttering to himself, "They can't all be bad, though." In the next moment, the classroom was eerily quiet. Aspen looked around, and all eyes were on him. *Did I not say that in my head?*

Mr. Gallafo looked him dead in the eyes and asked, "Aspen, what did you say? I couldn't hear?" His usual dull expression suddenly turned to a face of disbelief.

"Well..." Aspen was caught off guard and tried to come up with a response. Out of the corner of his eye, he saw his best friend, Niko, gesturing to him to lie and mouthed, *"Tell him it was a joke."* Despite his friend's warning, Aspen repeated his statement to the class, "W-well they can't all be bad, right? I-I mean, they have kids the same ages as us, so it's not like they could all be bad." Aspen suddenly started sweating with anxiety. *Oh boy,* he thought, *why did I have to say it out loud?*

Mr. Gallafo walked a little closer to Aspen. "Did you do your homework on the history lesson, Aspen?" he asked. "Because you should know that—" The school bell rang, signaling the end of the school day. "Well, I guess class is dismissed, we can continue this lesson next week," Mr. Gallafo said, already packing his things.

Saved by the bell, Aspen thought with a sigh of relief. He began stuffing his books in his bag so that he too could head home.

Before he could get up, Niko walked by Aspen's desk and sat in an open seat near him. "Gee, Aspen, can't you play it cool in class? Mr. Gallafo's lessons are enough torture as it is, you don't want to add him constantly being on your case, too."

This was Niko, one of the few people in this town who wasn't terrible and was his best friend in Grasalia—well, his only friend in Grasalia. Aspen was a shy child growing up, so it was his mother that he had to thank for setting up the many playdates between him and Niko when they were five years old. It was perhaps Niko's outgoing personality that made other kids draw to him, including Aspen, who was quite the introvert. Which is why it did not take long at all for Aspen to warm up to him; very quickly the two had been spending almost all their free time playing in the woods, hanging out at Old Man Willey's, or whatever mischief Niko had thought up. Despite his ever-growing popularity, Niko had still stuck by him for the last seven years. Though there were definitely times when he worried that Niko would wise up and leave him for cooler friends, which terrified him immensely. Because for Aspen, this friendship was one of the last few things he had treasured in this town.

Aspen gave Niko a soft punch on the shoulder. "Yeah well, he was so boring today, I thought I'd spice things up," Aspen counters, now with a slight smile.

"But anyway, happy birthday, Aspen," said Niko. He dug into his own backpack and brought something out. A book. "I know you're probably a little too old for it, but it's the book your mom used to read to you when you were young, right?" It was a children's picture book with a princess on the cover.

"Wow, man, I...I lost my copy a while ago and couldn't find another one anywhere else," Aspen said. He was astonished. "Thanks, Niko. No, this...this is great. Thank you." He took the book from Niko's hands, and clutched it tight. His mom used to read this book to him every night when he was only a few years old. Just by holding it, a flood of memories came back to him—countless nights where he and his mom were sitting on his bed with a candle lit and the book in hand. She must have read the book to Aspen almost every night for that year, but he didn't care, he loved that book, and loved it when his mom read it to him. Aspen carefully put the book in his bag.

"No problem," Niko said with a smile and a thumbs up. "Well, are you free right now? I found this really cool secret spot in the woods."

"Yeah, sure, I have no plans today," answered Aspen. *Wow, not having any plans for my birthday seems kind of sad. Thank you, Niko.*

"Well, well, well, did I just hear that it's someone's birthday?!" a familiar voice echoed from across the room.

Aspen mentally crossed his fingers, *Don't tell me that's...* Just then, he felt a forceful slap on the back. *Oh no, it is.* Aspen looked behind him only to see Gerard with a huge smirk on his face.

"I heard about your secret spot in the woods, Niko. I want to see it, too," demanded Gerard.

"Do you always have to butt into people's conversations?" Niko responded in a slightly annoyed tone.

"Come on now, we're all good friends, right? And it's my friend Aspen's birthday," Gerard snapped back. He put one of his hands on Aspen's shoulders, squeezed it tightly, and ushered his goon friends to join him. "We don't have any plans here. The more the merrier, right, Aspen?"

Aspen tried to think of what to say. *Just tell him to buzz off, I don't like hanging out with you, go away! Anything! Say something!* "Uh, sure I guess. The more the merrier," Aspen unenthusiastically repeated. *That wasn't what I wanted to say.* He slumped a little in his seat.

"Perfect. Well, boys, get your ass off those seats and let's go see it!" yelled Gerard.

And so, Aspen, Niko, Gerard, and Gerard's goon friends headed off to the woods to check out that secret spot.

CHAPTER

TWO

Aspen closed his eyes, feeling the gentle cold breeze as he walked on. Something about being outside, away from the town, away from the people, made him feel relaxed. He opened his eyes and looked around the woods, absorbing the views to the best of his ability, as if it was going to disappear at a moment's notice. He saw the white blanket of snow covering the ground, and smelled the crisp, damp pine trees.

Maybe I should just live in the woods, Aspen jokingly thought to himself, only to quickly forget about it after imagining how scary it would probably be to be alone here at night. Aspen heard gentle footsteps to his side and turned around. It was a baby deer. He extended his hand out to it, trying to convey that he meant no harm. The baby deer treaded slowly and carefully towards him with innocence and curiosity in the gleam of its eyes.

The baby deer came closer and sniffed his fingertips.

SMACK!

"What the—" Aspen said. A snowball had been thrown at the deer, startling it. Soon after, the baby deer was pelted with more snowballs and retreated into the heart of the woods. Hearing obnoxious laughter, Aspen turned around. He was not surprised to find Gerard and his friends behind him, snowballs in hand.

"Did you see that shot? That thing didn't know what hit him," Gerard howled.

"Wow, not cool, man," Niko condemned.

The snowflakes had begun to fall as the boys continued to march on through the woods. Niko was in the lead, followed by Aspen, then Gerard and his friends. As they continued to hike through the trail, the sky pelted them with hail and the cold winds slapped their skin with snow, like it was delivering a warning for them to turn back. Out of nowhere, a large gust of wind flung a pile of snow onto Gerard's face.

"Okay, who threw that!" Gerald yelled as he wiped the snow off. One of his friends let out a laugh. "You think that's funny, Butch?" Gerard asked as he scooped up a huge pile of snow with his hands. He chucked the snowball at Butch as fast as he could, and hit his mark.

"Ouch, man! What the heck was that for? There was a rock in that one," Butch said, rubbing his face to soothe the pain.

"Yeah, well, serves you right," Gerard laughed. He rubbed his hands together. "Can we freaking hurry this along, why the heck is it so far away?"

"Well, you didn't have to come, you know," Niko retorted; clearly, Gerard was getting on his nerves by the minute. Niko walked backward until he reached Aspen. "Why did you agree to letting him and his friends come along?"

"Sorry, I cracked under the pressure," Aspen guiltily replied. "But seriously, why is your secret hideout so far away?"

"You think I would actually show him where it's at?" Niko winked at Aspen. "If I actually show it to him, he'd probably steal it. I'm trying to get him to go back on his own."

"Sheesh, why didn't you let me in on this plan? All this time, I thought we were getting close," Aspen said, defeated. "But maybe we should head back soon? The snow is falling harder and harder." It was snowing so much that Aspen's face felt numb. Not even his scarf could keep him warm at this point. Just then, a huge pile of snow smacked the back of his head, and he heard snickers from behind him. Gerard and his squad were busting on the ground laughing.

"Nailed him!" Gerard yelled out. Aspen shook the snow off his head and ignored them.

"All right, I'm tired of this. I bet the base isn't even that cool anyway," Gerard whined. Aspen and Niko locked eyes and gave a silent cheer. Gerard looked around the woods. "There!" he said as he pointed in the direction across from him. "Let's play a little game."

Everyone looked in the direction that Gerard pointed and saw a small cliff with a jagged and thin path that looked like it could cave at any second. "Whoever can go the closest to the edge of that cliff over there wins, and whoever is the furthest is the loser!" he declared. Gerard's two friends looked at each other, a scared look on their faces.

"What's even the point of playing? That doesn't seem like fun," said Niko.

Aspen breathed a sigh of relief, *I'm glad Niko called him out. What's so fun about potentially falling to your death. I...I mean I'm not a chicken, but it's so scary being high up.*

"Don't be so lame, will ya?" Gerard was starting to sound agitated. He turned around to his friends, "Are you guys chicken? Or are you brave? Butch? Mitch?"

His friends looked at one another, and said in unison, "We ain't chicken."

Butch pushed Mitch forward and said, "You go first, man, or are you a chicken?"

"Me? Why don't you freakin go for it?" Mitch asked as he pushed Butch back.

"Man, you guys are a bunch of babies. If you were in a war, the demons would eat you alive," Gerard said with a smug look on his face.

"Well, it was your clever idea, Gerard. Why don't you go first?

Why don't you show us how it's done then?" Niko snapped back. He paused for a little bit. Mitch, Butch, and Aspen were all looking at him. Gerard knew he could not back down now.

"You think I'm a chicken? I'll show ya how it's done, and then I'm making all of you guys go next," he declared, pointing to everyone in the group. Gerard kicked some snow off his boots and marched towards the direction of the cliff. Everyone watched, some with agitation, some in disbelief. Gerard walked along confidently in an attempt to show off his bravado.

Oh Jesus, does this mean I have to go, too? Aspen's thoughts were racing in his head. *There is no way I'm going towards the edge of that cliff.*

From what the others could see, Gerard was at the near edge of the ledge. "See!" he yelled from a distance. "Let's see who's too chicken to go near a stupid cliff," he laughed. Gerard began to jump up and down, stomping the ground as hard as he could. "Look, nothing happened!"

Butch and Mitch clapped and hoorayed, Niko looked as if he didn't care, and Aspen's nervousness began to visibly show.

Gerard had a triumphant look on his face as he strolled back to the boys. "Ok, ladies, now who's next?" Gerard scanned the group, trying to pick the next person. Aspen tried to shrink his presence. He thought that if he didn't draw attention to himself, then maybe, just maybe, they'd forget about him. But Gerard saw through this and smiled. "Well, well, well, I think the birthday boy's gotta go next." He rubbed his hands together, reminiscent of a fly rubbing its limbs together.

"Huh? M-me?" Aspen blurted out. *Of course he's going after me. Why does he always have to go after me?* His palms now sweaty as the uneasy feeling in his gut rose.

"Yeah, why don't you go? Or are you chicken?" Mitch chortled. He pushed Aspen towards the direction of the cliff.

"Yeah, you're a chicken, aren't you?" Butch joined in, his arms no longer trembling as he gave Aspen a shove. The warmth and rosy delight on his face returned.

"I don't even want to go! I'm not part of this stupid game," Aspen gasped. He walked away from the others until Gerard gave him a huge shove that knocked him to the ground.

"Yo, can you guys just leave him alone?" Niko snapped at the group. He tried to walk over to Aspen to help him up but was blocked by Butch and Mitch.

Gerard looked down on Aspen, who was still on the ground. "You turned twelve today, think of this as a rite of passage. Don't be a chicken. Go!" he insisted.

"Come on man...I don't want to do it," Aspen stammered.

"Oh, I mean, if you *didn't want to*, Aspen, that's all you had to say," consoled Gerard. He extended his hand out to help him up.

Aspen looked at him with suspicion but ultimately accepted his gesture and grabbed Gerard's hand to help himself up. "T-thanks."

Just then, Gerard squeezed Aspen's hand tightly, as if trying to crush it with all his might. Aspen let out a quiet yelp. Gerard forcibly took Aspen's backpack off of him and grabbed hold of it. "Well, I guess you leave me no choice," he nodded in pity.

"Give that back to me!" Aspen begged. He could hear Niko call out his name, struggling to move past Gerard's goons.

"Oh, you want this?" Gerard's eyes lit up like he was enjoying every minute of his twisted game. "Well, I guess you better go get it!" he yelled as he chucked Aspen's backpack with all his might towards the cliff. Luckily, his backpack landed just at the very edge of the cliff, but unfortunately, Aspen knew he had to go over there and retrieve it.

Aspen stood up on his own, scraped the snow off his jacket, and started to walk. Everyone stood silent and watched. *Just get the backpack and go quick, it's nothing too scary,* Aspen thought to himself. He could hear the snow crunching from his boots as he marched on towards the cliff. The wind picked up again, pushing him down as if trying to make him go back. As he walked closer to the cliff and farther from the group, he could hear Gerard rambling on from a distance, but he chose to ignore it. *As long as I firmly plant myself on the ground, there's absolutely nothing to be afraid of,* he kept telling himself. Aspen was close to the edge of the cliff with his backpack in sight.

He inched closer and closer to the backpack. "Hurry up already, slowpoke!" Aspen heard from a distance. Aspen turned back to his classmates and could hardly make out their faces through the falling snow and just barely heard someone shout after him. He couldn't tell who it was, but he would have bet a week's worth of lunches that it was Gerard. He grabbed his backpack. Safe. Aspen calmed down a bit. He looked down at the bottom of the cliff. At that moment, he realized that he had a fear of heights. The cliff wasn't too high where a fall would guarantee certain death, but it was high enough to scare the living daylights out of him. Aspen turned to his peers, just barely making out their faces. It was a farther walk than he thought. *Crack.* Aspen heard a noise coming from beneath his feet. Before being able to react, his part of the cliff immediately broke off.

Aspen lost his balance and was suddenly airborne, plummeting straight down to his doom. At that moment, every single one of his thoughts stormed his head. *Oh crap.* Aspen helplessly extended his hand out towards the cliff, but the distance between the two of them gradually drifted apart. It felt like time was moving in slow motion. *Oh crap,* he thought again, feeling a flurry of regret rush through him.

Though Aspen had been falling for only a few seconds, within that time frame, his mind darted to everyone he cherished—his mom, his dad, Willey, Niko. Before his untimely death, he wanted to think about the happy memories with these people. *I still wanted to make more.* But the amount of regret he held outweighed any amount of happy moments in his life. *I should have done better.* Aspen wasn't quite ready to accept his end here; there were so many things he still sought to do, relationships he wanted to repair. *If only I had one more chance, I promise, I'll do...* He closed his eyes.

Am I going to die?

CHAPTER

THREE

All the thoughts that bombarded his head came to a stop as he heard the *thud* the moment he hit the ground. Aspen could hardly breathe, let alone move his body. At that moment, he couldn't tell if his vision was getting hazier or if he was losing consciousness. Aspen fought hard to stay awake, remembering that after an injury, people are supposed to stay conscious. *Am I alive?* The pain that surged throughout his body was excruciating, but was numbed somewhat by the cold weather. He extended his hand outward towards the sky, as if trying to grab hold of it, and noticed the bruises and scratches on his arms and hands. Aspen had landed on a pile of branches and jagged rocks that had softened his impact, but left him in a damaged mess.

Aspen heard yelling from the cliff above. He could see Niko peering down with a distraught look on his face. At this point, he could barely make out the conversation that the group was having. Niko peered down at Aspen once more, shouting at him. Though not entirely audible, Aspen swore he heard that he was getting help.

Aspen tried to let out a joking response, saying that he wasn't going anywhere, but it pained him too much to speak. Niko pointed at Gerard and his friends and then pointed at him.

He must be telling them to watch over me, Aspen thought. Niko ran off, disappearing from his view. As Niko's face disappeared, it was replaced with Gerard's, Butch's, and Mitch's ugly mugs as they looked down towards him.

∿

"OH MAN, GERARD, YOU KILLED HIM!" Butch stammered. He was violently chewing on his fingernails as he paced back and forth near the cliff's edge.

"Shut up, I didn't do crap!" Gerard argued. His typical confident visage was in shambles, now turned to one of distress. "Mitch, you saw it, right? I didn't do nothing, right?" Now turned towards his other friend, seeking validation.

"I-I don't know," stuttered Mitch. The muscles in his jaw tensed up, making it hard for him to speak.

Gerard grabbed the collar of Mitch's shirt and shouted, "I didn't do anything, right?" This time, threatening him to give the answer he wanted to hear.

"Y-yeah, he just fell," Mitch responded quickly. Gerard let go of his shirt.

Gerard then turned to Butch, "I was nowhere even near him, he just fell on his own, right?"

Butch calmed down a bit. "Y-yeah, it was just a clumsy accident."

"We need to get our stories straight here, you hear? We were all never here! You got that?" Gerard fretted. His voice started to tighten and crack under the pressure. Mitch and Butch listened to his hysteria as if it was a lifeline that could save them from this situation. "W-we have to book it."

"But what about Aspen? Didn't Niko ask us to watch him while he gets help?" Mitch asked.

"When Niko gets here with the adults, who do you think will get all the blame? And if he tries to pin it all on me, I'm gonna take you all down with me!" Gerard stepped towards Mitch and Butch intimidatingly. "I'm not standing here any longer, I'm leaving. If you guys want to stay and get punished, go for it." Gerard sprinted towards the opposite direction, out of the woods, much like the startled baby deer from earlier.

"W-we should stay...right?" Butch asked, his voice still shaking.

"W-we should," Mitch answered. He peered down at Aspen once more, the snow he was lying on was covered with his blood, which only made him queasy. "Y-you think they'll blame us for killing Aspen?"

"S-shut up! Aspen's not d-dead!" Butch yelled unconvincingly. He let out a strangled cry though dared not look down, "A-Aspen if you're alive, yell that you're okay!...Aspen!...Say something, you dork!"

There was no response.

Mitch swallowed dryly as he looked at Butch, "Oh my gosh, you don't think—"

CLOMP! CLOMP! CLOMP!

Before he could finish his sentence, Butch had sprinted off in the other direction.

"H-hey, don't leave me all alone!" Mitch hollered as he chased after him.

The two had sprinted off as fast as they could and disappeared into the woods, leaving Aspen all to his lonesome.

THE COMMOTION he'd heard earlier began to die down. Aspen couldn't really make out the conversation, but an argument definitely took place. He hadn't seen Gerard and the others for a while, and honestly wouldn't have been surprised if they ran off. Aspen couldn't do anything but lie on the ground, motionless, staring at the sky. The view of the sky was stained crimson red. He mustered his remaining strength to touch his face, then looked at the palm of his hand and saw red. It was blood. His blood. He groaned in pain as he set his hand back on the ground.

Lying on the ground, he couldn't stop thinking about the what ifs in his life. If he had been more assertive, and had just told Gerard that he could not go, would he still be in this situation? If he had not allowed himself to get bullied, would he be a different person? If he was able to find the words to talk to his dad, would their relationship be mended? If he had been a stronger person, could he have saved his mom?

Aspen made a silent vow: *I promise, if I make it out of here, out of these woods alive, I'll change, I'll be different. I'll stand my ground and won't waver anymore.* He let out a soft chuckle and sighed. *As if I can possibly change.* The world became quiet, now clearing his thoughts. All he heard was the breeze and the sound of soft snow falling to the ground.

It's funny, I finally have the peace and quiet that I wanted, but it only took almost dying to get it. Aspen began counting how much time had passed by, wondering if Niko would arrive with help before he kicked the bucket.

At that moment, he heard footsteps brushing against the snow on the ground in the direction of his feet. Footsteps. Aspen let out a sigh of relief.

He turned his head towards the direction of the noise of the footsteps. His heart sunk, his sudden feeling of relief soon turned to a moment of terror. Aspen locked eyes onto it as it slowly emerged from the heart of the woods. It was a wolf. The wolf approached Aspen with caution, as if trying to gauge whether he was predator or prey. He heard more footsteps, and two more wolves emerged from within the bushes. The wolves slowly walked closer and closer, growling in unison.

Aspen made a half-hearted smile and lamented at his luck; it was hopeless, everything was hopeless. *Can't this world, for once in my life, give me a break?* The first wolf attentively stared at him, not making a

26

single noise. Just straight focus, looking as if ready to pounce. Aspen closed his eyes as he heard the wolf leap off the ground. *Please just let this end painless and quick.*

Thud.

Expecting to hear the sounds of wolves gnawing on his soft flesh, he instead heard a wolf squeal in pain as it tumbled to the ground.

Aspen slowly opened his eyes. It wasn't his untimely death that he was staring at but a girl who had just kicked the pouncing wolf's underbelly. His vision was still hazy from the fall and the blood still in his eyes, but that didn't stop him from watching her in awe. This girl had long white hair, pure like the snow that was falling from the sky, flowing freely in the air. His eyes, still wreathed with pain and covered in his own blood, dared not look away, fully enamored by the sight of the angel that arose before him.

Only one word came to Aspen's mind as he watched her. *Beautiful.*

She gracefully descended to the ground between Aspen and the pack of wolves. Her clothes looked different from what he was used to seeing around town, as if they were handmade. *Who is this girl? Where did she come from?* Some part of his mind started to wonder, *Is this really some weird dream again? Am I going to wake up any minute?* The girl before him wasn't much taller than he was. She had a baby face, looking quite innocent and pure, that made her seem like she couldn't have been older than him.

The wolf's snarls and their footsteps atop the soft snow snapped Aspen back to reality. They were steadily approaching the two of them. Now wasn't the time to be distracted, one false move and they would be ripped to shreds. In front of him, the girl stood firmly on the ground, not showing any signs of wavering. Aspen tried to call out to her but couldn't muster the strength to speak.

Forget about me, leave while you still can, Aspen silently thought, anguishing in pain. He flipped himself over—if he couldn't walk, he'd crawl if needed to. *Don't you know what's going on right now? Don't you see what's in front of you? What can you even do?* He extended his hand out and grabbed a clump of snow on the ground to pull himself a few inches forward. He saw the girl in front of him, readying her stance as if she was going to fight back.

Are you crazy? You don't even know me. Aspen extended his other hand outwards to pull himself closer. The wolves paced around him and the girl. She didn't even flinch. He tried to pull himself forward once more, but this time, every ounce of his energy had dissipated. Soon enough, his adrenaline faded and was replaced with pain. Aspen couldn't move, all he could do now was watch this beautiful girl get mauled in front of his own eyes. He stared at her. Tears rolled down his cheeks. *How can you be so brave right now?*

The girl locked eyes onto the wolves and growled back. They stopped in their tracks. Two of the wolves stepped back, contemplating their next course of action. The wolf that seemed to be the head of the pack did not waver, however, and pushed forward. The girl picked up a broken tree branch and pointed it towards the direction of the wolves. As the wolf took one step towards the two of them, she swung the branch at it, so as to keep it at bay. The two other wolves followed its leader and moved along with it. One wolf charged at the girl, but she parried it off using the tree branch. As soon as one wolf finished his attack, the other pounced on her makeshift weapon and snatched it away.

The only weapon she had now was gone. Despite that fact, the girl didn't look worried—it was just the opposite, actually. Aspen could faintly see a smug smile grow across her face that screamed *Come at me if you dare.* The three wolves continued their formation, circling around them, waiting for a moment of weakness. One jumped and lunged at her, but she grabbed both of its paws and threw the wolf back into the direction of the others. But this only angered them, and they growled even more ferociously.

The wolves ignored Aspen, and now focused their attention towards the girl. As each wolf tried to sink their fangs into her flesh, she evaded all their attacks gracefully. It was as if she was outside dancing in the snow with them, and she was the lead dancer on stage. Snow continued to fall as the two groups stared at each other. All three wolves grouped up next to each other. The girl readied her stance again, expecting another assault.

Who is this person? Aspen wondered. Not only was this girl keeping the pack of wolves at bay, but she was fighting them with her bare hands. He couldn't help but admire her courage.

The three wolves sprinted towards her in unison. An aura wrapped around the girl's hands, appearing so brightly that it was almost blinding. This, however, didn't scare the wolves as they still rushed on for the attack. The moment all the wolves dove at her, a burst of light exploded out of the palms of her hands. For a brief moment, the chilly winter air became warm.

The wolves collided onto the snow, burned from the attack, their fur and skin now singed from the blast. The girl marched towards the pack as two of the wolves slowly retreated. It seemed as though the tables had turned, the predator had soon enough become the prey. The leader of the pack, still showing no signs of fear, stood its ground, brandishing its teeth and growling back at her. Her hands brightened once more as she aimed at them, like a bow and arrow.

The sight alone was enough to scare them again, as they bolted back into the woods and away from the girl. The girl seemed like she was about to chase after the wolves until she looked back at Aspen. Her hands returned to normal, as she turned her attention to him instead.

Aspen watched helplessly as the girl headed in his direction. *What's going to happen now?* He looked at the ground he was laying on, it was stained red with his blood. *Maybe I really will die after all?* Aspen slowly closed his eyes and opened them again, trying to combat his fading consciousness.

If this is a dream, you can wake me up now. All the pain was surging throughout his body again. *But if this...but if this isn't a dream...* Mid-thought, he watched her walk closer to him. *If this isn't a dream, there's so much regret I have in life.* The hair on his head down to his little toes hurt like hell. *At least let me live long enough to find out her name.*

Each time he closed and opened his eyes, she grew closer and closer to him. The girl knelt in the snow and gazed upon Aspen's face with curiosity and then with a bit of distress and urgency. She held his icy cold hands and pressed it upon the side of her own face; her cheek felt warm. Aspen forced himself to stay awake. If he was going to die, he at least wanted to look at her one last time. She lifted his head up and gently placed it on her lap.

Aspen locked eyes with the girl, enthralled by her very existence. In that single moment, the snow had stopped falling from the sky, the woods dared not utter a single sound, and the two of them were the only two in the world.

Waves of light suddenly sprouted from the ground, encircling them as it flung about in the air. The light looked like tentacles that spun faster and faster, but hummed like a sweet gentle nightingale, until it eventually wrapped together and enclosed them from the outside.

Her hands illuminated once more, like they had when she fought the wolves, though for some reason, he wasn't afraid. Maybe it was because he trusted her despite this being their first encounter, or maybe it was because he was just too exhausted to care.

She placed the palm of her hand on Aspen's forehead. He imagined that there'd be a hot burning sensation radiating from it, but surprisingly, it didn't burn. It was warm. It felt gentle in an indescribable way, giving him the feeling that everything was all right in the world, almost as if melting his troubles away. It also reminded him of spring—a springtime back in his childhood, a time where it was just him, his dad and his mom, where his only worry was making sure his dad didn't eat all the stew or catching more bugs than Niko as the cicadas chirped about. This warm feeling was something he hadn't experienced in a while, feeling almost too good to be true. And finally, Aspen saw his mother vividly and clearly in his head for the first time in a while. A few tears rolled down his cheeks, but this time, they were of joy.

Thank you, thank you for reminding me of this. If this is what Aspen got to feel in his final moments, maybe it wasn't all bad.

The girl mumbled to him a few words, but he couldn't quite make out what she was saying.

And just then, a thread of light from up above the veil that encircled them pierced through her chest. Aspen was startled, but the girl was smiling, showing no signs of pain. And then the same thread that pierced through her pierced through his own heart.

He gasped at first, but allowed it to happen. His body started to heat up to the point that winter felt like spring. *Maybe the world hasn't always been so cold after all.* Aspen managed to smile, moments before he fell unconscious.

CHAPTER

FOUR

D*rip.*

Where am I? Aspen was lying on a cold, damp surface.
Drip.

Am I at home? He steadily began to open his eyes, only to find himself surrounded by darkness. Aspen tried to recollect his thoughts as to how he got here. A drip of water from above splashed his face. Wiping it off, he was certain of one thing, and that was that this *wasn't* a dream.

His eyes began to adjust to the darkness, wherever he was, it looked like he was in some kind of cave dwelling. Water continuously dropped to the ground from the ceiling, each echoing to the other end of the cave. Aspen surveyed the area, and couldn't identify anything outright dangerous. The only thing here was himself, the water dripping from the ceiling, and rocks, lots of them.

"How am I alive right now?" he spoke aloud, trying to recollect what had happened to him once more. He still felt groggy, and had a dull pain throughout his body, but at least he was alive.

Come on, Aspen, think. Trace back to the events that happened, he thought. *I was with Niko and the others in the woods. Stupid Gerard threw my backpack near the cliff. I went to go get it, but a part of the cliff broke off and I fell. Then there were wolves. But I'm still alive... Because she saved me.* Aspen eyes widened in realization. "The girl!" he inadvertently yelled out. A sudden jolt of energy coursed through his body as he shot straight up.

He winced, preparing for the backlash that would come from suddenly moving after sustaining a serious and grave injury. But upon realizing that he wasn't in any pain at all, Aspen let out a sigh of relief, until the question hit him.

"Wait, why am I not hurt?" He touched his face and all around his head and looked at his hands. "Huh, I'm not bleeding anymore." Next, he moved his legs around and wiggled his arms, which were all functioning normally. Aspen let out a slight chuckle to himself. "There is no way this is normal." He remembered the warm light that embraced him before losing consciousness. *Did she have something to do with this?* Aspen decided that he needed to find out for himself.

He braced himself to stand up only to lose his balance. As his knees dropped to the floor, his scarf became undone and dropped onto the damp surface of the cave. One of the holes on his scarf had become noticeably larger, something he'd have to learn how to patch when back at home. Aspen grabbed it and securely wrapped it around his neck. He heard noises past a small tunnel behind him.

Ding. Crackle. Crackle.

It's her! Aspen felt both nervous and excited that he was going to meet the person who saved his life. *That* must *be her!* He stood up again, this time without falling over. His strength was slowly coming back to him now. Though still feeling a bit weak, Aspen headed towards the direction of the noise, using the cave walls to lean on as support. As he walked closer and closer, the crackling of a fire grew louder. *It has to be her, I just know it!*

Reaching the end of the tunnel, he entered the small cave. The fire was flickering brightly, warming up the entire enclosed space. He saw a small shadowy figure near the fire. *It is her!*

"I-I just wanted to say thank you for saving me from the wolves! If you weren't there, I would have been a goner for sure." He scratched the back of his head. "Sorry, I didn't even tell you my name." The shadowy figure came closer to the fire and peered directly at him. When Aspen was able to get a good look, terror overtook him. He took a step back and lost his balance, falling flat and landing on his butt.

What did Mr. Gallafo say in class again...? Aspen desperately tried to remember. An image of Mr. Gallafo popped up in his head and spoke in his usual dull tone. *"The distinguishing features of a Mogoniwai are the red pigmentation of their skin."* Aspen examined her, her skin was blush, light red. When he first saw her outside, he chalked it up to the fact that his vision was bleary from the fall and the blood in his eyes. But her skin was, in fact, red. *"They also have white colored hair."* As he checked off more and more items off the list, the more tense and filled with anxiety he became. *"Lastly, they all have horns growing on their heads and have slightly pointy ears."* Aspen looked at her, praying that there were no horns. But, to his dread, he saw her pointy ears and the small horns growing from her head.

That feeling of hope he felt was burned away like wood in fire, replaced now with fear. She leaned in closer to him, her two small fangs clearly visible to Aspen now. The fire cast her shadow onto the wall behind her, making her seem more gargantuan than she actually was. He kneeled, remaining very still. All the energy he had was gone, now once again drained.

Many questions and thoughts filled his mind, so many that it felt like there was a storm raging on in his head. The girl who saved him from a pack of wolves, the girl who somehow nursed him back to health and brought him back to this cave, the girl who he most wanted to meet as he lay there dying on that snowy day was a... Mogoniwai.

The girl was a demon.

Worried that any sudden movements might agitate her, Aspen slowly backed himself closer to the wall. "Don't show fear, Aspen, don't show fear. They might be able to sense those types of things," he quietly muttered. He couldn't hold the twisting knots in his stomach because his hands were trembling too much. Aspen kept thinking back about what all the townspeople said about the demons. One vivid thing that everyone mentioned is that they eat humans. Aspen took in a gulp of air, hoping that the rumors weren't really true. Even though he kept telling himself over and over that it was a rumor, Aspen couldn't help but look back at her fangs—the two little fangs that could probably rip his arm off.

Did she save me from the wolves because she wanted to eat me? Am I going to be the main course pretty soon? Aspen watched her cautiously from the other side of the cave room, still not sure if she saved him or was just saving him for a midnight snack.

I shouldn't be standing here, I have to move right now! He slowly stood up, eyeing the girl, half expecting her to pounce and attack. But as he stood, she approached him not with animosity but with curiosity. Aspen quickly dropped back down again quietly muttering, "sorry, sorry, sorry," repeatedly. She proceeded to stand in front of him, staring at him intently with her fangs on display. Aspen could tell from the glazed look in her eyes that she was hungry.

He closed his eyes in fear and rambled, "I don't taste good, I don't taste good, please don't eat me."

Aspen opened his eyes as soon as he heard footsteps rush out of the cave. His prayers had been answered and the demon had rushed out. "I'm...alive?" he mumbled in disbelief. Though his nerves started to calm down a bit, he was still on edge.

Where did she run off to? Does this mean I'm allowed to leave? Aspen peeked out to the tunnel exit; there was nothing in sight. In fact, he couldn't really see much as the caves were too dark and the only source of light was the fire that was lit in this room. It was time to strategize his next move.

"I definitely can't take her on, so my only choice is to escape this cave. This is her home, so she has the advantage. It's dark, so I can't really see where I am going. Plus, I wouldn't even know which direction is the exit," Aspen sighed. "I'm screwed, aren't I?" He brushed off some of the dirt that was on his pants. "Well, I'm better off taking my chances trying to escape this place, then staying in this room."

Making his way out of the room, he realized that something was missing. "My backpack. Where is my backpack?" Aspen searched around the room. "It's not here, where did she put it?" There was also the chance that the demon had completely left it outside. *I'll go look around the cave while she's still out to try and find it.*

Before he could set out to find his backpack, Aspen heard the pitter-pattering of footsteps from outside the room. *She's back!* Panicked, his first instinct was to hide somewhere, anywhere. With not much time until the demon returned, there weren't many places to hide on short notice besides the rocks bunched up together in the corner. *There, I can hide behind there until she leaves again.* He jumped from above and crouched between the rocks, thinking that he was now perfectly hidden. He held his breath and closed his eyes. The footsteps had entered the room.

Aspen could hear her scattered pacing and growling all around the room, until eventually the sound of footsteps came to a halt. *Did she leave?* he wondered. Aspen slowly stood up from his hiding spot and peeked out. Shoved in front of his face, to his absolute horror, and without warning, was a skinned rabbit carcass, still oozing out blood.

Aspen screamed from the top of his lungs, louder than he had ever screamed before. He quickly jumped out of his hiding spot, only to stumble to the ground. The demon girl held the rabbit by the ears, once again shoving it in front of Aspen's face. "Stop! No, I don't want it! Get it away from me!" he shouted, pushing the rabbit carcass away from his face.

"Asa ooo no rabbeese?"

"I...I don't know what you are saying," Aspen replied.

He watched as the demon studied the rabbit and then himself and then eventually retreated over to the fire to cook the rabbit.

Aspen let out a sigh of relief, calming down once realizing that the demon chose the rabbit over himself as dinner. The girl looked towards his direction again and walked towards him, this time holding something else. Before he could react, she threw the object at him.

"My bag!" Aspen joyfully squealed. He grabbed it from her with gratitude. The girl went back to roasting her rabbit.

Aspen clutched his backpack close to him and quickly unzipped it. He checked inside and ensured that everything was there and in one piece, especially the book that Niko had given to him, as it was a memento of his late mother. *Maybe, she's not so bad after all.* His stomach began growling aggressively. *I guess it's been a while since I've eaten something. Oh wait, I have just the thing!* He unzipped the zipper of his backpack and pulled out the chocolate bar that Old Man Willey gave him. *Thank you, Willey!* He excitedly squealed, holding the candy in the air and kissing the wrapper. He delicately unwrapped it, the caramelly smell wafted in the air, overpowering the smell of burned wood.

The girl looked back at Aspen; he could feel her eyeing the chocolate bar. "D-do you want to try some?" he asked. Though scared that she would rip his arm off at first, it was the least Aspen could do for her. He ripped the chocolate bar in half, and extended the piece to her. "Here, try it," he said, urging her to take it. He smiled at her. "I swear it's yummy." She walked towards him and grabbed half of the chocolate bar, and then returned to sitting by the fire.

The girl sniffed the chocolate bar and held it near her face to examine it. After rationalizing that it was safe to eat, she took a bite. Aspen watched as her red eyes steadily glistened and sparkled after the first bite. Immediately, she consumed her entire half in a second. Letting out a quiet, happy squeal as she kicked her feet out in the air, it seemed like she was happy dancing, barely able to conceal her delight. The girl put both palms on her cheek, as if trying to prevent the taste from escaping her mouth. The two looked at each other and smiled.

For the first time in a while, Aspen laughed loudly without a care in the world. He could feel the happiness glow inside him just from watching her. He took a seat by her next to the fire. Aspen had only eaten a portion of the half he had ripped for himself, but decided to hand her his piece.

"Here you go, I'm not that hungry anyway." He could tell that she was hesitant about taking it, exhibiting much better constraint and manners than nearly all of his entire classmates.

"Asa asa lo." The girl shook her head no.

"Don't worry, I want you to have it." In the end, she accepted the chocolate after Aspen insisted multiple times.

The girl ate the chocolate, this time letting out a much louder happy squeal. Happiness itself was dancing about within her. The room felt much brighter at that moment, her gaiety and merriment filling the room with this joyful, sparkling energy.

Soon after, the laughter that echoed in the room was replaced with the growling sounds of Aspen's stomach. "Guess I'm still a little hungry," Aspen chuckled, clenching his stomach.

"Asa rabbeese yoi yoi," the demon girl said. The girl looked at him again, pointing to the rabbit that was cooking in the fire.

He quickly gestured no, "I'm...I'm okay, really... it's not really my thing."

The girl became visibly frustrated with Aspen. She ripped off a piece of the cooked rabbit. This time not taking no for an answer, she shoved the piece of the rabbit in Aspen's mouth.

Aspen winced as he was chewing the forcefully-fed meat. "Huh..." he mumbled after swallowing the first bite. "You know, it's actually not too bad." Expecting to gag and vomit from eating it, but surprisingly, he did not hate it all too much. It was personally hard for himself to admit, but Aspen was known to be a bit of a picky eater among those who really knew him. Though, maybe the rabbit meat was only palatable due to his extreme hunger. Whatever the reason was, it definitely tasted better than some of the dishes his dad had made. "You know, can I have more of that?" he asked, pointing at the cooked rabbit.

The girl smiled. It seemed as though she understood him because she ripped another piece and handed it to him. Aspen took the piece without hesitation this time and started eating.

You know, I bet everyone in class won't believe that I met a demon, let alone ate dinner with one. Aspen chuckled. *The rumors weren't true after all. How can someone like her be so terrible? She saved me from the wolves, helped me feel better, gave me shelter, and even gave me some food. I mean, can someone so bad make a face like that when they eat chocolate?* Aspen deeply thought. *My whole life, the people I met, in the classroom, even the people closest to me, they all warned me about the demons. How they are animals, how they will kill and eat you on sight.* Aspen took a quick glance at her. *Sure, she looks different, she has that red skin, the white hair, pointed ears, and horns, but does that automatically make her bad? Take away what she looks like, and she's just like all of us.* Aspen sat content, and with a slightly bigger belly.

He furiously shook his head from side to side. *No, this is crazy, I'm letting my feelings get the better of me.* Demons are all evil and terrible; that was what he had been taught since growing up. He extended his hand forward to warm himself with the fire. *I'm not gullible, I know for a fact she's plotting something. Yeah I know she's...she's a monster.* Aspen held his head up to get a glimpse of her.

The demon girl swayed her body back and forth, still cherishing the chocolate that she had just consumed entirely. In the midst of it all, she noticed him staring at her.

Making eye contact with her, he spoke out loud, "With your fangs that eat human children and your magical powers that make you so strong, you are our enemy?" He corrected himself to form a statement. "You are our enemy. Why are you helping me? If I was Gerard, I would have a whole army here to capture you."

She did not consider his words a threat, however. Instead, the demon child had waved at him with a smile on her face.

Aspen nervously chuckled. "I guess you don't understand a word I'm saying." He returned a wave back, only to feel a burning pain on his fingertips. "Ouch!" His hand was slightly burnt, as he carelessly waved his hand too far forward. Though a first-degree burn was nothing compared to what he had already been through.

"Asa, ah. Foro! Foro!" The demon child looked even more worried than Aspen had been. She quickly shuffled herself towards him and took his burnt hand.

"It's okay, I'm fine," he reassured her.

Though she completely ignored him and gently held his hand. An aura appeared around her hand just as before, and soon enough, the pain of the first-degree burn was nothing more but a distant memory.

She turned to him, upset, and pointed to the fire, "Foro, non. Foro, non." The demon girl made a pretend hurt sound as she hovered her hand above the fire, as if he did not already know that touching fire equals great pain.

Aspen moved his fingertips and curled them into a ball. Just as before, she had healed him without hesitation. And here he was, still questioning if she was an enemy. "I'm sorry...I'm sorry..." Now feeling a bit of shame for how he was quick to label her as a monster again despite her generosity. "You're not a monster."

He gave thought as to how his dad, Willey, and Niko would react if they saw her with him. *Would they hurt her even though she was the one who saved my life? They wouldn't, right?* Aspen didn't even want to think about the possibility of someone else from town knowing of her existence. He lifted his head up to see the girl curled up like a ball, warming herself near the fire. *Can I even convince everyone at this point? That she's just like us?* No matter how hard Aspen wracked his brain about this, he couldn't see a scenario in which they'd understand.

I won't let them find her, I'll keep her safe somehow. Aspen felt a sense of determination, more determination than what he'd felt in a while. He sat upright again and called out to the girl until she was looking at him. "Hey, I didn't even get your name," he exclaimed. The girl stared blankly at him. "So...uh...what's your name?" he asked her. The girl continued to stare blankly at him.

He pointed to himself, "My name is Aspen, Ahhh-spen." He repeated it a couple more times, wondering if she could understand him. Aspen pointed to himself and to his mouth, sounding out his name once more for her, but his efforts were fruitless. He felt a little defeated, but decided to continue speaking to her anyway. "You know you looked pretty cool out there. When you fought those wolves," complimented Aspen. He started shadow-boxing the air, trying to mimic her fighting moves. She looked around and didn't see anything nearby, not only confused about what he was saying but also whom he was fighting. Aspen gestured to join him, "Come on, do it with me, too." She slowly stood up and awkwardly mimicked him.

"Hey, you know, do you think you could teach me how to be more like you?" His whole life, he'd been pushed around, always complying and always obeying. But when Aspen watched this mysterious girl out there, he couldn't help but feel a little jealous of how free and confident she appeared to be. This girl was in control of her own life, and nothing could stop her. Even when things looked grim, she stood firm and took the challenge head on. "With the wolves, even if I wasn't hurt, I wouldn't even be able to move. I would have been hopeless no matter how I see it. Even before then, with Gerard, maybe I could have made him leave me alone, I don't know, if I wasn't so scared or something." Aspen scratched his head, as if trying to shake out what he was trying to say. "Show me how to be brave like you, so that I won't ever back down from people ever again.

"Of course, you probably don't know what I'm saying, huh?" Aspen knew she didn't understand him, but for some reason talking to her just made him feel better. He pointed to her again. "You," then to himself, "teach me." And then, he proceeded to shadow-box, throwing punches and kicks in the air, as if he was fighting someone. "Fight."

She looked at him and punched the air slowly like he just did, still clearly confused.

He sighed. "This isn't going anywhere, is it?" Just then, Aspen spotted the discarded chocolate bar wrapper which gave him a great idea. "If you teach me, I'll be your friend and bring more of these," he tempted, pointing to the wrapper. Her face lit up, now wearing a smile filled with excitement. *Maybe she understood me this time,* he considered. "I'll introduce you to even more tasty things, and cool stuff!" he shouted. "I can show you a whole new world." Then, he threw his arms out in the air to show his enthusiasm. "And you'll be happier, too." The girl mimicked him and threw her arms out in the air with just as much elation.

"It seems like you're on board," Aspen nodded. It seemed surreal that he went from celebrating his birthday in the woods to becoming friends with a demon. It had officially become one of his strangest birthdays yet.

"In my town, we forge our promise with an unbreakable bond." The girl looked confused. "Come on, you guys must have something like this, too!" he groaned in disbelief. Aspen stuck out his pinky. "It's called a pinky promise; it's an unbreakable promise that all the kids and adults do. It's a promise to ourselves and to each other that we will keep our side of the bargain," he explained.

"Here, let me help," Aspen offered as he took her hand. The girl swatted his hand away, and immediately stepped back.

"Sorry, sorry, sorry," Aspen apologized. He approached her slower and raised his hands, "I mean no harm, seriously. If you let me...I can show you." Aspen extended his hand.

She extended her hand to his.

Aspen held it, stuck her pinky out, and closed the rest of her fingers. "And then you link each other's pinkies like so." Aspen then linked his pinky with her own. "There, like that!" he excitedly said, smiling at her with a goofy grin.

She looked at him, and then marveled at their linked fingers, and returned a smile.

"We cross our hearts and hope to die that you will teach me how to be brave and courageous like yourself and I promise that I will be your friend. I'll bring you more tasty things and cool things and make you even happier." After saying it out loud, Aspen did feel slight secondhand embarrassment. *It's a good thing that there is no one else around.*

The girl opened her mouth wide with excitement, "Ahh peen!"

From the water drips from the ceiling to the crackling of the fire, Aspen couldn't hear anything except the words that came out of her mouth.

"Wait, can you say that one more time? Did you just say what I thought you said?" Aspen couldn't believe it—maybe she did understand him after all.

"Ah peen, Ahh peen, Ah peen," she cheered over and over again.

His mind wasn't playing tricks on him after all. Aspen's eyes glistened. The words, her voice, it all played like a beautiful melody his ears had never heard of. "Yeah!" Aspen couldn't contain his smile nor the excitement that was bottling up inside him. "I'm Ahh peen."

CHAPTER 5
FROM HER PERSPECTIVE

The girl studied this person in front of her with awe.

What is he saying? She didn't understand at all. *These people really do speak a different language,* she thought to herself. *I guess my parents hadn't lied after all.* With her parents nowhere in her life anymore, this was the first time she saw a human in a very long while—and one that would converse with her at that.

This human looked different than herself. This person had dark hair, no horns, and smooth, rounded ears, something she never saw before in her village. The room was dead silent for a while, all that could be heard was the water drops echoing about in the cave and the crackling of the fire. Suddenly, the boy before her dropped to his knees.

Are you hurt? she wondered, approaching him with caution. The girl formed a smile to show that she meant no harm. She inspected him again. *The person doesn't seem hurt.* She tried to think of what else could be wrong. The boy started mumbling once more and quickly dropped to the ground again. She was in front of him now, face-to-face.

Her eyes lit up. *This person...maybe this person is hungry!* She felt a sudden sense of accomplishment and pride at deciphering his dilemma. *I will get this person something to eat and maybe he will feel better!* She rushed out of the room to bring her newfound guest a snack from her personal stash. The girl was excited; after all, it had been many years since she had interacted with someone that was not an animal.

She checked her stockpile of food and had a difficult decision to make.

"Wait, I don't even know what he likes," she said. The Mogoniwai child scavenged through her hunts of rabbit, birds, and deer. "Well, everyone likes rabbits, right? Oh wait, I should probably give him his bag as well" She picked up her freshest rabbit—nothing but the best for her guest—and his bag, hurrying back to the cave.

"Where did he go?" She came back to the room to find that the human had disappeared entirely. The girl dropped his bag on the ground, worried that something bad had happened to him. Though it did not take long for her to see his hair peeking out from behind large piles of rocks. *Is this some kind of hunting game that humans play? Maybe I'm supposed to find him.* The girl scratched her head. *Well, I don't want to make him sad by finding him immediately.*

She scampered around the cave, pretending that she had no idea where he was at. "Where are you? Oh, where are you? I have no idea where you are." The Mogoniwai could hear his breathing start to calm down and his stomach rumble slightly. She mischievously smiled and hushed her footsteps, tip-toeing towards his hiding spot.

The boy slowly peeked his head out from behind the rocks.

"Surprise! I found you!" She jumped out to scare him.

The boy screamed from the top of his lungs, louder than any animal she had ever encountered. He quickly jumped out of his hiding spot and tripped due to his own clumsiness.

She winced, "Stop shouting, I brought dinner." The Mogoniwai child showed him the fresh rabbit, only to have it pushed away.

"Do you not like rabbit?" The girl was perplexed. She held the rabbit to her nose and sniffed it. *It doesn't smell bad.* The girl knew for a fact that it was still fresh; she had hunted it this morning. She walked over to the fire, preparing to cook the rabbit. *Well, more for me then.*

Oh, that's right. I should give him his bag. She picked up his bag, walked towards him and dropped it in front of him.

The boy's smile grew in size for the first time since he had awoken. *I'm glad I brought it back with me after all,* she went back to cooking dinner.

Just then a sweet succulent aroma filled the cave, an aroma unlike anything she had ever smelled.

She looked back at him, finding the source of the smell. The boy ripped the sweet morsel in half, and extended the piece to her. He smiled.

My mom used to tell me not to take things from strangers... The girl thought to refuse, but smelled the sweet scent once more. *But it's also rude not to accept gifts.* She walked towards him and accepted his gift, and then returned to the fire.

She sniffed the light brown object and held it near her face to examine it. *This isn't some kind of poison, right?* She slowly nibbled on it. The next few moments felt like a blur because the food that the boy had given her had suddenly disappeared. Her body was instantly rejuvenated with energy. As the sweet taste lingered in her mouth, she couldn't help but kick her feet out in the air in delight. The girl put both palms on her cheek, wanting to preserve this taste forever. The two looked at each other and smiled.

For the first time since she had met him, the boy laughed, which gave her great relief.

He took a seat by her next to the fire and handed her his share of his sweet treasure.

"I can't take that." The girl shook her head no, not wanting to be a greedy host.

But the boy was insistent on giving it to her.

Well, if you really want me to take it... The girl took and ate the chocolate, this time letting out a much louder happy squeal. *How is it possible that it'd taste even better the second time around?*

She started laughing with him, happy that she was able to eat something so delectable and also happy to have been given a gift from her very first friend. Though their laughter would soon be interrupted by her friend's loud, gurgling stomach.

"Here, have some of this rabbit." This time it was her turn to be insistent in sharing her food with her friend. The girl looked at him again, pointing to the rabbit that was cooking in the fire.

He quickly shook his head no, refusing to eat no matter how much she urged him.

The girl felt frustration build up within her. "It's okay, you don't have to be shy." She ripped off a piece of the cooked rabbit, this time shoving the meat in his mouth, as her new friend probably did not want to be a bother. But to her, he was no bother as he had already shared his meal with her, so it was only right that she did the same.

She watched as the boy chewed on it, slowly as if trying to decipher its taste, until he swallowed it. It did not take long for him to want more, which made her grow a proud smile on her face.

She gave him another piece, and the boy took it this time without hesitation.

You see, this is how friends should be. Well, not that I would know... But this must be what friends do...right? The girl had no idea as she had been alone for quite some time now. *I wonder what his name is? I wonder what made him stumble into the woods? I wonder if he has a family?* Family. Family was something that she did not have. She and her parents had been attacked by humans despite being simple merchants. *Humans are the reason why I'm here alone. His people.* The Mogoniwai girl had not seen her parents for about four years now. *Why did I help him again?* Though, she already knew the answer. The girl had another good look at him, *I wonder if I was as scared as he was when I first got separated from my parents?*

What did ma and pa always say again? She swayed back and forth, reliving and remembering their voices that still resided in her heart. That was when the girl happened to lock eyes on him. She waved at him with a smile, *She always did say that not all humans are bad. I wonder if they were here with me now, they'd let me bring my new friend over to go play. I'm sure they'd say yes.*

She was disrupted midthought as her new friend shrieked in pain. He had accidentally waved his hand into the heart of the fire.

"Watch out! The fire!" His normally pale hands were burnt red. She gasped, worried that he was going to get hurt once again. The girl quickly rushed over to him. *Humans are a lot more fragile than I thought.*

The boy had opened his mouth but she completely ignored him, she needed to concentrate.

To Mogoniwais, magic was second nature to them. She was only a toddler when she was able to perform magic, like healing scrapes or summoning balls of fire—though at that time, she could only conjure a fireball the size of her fists. To trigger her magic, she and her people prayed to the spirits to will for things to come into fruition. Whether it was the workings of spirits or not, she had no idea, but regardless, she willed and prayed. Right now she had willed for her friend's hand to be healed. Her hand began to illuminate and her magic did as she willed it to.

She turned to him and pointed to the fire, "The fire, don't touch. The fire, don't touch. It hurts!" The girl hovered her hand over the fire and made an ouch sound, hoping that the boy would understand how foolish it would be to touch it.

The girl did not know if the message came across, but it seemed like he understood.

He sat upright again and called out to her. Of course, his words still made no sense to her.

She stared at him, trying to understand him. "What are you

saying?" The girl tried reading his lips but still they did not make sense.

He pointed to himself, "Aspen, Ahhh-spen." He repeated it a couple more times. The boy pointed to himself and to his mouth, sounding it out to her.

What are you trying to tell me? the girl wondered.

He started throwing weird punches in the air. She quickly scanned the cave and didn't see anything nearby, not only confused about what he was saying but also whom he was fighting. The boy gestured to her to come over. She stood up from her seat and awkwardly mimicked him, not knowing what or why he was doing this.

I wonder why he tries to keep talking to me when we both can't understand each other, she wondered. She patiently watched him talk and talk about something, something the boy was probably quite passionate about.

The human started throwing punches and kicks in the air, while pointing right towards her, as if he was challenging her.

She looked at him and punched the air slowly like he just did. *Why did he point at me just now? And who does he keep fighting?* the girl thought to herself and looked around at their surroundings. She couldn't see anyone nearby. *Maybe he actually wants to fight me.* She scoffed at that idea. *There's no way this person wants to fight me, I would beat him no problem.* The girl put her hands on her hips and held her chin high, knowing full well that she'd destroy him if needed. She stared at the boy who shared one of the tastiest foods in the world with her. *This person is strange, a bit of a scaredy-cat at times, but he seems nice. Maybe I won't hurt him too much if he gets out of line.*

The boy took a break from fighting imaginary animals and was constantly pointing at the chocolate bar wrapper to her once more. This time with much more enthusiasm.

The Mogoniwai stamped her feet to the ground with excitement. *Oh, I get it! Maybe if I help him he'll give me more of whatever this food was.* The idea excited her immensely. Never had she consumed something so sweet and delectable before, even the berries that grew in the springtime could not compare. "Do you want to make a deal? Is that it?" Her face lit up at the idea; it seemed like a fair trade to her, the sweet morsel for her help.

He nodded his head. Her assessment must have been correct.

Her new friend stuck out his pinky.

"Is that some kind of pact agreement?" the girl asked. She awkwardly stared on, not sure what she was supposed to do with his finger.

His lips were moving again, she was sure he was trying to explain the terms of agreement to her, but unless he could suddenly speak her language, it was all moot.

He suddenly took her hand, which she immediately swatted away.

"I didn't say you can touch me," the Mogoniwai child stepped back.

He approached her slower and raised his hands, conveying that he meant no harm.

The child watched as he tried to reach out to her. This time however she allowed him and had extended her hand to his.

The girl had been fighting for what seemed like her entire life. Out here in the woods, a moment of weakness, a moment of a lack of awareness and caution could spell death. But maybe she could trust this boy. The world had been so lonely after all these years that it felt unbearable to keep moving on by herself.

The boy held her hand, stuck her pinky out, and closed the rest of her fingers. For the first time in a while, she felt the warmth of another. It felt far warmer than the campfire she had made every night, and far warmer than the sunny mornings. It was a warmth quite familiar to her although from quite some time ago. She could not help but imagine her snuggling up to her parents every night.

She looked at him, and then marveled at their linked fingers, and returned a smile.

Unknown words were coming out of his mouth. The girl had no

clue what he was saying but she made up her own terms. *If you bring me more of those sweet things, I promise with all my heart, I'll be your best friend and protect you from anything dangerous and scary.*

This is my promise to you, to my new friend, my friend...

The girl opened her mouth wide with excitement, "Ahh peen!"

The boy became dumbfounded, and then suddenly bursted into a ball of excitement, he looked giddy as he kept shouting words.

I was right after all, that was his name.

"Ah peen, Ahh peen, Ah peen," she cheered over and over again. The girl began to think that maybe they'd be able to talk to each other after all.

So that was your name after all, Ahh peen. Ah Pen. She enunciated the sound of his name over and over in her head, practicing to make sure she was pronouncing it correctly.

The boy, who would soon become her very first friend, pointed to his chest in validation. "I'm Ahh peen."

CHAPTER

SIX

"So, do you know where the exit is?" asked Aspen.

"Ah spen?" she responded, confused as to what he wanted.

"Yes, do...you...know...where...the exit...is?" he repeated, now talking slower, as if it would help her understand better. The girl returned with only a blank stare. It was until performing various hand gestures and signals to get his point across did she eventually understand, now getting quite used to his charades.

Maybe I'm getting better at this, Aspen thought, already mentally congratulating himself for figuring out how to converse with a demon.

The cave was pitch-black, but somehow this girl was able to navigate through the cave as if it was bright as day. Aspen had a tough time following her through the cave at first. Thankfully, however, she quickly realized his lack of direction and held his hand to help set him on the right course. The two continued on, climbing over rocks, scaling the walls and going through various tunnels. Aspen had tried to mentally map their route, though gave up halfway, already knowing it would be impossible for him to remember. If he were to ever traverse this area again, he'd just have to leave it to luck.

Eventually, they were able to make it out of the cave. Outside, the snow had already subsided. It was night time; beyond the trees Aspen couldn't see anything else but the stars and the moon outside. He took a minute to take in the scenery, burning this mental image into his head. The moon and the stars shimmered brightly in the night sky. Aspen never really bothered to go stargazing before, but now, something about it looked different.

"Thanks for showing me to the exit," Aspen thanked the girl. However, she still stuck by his side. "Oh, uh...you can go now, if you want," he added, pointing back to the cave.

"Non." The girl shook her head and refused, probably because this was the first time she had conversed with a human in what seemed like forever.

Aspen heard her footsteps following behind him as he proceeded walking. Though, he didn't mind. "Well, I guess that's okay, too."

It was only but a few minutes until the footsteps behind him stopped. He quickly turned around, wondering if she had decided to turn back. Though, that was not the case. The girl stood in place, clasping both hands together and gazed upon the shooting stars up above with a twinkle in her eyes.

Though the sky was a sight to behold, Aspen caught a glimpse in which the beauty of the stars could not compare. The girl's silky, luscious white hair blew in the night sky, flowing gently like a calm river, and sparkled under the moonlight, like the very stars that captivated her gaze. If only he was able to encapsulate this moment, so that he'd have proof that stars are not only just found up in space. Aspen turned away as he found himself staring, feeling quite wonder-struck by her beauty.

"The moon is beautiful outside tonight, isn't it?" he muttered softly. Aspen walked back and stood with the girl so that they both could share the moment. The two locked eyes and smiled, then continued to gaze at the shooting stars together in silence until they disappeared off to the vast emptiness of space.

"Hey, so you know my name already, but I didn't catch yours," Aspen asked the girl. Though no matter how he tried to ask her, in the end, she shook her head. *Does she not have a name?* He thought, *surely even demons name their children.* For now, the fact of the matter could wait.

I should probably head back to town soon. It isn't like I can stay here forever. This got him thinking, wondering if anyone would even be worried about his disappearance or even realized that he was gone. Niko was probably worried sick about him, perhaps even Willey. His dad probably hadn't even noticed that he had disappeared, and Aspen wouldn't put it past him to not feel anything beyond anger or disappointment.

He peered through the woods; though dark, the moon reflected light upon a path straight ahead. Aspen turned to look at the girl, then back at the woods, then back to her with confliction, wondering if this might be their last time together despite their promise. "I guess it's pretty dark outside, I would probably have a hard time finding my way back right now."

Plus there's probably scary animals out and about, I don't think it'd be safe, he surmised, trying to persuade himself. "Maybe can I stay one more night? Just until it's morning again," Aspen asked her. The girl didn't understand at first, only until he pointed back to the path back and charaded his way did Aspen get through to her. Slowly but surely, she became accustomed to the meanings behind his acts and gestures.

He followed her down the cave, this time making sure to stick close so as to not get lost again. They reached the room, the fire still burning strong. This was the room where Aspen had first met this girl who saved his life and discovered she was a demon. It was only a little while ago that he tried to hatch plans to escape this place, but now here he was, willingly wanting to come back. Aspen chuckled at the irony of it all.

As Aspen set his backpack down, an object fell to the ground. He bent over, picked it up, and wiped some dirt off it. It was Niko's birthday present.

The demon girl walked over to Aspen with curiosity, having never before seen anything with such vibrant colors.

Aspen handed her the book. "Did you want to take a look?"

She took the book and stroked the illustrations on the cover. Staring at it intently, she was especially enamored by the princess on the cover, her hair white as snow—similar to her own.

"That's Princess Noelle on the cover," Aspen answered as he pointed to the character. "She's the main character of the story alongside the village boy. It was one of my favorite books as a kid."

"Ahpen?" The girl looked at him, pointing at the boy on the cover.

"No, that's not me," Aspen shook his head.

She tugged on his black hair.

"Yeah, I know he has the same black hair."

She pointed to his eyes.

"Okay, yeah he does have the same color eyes as me, but he's not me," Aspen swore. After taking a closer look however, the resemblance did seem uncanny.

"My mom used to read this to me every night when I was little. Before going to bed, that is. It was one of my favorites."

The girl flipped through the book, looking as if trying to absorb the beautiful illustrations. Judging by her reaction, Aspen knew she had no clue what this was used for, but was fascinated by it nonetheless.

"Ahhpee," she tugged on Aspen's shoulder.

"Huh, what was that?" Aspen turned to her. She held the book to his face and tugged on his shirt sleeve again. "Would you like me to read it to you?" Aspen asked as he pointed to the book. The girl nodded.

"Sure, I can read it," Aspen said. He settled himself near the campfire, because not everyone had nocturnal vision like the Mogo-niwai beside him. His face formed a tiny pout of jealousy, there was no end to what she could do. "Come over here," he said, gesturing for the girl to sit close to him.

It's not exactly as comfy as my bed back at home, but it will do. The girl handed him the book and took her seat, huddling near him with eyes gleaming with anticipation. *This sure does bring me back.* As he watched her, he was reminded of his younger self—the feeling of suspense and excitement as each page gets turned, the appreciation of the art that somehow dances into everyone's imaginations, and his eyes that sparked joy and elation. Suddenly, he was back to his old nighttime routine, where his mother would sit by his bedside and read to him, and his father would also step in with glasses of warm milk, often sticking around 'til the end. Sometimes, Aspen would fall asleep halfway through, and other times, the whole family would fall asleep in the same room. Those were great times. Amazing times, in fact. But now those times were a thing of the past. And here he was, the one telling the story.

"This is the story of The Village Boy and the Snow Princess," narrated Aspen. He turned to look at the girl, who dared not move in case she were to miss something and whose body fidgeted, waiting for him to start. He flipped the page and continued,

A long long time ago lay a village where the snow suddenly stopped melting and the sun stopped shining. All because of the appearance of one girl, the girl whose hair was as white as the snow that fell from the sky.

"Asa mo mo!" the demon girl cheered as soon as she saw the princess from the cover appear on the page.

This girl was named Noelle. Everyone in town called her Snow Princess Noelle, since snow seemed to fall wherever she lived. Snow Princess Noelle lived in the outskirts of the village, in the woods all by her lonesome. Initially, the villagers wanted to chase her away, so that spring would come again, but did not, in fear that she would retaliate. Eventually, all the villagers got used to living in an eternal winter wonderland.

Though everyone in town feared her, the village boy did not. Often he would visit Snow Princess Noelle to keep her company as she lived far away from the village. He would bring her hot chocolate and cookies, and talk to her about the daily lives of the people who live in the village.

One day, the princess asked the village boy, "Why do you visit me everyday? Are you not afraid of me?"

"How could I be afraid of someone who helps the village so much?" asked the village boy.

"How so? Because I live here, the snow never stops falling and the sun hardly shines," she remarked.

"Yes, but it is also you who provided all the wood that keeps our fireplaces always lit and you who provided the herbs that heals our sick and much, much more," the village boy explained

"Have you always been watching?" asked the Snow Princess.

"I have and I always will. The villagers may not see it now, but one day they will see, they'll see how beautiful the snow really is," reassured the boy.

The next night, however, a blizzard appeared out of nowhere, destroying many homes and crops.

"It must be that cursed princess!" yelled one of the villagers.

"We must get rid of her!" yelled another. Everyone in the village grabbed their pitchforks and torches, ready to push the Snow Princess away.

The demon girl became visibly upset at the sights of the angry mob of torches and pitchforks. Aspen took notice of this and wondered if she too experienced something similar.

Despite this, and despite not knowing entirely what was going on in the story, it seemed like she enjoyed it. Pictures probably played a part in helping her understand at least, as she often cheered when Noelle appeared on the pages and frustratingly scoffed when the angry mob showed up. At least one thing was for certain—the demon girl was completely enamored with Snow Princess Noelle.

The demon girl yawned, which in turn made Aspen yawn immediately after. It had been a long, eventful night, so being fatigued did not come as a surprise for the two of them.

Aspen closed the book, "Perhaps we'll end it here for now and pick up at another time. So, what did you think of the story so far... uh..." *That's right I still don't know her name,* he realized.

"Aspeen! Asa noi yo go go!" the girl excitedly exclaimed.

"I'm glad you liked it so far! Hmm. You know, it might be hard to talk to each other if you don't have a name." He took a slight pause and looked at the girl, "If it is alright with you, can I give you a name then?"

Taking a minute to think of what would be a suitable name for her, an idea arose as he glanced at the book's cover. "I've got it!" Aspen blurted out. He pointed to the girl, "Your name is Noelle. Just like the character in the book! Maybe one day everyone will see you how I see you."

The girl pointed to herself. "No elle?" She looked as if she was deep in thought, then her eyes widened. She looked at Aspen, smiled, and then pointed to herself, exclaiming, "No elle!"

Aspen smiled back at her. "That's right, my name is Aspen, and from this day forward, your name is Noelle."

CHAPTER
SEVEN

I t was morning again. Without even realizing it, Aspen had fallen asleep sometime after he had stopped reading the story to Noelle. She escorted him out of the cave and back to the cliffs where he had nearly lost his life. The sun beamed brightly on their faces, and it was warm outside, a far cry from the weather a few days ago. It felt as if he was getting embraced by the sun itself, and he thought that maybe this was the universe's lame way of apologizing for all the bad luck he'd received.

"Well, I have to go back now," Aspen informed Noelle. As he gathered his backpack, she followed him.

"Sorry, I have to go by myself," he said, gesturing for her to stay put. Aspen stuck out his pinky. "But don't worry, we made a promise. Remember, Noelle? I'll come back. I'll see you again. Back at the caves." She stuck her pinky out in response. "Goodbye for now, Noelle."

Noelle could hardly raise her head to look at him. *My first friend... is leaving already?* Just like her parents. Who knew if he would return or not.

Aspen took notice. He felt bad about leaving but it wasn't like he could live here in the woods forever. He unzipped his backpack and pulled something out. "Here, Noelle. For you. Hold on to this for me, will ya?"

She carefully held onto it like it was a delicate jewel.

"We still have to finish the rest of the book. I'll return for it later so, for now...keep it safe for me, okay?" Aspen asked. "Until next time, Noelle. Goodbye."

"Gud bee, Ahh peen," Noelle mimicked Aspen and waved. She stood there with a grin on her face, only showing her disheartened look when he disappeared from her view. The first human boy she had ever met was gone now, leaving her all alone in the woods once again.

WAS I ALWAYS THIS ATHLETIC? Aspen proceeded to climb up the cliff, surprising himself that he managed to reach the top without tiring out. He looked behind him, the demon girl, Noelle, was nowhere to be seen. It was time to come back to reality. Aspen recalled to the best of his abilities the route Niko had taken the group, though it was a little difficult considering the number of turns he had made them take to throw off Gerard and his goons.

"Aspen!" a worn out voice called out from behind him. He turned around, and to his relief, it was his father and Niko.

"He's found!"

"Aspen's right there!"

"Thank heavens, he's safe and sound!"

Other villagers scattered around the forest, shouts of great relief at his sudden emergence. A search party had been launched to find him. An act that greatly surprised Aspen, not thinking that anyone would even care at all.

"Aspen, it is you!" Niko rushed towards him, hugging him so tight that it felt like he was going to get crushed. "Where were you, man? We've been looking for you everywhere! When I came back,

Gerard said you just disappeared. There was blood from where you fell, but there was no trail and...that Gerard! That little snake already had half the town convinced that he was nowhere near the scene."

Of course Gerard would lie like that, he thought. Niko sank down to the ground, looking like a sudden weight of guilt slid off his shoulders.

His father approached him, almost stumbling at the very sight of his son, stashing away his flask in his back pocket. Ben wiped his mouth with the sleeve of his shirt and kneeled towards his son. The alcohol was evident on his breath. Ben covered his own face, though Aspen wasn't sure if it was because of relief or because his father was battling a migraine.

"Isn't it great, Mayor Chase?" Arthur said. "We found him safe and sound." Arthur was a tall, young tan man who recently started working for the mayor. There was no doubt in Aspen's mind that this guy wouldn't last too long as he imagined working for his father could not be fun at all.

Ben ignored him completely, his attention completely towards his son.

"Are you hurt? Niko said you fell from a cliff," Ben asked in his usual stern demeanor. "Y-you're okay, ri–," he halted as he combed Aspen's bangs back and inspected him, seeing no visible signs of an injury at all. Ben grasped both of Aspen's shoulders, his arms shaking and quivering, looking as if he was about to hug him, but quickly lowered his arms.

He was surprised at his father's question, as this was the first time he had felt concern from him in a long while. Aspen studied his father's face, something he hadn't done since he was young. His father had bags under his eyes, his clothes were riddled with dirt, and his fingernails were split from digging in the snow.

"I-I'm fine, I'm not hurt at all. Actually I—" Aspen cut himself off before he could finish his sentence. There was no way he could tell them that he met, and was saved by, a demon. "Actually, something

61

broke my fall, I was perfectly fine. And it was nighttime, so I slept inside a cave."

"You spent two nights in a cave?" Ben replied in disbelief.

I was unconscious for an entire day? Aspen's eyes widened at the sudden realization. "I-I...um, sorry, sir." He had trouble thinking of an excuse off the top of his head.

His dad sighed. "Well, let's just head back for now so you can rest." He turned back to the search party. "Thank you all for helping me find my son," taking a bow towards them, "I couldn't have done it without you."

The atmosphere was now calm as everyone headed home.

After traveling for about half an hour, they finally made it back to town. Niko said farewell to Aspen and his dad, telling him that they would meet up again after he got some rest. It wasn't long until another familiar voice called out his name up ahead.

"Hey, Aspen!" the voice yelled as he ran towards him. It was Gerard, who immediately turned to Aspen's dad and said, "Oh, um... good afternoon, Mayor Chase, I'm a friend of your son here. Boy, I was sure worried when I heard that Aspen was lost."

"Thank you for your concern, Gerard," his father replied, "and thank you for joining the search party yesterday."

Gerard leaned closer to Aspen and whispered in his ear so that only he could hear, "I saw you. Laying there, bleeding. And now you're good as new? Something happened out there. Something fishy." Gerard took a step back. "Well, I'll let you guys go. You need to rest up, right, Aspen?" He began backing away from them. "Glad to see that you're fine after all. Oh, and thank you for everything that you do for the city, Mayor Chase."

Beads of sweat rolled down his forehead. Gerard was the last person he wanted to find out about Noelle.

They arrived back at the house where Aspen instantly headed for his room to rest in his nice, soft bed. Though his bed was soft, his blanket warm, and his pillows plush, something didn't feel right. For some reason, the room still felt cold. It felt a tad bit lonely. It didn't take long for his eyes to droop. His scary journey had come to a close, and the gratification of prevailing through life's trials and tribulations had lulled him to sleep. Aspen didn't have any nightmares that night, as his mind was filled with nothing but thoughts of what he was going to bring Noelle next time they were to meet.

ASPEN LAZILY WOKE up and got out of bed. He headed downstairs to an empty kitchen; his dad must have let him sleep in and skip school today. "I wonder what I should do with my free time?" he asked himself as he ate breakfast and headed out the door. Aspen decided to go to Old Man Willey's store. Since he had been missing for a few days, Willey was probably worried about him. Well, that, and the fact that he wanted to buy some sweets.

He stepped into the store after a brisk walk and saw Willey jump out of his seat at the sight of him.

Willey rushed over to Aspen with a worried look on his face. "Are you okay? I heard what happened to you. I heard that you had fallen off a cliff because you lost your balance and they could not find you after that. Your father had been looking for you like a crazed madman, out there in that storm."

"Believe it or not, I'm fine," Aspen responded with a nervous laugh. He surveyed the store, trying to determine what sweets to buy.

"Well, as long as you're alright, then that's all that matters." Willey walked back to the counter.

"Thanks, Willey, I'll be more careful. Promise." He started looking through the store, aisle by aisle. "Ah, here they are!" he babbled, picking up a chocolate bar. *I'm in luck, he still has them! She'll like these crunchy milk chocolate bars. They always sell out fast.* Aspen headed to the counter to ring it up.

"Doing some light shopping, are we now?" asked Willey.

Aspen put the money on the counter. "Yup! I've been wanting to try them."

"Well, to celebrate your speedy recovery, here, I'll throw in a few of these, free of charge." Willey winked at Aspen. They were freshly baked chocolate almond cookies, the smell of melted sweet chocolate filled the air as he pulled them out from behind the counter.

"Thanks a bunch!" Aspen said as he grabbed the cookies from Willey. "I'll be back again!" He held the bag full of goodies, guarding it as if it was treasure, and briskly walked back home to avoid any of the questioning and curious townspeople.

ASPEN STEPPED into his house and noticed a note on the kitchen table. He picked it up and read it out loud, *Aspen, I'm going to the capital for the weekend for some impromptu meetings and to sort out some paperwork. I will be back on Monday. There's food in the fridge. Do not go out. Stay inside. Dad.* He stuffed the note in his pocket and rushed to his room, giddy with excitement. Aspen began packing his backpack again, stuffing books, a few clothes, and random supplies inside. He then ran downstairs and packed the sweets and all the food his dad prepared inside his backpack as well. It was a little before noon, meaning everyone would either be at work or at school. After finishing packing everything, he stepped outside and locked the door.

He headed out of town, away from the people, away from the commotion, and back into the woods. Aspen had remembered the path he took with Niko and Gerard, but this time there wasn't much snow on the ground, and the sun was beaming brightly. Aspen ran speedily through the path without stopping for breaks, the exhilaration was fueling his energy. The only thoughts he had were leaving this insufferable town once more.

In due time, he made it back to the cliffs. The cliffs that nearly killed him no longer scared him. How Aspen saw it, it's the first place where he met Noelle. He carefully scaled down the cliff, being extra cautious with each step as to not slip down.

"This is easier the second time around," Aspen said once reaching ground level. He hiked through the pathway to the cave. The pathway to Noelle's home had been camouflaged with a dense thicket that normally no one would travel through, except for now, that is. While walking, he saw many of the landmarks that he had memorized, using them as checkpoints to make sure he was going the correct path to the cave—like the giant tree with an *A* carved into it, the two neighboring boulders, and the river (in which he fell in once, still remembering how shivering cold it was).

Aspen made it to the entrance of the cave. "Noelle! Noelle! Are you here?" he called out. No response came from inside. "Hmm, is she out? What should I do now?" he wondered aloud.

Just then, he felt slaps on both shoulders and a voice yelled out, "Aspe!" in his ear. Aspen jumped and shrieked in fright, as it took him by surprise. He turned around and it was Noelle, who was giggling from her little prank.

"Ha ha, very funny, Noelle," Aspen said in a mockingly exasperated manner. "It's nice to see you again! This time, I brought tons of stuff to share with you," he continued, pointing to his backpack.

"Oh so lozzo cho to!" she thanked. Noelle didn't care too much about the gifts, she was simply excited that her newfound friend had visited her—and that was enough.

Aspen set his backpack down and took out some books. "I brought some of my old school books, I was thinking I could help teach them to you, we can start with the basics."

He and Noelle found a comfortable spot to sit and proceeded on with the lesson. "This is the alphabet, it's important for reading and writing. Once you learn this, you'll be able to read the books yourself. Here, just repeat after me." The two of them spent some time reciting the alphabet together. Noelle quickly learned the pronunciation of each letter, though she did have a hard time memorizing them all, often confusing M for N, and B for D.

Aspen slowly pointed to the letters and recited, "N-O-E-L-L-E, that's your name. Noelle. And A-S-P-E-N, Aspen is my name." She recited them back in perfect succession after trying for a couple minutes. "That's perfect, Noelle. You got it!" he congratulated her. Noelle became visibly proud of her achievement. They repeated their names and the alphabet many more times, until slowly but surely, Noelle started to memorize and get the hang of it.

"Since you seem to be getting the hang of the alphabet, let's move on to this," Aspen said, bringing out some paper and pencils. "You remember what the letters look like, so try writing your name on this paper. Write out N-O-E-L-L-E."

Noelle took the paper and pencil and examined it, then proceeded to write what seemed like scribbles. She looked at her scribbled attempt versus what the alphabet showed on the book and frowned.

"Here, let me help you out a little bit," Aspen suggested. He grabbed her hand and guided her as she wrote both her and his names on the paper. "There, now you try it."

As Noelle practiced her handwriting, Aspen's thoughts were adrift. This was probably the most relaxed he'd felt in a while. Away from the town, away from the people, no judgment, no conflict—this was something he could get used to. His daydream was cut short as he heard the sound of paper rustling to his face and Noelle's *humph* sound, indicating that she was finished.

"Oh, did you finish? Let me take a look at it." Aspen took the paper and examined it. It was a picture of himself and Noelle, a rather simple drawing, but it definitely had the distinguishing features correct. Below the drawing, she had Aspen's and Noelle's names written out. "That's amazing!" Aspen spoke with delight. "You're getting better and better at this." Noelle had a huge grin on her face, pleased with the results of her practice. He handed the paper back to her, but she gave it back to him. "Oh, are you letting me keep it?"

Noelle nodded.

"Thank you, Noelle!" Aspen took the drawing and stored it carefully in his backpack. "I'll treasure it forever."

"Oh, like I promised, Noelle, let's finish the story. Can you bring out the book I lent you?" She returned his book back to him, *The Village Boy and the Snow Princess*. The two sat comfortably next to each other and Aspen continued on from where they last left off.

And so, the villagers all marched to the woods where the princess lived. The village boy got word of the news and ran to catch up to them.

Once the angry mob found the princess, they all yelled out in a fit of rage, "We want you out of here! All you do is ruin our homes and our lives!"

The princess apologized, "This has been my home for as long as I can remember, but I shall disappear as the happiness of the village outweighs my own." And just like that, Snow Princess Noelle left without another word.

Noelle frowned once the snow princess left the pages.

The village boy had arrived too late, the snow princess had left the lands. He argued desperately at the mob, "She's not the monster that you all think she is, she's not!"

But was completely drowned out through the villager's own celebration of her departure. Realizing no one would listen to him, he alone chased after her.

Back at the village, their celebration is cut short, a blizzard raged furiously and hail dropped from the sky. It was a blizzard that was even harsher than anything they had all experienced before.

"I don't understand, we chased her out!" a villager shouted.

"The curse should have been broken!" another said.

With guilt weighing down on him, the village chief finally revealed his secret.

"The village had actually been cursed by a witch, a long, long time ago. It wasn't actually the snow princess' doing."

Aspen flipped to the next page, where it showed the village boy managing to catch up to her.

"*Snow Princess Noelle, you have to come back!*" *the village boy shouted at her.* "*Your home is back in the village.*"

"*I cannot,*" *she said.* "*Everyone would be much happier that I am gone, so I must—*"

A terrible gust of wind blew furiously, almost knocking them down. The two turned towards the gust of wind in horror, as they watched a blizzard form, blanketing the village the two called home.

"*Never mind, I must go back after all,*" *Snow Princess Noelle said.*

"*What are we going to do now?*" *a villager asked.*

"*The village will be destroyed at this point!*" *another shouted.*

"*No, it shall not.*"

The villagers turned around to see the village boy with Snow Princess Noelle.

"*Snow Princess Noelle, what are you doing here?*" *one asked.*

"*I will offer myself to the sky and end this harsh blizzard,*" *Snow Princess Noelle said.*

The village boy grabbed her hand, "*Snow Prin—*" *he choked on his words.* "*Noelle...You mustn't. Why would you do so much for a village that scorned you so? You don't have to do this!*"

But the Snow Princess had this to say, "*Because you had talked to me as if I was a normal person, and not a monster. Eventually from you and the stories you told I have inadvertently begun to love the village. As you have always watched over me, this time it is I who will watch over you.*"

The village boy woefully let go of her hand, knowing full well that nothing could stop her now.

"*I give myself to you!*" *Snow Princess Noelle shouted up above.* "*Please spare this village. The people here may not be perfect...*" *She turned back to look at the villagers one last time, but with a warm smile on her face,* "*but they are still good people.*"

The skies seemed to have accepted her offering as Snow Princess Noelle vanished into the sky.

The hail had turned into gentle snowflakes.

The harsh blizzard had stopped.

And the village was once again back to normal.

The snow was still never-ending at the village, but this time it was blanketed in a snow filled with the Snow Princess's warmth and love for them all.

And that had made the village feel warmer than any summer day.

Turning to his side, he managed to sneak a glance at Noelle wiping her wet eyes. She had sat in silence the entire time, not making a peep until now.

Aspen closed the book, "The end."

The atmosphere was filled with silence, the ending of the book hit much harder to him now then it did when he was little. It wasn't until their stomachs growled did it snap them out of it and the two returned to their normal selves. Aspen chuckled, "I guess it's time to eat." Before he could say another word, Noelle went back into the cave. After waiting for a few minutes, Noelle returned with a bow and arrow.

"Whoa, is that a homemade bow?" Aspen asked. "It looks super cool!" She handed him the bow and set of arrows and gestured for him to follow her. "O-oh I never really shot a bow before, I...I can't really—" But Noelle kept pushing him forward, not taking no for an answer. *This is crazy! I've never gone hunting in my life! I wouldn't even know the first thing to do.* He sighed. *I even brought enough food for the both of us this time.*

The two traveled into a deeper part of the woods, where wildlife was more abundant. This area was quite lively; the rabbits were hopping about, the deers trotted, the birds were chirping in the air. And of course, there were the two of them, trying to find supper.

"Here, you're better at this," Aspen urged Noelle as he attempted to hand her the bow. She, however, would not take it back but insisted on him handling it. He kept fiddling with the arrows, almost dropping them to the ground. Noelle turned Aspen's head to the right—a deer was standing out in the open.

"D-do you want me to shoot that?" Aspen stammered. He had never actually killed a living thing before, well, besides the bugs that crawled into his house. Noelle handed him an arrow, and then gestured to him to pull back the string of the bow and fire. Aspen awkwardly pulled it back and kept fumbling the arrow. It was only until she had helped him did he finally get into position. Noelle pointed at the deer, signaling Aspen to take the shot.

"Aspeen," she reassured him.

With the deer in sight, he took aim. A bead of sweat dropped from his brow. As Aspen aimed, flashes of images suddenly filled his head. He saw images of his mother when she was lying on her deathbed. Images of the time when he watched her from afar, daring not to look away for a second or else she'd disappear before his very eyes. Images of his fall from the cliff and the attack of the wolves appeared next. He felt like a ghost watching his very own death transpire before him. The thoughts of death filled his mind. Aspen shut his eyes in panic, shooting the arrow haphazardly. It landed onto a nearby bush, completely missing it. The deer galloped away and disappeared without a trace, living to see another day.

"S-sorry, Noelle," Aspen apologized. She ignored it and immediately pointed ahead. Something was rustling in the bushes, growing louder and louder. "W-what is that?" he whispered. The creature making the noise became more visible with each passing second. As Aspen squinted to get a better look, the little hairs on his arm began to stand. "It's a charging boar! We have to get out of here!" But before he could make his escape, Noelle held him in place.

"What are you doing? Let go of me, we have to run!"

Noelle did not falter; instead, she handed Aspen another arrow and positioned him again.

"I-I don't think I'm ready for this," Aspen stuttered. The boar was getting closer. "You should do this, not me." Noelle stood her ground.

Aspen took aim at the boar that was nearly within 100 meters of the two of them. He couldn't help but feel the looming shadow of death beside him, which made him instinctively shut his eyes. His arm was trembling, his whole body was shaking—he couldn't do this.

I'm not strong enough, Aspen thought to himself. He couldn't release the arrow, as if it was frozen onto him.

"Aspe," Noelle encouraged. She held his hand steady, guiding him straight ahead. Her warm embrace calmed him down.

He locked eyes with the charging boar, who was homing in on him. *That's right*, Aspen thought as he aimed the arrow and locked on to the boar. *I made a promise with Noelle that I'll be braver, that I'll move forward! With her, I can move on. I know I can move on.* He let go of the bow. *Whoosh!* Aspen's was hair tousled from the breeze of the arrow as it zipped through the air. A blinding light following the arrow's trail, as if preventing it from moving anywhere else but forward. It struck the boar dead center, stopping it in its tracks.

"I did it," Aspen said in disbelief. His eyes widened in realization. "Noelle, I did it! I was able to shoot! I was able to—"

His celebratory cheers were cut short, as he watched the life of the boar slowly leave its body. Blood poured out of its head, glistening bright red. Aspen felt his legs turn to jelly, as he heard the boar make its last squeal and realized what he had done. Thankfully, Noelle held him in place just as he was about to fall over. Instead of focusing on his unnerving guilt, he looked towards her. And doing so had calmed him down.

Noelle grinned profusely, congratulating him for a job well done and left him to marvel at his own achievement while she went to go collect their spoils of war. He panted slowly, taking it all in. It may not mean much for other people, but for Aspen, this meant much more than just a hunt or dinner. He shook off the last fleeting feeling of remorse, *I should be celebrating. For the first time...for the first time ever, I was able to stand my ground.*

Then, unable to control the excessive rumbling of their stomachs, they headed back towards the cave where Noelle was about to roast the pig by the fire, using various herbs found in the woods, until she had a great idea.

"Aspeen, foro. Bosa. Foro," she urged and pushed him forward to help her.

"What am I supposed to do with these sticks and pinecones?" Aspen complained. He tried to create friction between the two sticks in hopes that a small fire would ignite, but all it resulted was him being out of breath. "Can't you just do your magic powers and make one?"

Had Noelle left him to his own devices to figure it out, the boar would be spoiled rotten at this rate. She placed her hand over his, and guided them on the correct way to apply pressure and speed to the hearth board. There was a small plume of smoke from where the spindle struck the board until it eventually grew into a fire.

"I did it Noelle! Did you see that! I made a fire!" Aspen exclaimed.

"Aspeen bo bo co co!" she cheered.

Finally, it was time to cook.

Aspen gagged, immediately turning around at the sight of Noelle dressing the boar. And then felt squeamish once more at the sight of the boar's body charcoaling from the fire. He enjoyed eating meat like everyone else, but never had to sit staring at the face of what he was eating before.

The smoke flowed to the top of the cave, and it didn't take long for the room to be filled with the smell of roasted pig. Thankfully, Noelle had cut up the boar, so he did not have to stare at its whole body much longer. Preparing the meat ended up taking a lot longer than anticipated, but it was worth the wait, in Aspen's opinion, as she had cooked yet another delicious dinner. Coupled with his hunger and how delicious it tasted, Aspen ended up helping himself to seconds. Something this delectable was dangerous, Noelle was too great of a cook despite not having a stove.

Before he could fall victim to a food coma, Aspen remembered something. "Oh, Noelle, now that we had dinner, we can finally eat these!" He pulled out the chocolates and cookies that he received from Willey. Aspen handed Noelle a large cookie. Her eyes lit up and mouth drooled from the sight of the sweets right in front of her. As she was about to take a bite, she paused.

"What's wrong?" asked Aspen.

ASPEN AND THE DEMON PRINCESS

Noelle broke the cookie in half and gave the other half to him.

"Oh no, I'm fine, Noelle, you can have it all," Aspen assured her. He pushed the cookie back to her. But Noelle let out a *humph* and would not take no for an answer, pushing the cookie back to him.

"Oh okay, you win," he chuckled as he took the cookie.

They both ate the pastries at the same time, and grinned from ear to ear. Though it wasn't fresh out of the oven, the chocolate chips still melted with each bite. Noelle felt pure bliss again, as she savored the taste of every bite.

"And now that we also got dessert out of the way, here are the last of my gifts to you," Aspen told her. He put a bunch of objects out of his bag—stuff Noelle had never seen or used before.

"Here, Noelle, this is a sleeping bag, I figured it would beat sleeping on the hard ground. Oh, and here is a lantern, you can light a fire in it so you can see better in the cave. Oh, oh! And also here's some of my old picture books! I know how much you liked *The Village Boy and the Snow Princess*." Aspen described each item's use to her as he excitedly handed them off.

"T-tank you, Aspe..." she muttered quietly. Noelle wasn't quite sure if she was using the term correctly, but had noticed that Aspen used it a lot when accepting food from her. She held each item like a delicate little treasure, never before had Noelle received such gifts in her life.

"Are those your first words?" Aspen enthusiastically replied. "You're welcome, Noelle!" It was only a short amount of time, but he was already thrilled at the progress she had made. Noelle was surely a genius. Maybe one day he would be able to converse with her freely, without any language barriers.

"You learn so quickly, maybe one day you'll speak it better than I can," he joked, gently patting her on the head. Noelle was elated at the praise.

"You know, I also want to thank you for today," Aspen told her. He fidgeted with his fingers, looking down. "I know that you won't understand everything that I say right now, and maybe it's easier...

more comforting, since you can't understand me. But I think I would feel better talking to you."

"You see, my mom died when I was little, and ever since then, I've just been afraid. We can't prepare for it. We don't know when it will happen. We're just helpless. Death comes whenever it feels like it," Aspen paused. "It's a stupid thing to say, but I'm afraid of dying. I'm sure everyone is...I don't know. W-watching her suffer made me scared, scared that I'm gonna get hurt one day, scared that the people I care about will get hurt, I just don't want to see any more people get hurt. Even today, after killing that boar, it still scared me."

Noelle didn't know the context of what he was saying, but she did know that he was hurting on the inside. The shadows of his past kept Aspen in the dark, preventing him from moving forward. She placed her hand on top of Aspen's to comfort him. But no longer does he have to walk alone, she silently communicated. As long as she was here, she would be his beacon.

"But then I met you," Aspen continued on. He held his head up to match Noelle's gaze. "You gave me a second chance. I admire you, it seems like nothing scares you. Whatever happens, you confront it head on. I thought to myself that maybe I could stop being wimpy and scared all the time, maybe I can be a little brave, too. If I watched you, maybe even I can change. We barely know each other, but ever since I met you, I've finally felt like I can breathe again. Maybe even stare death in the face."

Aspen allowed himself to be vulnerable with Noelle, exposing every guilt, every fear, and every hope that he buried deep within. He laid it all out there, his secrets disclosed, just like the storybook he read to her. Perhaps all this time Aspen had wanted someone to read his story. Maybe it had to be *this* someone in particular. Maybe it only could have been Noelle all this time. His chest began to glow along with hers, however, Aspen paid no heed to it. The more he talked, the more he felt a connection to this girl, a connection that warmed up his world. So, he continued to focus on her, and only her, ignoring all else. And she carefully listened to him, soaking in every word that he articulated from his mouth. Whether or not she could understand his words, it was clear to him that she could understand his heart. Throughout that night, as the fire crackled beside them in the dim cave, a light was birthed between the two of them that shined brighter than any star or moon they'd ever seen in the night sky before.

PART TWO

[Four Years Later]

"Hey, wait up!" a voice called out, emerging through the bushes. The boy was already out of breath, trying to catch up to the person up ahead.

"You know what they say—the early bird gets the worm, right?" the girl responded back. Her silky white hair tousled in the air with every leap and bound as she rushed forward.

"You do realize that it's nearly the afternoon, right?" the boy complained in retaliation, finally catching up to her only because the girl leading the way had stopped to survey the area.

"Oh, do you have to be keen on the specific, Aspen?" retorted the girl.

"I wouldn't be a good teacher if I didn't correct you, Noelle," snickered Aspen.

"Wait, I think I hear it up ahead," she pointed ahead, "right over there in that direction. Can you see it?"

"Bless your insane hearing, I can see it, too. I'll take the shot." He took out his bow and arrow.

Aspen stood tall next to Noelle. They used to be around the same height when they were kids, but now Aspen was a head taller than her. His disheveled and messy black hair was now a little more kempt and longer now. And from the constant training and hunting with Noelle, albeit sometimes against his will, he'd become a bit muscular.

"Aim carefully. We have only one shot," Noelle warned him. She, too, looked different from her childhood days. Noelle's silky white hair grew in length to about the middle of her back. She stopped wearing the handwoven clothes that she used to wear as a kid, and instead wore clothes purchased by Aspen. Her nails were also now trimmed and her face clean of dirt, courtesy of the various household items that he had introduced her to.

Aspen took aim, his hand steady and confident. "I got this in the bag. You know I'm not a kid anymore," he exclaimed, shooting the arrow. The arrow whizzed through the air and hit dead center at a golden spotted boar a few meters ahead.

"Yes!" he shouted with excitement, immediately rushing over to the boar to collect his prize.

"I can't believe we found one!" cheered Noelle. "They're super hard to find, but when you do, it's the best thing you ever tasted." She followed after him.

"Even better than chocolate?" he inquired. Aspen took the arrow out of the boar and cleaned it with a rag.

Noelle smiled back in defeat. "Okay, okay. I guess it's the second best thing you could ever taste." She helped Aspen carry the boar back to the cave to prepare for lunch.

"I remember when I had to force you to hunt and eat," Noelle said as they were walking back. "But now you can finally do so on your own. I am so proud of you." She teased Aspen, pinching his cheeks, a routine that she enjoyed greatly through the years.

"I still remember you shoving a dead rabbit up in my face; don't think I've forgotten about that. I still get nightmares, you know," Aspen jokes, his body letting out a tiny shiver.

"It's not my fault that you were afraid of every little thing back then!"

"Hey, cut me some slack! I think it was fair to say that I was having a rough day that day." As soon as they sat the pig down, Noelle immediately went to work.

"Do you need any help with that?" Aspen asked.

"No, I'm fine, but can you bring me the spices?" Noelle replied. Aspen handed her a bunch of spices from the cave and sat back down. He took out a notebook, paper, and pen and went to work.

"This algebra homework is killing me," groaned Aspen, scratching his head with the eraser end of his pencil. He stared at the problem set, waiting for the answer to pop up in his head, but was completely dumbfounded.

"Here, let me see," Noelle offered. She stopped what she was doing and sat next to Aspen, glancing at the assignment. He handed her the book. Noelle scribbled on the paper as she began calculating off the top of her head. "And if you carry that one, then it should be this," she said, handing Aspen back the assignment.

Aspen took a look and was in awe. "You're already almost as good as me in writing, don't tell me you're going to beat me in math, too," he chuckled, now starting on the next problem.

"All it takes is a little studying," Noelle remarked with a proud look on her face. She began spicing up the roasted boar and crisped it to perfection, the air around them enveloped with the smell of fried, smoky barbeque. The scent wafted in the air, enticing even the fullest man to hunger. This in turn only made their stomachs grumble even louder. Aspen had a tough time focusing on his assignment as his mind lingered towards lunch.

Aspen glanced at the roasted boar, then back at his assignment, then back at the boar again. "How long will it be until it's done?" he asked, wiping a little bit of the drool that was coming from his mouth. "How am I supposed to concentrate with that smell just teasing me?"

"Just about done," Noelle replied. Her attention was fixated on the boar, making sure it was cooked to perfection. After all, it did take several months to find this thing. She cut the boar into strips of meat, which turned to a dark hue of red, becoming charred and crispy. "Okay, all done! Let's eat!" Noelle announced, setting the meat on a plate.

They each took a moment to appreciate the smell of freshly burned pork, the playful tease that danced around their nostrils was over. Every bite of the strip was met with the crunch texture followed by a combined flavor of saltiness and spiciness. Perfection. Both Aspen's and Noelle's faces glowed as they ate their lunch. Their plates were cleaned in a matter of minutes, not a single morsel left.

Aspen laid on the ground, suffering from an extreme case of food coma. "That was probably the best dish you've made yet." He closed his eyes; it wouldn't take any effort for him to fall asleep at this point.

"Probably true," Noelle agreed as she laid beside him.

"You know, Noelle, I've been thinking a bit about the day we first met. Why did you decide to save me?" Aspen asked with curiosity.

"Isn't that a silly question, why wouldn't I save you? Had I not, you would have been a wolf's dinner."

"Normally people shy away from danger. You know the Gerard guy I told you about? He ran off that day. Without hesitation, in fact."

"That reminds me, are you still letting him tease you?"

"I...uh...no comment."

Noelle sat straight up at Aspen's lack of response. "He is, isn't he? Why do you let him bully you still? You are surely strong enough to fight him in combat now."

"It's different, somehow," Aspen tried to explain. "When I'm only with you, I feel more confident and at ease, you know? But when I'm not...I still have trouble dealing with, like, people."

Noelle laid back down again and sighed. "You know, if I ever saw him do that to you, I would—"

Aspen cut her off immediately, "I know, I know. You would crush him in a second." He let out a soft laugh. "No one in the world could stand against you. You're the strongest in the whole world."

"That's right, and don't you forget it," Noelle confidently declared. The wind whistled in the sky among the silence between them. "It was that look in your eye."

"What now?"

"Why I saved you that day, right? It was the look in your eye," Noelle explained.

"The look in my eye? You mean the look of almost peeing my pants in sheer terror?"

"No, no. When I was passing by that day, I saw you. It seemed like your body had given up that day, but your eyes, they told me something different.They seemed like they were screaming that you wanted to live." Noelle stretched out her legs and extended her arm to the sun as if trying to grab hold of it.

"You know, I can never thank you enough for that day," Aspen replied.

"It's not like you haven't done anything for me," Noelle emphasized. "Because of you, I've gotten to try things like chocolate, and you taught me how to read and how to write. I am happy." She stopped short of what she was really thinking. *I was alone growing up, but ever since that day you've been by my side. These past four years have been the happiest I have of my life.* Noelle briskly glanced towards his direction. *And it was all because of you.*

"I guess we're good for each other," Aspen joked. He reached for her exposed hand but stopped himself short.

Noelle's cheeks turned a lighter flush of red, slightly embarrassed by his comment. "Though you can get on my nerves sometimes," she muttered so quietly that he could not hear.

"But you did save my life that day. I wouldn't be here today if it weren't for you." A circle appeared on his chest, glowing brightly before fading away slowly. After many years had passed, he had come to realize that when this happened, he could feel her emotions and her presence, whether they were a foot apart or miles away from each other.

Noelle had told him a few years back about what really happened on the day that she saved him. Aspen was lying on the red-stained ground with multiple broken bones and dying from blood loss. He was nearly at death's door. That day, she was focused on one thing—saving Aspen's life.

The Mogoniwais had always had these magical abilities ranging from enhancing one's strength or creating explosions, to even saving someone from the brink of death. Noelle instinctively healed all his wounds by using her abilities, inadvertently imparting a bit of her mana, the source of a Mogoniwai's power, into Aspen's body. His magical prowess could not match the average Mogoniwai, where the only magical feat he could muster was absorbing and imparting mana, though it only worked with Noelle and random bursts of strength. This, in turn, made Aspen feel like he was connected to her. Puberty was hard enough as it is, but having to control his ever-glowing chest was icing on the cake. Despite some very close calls and glowing in the worst times, he had been able to hide it.

Not only did he have to hide his feelings from Noelle, but he also had to hide his friendship with Noelle from everyone else. It'd been four years now, and they'd both successfully hidden their friendship from all of Aspen's peers. The war had ended quite some time ago, but the relationship between the Mogoniwais and the humans was still as tense as ever. Feelings of resentment and hate still lingered amongst the people, some even preferred another war rather than peaceful coexistence. If the town were to ever find Noelle, it would spell nothing but trouble.

"Hey, Noelle..."

"Yeah?"

"You—" Aspen bit his tongue. A part of him wanted to ask Noelle about her family, but stopped short. All Aspen knew was that they were no longer in her life when she was a small child. For as long as they knew each other, conversations of their family weren't discussed all too much. It seemed like an unspoken taboo. He feared that bringing up those personal memories would only evoke feelings that were better left closed. After all, that was how he felt about talking about his own mother.

"You know, we shouldn't have to hide our friendship," Aspen changed the subject abruptly. For so long, he'd wanted to show her around town, to introduce her to Niko, to stroll around the places he grew up, and to hang out with her publicly without any persecution. She shouldn't have to be shut out from the world.

Without batting an eye, Noelle rebutted, "You know how terrible that'll be. You and I would both be in big trouble. It's not like I hate how we're living now, it's not so bad at all."

The war between the two nations had ceased when he was about ten years old. Though too little too late, as most of the Mogoniwais had been wiped out and stripped of their homes. They say that only about forty percent of their people are left at the end of it all, now scattered all around the world. Those in power of the country had decided to "end" the war but that did not mean it ended society's hate and hostility towards Mogoniwais. In fact, people probably hated them more than ever. Six years had passed since the treaty was signed to end the war, but relations between humans and Mogoniwais haven't really progressed despite the various laws and acts some government officials had tried to pass, ones that made it illegal to harm them in any type of nature. There was a news article last year when a Mogoniwai was spotted near the Great Lakes of Orange. The next week he had been found, tormented and beaten to death, and no one batted an eye or said a damn thing. Because the government and the people are so split about their stance on whether Mogoniwais deserve the same rights as humans, most towns harbored their own jurisdiction on them. This town in particular conducts unsuccessful Mogoniwai hunts and are told to kill on site if they were to see one.

Aspen sat upright, becoming visibly worried for her safety. "Isn't it dangerous for you to live here? If one of the townspeople were to find you, they could hurt you."

"Unfortunately this place is all I know. I've lived here most of my life. This is home to me," Noelle spoke in a solemn voice.

Aspen clenched his fists, becoming distraught at the fact that she had done so much for him and made him the happiest he had ever been since his mother had died, but he couldn't reciprocate. Aspen knew more than anything Noelle wanted a community, a home, and a place where she could roam free without being in danger. He still lacked the strength to shape the world the two of them dreamed of. "I swear one day I'll make it so that you can happily live here in peace. The townspeople will accept you, and you'll be able to walk into the store and buy all the chocolates you want," he promised.

"Shouldn't you stand up to Gerard first before you stand up to your entire town?" asked Noelle.

Aspen slumped down in defeat. "Why couldn't we have grown up in a time where Mogoniwais and humans could coexist peaceful- ly?" he questioned in a soft-spoken voice.

"Maybe in the next life things will change," Noelle replied.

Aspen laughed. "What do you mean? Like reincarnation? Does that actually exist?"

"It's something that Mogoniwais believe in. My parents would talk about it when I was little. Those that move on to the next life eventually become reincarnated," Noelle explained.

"So, what do people get reincarnated as?"

"Who really knows? It could be as a newborn baby or even a fish in the ocean. Though, what my mother did tell me is that there are some relationships, relationships so powerful, that are bound by destiny, fated to always meet."

Aspen smiled. "Well, if I ever get reincarnated, I promise I'll come find you again." He raised his pinky towards her.

A smile began to form on Noelle's lips. "In that case, I'll wait for you until the day we meet again." She locked her pinky with his. The two of them continued to bathe in the sunlight and lazily lounge about, feeling quite drowsy after the meal they had just consumed.

After about half an hour of complete silence, he pulled out his pocket watch, realizing how late it was. "Oh shoot, I have to go before my dad comes back! He's been having these stupid meetings about segregating the Mogoniwais and I just—it's so stupid! He's just—" he blurted with a slight panic. Aspen started packing his belongings and stood up.

"Well, he is your father. I'm sure he'll come around eventually," Noelle said as she got up. "Goodbye, Aspen."

"Not him. Well, I'll be back in a few days. Oh, do you want me to bring anything else next time? More chocolate cookies?" Aspen asked.

"You know eating too many of those things are bad for you, right?" Noelle told him.

Aspen grinned. "So I'm guessing that you don't want any. Then next time I'm going to bring a dozen and eat it all by myself."

Noelle mulled it over but ultimately admitted defeat. "No, I want some too..."

"Perfect." After knowing her for many years, he knew her one weakness, it always helped him out whenever she was upset with him. Maybe one day Noelle would be able to meet the man who made them. Willey always did seem different from the other townspeople.

"Well, I'll be off now."

They hugged and held onto each other, both not wanting to be the first to let go. Aspen and Noelle pressed their foreheads together, now just a breath away from each other, so close that they could hear the other's heart.

"W-well, I gotta go," Aspen immediately broke off before his emotions resurfaced.

~

He skipped through the river without falling in, passed the neighboring boulders, and walked by the giant tree with an *A* and *N* carved into it. With breakneck speed, Aspen arrived at the town gate.

Aspen glanced at his pocket watch again. "I just barely have enough time to make it." He ran back home in hopes that he would arrive there before his dad. Not paying attention, he bumped into someone right by Mr. Donnoly's supermarket, hitting them square in the shoulders.

"Sorry, sir," Aspen apologized, turning back to see who he had bumped into. He froze. Standing tall was an army general, brandishing more medals than he could count. This person had a tall, opposing figure, and a stone-cold face that screamed, *don't mess with me.*

Oh crap. This was Gerard's father, the man who had led the army against the Mogoniwais in the war. He commanded respect wherever he went, and this was backed up by the many achievements he had, accolades he received, and the ferocity he exhibited on the battlefield, unlike Gerard who was all bark and no bite.

"I mean, s-sorry, General U-Ulger, sir," Aspen stuttered apologetically.

"Were you listening to what I just said?" Jack Bellard interjected. Jack is a balding, unassuming scientist who is known to be a recluse in town, ditching everything and everyone for his work. He is also a brilliant man whose scientific knowledge could benefit the world one day with his amazing inventions and ideas, but until then, he's attached to General Ulger's hip. "Using waves, we can broadcast it onto a certain frequency where it gets picked up by an antenna. With it we can communicate through long distances! Do you see the possibilities? First thing, long distance communication, next thing, perhaps transportation that doesn't rely on horses and—"

"Hush now, Bellard, you're rambling again," General Ulger waved his hand in front of his face, ignoring him completely to focus on Aspen. This shut him up entirely as he instantly dared not utter a single sound besides the nervous ticks he made. "And Aspen, no need to apologize so formally. You are Gerard's friend, after all." He brushed off the shoulder that Aspen bumped into, as if just the direct contact with him was enough to stain his clothes.

Aspen winced at the thought of someone thinking him and Gerard were friends, but he kept that thought to himself. He wasn't about to tell Gerard's father how his son repulsed him to his very core. "R-right," he nervously chuckled. Aspen continued to head back to the direction of his house, when someone forcefully grabbed his shoulder.

"Now, where are you off to so fast? You know it looked like you were spooked by something, like you saw the big bad boogeyman. Did you find something dangerous?" the general asked, though it seemed like more of an interrogation.

The only scary thing here is you, Aspen thought. "No, sir, I was just on my way home." He wanted to leave as soon as possible. Just by being near him felt like he was being mentally strangled to death. In fact, he had so much political power he'd be able to actually do it, hide his body, sweep it under the rug and move on with his day without a care in the world. The general lessened his grip on his shoulder.

"Well, you best get on your way now," he cautioned. "You know, it was quite the miracle that you came out unscathed years ago when you accidentally fell from that cliff. My son told me all about it. Quite the miracle indeed." General Ulger took a brief pause and then slapped Aspen's back forcefully. "Well, off you go then. You don't want to keep your father waiting, you hear? Oh, and if you do find something out of the ordinary, let me know." He shot Aspen a half-hearted smile that looked quite forced and out of place and walked the opposite direction.

Aspen rubbed his back and continued walking back home. "Sheesh, now I see where Gerard gets it from." He hardly talked to the general one-on-one, and hopefully he'll be able to keep it that way. Aspen made a mental note to increase efforts to never cross paths with that man again and avoid being around his general vicinity at all costs. General Ulger was definitely the one person who should never know of Noelle's existence—no matter what.

As Aspen quietly crept into his house, he was immediately met by a stern gaze from his father.

"Where are you coming back from?" Ben questioned. Aspen's face was still covered in sweat and his hair was tousled in a mess.

"W-when did you get back? How did your meeting go?" Aspen asked, trying to tip-toe around the question.

"Just now, and not good." his father's face was stoic. "People at the capital still don't realize the dangers of those demons. We have to separate ourselves from them before it's too late."

Mayor Ben Chase had been leading the movement for years now; to find, segregate and contain the Mogoniwais into special zones so that they would be able to watch their every movement and ensure that a war between them would never happen again. Though, all this did was spread the hate and persecution of the Mogoniwais. Desperation and hatred were the only things that fueled his ambition.

Aspen wished that he could convince his father otherwise. It had been about six years since the war ended and enough blood had been spilled, especially on the Mogoniwais' side. But his father always turned a blind eye to rationality when it came to this subject.

"I'm asking again, where are you coming from?" Aspen's father clearly wouldn't accept anything less than an answer to his inquiry.

Crap, if I wasn't stopped by Gerard's dad, I probably would have made it back in time. Thanks a lot. Aspen knew his father wouldn't budge. "I was with...Niko. Yeah, we were hanging out earlier," he explained, using the first excuse that came to his head.

"Really? Because he came by earlier looking for you." Aspen's father raised his eyebrows, now with raised suspicion since he obviously caught Aspen lying. "You wanna try that again?"

Darn it, I messed up. "Oh, y-yeah, we were hanging out earlier today but then I went to school to study in the library, you know, to work on assignments and stuff." He hoped that his father would buy into the lie and give up on finding the true answer. There's no way Aspen could tell him the truth, that he'd been secretly hanging out with a Mogoniwai for all these years.

His father took a deep breath and sighed. "Well, Niko wants you to meet him at Willey's shop in about ten minutes. Don't keep him waiting too long." He rubbed his sore neck and wobbled up the stairs to wash his sweat off.

Aspen breathed a sigh of relief once his father disappeared upstairs. *I better start coming up with better lies.* Ever since that day he fell off the cliff, his father had paid him more attention, though in this case, this wasn't the type of attention that he wanted. His absence and disheveled state had just made his father's paranoia skyrocket. Aspen worried that from now on, his father would always be asking where he was all the time, making it that much harder to freely meet up with Noelle.

He set his backpack down in his room and washed up before getting ready to go to Willey's candy shop. From all the hunting and lying on the dirt, his clothes were a mess. But the more looming thought in his head than his dirty laundry was the uneasy feeling that General Ulger gave him. Though that problem would have to wait, as Niko was waiting for him at Willey's.

On his way to the store, he saw Kenny, Jeremy, and a soldier lounging about in front of a liquor store, at their usual spot.

He looked at Jeremy, alcohol in hand. *Drinking four years ago, and still drinking now, some things never change,* Aspen thought.

"Did you hear about the man secretly harboring demon children in Taylor? He had about four of 'em until some of his neighbors found out and spilled the beans," Kenny said.

"So, what happened to them?" the soldier asked.

"His whole house got burned down, him and them demons along with it. No one got charged for it, when the authorities came by, no one dared rat on whoever did it," Kenny said. "Sheesh. Can you imagine that? Harboring a demon?"

"We need another war! We had 'em on the ropes, we coulda won and beat 'em," Jeremy declared. "I keep telling everyone, we have to attack first before they get us." He took a large gulp and belched.

"Well, when the war happens, I bet I can take out a hundred of them, just like you, Jeremy," the soldier replied with confidence. The soldier's name was Abe, the same one that was often dragged into their conversations. His uniform didn't seem to fit him; years ago he had the problem of it being too large on him, but now he had the opposite problem. It looked like he'd been eating and drinking a bit too well. And it seemed like after all those years, this person became just another version of Jeremy, another product of this town's racism and hate.

Aspen walked on, not caring about their conversation. There was no point. Despite how many years had passed since, this town would never change how they view things. He thought about how the town might perceive Noelle. They'd blindly hate her and the Mogoniwais because of their red skin. They'd hate her because they think she eats humans, when really she prefers to eat chocolate. And fear her because they think she'll kill them, when in actuality, she's one of the nicest people you'd ever meet.

He walked into the entrance to Willey's store, the bell on the top of the door rang.

Niko peeked out of the corner of the store, "Aspen!" he yelled out, "Over here!" gesturing him to come over. Aspen walked over and sat down at an empty seat beside him in the lounge area. The lounge was located off to the corner of the store that had sets of round, colorful tables and brand new swivel chairs for customers to chat and enjoy their desserts.

"Where were you today? I was looking for you everywhere. I even stopped by your house and your dad said you were out," Niko asked.

Aspen rubbed the back of his head and chuckled. "Well, you know, here and there. I was working on some errands, doing some chores."

"Working on errands, doing chores, traveling with your dad to work meetings, visiting your grandparents...I've heard it all man. You've been using these excuses for the past four years. Are you hiding something that you can't even tell your best friend? What are you hiding?" Niko asked.

"You're my best friend, of course I'd tell you if something's up," Aspen confirmed, "but nothing's up, I swear."

"Are you sure it isn't because of a girl?" Willey chimed in as he stepped out from the back of the store to greet Aspen.

"Oh, so *that's* what it is, and why you're always so secretive. Did you have a secret girlfriend for the last four years?" Niko teased with a sly smile. "So, when do I get to meet her?"

Aspen instantly shook his head no. "N-no way, you think someone would be interested in me." He laughed nervously.

"Come on, everyone has a boy or girl waiting for them, they're just somewhere out there, all you need is the right timing," Willey proclaimed while reorganizing the candy on the shelf.

"Wise words of Willey," Niko mumbled as he took a bite of his cookie. "Aspen, I've known you for most of my life. Something's up. We used to hang out all the time, and now you're suddenly so busy, but whatever, I guess this is a part of your rebellious phase. Whatever happened to the shy and timid Aspen? You'd tell me if you're hiding someone, right?" Niko jokingly asked.

Aspen let out a nervous laugh. "Of course, I'd tell you, man," he reassured him. *If only I could actually tell you, but it's just not safe. I have to hide Noelle at all costs—for her sake.* He avoided eye contact with his best friend, as Niko always had the innate ability of knowing when something was on his mind.

"Hey, Willey, could I order some iced tea?" Aspen called out.

"Sure thing, coming right up!" Willey yelled from across the store.

Within a minute, Willey set down the iced tea on the table. He collected the change that Aspen handed him and stuffed it in his pocket.

"Boy, it sure is nice, seeing you guys grow up. It seems like it was yesterday that you guys were yea high. Pretty soon, I'll be too old to remember ya," Willey spoke and laughed out loud.

"That'll never happen, your memory is as sharp as a needle and you don't look a day over forty," Aspen reassured him. "Plus, I'm still the same old Aspen, nothing changed much."

"Oh no, don't sell yourself short, Aspen. You've changed alright."

"For the better, I hope," Aspen added, taking a big sip of iced tea.

"Of course, Mr. Aspen. I can't really put my finger on it, but you seem more confident than you did a few years ago. Confidence can do a man good, ya know. In time, you just need to find a reason to be confident, but that will come to you eventually. I know it," Willey said as he hobbled back to the front counter, "Just make sure you stop letting little ole Gerard pick on you."

"Riiight," Aspen promised with weak affirmation.

"Don't worry, man. There's just no stopping Gerard sometimes, he's just an entirely different species," Niko reassured him, finishing the last bite of his cookie.

Aspen chortled in agreement, then he remembered the day's events. "Oh, right. Did you need something from me? Why'd you call me over here?"

"Oh, you're right, I totally forgot," Niko replied. "Yesterday was yet again one of your *busy* days so I didn't get to ask. I was wondering if you wanted to talk about the festival?"

"The festival...what festival?" Aspen asked with confusion.

Niko shook his head in disbelief. "Come on, man, it's what everyone's been talking about all week. You even got a paper ad about it. Since Grasalia is at the center of everyone, they decided to host it here. Well, I mean, this town is probably the best choice because who would want to even visit Chagus or Tortaville. So, people from Taylor, Chagus, Tortaville, and even those from Cresnough are all coming. It's *the* biggest festival this year."

"The paper..." Aspen muttered. He remembered using some papers as fuel for the fire today, which may or may not have been mixed in by accident. "Riiight...right. So, what about that......uh......paper?"

"The flyers, man! The mailroom has been sending out flyers constantly for the past week throughout town, and unfortunately, that meant my dad had me go door-to-door passing out these flyers for the festival," lamented Niko.

Niko's father had owned a postal service in this town; letters and packages were sent in and out from his business. His dad always took pride in the fact that not a single letter was ever lost or not delivered, as everything was always under his company's watchful eye. Lately, his father had been forcing Niko to work under him, showing him all the ins and outs of postal service, in hopes that one day he'd take over the business.

"It's supposed to be a celebration of peace between Mogoniwais and humans, but really it's just a convoluted way to brag and celebrate on how we beat them."

Niko pulled out his pocket watch and groaned. "Whoops, I have to go. I still had to help my dad deliver some packages around town." He stood up and headed for the door. "It's the first ever Founder's Festival. There's food. There's games. People dress up in costumes. Just be sure to pay attention in class tomorrow, okay?"

Aspen nodded and watched as his friend left the store. It was getting late, and he realized he should be going as well. After collecting his belongings and cleaning up after himself, he too made his way to the exit.

"Bye, Willey, I'll stop by again," Aspen called out before leaving. Willey, who was preoccupied in the kitchen, bid him farewell.

Aspen walked home; it was around that time of day when the sky had just started to transition to a golden-orangish tint as the sun started to set. *Founder's Festival, huh? I wish I could take Noelle, she'd love something like that. Technically, it's to celebrate peace, so a Mogo-niwai should be allowed to go. If I could take her, we could try every single food stall and play games until we run out of money. Man, it'd be so much fun. Maybe, I can find a way to sneak her in. If only...*

CHAPTER
EIGHT

Aspen sat in class, bored out of his mind. Standing up front was his least favorite teacher, Mr. Gallafo. He thought that he'd finally be able to escape him, but somehow Mr. Gallafo managed to follow and bore him in yet another grade.

Aspen rested his head on his desk and looked out the window. The leaves were already fading to different shades of yellow, orange, and brown; clear signs of the ending of summer. *I wish it could be summer again, then I could spend less time in class and more time with Noelle.* Aspen sighed.

"So, now let's talk about the Founder's Festival..." Aspen sat upright once Mr. Gallafo mentioned the word. *This was the thing that Niko was talking about last night.*

Mr. Gallafo continued on, "The first ever Founder's Festival will be in a few days. In celebration of the peace between the Mogoniwais and us, we are hosting a festival with food, music and such for the general public. It's a time for celebration and to be merry. Also, in good spirits, feel free to dress up as a Mogoniwai or in uniform. Paint yourself red, color your hair white. Let us embrace both cultures, so that one day we can be at peace."

Peace? What a joke. You have people hunting them down for fun like a damn sport. You guys hate them so much that they're scared to even show themselves to the public, Aspen thought.

"You betcha, I'm gonna paint myself into those ugly demons, and then I'm gonna scare the shit out of the kiddos," Gerard bellowed from the back. His goons snickered along with him.

Aspen rolled his eyes. Of course, along with Mr. Gallafo, Gerard somehow managed to follow him as well, being classmates in the same homeroom.

"Thank you for that Gerard. It is always such a pleasure to have your feedback," Mr. Gallafo remarked in an unamused tone. *BUZZ BUZZ RING.* "Well, class is dismissed. Be sure to have your assignments ready tomorrow," he said, already halfway out the door.

Niko walked over to Aspen's desk. "So, what do you think? Are you gonna dress up as a Mogoniwai?"

"Dress up?" Aspen repeated. He jumped up from his desk, "Dress up!" Just then, a clever idea popped up in his head. *This is it! It's our chance,* Aspen grinned fanatically. He gathered his things quickly and stormed out of the classroom. "Sorry Niko, I have to...water the plants at home!"

Niko watched in confusion as Aspen rushed out of the classroom. "Well, okay...alright, man," he chuckled, packing his stuff, knowing full well that he was up to something yet again.

~

ASPEN RAN, passing by Willey's store, passing by his house, and heading straight to the woods again without stopping. *If people are going to dress up as a Mogoniwai, I can sneak Noelle into town. She can blend in with the rest of the people. She'll finally be able to experience life outside that cave, outside of the woods.* The whole way towards Noelle's place, he ran with a slight skip in his step, excited about the news he was about to share.

"Noelle! Noelle! Where are you!" Aspen eagerly yelled out,

approaching her home. He called out for a few minutes until footsteps could be heard from the cave.

Soon enough, Noelle appeared with a book on hand. "I'm here, I'm here. What's got you so excited? I wasn't expecting you to come by so soon. Also, shouldn't you be in school? Don't tell me you're ditching again."

"Give me a minute, I ran over here the entire way," he panted. Aspen took some time to catch his breath. "So, I just got out of school and ran over here because I have exciting news to share. We're going to have a festival in the town, and I want you to come with me!"

Noelle's face was visibly skeptical about Aspen's invitation. No doubt her attendance would bring trouble for the both of them. "You and I both know how much of a bad idea that is."

"Yeah I know how it sounds, but there's a catch. It's something called the Founder's Festival. It's a festival that is meant to celebrate the peace between humans and Mogoniwais. People are supposed to dress up as soldiers or Mogoniwais," persuaded Aspen.

Noelle raised her eyebrow. "Dressing up as Mogoniwais? Doesn't that seem a little crude?"

"Yeah, I know what you mean..." Aspen agreed. "But, because people will be dressing up as a Mogoniwai, you can blend in with the crowd. No one would suspect a thing!"

"Then that means...I get to see the place where you grew up," she added. Noelle began to understand where Aspen was coming from, slowly becoming excited about the idea. That was until she realized what going into town could entail, leaving her also in an apprehensive and cautious state. Mogoniwais treading into enemy territory was suicide. Noelle held her hands in place to calm its jitteriness.

"Exactly! I'll be able to take you everywhere that we've talked about throughout all these years." Aspen's face gleamed with exhilaration. "We can stroll through the town! There will be tons of games there! And the food! Oh, the food! We will eat so much tasty stuff there that you won't be able to stomach anything for a week. And then there will be a fireworks display I heard, kinda like the stuff you shoot out of your hands, but it'll get shot out in the sky. It'll be the best time ever, I promise," Aspen gushed.

She stared into Aspen's eyes and saw nothing but excitement. She swallowed her anxiety for him. Noelle did not want to spoil the moment with fear, when she could revel in this moment with a shared enthusiasm. Besides, at the end of the day, she was completely confident in her abilities and in herself if any trouble were to arise.

"So..." Noelle clasped her hands together with delight, "can we visit the sweets shop that you go to?"

"Of course! You yourself can pick out what you want to try!" he promised.

"So, it's really alright if I can go?"

"Of course! You'll blend right in."

"Okay, I'm in. Please let me accompany you to the party." Noelle smiled, marveling at the thought of being able to have fun in Aspen's hometown.

Aspen was ecstatic. "Sounds like a plan, I'll be here in two days to pick you up and we'll go together. We'll blend in with everyone and then enjoy it together."

"I can't wait," Noelle hummed.

Aspen headed back home, planning out the festival activities in his head. He watched every minute and every hour on the clock, as the day of the festival came closer and closer. Excitement of the festival filled his head to the point where he found it hard to concentrate in school and sleep at night. It was going to be Noelle's first time in a town, and he wanted her visit to be as fun as possible.

FINALLY, the day of the Founder's Festival had arrived, and Aspen woke up bright and early, packed all his stuff, wrapped his white scarf around his neck, and headed out the door. He saw many of the townspeople putting up banners and building booths in preparation for the festival. He could even see little red children run around the grounds trying to catch each other. *Hopefully more people will dress up as a Mogoniwai,* Aspen thought. The more people dressed up, the better Noelle would blend in.

As he walked towards the town exit, Aspen spotted Niko coming from the opposite direction waving to him.

"Yo, Aspen! Pretty cool, right?" Niko exclaimed, pointing to the unfinished booths and decorations. "I wonder how it's going to look at night."

"Yeah, everyone's putting their all into this to make it look amazing."

"So what time do you want to go hang out at the festival? There's a couple of us from class going as a group," Niko asked.

"Oh, I...kinda already had plans to go with someone already," Aspen answered with a blushed face. He knew how it sounded, and knowing Niko, he was bound to tease him about it.

Niko suddenly grew a huge grin on his face, "Oh ho, Aspen, how did you sneak that one past me? Do I know her?" He gently elbowed Aspen's shoulder. "Well, no worries. I wouldn't want to spoil your date, but let me meet her, will ya? I have to make sure she's someone that would treat you right."

Aspen laughed nervously, "She's not a date and she's from somewhere far, far away. She's from...Cresnough! Yeah, that's why you don't know her. But hopefully you can meet her...possibly."

Niko gave Aspen a thumbs up and smirked. "Sounds good, you better keep your end of the bargain, or else one of these days I'll make your letters magically disappear." He stretched his arms as much as he could and sighed. "Well, I was supposed to help with setting up some booths, so maybe I'll see you later tonight."

"They better-double check them if you're setting it up," Aspen joked. "See you later, man." The two then parted ways, off to their own devices.

Aspen trekked through the woods and was back at Noelle's cave exactly two days later as specified.

"So, I brought you something to wear," Aspen said, handing her a sun hat. "It'll hide the horns."

"So you really did think of everything, huh?" Noelle complimented him as she placed the hat on her head.

"But that's not all," Aspen added. "A special day also calls for a special outfit!" he exclaimed, pulling out a new, white summer dress and sandals to match.

"Wow, it looks wonderful, thank you so much! I'll try it on right now!" Noelle gushed with joy. She took the clothes with her inside the cave to try them on and reemerged with her new outfit. "So, what do you think?"

He had never seen her wear a dress before. Aspen bit his tongue at first, worried that he might say something embarrassing. She was a view that took his breath away, leaving him with nothing but blank words and blushed cheeks. Needless to say, Noelle's gentle red complexion and white silky hair was a perfect match for the summery dress. "Y-yeah it looks great on you," he stammered.

"Wonderful." She smiled with glee. "Well, shall we head off to the festival now?"

For the first time ever, Noelle followed Aspen back to town. She felt both nervousness and excitement, not knowing what to expect. She had never stepped foot into a human town before, having only the knowledge of how Aspen described them to her and from storybooks.

As they were walking through the woods, Noelle could see the gates of the town from a distance. Her eyes were filled with childlike wonder and exhilaration. Noelle's heart was beating so fast she placed one of her hands over it, trying to dampen its loud pounding. *I'm here. I'm actually here.*

Before she could approach the gate, Aspen grabbed her hand, stopping her from proceeding any further. "Just to be safe, we should wait until it's closer to dusk and when more people are out." Noelle gave a little pout but understood why it was necessary. The two huddled together, waiting behind trees and bushes, killing time until they could enjoy the festivities.

"This is meant to bring our peoples together, but I bet not a single Mogoniwai would set foot in these festivals," Aspen said.

"Is this not a celebration of peace?" Noelle asked.

"They said this is a celebration of peace but it's all just a facade to mask their grotesque victory over Mogoniwais. In this town, there are drunks who love to gush about how many they've killed. And kids who are taught at a young age that the color of your skin determines how terrible you are. There was even a Mogoniwai activist at Taylor, about twenty miles south of here, that got beaten, just for leading the campaign to promote better rights," informed Aspen. "Needless to say, there are risks coming here. In the best case, if we're found out, the town gets scared shitless and panic ensues where we can use that to escape."

"Well, then what's the worst case?"

"Well...worst case is..."

"Death?" Noelle finished his sentence.

"Yeah, but it's very unlikely..." Aspen rubbed his neck, wondering if this was a bad idea after all, "We can still turn back. We can just celebrate the night back in the woods if you want?"

Noelle shook her head, she had already resolved her nerves days prior. She wanted to come here more than anything now, so she was willing to risk it all. Even if her identity was found out, she kept telling herself that she'd be able to easily escape. "No, no, I want to go."

"Alright then, while we wait we should go over some ground rules so your identity doesn't get exposed." Noelle nodded her head in agreement. He cleared his throat, and said, "Okay, so first, obviously, you have to keep your identity a secret at all costs, even lie if you have to. Second, stick close to me. People might come up to you or be suspicious, and when that happens, I can talk our way out of it.

Third, do not use your powers or pick fights with anyone under any circumstances."

"Even if they make me upset?" Noelle chimed in.

"Especially if they make you upset," Aspen added, wagging his finger. She agreed to his terms.

They watched the crowd of people going into town become larger and larger; it seemed like families from nearby towns opted to come here to celebrate the festival as well. Most even dressed up as a Mogoniwai, painting themselves red from head to toe and dyeing their hair white.

It was finally near dusk, and Aspen decided that now was the time to make their move. "Let's go in, Noelle."

They both stood up and walked towards the entrance, doing their best to blend in with the hordes of people. Noelle was at a loss for words—for someone who had lived in isolation in the woods for the majority of her life, she had never seen this many people before. From little ones to tall ones, to female ones to large ones, the people came in all sorts of shapes and sizes. She began to feel a little nervous, her body shook with apprehension. The chortle of dozens of people were scarier than the sounds of a pack of wolves. Her throat tightened. *Maybe I should go back before it's too late. It was enough for me to see this much, it's enough for me.* Noelle felt a nudge on her arm and saw Aspen offering his hand to her.

"Nervous?" Aspen whispered to her. "Just hold my hand, we'll move in together."

She held his hand, gripping it tight, feeling the tension and anxiety slowly fade away like hot water down a sore throat. This time, it was Aspen who kept her steady. He was an anchor that kept her from drifting ashore.

Despite putting up a strong front, Aspen was all sorts of nervous and timid. His thoughts were darting back and forth, wondering if Noelle would be outed as a real Mogoniwai and whether Noelle had noticed the excessive amount of sweat protruding from his palms. *If it doesn't work out, should we run? Should we talk our way through? Just a couple more feet, Aspen, then you're in the clear.* Slowly but surely, they moved in with the crowd, doting parents were distracted due to their crying children and teens too preoccupied with talking to their crushes and looking cool in front of the other. The entrance was only but a foot away now. A bead of sweat dropped from his forehead as he held onto Noelle's hand like his life depended on it. If there is any slight hint of danger, they'd bolt out of there. Half expecting alarms and whistles to go off, the two crossed the gate entrance without a hitch, as if they were two normal, completely ordinary people. *Safe,* Aspen sighed with relief.

"Hey! You!" someone yelled, grabbing his shoulder just as the two of them stepped through. They had barely passed through the gates before getting caught. Aspen turned around, locking eyes with a soldier.

Oh crap! We're screwed! We're already caught! Aspen screamed internally. "Y-yeah, is something wrong?" he stammered.

The soldier intently stared at the two of them. Noelle squeezed Aspen's hand even tighter. His visage was stern with eyes that were stone cold.

"Wow, her demon costume is really good! Nice going," the soldier complimented. His demeanor took a complete one-eighty as his stoic face sprouted a smile, and rather than holding the rifle currently resting on his shoulders to their faces, held a thumbs up.

"R-right...thanks," Aspen responded. As they stepped into town and through the gates, they both let out a huge sigh of relief. *Thank goodness no one has really seen a Mogoniwai in person.*

"We're in, Noelle! Welcome to my hometown," Aspen whispered in her ear.

Noelle's jaw dropped. The stories he had told her had never prepared her for how beautiful this quaint little town was. The abundance of light brightened the streets like stars in the sky. Beautiful decorations hung from house to house like royal galas she saw in picture books. There were also different booths where people were playing games and the food stands where people were stuffing themselves with all sorts of sweet and savory foods. Noelle could hardly hear herself due to a combination of the live music and crowds of people cheering and laughing loudly with one another, drunk on each other's gaily stupor. She didn't mind the noise, though. In fact, despite being in a world vastly different from her own, despite how her very presence here could spell danger at any minute, this town felt comforting. Noelle drew comparisons to her cave in the woods, realizing that the differences were night and day, and now couldn't help but feel a little lonelier.

Just then, two kids brushed past her, with skins painted red. "Did you know I saw a demon in the woods?"

"No, you didn't," the other responded, sounding more frightened than in disbelief.

"I did, too! It was real quick, though! If you don't believe me, I'm going to make it eat you in your sleep!" the kid warned.

"Stop it! I don't like demons! That's not funny!" the other cried out, running away with the other chasing after her.

Their conversation played back in her head as Noelle watched the two kids disappear into the crowd. Reminding her that this wasn't a world in which she belonged. No matter how much she yearned for it, the people here wouldn't accept her.

"Wow, it looks better than I thought it would," Aspen said, gazing at all the booths and decorations.

"S-sorry, what was that?" Noelle asked, not paying attention.

"It looks pretty good, right?" Aspen repeated. "So, what do you think of it, Noelle? Is it like you imagined?"

Noelle buried her true feelings, there was no way she could let Aspen know how she really felt. "It's definitely better than you described it, I've never seen anything like this in my entire life." Her eyes shifted from one booth to the other, looking for a distraction for the bottled-up emotions that shook inside her. *Now is not the time to feel this way, now's the time to have fun with Aspen.*

"Come on, Noelle, let's try that one." Aspen dragged her to the nearest game booth.

As they approached the game booth, the man running it turned to them unenthusiastically, "Throw the ball and knock all three blocks. If you knock all three blocks you win a prize."

Aspen looked to Noelle, "Do you want to try this one? Let's see who can win."

Noelle, never backing away from a challenge, accepted. "You know you never have once beaten me at something," she smugly remarked.

"You've never played these games before, this time I have the advantage. Victory is mine now!" Aspen smugly remarked back at her. He turned back to the guy running the game booth and requested a round for each person. The guy handed Noelle and Aspen two balls each, then went back to reading his book.

Aspen went first. He eyed the blocks in front of him, wound up the pitch, and threw as hard as he could. The ball smacked too far to the right, missing the blocks entirely. He could hear Noelle sarcastically clap and cheer him on from behind, which only made him feel embarrassed.

"That was a warm up." Aspen picked up his second ball. This time his concentration was solely on the blocks. As he was getting ready to pitch, he adjusted his position multiple times, making sure it aligned just right. He wound up the pitch again, and threw it with all his might. The ball zoomed straight, knocking two of the blocks down with one block barely on the ledge. He looked back at her, and her back at him, now slowly clapping. Aspen hung his head in defeat and whined, "It's rigged, there's no way someone can beat it."

"I guess I'm up now." Noelle was feeling smug, a smugness that exudes the utmost confidence in oneself, just as how it looked when she faced off those wolves and saved Aspen's life many years ago. She picked up a ball and tossed it lightly in the air to get a sense of the weight of it. She gazed upon the blocks as if it was another hunt, and chucked the ball with much force. The ball whizzed in the air and curved in the last second, knocking all three blocks off the platform.

"My advantage..." Aspen whined. He jokingly half bowed

towards Noelle. "I still have a ways to go before I can take you on, master."

Noelle laughed softly. "Don't worry, maybe in a few years you might be able to take a win off me."

The game booth guy apathetically handed Noelle a large stuffed teddy bear and Aspen a medium sized stuffed wolf. "Here are your prizes."

Aspen took his prize and glanced at Noelle's. "Well, I was trying to win first place for you so I could win you that prize." He tousled his hair. "Would you take this as well?" he asked, handing Noelle the toy wolf.

She looked at his prize then back at hers. Noelle couldn't help but smile profusely. "Actually, I think I would much rather have this wolf. But I'll only take it if you keep this," she handed him her stuffed bear.

"Wait, why are you giving me this? You won first prize."

"Because this way, it's like we're exchanging gifts with each other. So, when you hold it, you'll think of me, and when I hold this one, I'll think of you." Noelle gave him a smile so innocent he couldn't help but accept her proposal.

The two happily exchanged gifts, and Aspen could hear the game booth guy scoff and jealously mutter, "Couples..." under his breath.

"That's why everyone thinks you're weird," Niko mocked.

Aspen's heart almost leapt out of his chest, when he heard his best friend's voice. His eyes slowly drifted to the left to where Noelle stood. *This is bad. Really bad.* He turned around to see his friend's back turned from him, and surrounding him were about five more of his classmates.

"What's weird is your friendship with Aspen," someone from the group had said.

"Can it," Niko lightly punched him on the shoulder. "He's a better friend than you, that's for sure. You've eaten way more of the food that we've bought to split."

"Whatever, man."

Noelle scanned the nearby stalls, "What should we do ne—"

Without warning, Aspen had grabbed onto her wrist and dragged her in between the corn on the cob and hot tea bar stall. Not a single light touched this area, the darkness obscuring the two of them from the heavy crowds.

"What are you—"

Aspen put a finger to his mouth, gesturing to her to shush for the time being. "Sorry, I know them from school. It might be bad if they see you." He had his back facing the crowd as he covered Noelle entirely with his body. Aspen shut his eyes, as if it would help him become unseen and invisible.

Noelle could hear his rapid, deep breaths. It was quick and erratic. She looked up and studied his face up close. She hadn't noticed that his long bangs nearly covered his eyes now. One of his arms grabbed hold of her, holding her so tightly it'd take the world to pull them apart, which gave her a sense of protection. She leaned her head forward, resting it on Aspen's chest, and closed her eyes as well. Ignoring the clamoring of the crowd, to hear his heartbeat. *Ba-dum. Ba-dum. Ba-dum.*

"Let's move on already, I wanna check out the music venue," Niko lamented. "We're not gonna wait here all night and watch you try to knock down all the blocks."

"I swear it's rigged!" the other boy complained.

Niko and the group of friends walked past Aspen and Noelle, their voices now joining the other festivalgoers until eventually their echoes were no longer audible to the two of them.

Aspen breathed a sigh of relief as he poked his head out to see that his friend was no longer there. He walked out and gestured to her to come out of hiding as well. Somehow, he had managed to hide her once again. *Hide.* Aspen quickly turned to Noelle, hoping his actions were not misconstrued.

"Sorry I panicked. It's not like I wanted to hide you because I'm ashamed or anything. It's just...I don't know if they'll realize what you are and...I got worried that they'll—"

Noelle placed her index finger atop his lips which immediately caused him to be quiet. "I know, Aspen, I know. You don't have to explain yourself. Not to me at least, not at all." She smiled. "So, what other games shall I beat you in?" Aspen returned a smile as he led her to the next stall.

The two of them continued to play game after game at various different booths. Most games ended with Noelle's victory, but neither of them really cared. They were both too busy drunk in each other's company and having the most fun they'd had in a while. Aspen and Noelle played for hours until the smell of smoked meats and fried pastries captivated their noses. Almost in unison, both of their stomachs growled immensely, and they both looked at each other.

"Food?" Aspen asked.

"Food." Noelle nodded.

Aspen surveyed the food stands until he found what he was looking for.

"I found it!" he exclaimed. "It shouldn't take too long, I'll be back in a minute," he promised, rushing off to find something to appease their hunger.

Noelle sat down at a bench and looked out at the crowd. She watched the kids run around and the adults chatting while filling their bellies. She had been separated by her parents ever since their carriage was attacked by humans. Because of this, she had always been by herself, well, until the day Aspen entered her life. Growing up, isolation and silence were commonplace, but lately Noelle resented it. Her eyes were a little melancholic, wondering if she too would ever find a home similar to this in the future.

While Noelle was lost in thought, Aspen sat next to her, carrying a bowl of something unknown to her. She could feel the heat from the steam warming up her face. And the spices were so strong that it pierced her nostrils, though it still felt oddly comforting.

"It's beef stew," Aspen said. He handed her a spoon. "It's actually something my mom used to make for me often." He took a spoonful of the stew and ate it, looking slightly disappointed. "No matter where I go and how many stews I eat, nothing has ever beaten my mom's stew. I even tried replicating it once, but I could never find out the secret ingredient."

"Your mom..." Noelle muttered quietly. Aspen never really mentioned his mom much to her, he usually tried to avoid the topic whenever he could. She took a spoonful of the stew as well. "This is really good, I must know how they make this," Noelle carefully examined the contents of the stew, already thinking about how she could replicate it.

The stew had filled both their appetites and warmed them up, bite after bite. Aspen suddenly stood up, "Noelle, I have to make a quick stop to the restroom, I'll be right back here again in a few minutes." She watched him scurry off hastily, locating the nearest restroom. As Noelle watched him, she let out a slight giggle, reminiscing about their younger days. On one of the first nights they spent together, Aspen had a tough time getting used to the fact that restrooms did not exist in the woods.

"But I want it!" a high-pitched, shrill voice screamed loudly. Noelle turned around to find where the voice came from, spotting a little girl lamenting over a stuffed animal to her sister at a game booth.

"We have to win it fair and square first," the older sister tried to explain. But the younger sister threw a small tantrum, not taking no for an answer.

Noelle got up from her seat, took a few steps towards them, and froze. She had never spoken to another person besides Aspen before. Noelle agonized over whether she should actually help them or not; what should she say to them? How would they react to her? Would they be afraid of her? Noelle held back the urge to help the sisters and walked back to her seat. As she was about to sit down, the little girl cried out again.

"Can we please try one more time? The cat looks just like the one we used to have."

"I know you miss her, but it's just not possible," her older sister apologized. Just as the two sisters were about to leave the booth, Noelle appeared right behind them.

Noelle knelt down to the little girl and extended her hand, "D-do you want me to win that for you?" The little girl instantly hid behind her sister. She withdrew her hand with a dejected look. *I knew it. She is afraid of me.*

As Noelle was about to turn away, the little girl peeked her head out, and asked, "Could you really?"

"We'd really appreciate it if you were able to win it," the older sister added, and then, looking at her sister, said, "We used to have a pet cat that snuggled up with us every night, but it died. And that stuffed animal looks nearly identical, which is why my sister is so obsessed with it."

Noelle knelt down to the little girl and smiled. "I'll certainly try my best." She turned towards the game—the goal was to shoot the plastic arrow in the bullseye, something Noelle was definitely confident she could do. She laid money on the table. "I would like one round please."

The plastic arrow was a lot lighter than what she was used to, so it took time to get acclimated with the bow and arrow. As Noelle prepared to shoot, she could hear the two girls cheering her on from behind. The distance between her and her target wasn't too far, she had definitely hit targets much harder than this. Noelle took aim and shot the arrow like it was second nature to her, the arrow zoomed in the air and hit dead center of her target.

"Congrats, here's your prize," the man said, handing her a stuffed cat.

Noelle held a great sense of pride on her face as she offered the little girl the prize. "Piece of cake," she humbly bragged to them. The little girl's eyes lit up as she excitedly jumped for joy, holding the cat in her arms.

"Thank you, thank you, thank you!" the little girl repeated. She jumped into Noelle's open arms and hugged her tightly. "I'll take good care of Francie Two."

Noelle froze at the little girl's sudden embrace, her muscles became too rigid to move. The voices of the crowd faded away, only being able to hear the gratitude of the little girl. *Maybe, it's...it's alright for me to be here,* Noelle thought. She was hesitant at first, scared to even touch her. *Maybe it is okay after all.* Noelle reciprocated and hugged the girl back. *She feels warm.* In fact, the area where Noelle knelt felt as if a ray of sunshine beamed down from the night sky. The little girl walked back to her sister, letting in the cold, fall breeze once again.

Glimpses of her memories—that she did know she had—resurfaced.

"We're so proud of you!" her father gave her one giant hug. It was winter time, the snow was falling, but the warmth of her father was enough to keep her away from the cold. She was holding onto a tiny rabbit in one hand and a bow in the other. By now, the strength of her father's hug was crushing her, though she did not mind it at all.

"I'll cook it for you," her mother came by.

"No, I wanna help momma cook it, I wanna help!" The six-year-old Noelle managed to squeeze out of her father's grip and hugged her mother's leg.

She picked her up and snuggled up to her, pressing her cheek with Noelle's. "How did I get such a smart and beautiful daughter?"

Her father joined in on the family hug. Noelle was able to remember how close she was to them. *"Our beautiful daughter, our amazing daughter, our incredible daughter. We love you N—"*

"By the way, your hair is so pretty, hopefully mine can be as pretty as yours one day," the older sister complimented her.

Noelle suddenly snapped out of her flashback and was facing the two sisters once again.

The two sisters bowed a thank-you to her one last time before they headed off. As the two sisters walked away, Noelle could hear the little girl thank her profusely one more time before vanishing and becoming just another memory.

Without saying a single word, Noelle walked back to her seat and waited for Aspen. He came rushing back towards her just a minute later. "Sorry I'm late, Noelle, there was a long line. Was everything al —" Aspen stopped talking when he locked eyes on hers. Noelle's heart was beating as fast as the streams of tears that were rolling down her face.

"What happened? Who did something to you?" Aspen looked around, flustered, trying to find the culprit.

Noelle shook her head. "N-nothing happened." She turned away, covering her face once noticing her tears drop to the ground.

Aspen sat beside her. "If something happened, you can talk about it with me. I'll wait as long as you need to."

Once her nerves died down and the teardrops subsided, she opened up to Aspen about what happened. "Nothing bad occurred," Noelle explained. "In fact, I was so overjoyed for them, and before I knew it, the tears came without warning." She couldn't put these newfound emotions into words as well as she would have liked, but in a way, it was as if it was too much happiness that she could handle. All those years of loneliness, those years of doubting whether she belonged, those years not knowing whether she was a monster or not, were validated by one little girl. Aspen gave her happiness and purpose in the world, but she had given her a sense of community and belonging. Noelle had told herself that all she ever needed was Aspen, which was true. She'd trade the world for him in a heartbeat without a second thought. So, why was she crying now?

"Maybe this place was too different from what you're used to?" questioned Aspen.

"No, no, this town is great. All these foods taste amazing. Everyone here seems so close, talking and having fun. Why does this place feel so warm and beautiful?" Noelle looked down at her red-skinned hands. "So beautiful..." she quietly mumbled.

Slowly but surely, Aspen began to understand. "When you

helped out those sisters, you must have felt good, right?" He gently touched her hand; it was cold. "I'm sorry I didn't notice sooner, it must have been pretty lonely after all those years...living by yourself in that cave. I know it hasn't been easy for you." He wiped the tears off her face. "One of these days, Noelle, I swear, you'll have a warm home, where you don't have to be alone. You'll be able to stroll into town every morning and greet whoever you see. You'll be able to make new friends and get sick of your neighbors like everyone else. And whenever you feel like it, you'll be able to buy sweets on your own accord. I swear on it."

Noelle looked at Aspen, yearning for the day that his words would become truth. "Do you really think that some place would accept me for who I am? They won't be afraid of me?"

He placed her hair behind her ear. "Of course. One of these days, everyone in the world will see you how I see you."

"And how do you see me?"

Aspen smiled. "Well, you're a girl who has the biggest sweet tooth I know. A girl who's too stubborn to give up on any challenge, a girl who hates it when you wake her up, a girl who's hard-headed at times." He gave a slight chuckle and continued on, "You're also someone who's selfless, someone willing to help out anyone in need. Someone who can be depended on no matter what, through hell or high water. And someone who's so warm, you can't help but be happy when you're with her. No one can ever compare to you."

Hearing Aspen gush about her made her flustered. "That's so embarrassing..." Noelle mumbled quietly.

Crowds of people started gathering at the center of the town, and were excitedly staring at the sky. "Oh no, is it time already?" Aspen gasped with a slightly worried look.

"Is something bad happening? Do we need to leave?" Noelle whispered.

He grabbed her hand. "Let's hurry, we need to go somewhere— somewhere special— before it's too late!" They both started running, zipping through the crowd towards a destination only known to

Aspen. While navigating through the horde of people, he bumped into a soldier by accident. Aspen raised his head to apologize to the man, only to have empty words. *I have such bad luck. Out of all the people I had to bump into, it had to be him.* The man was General Ulger, Gerard's dad.

"Aspen? Now who is th—" but before the general could utter another word, Aspen tightened his grip on Noelle's hand and ran right past him. She turned back to apologize to the general before they both disappeared in the crowd.

"Who was that man? Do you know him?" Noelle asked.

"You don't want to know," Aspen replied, currently praying that he was not able to get a good glimpse of the two of them.

"Ok, so where exactly are we going? What's going on?" she asked, still being dragged along by him.

"It's finally time!" Aspen excitedly yelled out, "It's the grand finale!"

CHAPTER
NINE

Noelle blindly followed Aspen, without a single clue of where he was taking her or what was going on. She looked at the crowd—kids and adults alike were all gathered together, all eagerly staring at the sky. "Are we almost there yet?"

"Just a little bit, up that hill," Aspen replied.

They threaded upwards, hiking farther away from the crowd. This place didn't seem too special, with nothing but trees and an abandoned bench. Noelle peered down; from this height, she could see the entirety of the town.

"Such a nice view, isn't it?" Aspen joined Noelle in admiring the town that looked quite small from here. "I spent hours yesterday trying to find the perfect spot, and best of all, it's secluded so we don't have to deal with the crowds." He took a seat on the bench and gestured to her to sit down beside him.

Noelle sat down. "It certainly is a beautiful view, you can see the entire town from here. Everyone down there looks so tiny." The wind sent a slight chill down her spine, it was so cold that she could see her breath in the air.

Aspen fiddled with the ends of his scarf.

"You know this scarf is one of the last things I have to remember my mom by. She sucked at sewing so she was bursting with joy when she finally was able to make this. Can you imagine? My mom made it for me for my fifth—or was it my sixth?—birthday so that I'd stay warm in the winter. It was far too large for a small kid back then." Aspen took his scarf and wrapped it around the two of them, "But now, it's the perfect size for just us...it'll keep the two of us warm, and it'll keep us warm for many years to come." Blanketed underneath the stars, they were now as one, connected with nothing but a pile of stitched wool. It was one of his most treasured items, which only made Noelle even happier that he'd shared it with her.

He brushed his fingers against hers by accident. The cold sensation emanating from her hands was enough to cool off a drink on a hot summer day. Aspen nudged her shoulder and handed her his gloves. "Here, use these. My hands are getting too warm."

"No, it's okay. I wouldn't feel right to take them from you. Plus, I already feel warm underneath this scarf," Noelle replied. Though he wouldn't take no for an answer, insisting on letting her have them. Eventually, after some back and forth, she gave in and slipped on the gloves.

He took out his pocket watch. *Looks like we still have some time before it starts.* Aspen rubbed his hands together; they were freezing, he regretted not packing another set of gloves. "Hey, Noelle, so how was it today? Did you have fun?"

"It was the most fun I've had in a while," Noelle smiled. She clutched onto her stuffed animal; she definitely would not forget this day ever.

"I'm glad you did," Aspen twiddled his thumbs. "Sooner or later, you'll get to live your days like this everyday. I promise you."

Noelle gently placed the palm of her hand on his cheek, "I believe you." She stared up above, the stars and moon had looked the same as every other night, but tonight, they were particularly more idyllic and beautiful. She rested her head on Aspen's shoulders and closed her eyes; she hadn't been this tired in a while. However, it wasn't physical exhaustion, she was more so drained from experiencing all these new firsts. From the moment Aspen invited her to the festival, it was the only thing on her mind. And today, she experienced many firsts—going into a town, seeing new people, talking to strangers, enjoying life with Aspen without being confined to the woods. It really felt like she was a part of a community. And she was glad Aspen was right there with her. "The moon is beautiful tonight, isn't it?"

Aspen took a glance at Noelle, then shifted to the night sky. "It sure is." He gently patted her on the head. "Hey, Noelle," he whispered, "You might want to open your eyes for this one."

She opened her eyes, once again enveloped by the night sky under the light of the moon. "Why is that?"

"The grand finale," Aspen told her, pointing to the sky. Noelle watched intently, but didn't see anything. Seconds later, out of nowhere, a huge ball of fire catapulted towards the sky and erupted into magnificent colors. *BANG!* A loud boom could be heard from where they were sitting as the fire dissipated.

"What was that? Are we being attacked?" Noelle awoke in surprise, eyes widening, still fixated on the explosion. She got up and was readying herself as if preparing for an ambush.

Aspen gestured her to sit down and chuckled. "It's okay, we're perfectly safe. They are called fireworks. Every so often when we have big events, the town shoots these fireworks up in the sky...well... to end things with a boom," he reassured.

Noelle eased up and sat back down beside him. "Fireworks? Your people never cease to amaze me. It's almost like you have your own kind of magic."

"Magic? Well, I guess it could be, in a way." Aspen placed his hand on top of hers, while continuing to admire the view.

A trail of light could be seen as the next set of fireworks shot up into the sky and whirled in a spiral filled with all sorts of bright vibrant colors of red, green, blue, and yellow. The roar of the fireworks echoed throughout the area, almost deafening those that were in its vicinity.

Noelle couldn't avert her gaze from the fireworks display, it was captivating. To her, it looked as if the colorful explosions were dancing in the night sky. It was amazing that something so destructive and dangerous could be so beautiful. She turned to Aspen, who was giddy with excitement as he too was mesmerized by the fireworks. *If it weren't for you, I probably wouldn't be seeing this here today, or would not have experienced a lot of things for that matter.* Aspen had told her countless times that if it wasn't for her, he wouldn't even be here to this day, but she always thought that the same could be said about herself. Noelle watched on as the next set of fireworks shot straight up and fragmented into thousands of colorful sparks then cascaded down like a waterfall. As she stared at the fireworks, Noelle couldn't help but reflect back to her life before she met Aspen. She lived her life just for the sake of living. Everyday she would hunt, eat, then sleep routinely. Her world was dull and gray. It was only after she saved Aspen did her gray life start to brighten. In time, he brought color into her life, colors as vibrant and wonderful as the fireworks that are in the sky now. If her life was displayed on a canvas, Aspen was the paint that brought it beauty.

The fireworks died down, but the audience was still in an uproar from down below. "Is it over already?" asked Noelle.

"No, no, there's still one last big explosion, one that would really end it with a bang," he replied. Noelle couldn't help but think how the fireworks display that was shown earlier could be topped with something even more grand.

"It's sort of like a customary tradition, but at the peak of the firework's explosion, when it's at its loudest, everyone usually shouts out their desires, their dreams, or their secrets. They let it explode just like the fireworks in the sky. It kind of acts like a relief, so that they are not bottled up inside of us forever," Aspen explained. He got up from his seat and stood at the edge of the hill. "Come on, let's go do it, too!" Noelle got up from her seat and stood next to him.

"Could you maybe stand a little farther away?" he pleaded. "It's kind of embarrassing if you were to hear my secret."

Noelle gave a sinister smirk, "Why? You don't want me to find out more about your irrational fears?" She walked a couple feet away from Aspen as the last firework began to shoot up to the sky.

A barrage of lights skyrocketed into the sky until it halted to its peak. *BOOM! BANG! POP! BANG!* In a much bigger display than before, the fireworks shattered into hundreds of thousands of sparks and whirled in a spiral. The sky was showered in luminescent bright colors, as many colors as they could imagine, being so bright that for a brief moment it felt like the sun had risen up from slumber. The town shouted out loud screams of desire and dreams but were drowned out by the loud eruptions in the sky.

She looked across from her and stared at Aspen as he too was shouting something with all his might. Noelle covered her mouth, shielding her smile. A few of her tears snuck out and began trickling down her cheek. Normally, the average person would not be able to hear anything but the fireworks, as they were too clamorous and ear-splitting. Perhaps Aspen underestimated Mogoniwai's naturally great hearing, because she could hear him. She heard everything. His secret played back like a charming melody. At that moment, she heard him say just three words, masked within the explosions. Aspen had yelled out, "I love Noelle."

Noelle wiped the tears off her face and couldn't stop smiling. She turned back to the fireworks and yelled off the top of her lungs towards the sky, "I want to stay with Aspen forever and ever!" Her desire was drowned out, like the rest of the town, by the fireworks. Eventually, the loud booms turned into silence as the sparks in the sky faded away. And just like that, the two of them were once again enveloped in darkness. They turned to each other. Noelle immediately rushed over to Aspen and hugged him with all her might. Though confused at first, he quickly reciprocated and hugged her just as hard. Her emotions suddenly became unchained as she kissed him on the cheek. Both their chests were now shining amongst each other, brightening the darkness that surrounded them.

He then stared at her lips and inched himself closer to her face. They lovingly stared into each other's eyes, not daring to look away. Aspen brushed her hair behind her ears, "Noelle, I—"

"So, what is going on here?" a voice yelled out from across the hill. The voice cut off Aspen before he could finish his sentence.

The sudden outburst startled them, and the two immediately let go of each other, trying to find out the culprit. Aspen could hear a group of snickering as they emerged from the shadows.

Of course, out of everyone who it could be, it has to be him, Aspen groaned as he saw Gerard on the hill with his friends laughing behind him. "How did you even find me here, Gerard?"

"I saw you at the fair and thought about how much I wanted to hang out with my dear friend Aspen, so I tailed along." Gerard had a smirk on his face. He started walking closer.

Noelle leaned in and whispered into Aspen's ear, "So that's the Gerard that you mentioned?"

"Yup," he begrudgingly responded. Gerard always seemed to weasel his way into Aspen's life at the worst moments and when he least suspected it, which was mostly all the time.

Gerard directed his focus towards Noelle. "Who's this girl here?" He began inspecting her from head to toe. "Why don't you ditch this fool and come hang out with us? Though make sure you wash off that makeup first." His goons followed suit and hollered at her to hang out with them instead.

Aspen clenched his fists and couldn't form any words, wishing Gerard would just go away. *I'm hopeless after all.* Gerard had always been the puppeteer and Aspen the puppet, controlling him for years. No matter how many times he'd rip the strings off, more would sprout on his back, burrowing deeper within each time. Even now, with the person dearest to him standing by his side, Aspen couldn't find the courage to move.

Noelle turned to Aspen who silently stood in place. Unfortunately, she promised him that she wouldn't start any fights. Noelle looked at the bully with clear disgust. "You're Gerard, I presume? I was hoping that we would never meet, so if you could go away, that would be much appreciated," she said while shooing him away.

Gerard laughed. "You really want to hang out with a loser like him?"

"The only loser I see here is you. You're the one who's trying to insert himself into other's lives when it is clearly not wanted," Noelle responded. The more Gerard opened his mouth, the more Noelle thought about how difficult it would be to keep her promise to Aspen.

"You know, it's a shame you're dressed up in that ugly demon costume. Maybe you'd be a little cuter." He pointed to Noelle's hair and skin, "Hey, maybe you really are a stupid demon. You look the part alright. It's too perfect!" Gerard and his friends all cackled like hyenas with their unsightly crooked, toothy grins.

She took a step forward, with a clenched jaw and a crinkled nose, her fists ready to be raised. Noelle knew that she promised Aspen that she wouldn't cause any problems, but Gerard was pushing her limits. Aspen grabbed her shoulder, stopping Noelle in her place, and marched towards Gerard.

With a cocky attitude, Gerard looked amused as Aspen approached him. "Oh, is Aspen gonna be sad that I'm making fun of—" *SMACK!* Before Gerard could react, Aspen punched him straight in the face, knocking him hard to the ground. Blood gushed from his nose as he lay there sprawled on the ground, still shocked as to what just happened. Everyone else froze. Aspen's chest faintly glowed along with the surge of power that suddenly ran through his body, but everyone was too surprised from the punch to notice.

Noelle couldn't help but smile.

We cross our hearts and hope to die that you will teach how to be brave and courageous like yourself and I promise that I will be your friend. I'll bring you more tasty things and cool things and make you even happier.

She recounted the promise they made back when they were children. *I think you're finally headed there.*

Aspen's left fist hurt, as he had stored up all his pent-up anger and directed it into Gerard's face. Gerard could bully him all he wanted, but insulting Noelle was where Aspen drew the line. *I'll probably suffer the consequences later, but boy that felt good.* Though he didn't care all too much, he would've done the same regardless of what the punishment may be, plus it felt gratifying to knock his bully down for a change. He stared down at Gerard and watched as his face turned from shock to anger. Aspen grabbed Noelle's hand and grinned at her. "Let's get out of here."

Noelle smiled back. "Yeah, let's go." They could hear Gerard yell obscenities directed towards both them and his friends. Faintly, the two could hear him command his goons to chase after them, but they didn't stick around to find out if that was the case. Together, they precariously ran down and back towards town, laughing under the night sky like they had when they were young children years ago.

They ran through the town looking for a place to hide from Gerard and his friends. Many people were cleaning up and storing stuff away, the festival was about to come to a close. The crowd was beginning to thin out, so they needed to find somewhere to hide, and they had to find it fast. Aspen could hear one of Gerard's friends catch up to them; he knew that if they didn't find a place to hide soon, they'd be caught.

"That place looks secluded," Noelle exclaimed, pointing to an alleyway. They ran towards that direction and hid behind a discarded pile of broken wooden planks from an old food stand.

"Where are they? They're both dead!" yelled Gerard. He had stuffed an absurd amount of tissues in his nose to stop the bleeding.

"I don't know, I saw them a minute ago but I lost sight of 'em," one of his friends said.

"You all go block off the exits! If he tries to leave we're ambushing him! I'll camp at his house just in case he goes back! None of ya are going home until he gets caught, even if it takes all night!" Gerard bellowed. Him and his friends went their separate ways.

Aspen peeked to look around the area. "I think the coast is clear for now," he whispered. "But we'll have to find a place to hide for a couple hours."

"Why not just charge through them? It's not like they'd be able to stop me," Noelle asked.

"There's already been a lot of attention drawn to you, Gerard's probably the worst person you'd want snooping around. He's always been persistent. Somehow he'll find a way to follow us and find your cave. It'd be safer to just wait it out for now."

"Where would we go? It seemed like they were going to block off any of the places you might think of."

Aspen considered this, trying to come up with the best solution for their problem. They could always wait outside, but it's freezing, and who knows how long they'd be waiting. He thought about staying at Niko's, but his parents might ask a lot of questions, or worst of all, tell Aspen's father about it. He wrapped his head around where they should go *Think Aspen, think.* Just then, an idea sprang into his head, and he wasn't sure if it was the best solution, but it was the most plausible as of right now. "Come on, Noelle. Follow me, I think I have a place where we both can stay."

She nodded her head, and grabbed hold of Aspen's hand, and followed him. They dipped, ducked, and covered every so often, just in case Gerard and his friends were nearby, and eventually, they made it to the front of a building.

"What is this place?" Noelle quietly asked.

"I guess...you could say he's an old friend of mine." Aspen heard the bell ring as he gently opened the door. "You always said you wanted to come here, right?"

As soon as Noelle stepped in, she was hit with the alluring aroma of melted chocolate and roasted almonds. Her eyes were filled with exhilaration as she looked around the building— hundreds of chocolates on display, freshly baked cookies on the counter, and more sweets than anyone could imagine. "Whatever this place is, I don't think I'd ever want to leave," she muttered quietly. Noelle could feel herself salivating, overloaded from the selection of different sweets in this store.

"Why, who is it?" someone from the back said. He turned around and walked towards the two. "Aspen? Is that you?"

Aspen nervously laughed. "Hi Willey....yeah, it's me, Aspen. We're kind of in some trouble...so I was wondering if we could hide out here for a few hours?"

"What kind of trouble could you have..." Willey noticed the red-skinned, white-haired girl beside him, "gotten yourself into?" He stared intently at the two of them.

Aspen immediately took notice of this. "Oh, this is my friend, Noelle. She's from out of town but came here for the festival. She... dressed up for it..." Aspen wondered if Willey was buying into the lie as he continued on. "It's the Gerard type of trouble. Well, he was bothering us, he was making fun of Noelle, so I...punched him...and now he's chasing us."

Willey laughed heartily. "Well, it's about dang time, isn't it? How'd he take it?"

"He fell to the ground and his nose bled."

Willey sprang up and gave Aspen a huge hug. "I couldn't be more proud of ya, finally becoming a man and standing up for yourself." Aspen breathed a sigh of relief when the attention turned back to him rather than Noelle.

"He definitely was brave. Standing up to him just for me," Noelle chimed in.

Willey turned his attention towards her and extended his hand, "I'm sorry, where are my manners? My name is Willey, and I own this dessert and candy shop you see here."

She shook his hand. "My name is Noelle, I'm Aspen's friend. He was nice enough to show me around the town. You have the most amazing shop, by the way. I couldn't think of a better place to be than a place filled with these delicious chocolates and sweets. How do you stop yourself from eating all these chocolates?"

Willey let out another hearty laugh. "Why thank you, Miss Noelle. And you know, I try to constrain myself but it never ends up happening," he said, pointing to his round belly. He gestured to them to come inside. "Well, come along now, you don't want to wait at the doorway all night. Aspen, why don't you show her around while I go check on things in the back?"

The two of them walked and explored the store. Noelle was bewildered at the massive selection of desserts, some she recognized because Aspen would bring them, but most of them were new. This place seemed like heaven to her, from milk chocolate, to gum drops, to peppermints, to brownies and cookies, it had it all.

"I'm glad that Willey doesn't suspect anything," Aspen whispered to Noelle. Though she was more preoccupied with looking around the store than worrying about having her secret outed.

"Look Aspen, look!" Noelle babbled, pointing towards a chocolate bar on the shelf. "You brought me this one time!"

Aspen walked over to her. "Oh, right. I did, didn't I?" he said, picking up the chocolate bar. It was the chocolate that Willey gave him a few years back on his birthday, the one he shared with Noelle on the first day that they met. He set the chocolate bar back onto the shelf.

Noelle turned to him with a perturbed look on her face. "Wait, I just realized, if you're here with me, won't your dad be worried about you?"

"Luckily for me, he's out for a few days, holed up in his office this time, to deal with all the logistics that follow after a huge festival like today's. Though, it's nothing new. He's always been away from home. From meetings out of town at the capital, to pushing his Mogoniwai hate agenda to everyone, to reading and signing bills and letters; sometimes I feel like he's using it as an excuse to not come back to the house. On most days of the month, he's hardly home. It's been like that for a while now..."

"Oh, I see." Noelle felt bad for Aspen. She knew he and his dad had a rocky relationship after all these years, though she was hopeful that they'd work out their problems eventually and become more of a family again. "So, is this where you get all your desserts and candy from?"

"Yeah, I've been coming here ever since I was little," he said as he ran his fingers through the shelves. "I've been friends with Willey ever since I started coming here. He's always looked out for me."

"I can already tell that he is a really nice man."

"He's always checked up on me, always giving me advice, and helping me whenever I need it." Besides the woods where Noelle lived, this was the second place that he had always retreated to when he wanted to escape, be it because of family matters or just life in general. Aspen quietly muttered, "He's probably more of a father figure than my actual one..."

Willey popped out from the back with a tray of freshly baked cookies. "Well, why don't we all just wait upstairs for the time being so you guys can rest up." The two looked at each other, and both agreed that they were pretty tired from today. Aspen and Noelle followed Willey up the stairs, where he opened his door for them. "Welcome to my humble abode." He set the tray of cookies down onto the table, "Here, go ahead and sit here and help yourself to some cookies."

"Oh no, we couldn't possibly. You're already letting us rest here at your home," Aspen said.

"Yeah! And we don't even have any money!" Noelle interjected. Aspen had also taught her the value of currency in the world.

"Oh, no, it's perfectly fine! I've baked far too many, a bad habit of mine. It'll just go to waste if you don't. Just rest up while I go lock up the store," insisted Willey as he proceeded to leave.

Aspen heard Willey hobble down the steps to the first floor. He surveyed the room, having never actually been upstairs before, let alone knowing that there even was an upstairs. From what he could see, there was a kitchen, two bedrooms, and a bathroom. "So, this is where Willey lives."

Noelle grabbed a cookie and took a bite. "Aspen, these are even better when they are fresh and warm!" She became giddy with excitement, making a joyful squeal after each bite.

The expression on Noelle's face made the cookie seem so delectable that he himself couldn't resist anymore and grabbed a cookie as well. "I guess you never got to try freshly baked cookies before, right?" Another first to add to the list.

Willey came back upstairs and closed the door with two mugs in his hand. "Here you go, something warm to keep you warm. Hot chocolate." He placed each mug in front of Aspen and Noelle. "A warm body is a happy body."

"Thank you for the drink, I've never had this hot choco before," Noelle excitedly gushed out. "Oh and the cookies were the best I've ever had!"

Aspen took a sip of the hot chocolate, and he could feel his body getting warmer already. His muscles now relaxing. It was an elixir, soothing both his body and soul.

"So, Aspen, when were you going to tell me that she is a Mogoni-wai?" Willey asked, glaring intently at him with an eyebrow raised.

He knows. Aspen started coughing, almost choking on his drink. He set his mug down. The muscles in his body couldn't decide whether to freeze up or shake with anxiety as it slowly turned towards Willey. *Oh crap, this isn't good! This is not good at all!* Aspen's eyes widened as they locked onto the man before him. His heart pounded faster than the exhilaration rush he had when punching Gerard right in the face, and beat louder than the fireworks display from the festival much earlier. *He knows she is a Mogoniwai.*

CHAPTER

TEN

"I-I don't k-know what you mean? I m-m-mean that's crazy talk, why would I even be with one, let alone in the city?" Aspen nervously tried to explain. "I mean, the costume is very realistic, right? She dressed up in a costume." All those news stories that told of what happened when a human hid or befriended a Mogoniwai flashed in his head. In those stories, it never ended well — from being chased out with rifles to being tortured, to even death on both sides. He glanced over to Noelle, who was still so preoccupied enjoying her hot chocolate and cookies that she didn't yet grasp the severity of their situation.

Willey took a seat and sat beside him. "Aspen."

Aspen stared at him, and from the look on his face, he could tell that Willey had already discerned the truth. He stared back at his mug, the steam from the hot chocolate was gone, his drink now lukewarm. "She...she didn't do anything wrong, Willey."

"If there is anyone to blame, just put the blame on me," Noelle set down her cookie and mug and walked over beside Aspen. She placed her hand over his to comfort him, to calm his shaking hands, but they were relentless.

"What! Are you crazy, Noelle? What did you do wrong?" his voice quivered. Aspen hated it, becoming intensely frustrated over the many misinterpretations of the Mogoniwai. *The town all fear them, hate them, kill them, what did they do wrong?* Aspen banged his fists on the desk, almost knocking over his mug. "Is it really such a crime to be born differently! Inside...they feel how we feel." Aspen stood up and grabbed her hand. "Willey, if you're going to keep us here until soldiers show up, we're going to run out before you get the chance. There's nothing you can do to stop us."

"Calm down, Aspen, it's okay. I won't tell anyone about this. You have no need to be worried," Willey pleaded.

Aspen looked him in the eyes. He had known Willey for years, and what his heart was telling him was that there was no deceit or insincerity in his words. If there was someone who he could share this secret with, it would be him. Aspen slowly sat down back in his seat, with Noelle pulling up a chair beside him.

"I don't share the same opinion of the Mogoniwais like the rest of the town," Willey continued on.

"You don't?" questioned Aspen.

"I don't," confirmed Willey. They sipped their drinks in silence, until the tension dissolved shortly after.

"So, where did you two meet? Is there anyone else who knows?" Willey was intrigued.

"No, no one else knows except you," Aspen replied. He recalled the day he first met Noelle and told Willey his story, with Noelle interjecting at certain times. He told him about how she saved his life that day, how he started teaching her to write and speak, and how they have lived and kept this secret going on for many years now.

"Wow, after all this time, frankly I can't believe you were able to keep this secret among yourselves for this long, especially Aspen." Willey eyed him in disbelief.

Noelle giggled. "Yeah, there were times where I even thought Aspen would break." She playfully tousled his hair.

"No way! I was not going to!"

Willey laughed. "Well, Aspen, you certainly have changed. I didn't know the reasoning then. But I think I know the reason now."

"Changed? How so?"

Willey took a minute to consider his answer. "Ah, let's see...how could I put it? You've changed. It's a good change. It's like...there's a light in your eye. You seem happier, more confident now." Aspen turned to Noelle, who then gave a proud look of accomplishment towards the both of them.

"So...how did you know anyway? That she was actually a Mogoniwai?" asked Aspen.

"It was obvious to someone who saw them in person," remarked Willey.

Noelle jumped from her seat, "You have seen my people in person before?"

"Yes, I have actually. But it was a long long time ago. Before the war that transpired years ago, whether due to fear or power, there had always been tension between the Mogoniwais and humans. I used to live in a town where humans and Mogoniwais coexisted. It was, let's see...maybe forty miles north of Cresnough. It's a small town, Junidad was its name, which is why you probably haven't heard about it, but it was a great town nonetheless." Willey recalled.

"There were places where we all lived together?" Aspen and Noelle both spoke out in unison. They looked at each other, questioning if such a place could actually exist. Aspen had never heard of Junidad before, never bothering to know neighboring towns beyond Cresnough for that matter. But that did not stop his thoughts from instantly jumping to whether Noelle could start her new life in such a town.

"Yes, there were, but I think those have been long gone by now," Willey continued on. "I lived there with my wife and my daughter." He stared at the bottom of his empty mug and gently rubbed the rim, "It's long gone by now."

"I...I didn't know you had a family, Willey." Aspen had known him for years, but never did he hear Willey talk about them.

"My daughter was friends with the local Mogoniwais in town. I am and will always be so proud of her—she didn't care about their skin color or their horns. She didn't care about any of that. What mattered to her was what they were like on the inside. It was nice and peaceful for quite some time in town. We laughed together, we worked together, we existed together." Willey took a long pause, it was hard for him to reminisce about what happened. It felt like he was being stabbed in the heart, yet he continued on. "One day, our town became the battleground of a fight between the ongoing conflicts of the humans and the Mogoniwais. The soldiers thought that the town was a cover for exchanging secrets to the Mogoniwais, so they attacked. The town was destroyed as a result. No lives were spared that day—the elderly, women, even children..." His voice trembled, "My wife and daughter died that day. They were protecting her friends from a couple of soldiers. I would have died that day too, had a fellow Mogoniwai not saved me. It's the reason I walk with a limp to this day."

His eyes began to fill with tears, "I...I moved out far, far away to try and forget. To start fresh. Could you believe that I used to not like desserts? It was my daughter who liked the sweet stuff." The tears now coursing down his cheeks. "It was my daughter's dream to...to own a bakery, you know. She was always baking...enough to feed an entire town." Willey wiped the ever-flowing tears from his cheeks, "I'm sorry, you shouldn't have to see me like this."

Aspen was at a loss for words. After all this time, he assumed Willey was just this happy-go-lucky man. Throughout his entire life, Willey had been there for him, whether it was to cheer him up, give advice, or lend an ear. And he had been hurting deep down inside all these years. *Some friend I was.* Aspen clenched his fists and gritted his teeth in anger towards his own ineptitude. "Willey, I'm so—" but before he could finish his sentence, Noelle ran over and knelt in front of Willey.

Noelle gave Willey a warm hug and patted him on the back. "I learned today that hugging someone can make them feel better. When someone hugged me today, I felt warmer on the inside. I haven't had a family for years now, so I don't know if I can relate to how you're feeling. But...I know what it feels like to be alone." She looked him in the eyes. "You don't have to be alone anymore."

Aspen walked over to him, knelt down beside Noelle, and put his hand on Willey's shoulder, no longer should he have to go through this alone anymore. "You can rely on me a little, you know. I'm older now, I can lend you an ear if you need it, I can help you if you request it. Am I not your friend?"

He looked at the two of them, still with tears, and smiled. He pulled them closer and tightly hugged them both. "We *are* friends, Aspen, and now...Noelle. How could I have forgotten?"

After a short while, Willey calmed down a bit, wiping off his remaining tears. "Well, you shouldn't have to see an old man weep about the past all night." He smiled, "I'm fine now, thanks to you both. Why don't you kids just stay the night? Go ahead and wash up in the bathroom, I will set your beds."

Aspen went first. He was covered with dirt and sweat, more so than Noelle somehow. He dipped his fingers in the tub to gauge the temperature; it was nice and hot. Once submerging himself in the tub, the hot sensation of the water relieved the soreness and stiffness he felt all throughout his body. His stress was washed away along with the dirt and grime. The water was like quicksand, the longer Aspen stayed in the tub, the more submerged he became. If he had a choice, he'd probably stay in there forever. Aspen raised his hand in the air, and stared at his bruised up knuckles from when he punched Gerard. Had this been the old Aspen, he'd be stressing about the consequences of his actions today. But right now, not a care in the world was floating in his head, today had been quite a long day and there were better things to think about. He got out of the tub twenty minutes later, worrying about falling asleep from the therapeutic bath.

As he came out of the bathroom, Noelle came running to him with excitement. "Aspen, Willey was showing me around the house! There's something called a stove where you can cook stuff without branches or leaves! He said I could try it out tomorrow!"

"That's great, Noelle! I can't wait to try your cooking tomorrow." Aspen plopped down on the couch. He could hear Willey show Noelle how to use the running water for the tub then promptly left to go fix up the other bedroom for her to sleep in. He rested his head on the couch and stared at the ceiling, grinning from ear to ear. It was probably the most fun he's had in a while. Not only was he able to spend time with Noelle at the festival and show her around town, but he also was able to tell someone about his secret relationship with her. It was a big load off his shoulders. Willey set aside some pillows and blankets for Aspen and joined him on the couch. "Thanks, Willey, I really appreciate it."

"Don't even worry about it, it's just a couple of pillows and blankets," Willey remarked.

"No, I meant thanks for everything you're doing for us. For keeping our secret. I know Noelle's probably really happy to be here right now." Willey nodded his head in affirmation. "I realized today that she's been pretty lonely. I mean, she's lived alone in a dark cave for years now, who wouldn't?"

Aspen faced him, now seeking advice, "What can I even do to help her?"

"I think deep down, you already know the answer to your question. Follow the choice of what you truly believe would make both yourself and Noelle happy." Aspen sat in silence, not knowing how to respond. Willey stood up and patted him on the back. "Noelle is a nice child who still doesn't know much about the world. Keep protecting her, Aspen, even the toughest people need help once in a while."

Willey yawned. "Well, these old bones need to rest, lots to do tomorrow." And then, he waved good night before disappearing into his room.

I already know what I need to do? Aspen racked his head about it until he heard Noelle walk out of the bathroom. She sat beside him, dressed in Willey's daughter's old clothes, which, luckily, had fit her.

"Aspen, the running water was amazing! In an instant, it was nice and warm! It felt so good, it beats bathing in the cold river anytime!" Noelle ecstatically proclaimed.

"I'm glad you liked it." There was a hint of guilt and pity in the tone of his voice. Hearing her gush over an everyday household item reminded Aspen about the fact that she lived most of her life in the woods ever since she was a kid. *It must have been hard living by yourself, wasn't it?* It was difficult for him to ask her these questions in fear that he'll resurface bad memories that she might have tucked away. *How many years was it that you had to fight for survival with no one by your side?* Aspen desperately wanted to know more about her; any burdens of the past, any hardship she had faced, any troubled feelings she locked away—*everything* so that he would be able to support her through it all.

"Hey, Noelle...you don't have to tell me if you don't feel like it, but can you tell me what your...what your parents were like?"

"What brought this on?" Noelle looked at him. Never had Aspen ever asked about her family.

"Nothing really. I just...want to know more about you."

"Well, my dad was huge! He may have looked scary at first, but deep down he had such a gentle soul. Whether human or Mogoni-wai, my father would always help out those who needed it. There was a time when he pulled a human's cart, full of supplies might I add, for twenty miles when their horse had run off." Noelle seemed to be glowing as she proudly bragged about her father. "And my mother, she was the strongest lady I had ever known. Nothing scared her. And not to mention she was the brains of the family, always the one who handled the more business side of stuff."

"They sound kinda like you," he smiled.

"Do they?" Noelle lightly chuckled. "They would always spoil me rotten, always going along with any of my stupid selfish desires and tantrums. One time, my father and mother hovered over me when I was sick, caring for my every whim all day, because I didn't want to get up. And also, the two of them would always carry me around like I was some princess when I cried—and let me tell you, I used to cry *all* the time. But don't get me wrong, though, that was way back then, I'm not such a crybaby anymore. We were quite close. I still remember those nights where we'd sit by the campfire to watch the night sky or...or when we would go on these business trips. I vividly remember one trip where we all sat in the front, my father taking the reins with one hand and stroking my hair with the other, while my mother would sing with a voice so beautiful the animals would stop to listen." The more she talked about them, the more she wanted to gush, to try and keep her memories of them alive.

"I wish I could have met them, I truly wish I could have." Aspen said.

"Yeah...I wish...I w-wish you could have met them, too," Noelle spoke, with a tremor in her voice. "They were the greatest parents in the world. Even though I lost them early on...I wouldn't trade my time with them for anyone else."

"You mentioned that you lost your family. Do you mind telling me about what happened to your parents?" Aspen asked abruptly. He needed to know more about her, as if not knowing would gnaw at him forever.

"Well, the details are a little fuzzy, since I was only a couple years old, so there's not much for me to tell." Noelle fidgeted with her fingers, taking a minute to remember the specifics. "My father used to be a traveling merchant, selling stuff from town to town, with a bunch of other merchants. My mom and I would always come with him. We'd travel everywhere, so I never really had a *home* home." She had a drooped posture, tucking her chin behind her knees. "But my dad would always tell me that home is wherever family was, so I was happy. One day, we were attacked by humans, soldiers in uniform who belonged to the general army. It was after our trip from Cresnough and when we were en route to Grasalia when the attack happened." Her chest pulsated in a soft glow. Noelle grabbed the nearest pillow and hugged it tightly against her chest, "I don't even know why. All we were doing was minding our own business. During the attack, my parents shouted at me to run and hide, and told me that they'd catch up later. I ran, farther and farther into the woods, until I was out of breath and my legs wouldn't move anymore. And then I waited, and waited, and waited, and waited. Hours turned to days, and days to weeks. In the end, they never came for me."

Aspen turned away from her, not wanting to show the look on his face. *Noelle was alone, alone after all this time. When I was a kid, all I worried about was how to tie my shoes and what toys I wanted to buy, and here she was just trying to survive on her own. How cruel can the world be to one person?*

"But it's okay, though. Really." She grabbed his hands and held them, "Maybe I was meant to wait all those years...just to meet you. Even if I had to do it all over again, I'd wait years and years if it meant meeting you in the end."

Aspen embraced her so tightly, as if to make up for all the lost time when she was alone. It was so abrupt that it took Noelle by surprise. He could feel her pain, he could feel her loneliness. "I'm sorry that I took so long to find you, I should have came sooner."

Noelle smiled and rubbed his back to comfort him. "Don't be silly, you were only a little kid then. What could you have done?" After a while, she stopped hearing Aspen's whimpering. "Aspen?" He was asleep. She set him down, rested his head on the pillow, and covered him with a blanket. She sat beside him and gazed upon his sleeping face. *I never noticed this before, but Aspen's face looks so delicate when he's sleeping,* Noelle thought. She ran her fingers through his hair, "You don't have to worry about me anymore, Aspen," Noelle spoke softly. She combed his bangs back and softly kissed his forehead. "As long as I have you, I'll never be lonely again."

Noelle walked into the spare room that Willey provided for her; it was fairly empty aside from a few pieces of furniture. She laid down on the bed and buried her head in the pillow. It was soft, it was probably what lying on a cloud would feel like. *How could I ever go back after sleeping on something like this?* she thought, burying herself underneath the warm covers and the plush pillows. Ever since arriving in this town, Noelle made a mental checklist of things she'd bring back to the cave. Though, there's no way she could possibly haul a bed way over there. She tried to relive the day in her head, remembering every small tidbit so that she'd be able to replay the best time of her life in the future. Noelle noticed her stuffed animal off to the side of the bed, and reached over to hug it. At least, when she had this toy, she'd be reminded of this day. Initially, when they arrived in town, the festival and the community of people overwhelmed her. Everyone seemed to be having fun together with not a worry in the world. Without ever realizing it before, this sense of community in this quaint town was something Noelle yearned for, feeling jealous of everyone here. But after talking to Willey and Aspen, Noelle realized that even in this town full of people, there are others who are still alone. She remembered what her parents used to tell her when she was little. *Home is wherever family is.* The more Noelle thought about home, the more Aspen popped up in her head. *I really can't live without you anymore, can I?* Her eyelids started to feel heavy, the fatigue from today had finally caught up to her until she eventually drifted off to sleep.

NOELLE FELT a gentle tug on her shoulders. *What is it now? I had just fallen asleep.* She turned her body towards the other direction. However, the tugging kept persisting to the point that she was about to get very annoyed. Noelle made a little groan. *Can you go away?* Someone was now tapping on her shoulder harder. *Whoever this person is, they better say their prayers!* Noelle sat upright in a jolt and hissed in an annoyed tone, "Who keeps bothering me while I'm trying to sleep?" She rubbed her eyes to get a closer look at the culprit. It was Aspen. He was already awake. *Was he not asleep just a few minutes ago?*

"Willey told me to wake you up. It's your fault, Noelle, you're the one who said you wanted to help and learn how to bake in the morning," Aspen remarked. He sat at the corner of the bed, waiting for her to get up and get ready.

"It's morning?" Noelle asked in disbelief. She got out of bed and looked out the window, and sure enough, it was a little before dawn. The minute after laying her head on the pillow soon turned into hours without warning. Noelle hadn't had a good sleep like this in a while. "Beds are dangerous," muttering to herself. She turned to Aspen, "I'll go get ready right now. Tell Willey I'll be down in a bit."

"You got it," Aspen replied.

Noelle stopped him. "Oh, I still have your scarf upstairs, should I bring it back down for you?"

"It's okay, just hold onto it for me," Aspen replied. He proceeded to walk down the stairs and back to the store.

Noelle was left smiling. Today had already started off as a good day. She quickly got ready and ran down the stairs with excitement. Since living in the woods, she never had the necessary tools and ingredients to bake sweets, nor had she possessed the knowledge to do so. Noelle stepped into the back room to the kitchen, and instantly, the aroma of melted chocolate, blueberries, and freshly baked bread filled the air. She saw Aspen, dumbfounded, in an apron with powder all over his clothes and face.

"Here you are. Wear this," Willey said, handing her an apron. He was brimming with joy and feeling more refreshed than usual this morning.

Feeling quite ecstatic, she quickly put on the apron and went to work. Willey was showing the two of them how to bake simple pastries like cookies and muffins. No matter how many attempts Aspen made, they just didn't taste as good as Willey's, often due to him making mistakes such as adding way too much sugar, or accidentally using salt. Noelle, on the other hand, was a natural. Willey's pastries were the best in town, though this may not be the case soon after. They spent the morning baking, laughing, and comparing who's muffins tasted the best.

Willey took the batch that Noelle baked and put them on display. "Well, I think these are about ready to be sold now."

"Are you sure they taste alright?" Noelle asked with a concerned look on her face.

"I've eaten about a dozen now, and I can certainly say that it earns my approval," Aspen chimed in, giving her a thumbs up.

"Aspen's right, Noelle. You certainly have a knack for baking, all right. Pretty soon you'll be better than me," Willey added.

"There's no way I could be better than you," Noelle bashfully interjected. Though, Aspen and Willey both still held true to their claim.

"Well, we should probably head out soon before the rest of the town is awake," Aspen pointed out, taking off his apron. People will be waking up and swarming outside the town soon. He handed Noelle an extra blanket to cover her head.

"You're right, let's go soon," she said, though her face revealed otherwise. Her time here was short lived and finally coming to an end, and deep down, Noelle wished that she could stay a bit longer.

The two left the kitchen and picked up their things. As they were ready to leave, Willey stopped Noelle with a bag full of cookies and muffins, "As thanks for helping me out this morning."

"I would have done so for free," Noelle graciously accepted the cookies. "If anything, I should be thanking you. I had fun learning how to bake." She and Aspen headed for the door, but before leaving, she turned back to Willey one last time, "Well...I guess this is our final goodbye."

"H-hey!" Willey stopped the two of them before they twisted the doorknob. "You know, I could always use more help from time to time. Why don't...why don't you stop by more often and help bake? Plus, I still promised to show you how to make my special almond butter cookies. You can stay in the spare room if you'd like, whenever you want."

Noelle looked back, grinning from ear to ear. "Do you mean that? I'd love to!"

"Of course, Noelle. What are friends for?" Willey stated while smiling back. The two of them thanked him profusely as they left his store.

Not a single person was out and about this early in the morning, probably too tired from yesterday's festival. They exited the town without a hitch. *Gerard and his friends must have been too tired to wait all night,* Aspen let out a tiny chuckle as he imagined him standing there freezing in the cold.

Noelle took one final look at the town. With scattered confetti on the ground, piles of discarded cups missing the trash bins and old buildings that didn't quite shine like they had last night, it still looked beautiful in her eyes. This might be her last look in a while— the town that she loved but didn't love her back.

Noelle turned around as they made their way deeper into the woods, she could hardly see the town now. And all that was left to remember it by were the warm muffins on one hand, stuffed animal in the other, and the memories of last night. Noelle held onto the hope that it wouldn't be long for her to return to this town.

"Right here's fine, you don't have to go take me back all the way," Noelle assured Aspen, after he had escorted her to the cliffs.

"Okay, I'll be back in two days. And maybe I'll bring my best friend along this time, he's a really nice guy, you'd like him. I'm sure you would. Like Willey, I know I can trust him." Aspen thought that since Willey could accept Noelle as who she was, maybe Niko could, too. After all, Niko was one of the few who weren't like the other people in this town. If people get to know Noelle little by little, maybe they'd all accept her eventually.

"I'd like that," she turned around and prepared to scale down the cliff but Aspen grabbed her hand, stopping her.

"H-hey, Noelle, I was thinking," Aspen stammered. "Maybe that... w-what would you say..."

"Say?" Noelle was confused as he kept fidgeting with his fingers, not looking her way.

Aspen took a deep breath, pinched his arm, and raised his head. "What would you say if I asked you...if you wanted to live together?" His face was beet red. "We can find a town...a town that would accept both humans and Mogoniwais alike, so that you wouldn't have to hide anymore. I don't want you to hide anymore. I want to take you away to a world that'll accept the both of us. You told me that home is wherever family is...and right now, that's with you. "

She covered her mouth as his words danced around her heart. Aspen was stammering, but Noelle did not pay heed to it as her mind was already adrift. His words beat at the same rhythm of her heart, fast in fluttering, sporadic periods.

Aspen continued on, "I know it'll be tough in the beginning...but I'll make sure we have money. I'll work and find a job, it'll work out somehow. You could even try bak—" Before he could finish his sentence, Noelle had tackled him to the ground.

She wrapped her arms around him and buried her head on his chest. There was no need to even think about it as the words came naturally to her. As if waiting for this moment for all of eternity. Her eyes glimmered with joy, "My answer is yes. Yes. Yes. One million times yes! I want you to take me away!"

However, no words came out of Aspen's mouth as he embraced her. No more words were needed anymore. The two basked in this shared mutual feeling of longing and needing. He felt relieved, though not knowing what the future may hold for the two of them, he did know that he wanted to spend it with her. And for now, that was enough. *This is my answer, Willey. From now 'til forever, I want to spend it making Noelle happy.*

Though reluctant to leave each other, the two eventually went their separate ways, both sharing excited thoughts of their future together. They'd lasted days, weeks, and sometimes months away from each other before. But at this moment, right now, after going their separate ways, each passing second felt desolate and unbearable.

CHAPTER

ELEVEN

"So, where are we going again?" Niko asked, blindly following Aspen into the woods. No matter how many times he'd asked, his friend wouldn't say where they were headed. In fact, Aspen had seemed nervous and hesitant the entire way going there.

"You'll see, man. If I tell you now, it'll just ruin the surprise, so just keep following along," Aspen hollered at him. He could feel his palms beginning to sweat; this was going to be the first time Niko meets Noelle. Aspen wondered how he'd react all morning—would he be willing to be friends with her? Would he be afraid of her? Would he tell everyone back in town that a Mogoniwai was near them? He shook those thoughts out of his head. *There's no way Niko would do that, I just have to trust him.*

"You're lucky I'm such a good friend," Niko yawned, "what weirdo chooses to go on a hike in the morning on the weekend?"

"Yeah..." Aspen mumbled. He recalled back to the festival where their fellow classmates questioned their friendship, something that happened many times over the course of knowing each other. "Why is that?"

"Why did I decide to go along with you and do this dreaded hike?" Niko began to sweat, "I don't know, maybe I like torturing myself."

"No, I mean why did you decide to be best friends with me?" Aspen asked, stopping in his tracks. "Surely you have many other friends, cooler friends, that are probably more fun to hang out with. I'm just a shy, introverted loser."

Niko walked in front of Aspen and gave him a playful, but hard whack to the forehead with his finger.

Aspen rubbed his forehead, "Ouch, what was that for?"

"That was to knock that nonsense out of your head," Niko answered. "I'm best friends with you because we're best friends."

"What does that even mean?" Aspen continued walking forward. "What do you get from being friends with me?"

"Being friends isn't some give or take exchange, man," Niko said, now following closely. "It means you have fun regardless of what they have or who they are and you can trust them with whatever in life. They'll stick by you, no matter what happens. And in my life, that person is you. You got it?"

"I got it, I got it." Aspen closed his eyes and chuckled, *I know having Niko meet Noelle was the right choice after all.* "Please keep continuing being friends despite the fact that I'm a lose–"

Aspen nearly tripped on a large tree root, but Niko had grabbed his hand and pulled him up before falling to the ground. "You're not a loser, Aspen. If you keep saying that about yourself, I'll seriously get pissed."

"I won't from now on," Aspen thanked Niko, patting him on the shoulder a few times.

"So, we're back at the cliffs from a few years ago? Is this where you wanted to take me?" Niko stood stiffly, crossing his arms. "What's the point of coming back here?"

"We still got some ways to go, just watch your step as you scale down," Aspen warned. "I of all people would know how much it hurts," he said, snickering.

They both carefully scaled down the mountain, crossed the river, and walked through the trail, eventually reaching their destination.

"Okay, so...we walked here to go into some cave? And why exactly?" Niko peered inside the cave, which didn't seem so special. "Whatever this big secret was, I can't say I'm too impressed."

Aspen fidgeted with his fingers, fighting back the nervous tick. "Just try not to freak out, okay?" He yelled into the cave. "Noelle, we're here!"

This only invited more questions. Niko stood there with a bewildered look and a tingling in his chest, "Okay, why would I even freak out? And who the heck is No-o-oe...holy shit!" Emerging from the cave, he saw a girl with red skin and pure white hair. He closed his eyes and opened them again, just to make sure his mind wasn't playing tricks on him. The red-skinned girl, with horns sprouting on the top of her head and ears pointier than normal, slowly approached the two of them.

Niko stumbled over his feet and landed on the ground. "W-w-w-what is g-going on here?" The color of his face quickly became pale. His entire body trembled like a stray cat in the rain and his eyes widened in terror. "W-what is a d-d-demon doing here?"

Noelle brandished her fangs towards Niko. "I'm here to eat you of course." She began licking her lips as she crept towards him.

Niko's legs failed, still paralyzed from the very presence of the predator in front of him, so he tried pushing himself away with his arms. Though he didn't get far, as Noelle walked up in front of him, now face-to-face. "P-please don't eat me!" Niko shouted in terror. He closed his eyes shut, afraid of seeing what was going to happen next.

Whack! Aspen gently hit Noelle on the head. "Could you stop teasing him before he wets himself?"

Noelle backed away, crossed her arms, making a little pout. "Well it's his fault for thinking that I would eat him."

Niko slowly opened his eyes, still on edge because nothing in the world right now made sense. "A-Aspen there's a demon, you have to get away from here."

He knelt down next to Niko. "It's okay, she's not dangerous at all."

"I'm plenty dangerous," Noelle chimed in.

Niko kept shifting his focus, darting his eyes to Aspen and then Noelle. "Tell me right now, what is going on here?"

"If I do, you have to promise you will stop freaking out. Deal?" Aspen extended his hand out to help him up. Niko nodded, adhering to his request, swallowing the internal screaming that was going on in his head.

"So, this is my friend, Noelle. Noelle and I have been friends for years now," introduced Aspen.

"Hello. Aspen told me a lot about you! Sorry for scaring you in the beginning," she reached out to shake Niko's hand.

"You can speak?" Niko stood in place, rejecting the hand that extended towards him.

"Yep! Aspen was the one who taught me for the past few years."

He turned towards Aspen. "You have been *what* for how many years now? Aspen, what have you been doing for all these years? How did I not know? You better start explaining yourself now or else I'm about to freak out again." Nothing was making sense to him—how and why was his timid and scaredy-cat friend involved with a demon? As his best friend, he knew him all too well, and he knew that his friend would be far too afraid to do something like this. Niko was half expecting a prank reveal, that this was just some elaborate ruse, but the punch line never came. This was all true—Aspen had really been living this double life and he was none the wiser.

Aspen calmed Niko once again, "I promise, let's just all sit down somewhere. I'll explain everything to you." And once more, he told his story to his friend, right from the beginning from when he was saved by Noelle at the cliffs, to spending time with her all those years, up to when he brought her to the festival.

"So, after all this time, this was what you were doing? Why didn't you tell me any of this?" Niko raged. He felt blindsided. Here was one of his best friends telling him that he had been living with a dangerous secret that could only bring trouble, or something much worse. Niko didn't want to think about the worst.

"I couldn't tell anyone back then, it might have put Noelle in danger," Aspen fought back. "What if you were to accidentally tell someone about her?"

"You think I'm the type to do something like that?" Niko grew offended. Not only had Aspen kept a secret from him for all these years, but it turned out that his friend didn't even trust him.

Aspen bit his lip, that was the wrong choice of words. "Come on, man, I didn't really mean it like that."

Noelle was silent, not knowing whether to interject or not, in fear of making matters worse. She sighed. *I guess that should have been expected.* Of course, not everyone could be as understanding as Willey. It was only natural that Aspen's friend would be mad. In the end, all Mogoniwais were hated by humans, a fact carved in stone.

"And you took her in town for the festival? Regardless of whether she was dangerous or not, don't you think it was risky to do so? I mean, come on, man. Not only would you be in trouble, but she would, too," Niko pointed out.

"You...you have a point," Aspen replied. Niko always had his best interest at heart, and what he said made sense. It was selfish of him to bring Noelle into a town that had a deep hatred for Mogoniwais. Luckily, Gerard and none of the other people attending the festival realized that she was an actual Mogoniwai, but what if they had? Was it selfish of him to bring her along? It all came down to what he valued more—her safety or her happiness.

Noelle pushed forward with her back now in front of Aspen. "What makes you think you have the right to judge whether it was right or wrong? I accepted the risk when Aspen asked me, I know what could have happened. And frankly, it was one of the best times of my life. For the first time in my life, I was able to play games, try new things, and meet new people! Am I not allowed to do these things because of how I was born?"

"Noelle..." Aspen spoke softly. The two boys froze. One thing was certain, and hearing her words validated it, that bringing her was the right choice after all. "That's right, Niko, it was a selfish decision. But you know what? I'd do it again if it made her happy. If we end up running into trouble, I'll be there to protect her like she has protected me!" Now was not the time to waver. If he couldn't stand his ground in front of his friend, then how could he expect to stand towards everyone else.

"Have you gone mad, Aspen? I've known you all my life. How are you going to protect her when you can't even protect yourself? Why are you risking your livelihood for her?"

Aspen grabbed Noelle's hand. "Because I love her. We're planning on moving away together, somewhere that will accept Mogoniwais. Where we can both live safely and freely. I'm telling you this because you're my best friend. I thought that you'd understand." Aspen opened up to his best friend, letting loose lips reveal true feelings. "Growing up, I've always been afraid, afraid of the unknown, afraid of getting hurt, afraid of getting into trouble. But, when I'm with her...it's different. She gives me the confidence and strength to move forward. I'm free now. I'll choose how to live my own life now. Whether I take the thorn-stricken path or if I have to lay each individual brick down the road in front of me, as long as I have Noelle, it's the path worth taking."

Niko looked him in the eye. At the moment, Aspen seemed as gargantuan as his stretched shadow behind him. This man looked like he was ready to take on giants, though he'd need to be ready to face much worse. Nothing good could come of this. Knowing Aspen for a good majority of his life, Niko always saw him as the scared little boy, content in his little bubble. Other kids bullied him, most took advantage of him—that is, other than when Niko was around to defend him. Like a watchful guardian, he'd keep one eye on him, especially ever since that day on the cliffs. But now here he was, standing so strong that Niko could do nothing but buckle down. Aspen no longer needed his best friend to watch over him anymore. He sighed in defeat. "When did you grow up so fast?"

He walked over to Aspen and gave him a light punch on the shoulder. "I still don't like it, nor do I trust her too much...but I'm your friend, and I'll support you in your decision," Niko muttered.

"Niko..." Aspen eyes glimmered like fireworks. "Don't worry. In time, you'll grow to love Noelle, too." Both looked at Noelle, who had shot the two of them a huge cheesy smile.

"Man, I still can't believe I didn't realize something was up. I mean, you said you were studying most times...you don't even like studying," Niko sighed. "You don't even get good grades."

"I mean, there were times I'm surprised you didn't catch on," Aspen joked.

"So, she gave you, like, mana or something? Whatever that is. Does that mean you have powers? Is your skin going to start turning red on me?"

Aspen looked at his hand. "No, not really. I haven't felt all that different these past few years. I mean, I randomly get strong at times and my chest glows where I can feel Noelle's presence, but that's just about it." He turned to Noelle, "Did you ever find out why that happens?"

She gave a puzzled look, shrugged and started rambling to herself, "I honestly still don't know...unless...no, no, that couldn't happen."

"What? What is it?" Aspen asked.

"Well, it's probably not your chest glowing but your heart," Noelle said. "The mana I imparted to you is resonating with my own. When I feel distress, or anger, or sorrow, you can feel it too, and vice versa. I would see it happen to my father and mother. There was one time when my father was injured in the woods and my mom, sensing that he was in trouble, was able to rush over and find him immediately. She described it like an unbreakable rope that pulled her towards him. No matter how lost they were, they'd find each other in an instant. It's another common magic that our people use."

"Why haven't you told me something like that years ago?" Aspen asked. Now that she had told him, the moments where his chest glowed did make sense, as Noelle seemed to always be the reason.

"Well...that's because this practice is reserved for..." Noelle bashfully whispered, "for husbands and wives."

"What was that?" he could not hear the last few words out of her mouth.

"Well, that aside for now, how are you going to tell your dad about this?" Niko interrupted.

"I...I wasn't planning to, to be honest." Aspen never really considered telling his dad the truth, somewhat hoping to leave without being noticed. Just as equally as the rest of the town, his father hated the Mogoniwais. Though the difference was that he didn't hate them because he feared them, he hated them for far more personal reasons. And there's nothing that could make him change his mind.

"I see..." Niko rubbed his furrowed brow. "Things are going to get complicated."

"What the hell is going on here!" yelled a voice from a distance. The voice sent a chill down everyone's spine, not only because there was a fourth voice out here in the middle of the woods, but because they recognized that fourth voice.

The color on Aspen's face quickly became pale white. Aspen and Noelle locked eyes onto the uninvited guest. It was none other than Gerard, who didn't try to hide the mixed look of terror, disgust, and anger on his visage.

"W-what are you doing here, Gerard? How did you know we were here?" Aspen yelled out. For the past couple years, he had double checked—no, triple checked—the area when visiting her, making sure no one was following him. He turned to Noelle. *How could I be so careless?*

"I knew something was up, but this...this I didn't expect. All this time you were fraternizing with the enemy, a filthy demon!" Gerard began laughing maniacally at the thought of how much trouble Aspen would be in, completely ignoring Niko. "I got you now, you're screwed! I'm gonna make sure you don't get off lightly and I'll personally see to it that you get the punishment you deserve!"

"Hold on now, it's not what you think, Gerard," Aspen argued. His heart rate skyrocketed, knowing all too well that trying to persuade him would be fruitless, but it felt like he had no other options.

Gerard still maintained his distance between the three of them, just in case he needed to escape, still wary of whether the demon would kill him or not. "That day...when you fell off the cliff, I saw you! You were bleeding out, but you came back perfectly normal! You were going to die! Did that demon over there save you?" All the pieces of the puzzle slowly started to come together in Gerard's head. "I bet you really had fun at the festival didn't you? Are you scheming to attack the town? Did you bring her in to plan out your attack? Bringing a demon along into town...I'll admit, you fooled me but you didn't fool my father!"

His father? Aspen's eyes widened in terror. *From that brief second at the festival?* Willey realized at an instant as well. Of course the general who led the massacre would have realized. He lamented at his own carelessness. *How could I have been so reckless?*

"I'm reporting back to my father, you and your little demon friend are dead!" Gerard taunted as he sped off back to town.

"If I run fast, I can still catch him before he reaches the town!" Noelle proposed. As she was about to run off to chase after him, Aspen grabbed her hand. "What gives, Aspen? I can still catch up to him!" Distress was in her voice as time was of the essence.

"Even if you caught him, his father still knows." His grip tightened, as if she'd disappear at any second if he let go. "It would be a different story if he wasn't involved."

"His father was the general that led the massacre of the Mogoni-wais," Niko informed her.

"If his father sent Gerard to scout out, he could be leading you to a trap. It's too dangerous." Aspen slammed his fist to the ground in frustration, so hard that his knuckles bled. "He might have soldiers at the ready."

"Then you two need to leave while you still can! I know the woods better than anyone, I can fend for myself," Noelle put up a brave front.

"These aren't some animals, Noelle, they are trained soldiers who will hunt you down day and night!" Aspen shouted.

"Murder, torture, practically anything unlawful, he's above the law...not to mention he'll get his soldiers to submit to his bidding through loyalty or fear," Niko pointed out.

"I won't let you be in danger because of me!" Noelle refuted.

"You think I'd be able to live with myself if I leave you here all alone?" Aspen snapped. He headed her way and hugged her tightly, "I promised you...never again, Noelle. You'll never be lonely anymore. Not as long as I'm here. Remember?"

Noelle was speechless at his unwavering fortitude. At this point, he was too stubborn to listen. Tears of frustration welled up as for the first time in her life, she cursed her own birth.

He closed his eyes. *Think, Aspen, you have to think. How are we gonna get out of this? Where can she hide?* Just then, an idea popped up in his head. Letting go of Noelle, he turned to his friend, "Niko, you have to bring her into town."

"Aspen, are you crazy? Wouldn't that be the last place you'd want her to be?" Niko asked.

"Gerard doesn't care about you. Throughout the entire time he hadn't even acknowledged you, he only wants me. So, only you can take her there. If we cover her up, she can blend into the crowd. Just take her to Willey's, I know he won't mind. She can hide at his place until this whole thing blows over."

"Aspen, tha—" Niko stopped mid-sentence when his eyes met Aspen's. The brave face he wore was nothing but a mask, ready to split in half. Aspen was scared. "We can talk about this later, I guess now's not the time to argue. Okay, I'll help any way I can, only because my best friend needs me right now."

"Thank you, thank you, man. I owe you big time." The tension on Aspen's shoulders waned just a bit. He turned to Noelle next. "Go pack up your stuff, pack anything that you don't want to leave behind. Gerard has seen this place, so it's dangerous to come back. I'm sorry to say this but...you might not be able to return here anymore."

Noelle nodded and rushed inside the cave. Luckily, she had always kept her essentials and personal treasures in a backpack that Aspen gave her. She re-emerged after only a couple of minutes with a backpack all packed up and ready to go. Noelle took one last look back at her cave.

Just like her parents, the only *home* she had ever known was gone in an instant. This home was not the warmest, nor the nicest, but it was the place that sheltered and protected her when she was a scared and lost child. It had accepted her where most places would not, and even now the world was stealing this from her, making her homeless once more. Noelle clutched onto her backpack, after having to leave behind a majority of her stuff, her entire life was reduced and squeezed into this bag. "Goodbye forever," she whispered, "and thank you."

"Okay, we can all go now. I'm ready."

Aspen was stoic. "I'm staying here, Noelle."

She dropped her backpack to the ground. "What do you mean you're staying here?"

"They'll be on the lookout for me. I'll be bait and stay here while you guys hide in town."

"It's the logical choice, Noelle. Aspen will be fine," Niko chimed in.

"B-but I don't want to leave you," Noelle still felt guilty of the trouble that she caused him. And felt just as he did, that she couldn't just leave him behind.

He leaned forward until his forehead touched hers. "I'll be fine, Noelle. I can't guarantee your safety right now if you're with me. I promised you didn't I? That you wouldn't be alone. You have to trust me. I'll be back."

Noelle knew he was right, but it still pained her to leave him there alone by himself. With great reluctance, she picked up her backpack and hugged him one last time. "Okay, Aspen, I'll wait for you."

Noelle and Niko ran off towards the town, leaving Aspen behind. What should have been a sweet day turned sour in an instant. She gave one last look at him until he disappeared from her sight, wishing him good luck for whatever came his way.

THE TWO RAN with all their might, cautious as to not get caught. It didn't take too long for them to reach the outer gates of town. Though, there were too many people outside the surrounding area, so they stayed hidden for the time being.

"So...uh...you've known Aspen for a while..." Niko said.

"Yeah," she answered. The two sat in awkward silence as the only thing that connected them to each other was Aspen, and he was nowhere near them.

"I just wanted to say that, um...it's not like I hate you or anything. Or I hate Mogoniwais, but I just..." Niko had trouble getting his words out, "I just have been protecting Aspen since we were kids. You're different from us, so nothing good could come of this—no offense and all. As his friend, I'm gonna look out for him and his best interest."

Noelle gently patted his shoulder, "It's okay, I understand." Her mouth formed a smile, "Aspen's my best friend, too, and I'll do whatever it takes to protect him and keep him safe. I probably would have the same initial reaction." She took comfort in the fact that Niko was not like the other humans in town that Aspen had mentioned in the past. He did not hate Mogoniwais, just hated the relationship between her and his best friend. Though the two had only met each other today, she felt a greater connection to Aspen's friend now after understanding his intentions. They both will do whatever it takes to protect Aspen. Perhaps she and Niko weren't too different after all.

"Wait...we should take the long way around. The soldiers will be in a hurry so they'll probably go through the main entrance. I know a hidden entryway that not many know about," Niko suggested. Bypassing the obvious entryway, they took the time to go through the longer route into the town, and sure enough, the entrance was free to pass. Noelle made sure her face was covered entirely as they threaded inside.

"Stay close to me," Niko whispered to her. Not a single soul was around as they snuck back into town. They were in a back alley that was less traveled by the fellow townspeople, covered in shade and old discarded barrels. It was the perfect hiding spot.

"Go now, before it escapes! On General Ulger's orders, go out and find that demon! You won't like him when he's pissed off," a soldier yelled out to another.

"Won't we get into trouble for hunting a d-demon?"

"General Ulger has done this time and time again, he'll just clean this up like he always does. Now, shut up and go!"

The soldiers headed towards the main entrance in the opposite direction, armed with weapons, completely ignoring the two of them. It didn't take long for two, four, then six more soldiers to charge out of town, following the one in front.

"Thank goodness we went the longer way." Niko let out a huge sigh of relief.

"Yeah," Noelle nodded in agreement. Though they were safe for now, there was another whose livelihood was still uncertain. "Do you think he'll be alright?"

"Yeah...yeah, he'll be just fine. The soldiers won't harm him without any clear evidence," Niko hoped. The distress that Noelle wore seemed to lessen upon hearing this. The two continued navigating through the town, taking a lot of hidden routes that only Niko had known until eventually reaching Willey's store.

Niko and Noelle entered the store, the doorbell rang and out popped Willey's head from the counter. "Oh, hello, Niko. What brings you in today?" He looked at the person beside him who was covered from head to toe. "Who's this here, a new friend?"

"Not so new, Willey." Niko scanned the store for any customers. He turned to Noelle, "Go ahead, it's safe right now."

Noelle unraveled the scarf and took off the hood, revealing her red face and white hair. Willey, wide-eyed, quickly jumped from his seat and rushed towards them. "What's going on here, Niko? How do you know about Noelle? Wait a minute...where's Aspen?"

"I'll answer whatever I can about the situation," Niko replied. Though before he could start answering questions, Willey stopped him.

"Wait just a minute." He flipped the sign to closed and locked the doors. "Okay, let's speak upstairs in private." The three of them headed up the stairs and all took a seat in the living room.

"So, what is the situation right now, Niko? Is Aspen okay?" Willey asked, worry lining his voice. The fact that Niko was the one who brought her here could only mean trouble.

"Aspen should be fine. He stayed behind in the woods so that he could be bait," said Niko.

"Bait? Bait for what?"

"Gerard found us in the woods, and he saw Aspen and Noelle together. Who knows when he'll come knocking at my door. He doesn't know your involvement in all this, so maybe this will work out...and I didn't know what...what to do..."

"Gerard found out about all this? That's not good at all."

"Even worse, Willey. It was his dad that told him to follow Aspen. It seems like he's involved in some way."

Willey turned his attention towards Noelle, "Are you okay? You're not hurt are you?"

"I-I'm fine. We left as soon as Gerard found us," she reassured him.

Niko continued on, "The woods weren't safe anymore for her, so Aspen told me to bring her to you."

"I see..." Willey took one look at Noelle, no doubt she blamed herself for this situation. "Noelle, stay here with me where it's safe. You can have the second bedroom."

Hearing his generosity made Noelle abruptly stand up, first surprised by his offer, then taking a second to process what he just said, until ultimately becoming quite vehemently against it. "There's no way I can accept your offer. I don't want to put you in danger as well. Once night falls, I can escape and I—"

Willey cut her off. "There's no way I'll let you go out there alone with those brutes out there. Gerard's father is a ruthless man, especially towards the Mogoniwais. He would scour the entire woods and cut down every tree just to find you."

An involuntary whimper escaped her lips. Noelle didn't care about what happened to herself, but putting those she cared about in harm's way pained her more than any amount of physical pain. "That's even more the reason why I should leave. What if he comes after you next? Why do you want to help me so much?"

Willey stood up and slowly walked over to her, and for a second, saw an image of someone quite familiar to him. He knelt down and looked her in the eyes. "You know, Noelle, you remind me of my daughter."

"Your daughter?"

"Yeah, she was thoughtful and kind-hearted, often putting others over herself, and often unwilling to accept help. But just as *she* had to realize, *you* must also realize that you're not alone anymore. You have people that care for you. And it's okay to accept the gratitude that they're offering." He handed her a handkerchief so that she could wipe her tears. "Besides, I promised that I'd teach you how to bake again, didn't I?" Noelle buried her face with the handkerchief and nodded reluctantly.

"Aspen will be alright. I know it," Willey said reassuringly. "He'll be alright."

CHAPTER
TWELVE

"I hope Noelle will be safe," Aspen said aloud, now sitting down as she left his sight. Though he knew he would be in quite the predicament soon, his mind was still preoccupied with her well-being. He tilted his head towards the sky, the clouds were calm with a slight breeze that cooled the spring heat to the perfect temperature. "It would have been a great day to have a picnic." He reached in his pocket, realizing he had forgotten his watch. *I wonder how much time has passed? Fifteen minutes? Thirty minutes?* Aspen had no plan beyond Noelle's escape, and thought that maybe if he got lucky they wouldn't even show up, or perhaps get lost on the way. His chest glows iridescently, shining and flickering brighter and brighter. The brighter it glowed, the more he felt Noelle's presence in an unexplainable way. Though he didn't know where she was, he could sense that she was at least safe.

He clutched onto his chest. "Now's not the time to glow, I'll be screwed if anyone sees this." After a couple minutes, his chest stopped glowing as if on command. And he heard the leaves rustling from a distance and the sound of boots stomping on the ground.

He looked up, now staring down the barrels of a dozen soldiers' rifles. *Don't tremble, don't freeze up, Aspen,* he told himself. A bead of sweat rolled down his face. The soldiers kept their distance, screaming in his direction. Aspen wasn't sure if they were all barking commands at him, but if they were, it all just sounded like incoherent jargon.

"Silence!" a loud commanding voice echoed behind them, and immediately, the soldiers were dead silent. A figure walked forward through the soldiers that stood like statues. The man emerged in the front of the crowd, standing out from the rest due to his tall stature and stone-faced demeanor.

Aspen gulped when he locked eyes with this giant—*General Ulger.*

The general smiled down at him, a wicked smile that sent a shiver down Aspen's spine, resembling that of a predator that had just cornered its prey. "Aspen, long time no see," he said coldly, heading towards him, "I haven't seen you since...the festival, am I correct?" Aspen stood silently as General Ulger continued staring. "You were in such a hurry that I didn't get to meet your new friend."

"Sir, I don't know what you are talking about." Aspen attempted to appear as unfazed as he could, ignoring the rifles pointing at him.

"Oh, I think you know who I'm talking about. You can help me, Aspen. Can you imagine what we humans can do if we can harness their power? Humanity won't be limited to what they can do. We'd be able to do the impossible. So tell me..." He leaned in closer to his ear. "Where are you hiding the demon?"

Aspen stared up into his eyes, first in disbelief and then in fear. Most people know that Mogoniwais possess magical abilities, but not very many knew about how their powers were transferable to others. General Ulger's plan was something unheard, that no one in history had ever thought to do. And he needed Noelle for this plan. That alone was enough to chill him to the bone.

"I don't know what you mean, sir. I was just out in the woods. You know, just enjoying nature." *If they are all here, this means Noelle and Niko should be free to escape to Willey's house. I just need to keep stalling for as long as I can.*

"My boy happened to run into you in the woods, said you had… *company*…" General Ulger emphasized.

"He must have been seeing things, because as you can see in this neck of the woods, I am here all by myself," Aspen retorted in a slightly smug tone. He wasn't going to let the general scare him, not anymore.

"I'm not playing around here! You are going to start answering the questions! Where is she now?" The general raised his voice, now visibly pissed off. Even with the general screaming in his ear and the rifles pointed at him, Aspen still kept quiet, not letting out a single clue of Noelle's existence.

Jack Bellard finally came from behind the soldiers, now catching his breath. "Did you find her? We need to see if she's the right one."

One of the soldiers walked over to the general's side, pointing out, "Maybe it left the area, sir. She couldn't have gotten far." General Ulger pondered his next course of action. Aspen took a quick glance at the cave, making sure he was caught peeking.

"Is she in that cave? Is that where you're hiding her?" asked General Ulger. "Go check out the cave, report any findings to me," he demanded to the soldiers behind him. Without hesitation they followed his orders and stormed the cave.

Great, hopefully that keeps them here longer. The more I can stall for Niko and Noelle, the better chance we have. I just hope they aren't running into problems on their end, Aspen thought, watching the soldiers rush in.

Ten minutes later, the soldiers come back holding Noelle's sleeping bag, lantern, and other household items such as cooking pots and silverware. General Ulger snatched the sleeping bag from his hand and held it in front of Aspen. "Can you explain what these items are doing in a cave?"

"I camp here often, you know it's nice out here in the woods. You can see the stars very well at night."

Another soldier came out from the cave and held out a dress. The general looked at it and then stared back at him, waiting for a response.

"It's....very comfy..."

General Ulger's eye twitched as he smiled and let out a soft cackle. *BAM.* Without warning, he punched Aspen in the gut. It was so fast that he couldn't react at all. Aspen gasped for air, feeling the wind knocked out of him, and tumbled to the ground. The general followed up by punching him so hard in the face that it felt like Aspen just ran into a stone wall. His lip and nose began to bleed. General Ulger took a handkerchief out, wiped the blood off his knuckles, and stuffed it back into his pocket. He picked Aspen up by his shirt collar, and said, "I'm not here to entertain you. Do I look like I have the patience?" Aspen tried to loosen his grip on his collar but couldn't break free. The general continued on, "You don't know how dangerous those things are, do you? They can enhance their own strength and create explosions from their fingertips. Those demons have the power to wipe us out, so we must kill them before they kill us. Do you understand? Humans are the apex predator, not the prey." He whispered into his ear, "I have been very patient with you, Aspen. You are going to tell me where she is or else I am going to beat the answer out of you myself." General Ulger loosened his grip on his collar to let him speak.

Aspen held part of his beaten face. One of his eyes was starting to swell up, but nevertheless, he only had two words to say.

"Screw you."

Shoving Aspen to the ground, Ulger yelled out to the crowd of soldiers, "Rifle! Hand me a rifle! You wanna play games? Okay, let's play games, you'll see...I'll show you, I'll show you not to mess with me. I'll, I'll..." The soldiers looked at each other, all hesitant to follow his order. Ulger kicked the earth as he looked back at his men in disbelief, "Why are you all just gawking at me like a stupid herd of animals! Did I just stutter?! Give me a fucking rifle! Or else I will...I will..."

"General Ulger, this m-might be a bit excessive," Jack quietly raised his point.

A soldier stepped in, "Sir, he's just a—"

"Did I recall asking? Next time you step out of order, I'll shove the next bullet in your skull!" he snapped at the soldier. General Ulger snatched the rifle out of his hands and held the gun by the barrel like a bat. "I'm going to beat some sense into you!" he said, holding the rifle high, readying himself to strike.

Aspen shut his eyes tight, preparing for what was about to follow. At that moment he truly thought about his death. It was definitely something Ulger was capable of, and the worst of it all, he would get away with it scot-free by pinning the blame onto his loyal followers if the government would dare to sanction him.

"Richard Ulger!" an angry voice yelled out from behind. General Ulger lowered his weapon to see who was calling out his name.

I'm saved, Aspen thought, breathing a huge sigh of relief. Though, as he opened his eyes the feeling of dread instantly came flooding back to him. *Never mind, I'm dead, I'm dead, I'm so dead.* Of all people Aspen expected to see, the person approaching was the last person he thought would come to his aid—his dad. His dad walked towards the general, confronting him face-to-face.

"Richard..." Aspen's dad called out once more. He looked at his son, who was on the ground, then back towards General Ulger.

"Ben..." General Ulger stood his ground, not feeling fazed in the slightest. "So, what are you doing here in this neck of the woods? A little far from town for the great Mayor Ben Chase, isn't it?"

"Soldiers running around town causing a commotion about a demon that was spotted with a human. Something about a demon hunt," Ben said. "And on your command at that. You think I'll let you do whatever you want in my town? Those demons are a menace, but that doesn't mean I'll let you destroy everything in your path just to find one."

"So, entertain me...you mind explaining why you're using my son as a punching bag?" Aspen's dad looked furious, looking almost as scary as the general himself.

"Did you know, Ben? Your son has been acquainted with a demon girl."

Aspen's dad turned and glared at his son, causing him to shrivel up. He turned his direction towards General Ulger once more. "Well, it looks like whoever you are looking for isn't around. Take your men and leave here, I suggest you look elsewhere."

All the soldiers watched the confrontation in silence, not knowing what to do. One of the men in the back whispered to a nearby soldier, "I've never seen anyone talk to General Ulger like that."

"Apparently, they fought together in the war, I think they go way back," answered the other.

General Ulger and Aspen's dad locked eyes, it was like they were playing mind games with each other, waiting for the other to back down or waver. The fiery tension between the two was enough to spark and burn the whole forest down if it went on any longer. An altercation was bound to explode, it was just a matter of how long the fuse would last.

Without breaking eye contact with Ben, General Ulger called out to his soldiers, "Men! Fall back!" The general walked away with his men tailing behind him without skipping a beat, all in retreat. It didn't take long until Aspen and his dad were the only two left.

Aspen looked at his dad, who was still turned away from him and avoiding eye contact, "Dad, I—"

His dad cut him off, "Not another word until we get back home."

Aspen kept silent as the two of them headed back to town. He followed his dad, making sure he was at least two or three feet behind. Though he was thankful that his father had saved him, he was still afraid of what was to come and how much trouble he was going to get in now. Though it was a small price to pay, it should have bought Niko and Noelle enough time to escape to Willey's. *They should be fine, right?* Aspen quickly shook any concerning thoughts out of his head. *I shouldn't think like that, of course they are fine. There's only one thing that I should be thinking of, and that's how I'm going to deal with Gerard's dad later on.* Having experienced how ruthless and violent General Ulger was in regards to Mogoniwais, there was no doubt that his desperation in capturing Noelle wouldn't end today. General Ulger's views on them extended beyond the blind systemic hate that everyone in town shared. It's one thing to hate them because they falsely believed Mogoniwais were dangerous, but for the general, it seemed much deeper than that. It seemed like his motives were fueled more by intense obsession rather than hate.

His father walked forward as if there was a weight that slowed him down. Perhaps his mayoral duties had tired him out today, or maybe it was the confrontation he had with General Ulger. Aspen realized that being mayor did have its perks. After all, he made Ulger stand down—and the general never adhered to anyone's command but his own.

To Aspen, it seemed like his father and Gerard's father were somewhat similar people. They both worked for the government, they both were in the war, they both were way too serious, and last of all, they both hate Mogoniwais. The only difference was their ideologies about how Mogoniwais should be treated. It is clear that Richard Ulger abused his power to unlawfully do whatever he wanted to Mogoniwais—kill them, hunt them, experiment on them —bypassing any laws or officials that stand in his way. Although his father hated them, he did things by the book, using his stance as mayor to lawfully push away any Mogoniwais that hide around towns and into their zones. This stark contrast made Aspen believe that maybe his father was not a lost cause after all.

The sun was starting to set by the time they arrived back into town. Aspen looked around, noticing the townspeople gawking at him and whispering to one another as he passed them on the streets. Initially, he thought that it was a coincidence, but quickly realized how wrong he was as it happened with each and every person they passed. Word must have traveled fast.

Out of nowhere, Jeremy rushed over to Aspen, shaking his shoulders vigorously. "Are you with them, boy?" He had a crazed look in his eyes. "I heard you a demon-lover, are you crazy? Make it right, and tell me where they at? We have to strike while we still can, boy." Aspen loosened Jeremy's grip on his shoulders and pushed him aside, ignoring him completely. Jeremy was still persistent in finding out the truth, though his interrogation was quickly put to a halt as soon as his eyes met the scowl of Aspen's father.

What's going on? Aspen thought. *Did Gerard end up telling the entire town? Or was it the general? I wouldn't put it past either of them to do it.* He lowered his head to avoid the constant stares on the streets that looked his way as he walked by them. Aspen didn't mind that his secret about being friends with a Mogoniwai was exposed, but now this just meant many more eyes will be looking for Noelle, making it that much more dangerous for her to still be here. This was something he definitely wanted to avoid, especially since she was currently at Willey's place.

As they passed by Willey's store, Aspen tried to peek through the windows but couldn't see a thing. If he could, Aspen would rush right in there to check up on Noelle. He still had no idea if she had made it there safely. But with his father with him, it would be nearly impossible to go there now without raising suspicion.

The two finally arrived home. Without delay, his father sat him down in the living room demanding answers. "Aspen, tell me the truth about what is going on right now."

Aspen had much preferred the awkward silence on the way home then this one-on-one confrontation. He debated on what he should tell him—should he lie? Should he tell the truth? Maybe there was a chance his dad might understand.

As he was about to open his mouth to speak, his dad interrupted him again, "The truth, Aspen." It was like he had already known that Aspen was about to lie.

Twiddling his thumbs, Aspen tried to find the right words, but nothing came up. Aspen looked directly into his dad's eyes, not averting his gaze for the first time in a while. His father had crow's feet beside his eyes. *Did he always have that?* Aspen tried to remember, but couldn't recall. His dad looked furious, though not as furious as when he confronted General Ulger today, but probably the most he had been towards him in a while. For some reason, Aspen couldn't do it. He couldn't, no, didn't *want* to lie to his father anymore.

"It's true," Aspen affirmed, "I have been hanging out with a Mogoniwai. For years now. Her name is Noelle. For the past few years, I've been spending time with her, teaching her how to read and write while she taught me how to do stuff like fight and hunt."

"Aspen, are you crazy? Why the hell would you even do such a thing?" his dad bellowed. "How could you keep such a thing a secret?"

"She saved my life, Dad. I wouldn't even be here, sitting here, talking to you, if it wasn't for her. I'm living off of a second chance, and I want to spend it with the person who saved my life." His dad froze for a second, not knowing how to respond. "They don't deserve this treatment, Dad. They're just like us."

"Just like...you don't know how dangerous they are, Aspen! We went to war against these monsters! Do you know how many people died? If they are left unchecked, who knows when another war will happen. We fought out there so our children didn't have to experience such a thing ever again. Our brethren. Our friends. All slaughtered one after the other. We dirtied our hands, sacrificed our humanity...lost loved ones...and still only won by the skins of our teeth. They. Are. Monsters."

The word "monster" screeched in his ears like nails on a chalkboard. Noelle was not a monster, she wasn't. He was tired of everyone labeling her as such. "Well, the same could be said about us! Can't it? We massacred their people and forced them into hiding! Noelle had to grow up without parents, they were killed by us. While we children were comfy in our beds, she was out there fighting to survive everyday, not knowing when she'd eat or when she'd get attacked. She didn't have a family because of us. In their eyes, *we're* the dangerous ones, *we're* the monsters!"

His dad let out a huge sigh, "You're just a kid, you don't know any—"

"Just a kid? I'm sixteen years old! I'll be old enough to move out soon. I'm tired of the adults thinking they know everything and I'm sick and tired of this town's xenophobic behavior! I just don't understand, Dad. I'm the kid here and you're the adult, then why can't you see how wrong you're acting towards them? Why do you hate them so much?"

"Do you realize how much they ruined our lives? Because of them, I couldn't be here when your mom was sick! I couldn't be here for our family!" His dad looked broken, like a shattered vase put together again with tape. Aspen knew that his dad blamed himself for not supporting his mom at that time, but didn't know it was to this extent.

"Dad, it's not your fault," Aspen comforted him. "Look, Mom and I could never blame you for what happened. It was out of your control. At some point, you have to move on."

"How am I supposed to move on? She was my world. I wasn't there, she couldn't lean on me. I couldn't even console her, tell her that everything would be okay. Your mother put on a brave face for everyone, but deep down, she was scared. She didn't want to leave this world prematurely, to leave you alone, she still wanted to watch you grow up." He wrapped the guilt in his hands and clenched his fists. "It should have been me instead of her..."

Aspen averted his eyes from his father, opting to stare blankly at the coffee table. The feeling of uselessness felt all too familiar to him, perhaps it was in their genetics, passed down from generation to generation. The sound of the clock ticking echoed in the room, the hour hand had been broken for years now, neglected of that much-needed care. It was just like father in a way, both stuck in the past.

"Noelle is my world," Aspen declared. His dad looked up at him with a confused look on his face. "Just like how Mom was your world, Noelle's mine. Without meaning to, slowly but surely, we became a part of each other's lives. I don't think I can live without her anymore." Aspen's feelings solidified after hearing his dad speak. He'd do anything to keep Noelle safe, to keep her happy, to protect her just like his dad was with his mom. Although Noelle was strong, she still got scared sometimes, too. She tried to hide it, but he could read her like an open book. Noelle was afraid of being alone forever or hurting those close to her or losing those that she cherishes. In one day, her world was flipped upside down. Aspen couldn't help but think about how scared Noelle must be feeling, not knowing whether she'd be killed or what the future had in store for her. He needed to see her right away.

His dad turned to him with a concerned look on his face. "Aspen, do you realize the repercussions of what you just said? Do you realize how hated the demons are throughout all the towns? The people will treat you with scorn, they will torment you while you're just walking the streets. The life you have with her will only be filled with misery."

"Then Noelle and I will move. We'll both keep moving until we find a place that can accept the two of us. I won't stop until she's happy, until she finally has a place she can call home!" Aspen shouted. It didn't matter to him if it took months or even years; they'd travel from town to town until they found a place where she'd belong. Noelle deserved at least that much in life.

"You'll move? And how would you support yourself? You don't have any money. You don't even have skills for a job. Can you honestly say that you'll be able to protect her? Even in other towns, they share the same sentiment as us, no one will accept you. What you're saying is just an idealistic dream."

"It'll...work out somehow. I'll make it work." His words didn't sound promising, not to his dad nor to even himself.

Aspen's dad shook his head, looking quite disappointed with himself. "You leave me no choice, Aspen."

"Leave you no choice to what?"

"I know an old war buddy who runs an academy for boys, located just short of Cresnough. They live and learn at the school, and are watched by the teachers and faculty to make sure that they aren't getting into trouble. I am contacting him first thing in the morning to enroll you there immediately."

Aspen stood up in protest. "That's not fair! It's my life! You can't just send me away just because you can't accept the idea of me and Noelle! You just want to separate me from her!"

"Your life with her will be only filled with hardship and suffering. It's best for you, maybe even for her. As your parent, I am only doing what I see fit to protect you, even if you'll hate me for it."

"As my parent? Where were you in the past decade? You never acted like one before! When I was getting bullied at school, what did you do? Nothing. When I was devastated and needed someone to comfort me when Mom died, where were you? For all those birthdays, all those times when I was feeling like crap, all those times when I just wanted you to talk to me, all those times when I needed a parent, you were never there when I needed you!" Aspen started choking up—it wasn't fair to him, it wasn't fair at all. He continued on, "Where were you? Where were you then? And you choose now to suddenly become concerned with my life? To become a so-called parent?"

His dad's decision did not waver, Aspen's words passed through him like wind in the air. "I know I haven't been a parent. I'm probably the worst parent in the world. I failed your mom, most importantly, I failed you. But it's time I start trying now. You'll hate me but I will gladly accept it if it means protecting you from the harsh reality that will be your future if you continue to stay with her."

"H-how could you do this to me? I hate you!"

"Be sure to pack your bags," Aspen's dad declared, his resolve hardened on this decision, making his son's fate sealed. "It's what's best." It was not just because she was a demon, but the fact that being with her meant potential danger to his son wherever they went. By association, he'd be no better than a demon in the eyes of the people.

Aspen didn't mutter another word as he stormed into his room, letting the loud stomps up the stairs speak for themselves. It seemed as if the world was hell-bent on separating the two of them. If the world was up against him, he thought that maybe his dad would be by his side. But he was wrong. Completely, hopelessly, utterly wrong.

Aspen's father stood up and poured himself a drink. The living room downstairs was once again quiet except for the sound of the clock ticking and the splash of alcohol being poured into the glass. He took one long gulp. It was bitter. He poured another and another and another and another. The bitter taste still had not numbed the pain that struck him to his very core. The tears forming in his eyes as he questioned the validity of his choice. "I can't do this without you, Maya," Ben spoke softly. "I don't know how to be there for him anymore. Am I wrong?" His eyes felt drowsier, the fine line between consciousness and weariness now started to blur. This was the part that comforted him, this blissful slumber that followed after was the only time when the pain subsided for just a fleeting moment. Ben finished his drink and stared at the empty glass. "It... should have been...me instead."

ASPEN THREW a fit in his room, thrashing and throwing anything near him to the ground, nothing escaped his wrath. He grabbed a picture frame, stopping himself short from throwing it at the floor. Aspen stared at the frame. It was a picture of him, his dad, and his mom at a picnic; they were all laughing and enjoying themselves, like the happy family that they should be today. He sat on the floor slumped over with a defeated look on his face.

"Why can't I hate him?" Aspen questioned himself. More than anything, he wanted to hate his father, to curse his name for separating him from Noelle. Despite that, he still couldn't truly hate him.

He crawled over to the other side of the room and picked up a large stuffed teddy bear that was sprawled on the floor, hugging it tightly. His chest began glowing again. Aspen didn't know why but the more he hugged the teddy bear, the more he felt Noelle's presence.

"Noelle..." Aspen didn't know how he was going to break the terrible news to her. Now that he thought about it, once he's sent away it'll be the longest he'd be separated from her. *Click.* Aspen stood up, he heard a noise coming from his window. *Click.* Someone was throwing a pebble at his window. He opened the window and peered down; it was Niko, gesturing to him to come outside. Aspen left his room, slowly crept down the stairs and peeked to see where his dad was. *Dad's passed out drunk on the couch, now's my chance,* he thought. Aspen used this opportunity to sneak out of the house and headed out to Willey's with haste. What very little time he had left, he wanted to spend every second of it with her.

CHAPTER

THIRTEEN

Aspen followed Niko to Willey's store. The good news was that she was safe and hadn't been spotted, and the better news was that she was going to stay with Willey until the hunt for Noelle cooled down. A huge weight was lifted off his shoulders for the time being, he was so relieved that he'd almost forgotten that he'd have to move soon.

"I know that she's a demon, but it seemed like General Ulger was quite obsessed with capturing her," Niko said after Aspen had recapped him about what happened earlier today.

"He was. Gerard's dad was willing to torture me just to get information. He wants Noelle for some crazy plan. Even not knowing what it is, I know it can't be good." General Ulger was definitely hiding something, and Aspen had a hunch that it was much deeper than he had anticipated.

"How are we going to stop Ulger now?" Niko asked.

"I don't exactly know how. He's stronger, more cunning, and has all the resources at his disposal. All I can do now is hide Noelle away and take her somewhere where Ulger will never find her. Today showed that I'm not strong enough to stop him, I'm just lucky my dad showed up before the general was going to beat me half to death."

"Your dad showed up? How did he take it?"

"He's sending me away. Shipping me off to some school for troubled boys," Aspen irritably grumbled.

"He's sending you away?!" The news shocked Niko so much that he almost yelled it out for the whole town to hear.

"Yeah, he's sending me away as soon as possible. I have possibly a few days left. He went on saying that being with Noelle would only make my life like hell."

Niko didn't respond.

"Are you not going to say that he's wrong?" Aspen looked at his friend, "Don't tell me that you agree with him?"

"Your dad's right, Aspen. You have no money, no plan, and you don't even know how the adult world works. Even more, no town will allow demons to live there. You'll face persecution wherever you go. I know you care about her, I honestly do. But as your friend, I think you and Noelle are better off going your separate ways," advised Niko.

"Not you, too..." Aspen pouted. "When I do get sent away, I'll have to find a way to communicate with Noelle."

"You're still going to try and send messages to her? Didn't you just get in trouble because of that?" Niko scolded. "Shouldn't you just lay low until the dust settles?"

"I'm still worried about Noelle." Aspen tried to wrap his head on what he should do. "Maybe I can send her letters and address them to Willey."

Niko gave him a disapproving look.

THE TWO EVENTUALLY ARRIVED IN front of Willey's store, which was closed for the day. Niko knocked on the door a few times until Willey peeked his head out from the curtains. With haste, he unlocked the door, let the two of them inside, and locked it back.

"Aspen, I'm so glad you're safe. Niko and Noelle filled me in on what happened. How are you feeling?"

"Aside from the eye, I'm fine, Willey, thanks for asking."

"That's good to hear, Very good to hear. Well, let's head upstairs and join Noelle, shall we?" he said, gesturing to them to walk up the stairs.

"Actually, it's getting late," Niko interjected. "My parents will probably worry about where I am if I don't head home soon. Fill me in on the rest of the details tomorrow, okay?"

"Sounds good, man. Thanks for today," Aspen gave him a short hug.

"Of course, what are friends for, man?" Niko said his goodbyes and left the store.

Aspen and Willey went up to where the hearty aroma of beef, carrots, and roasted potatoes filled the air.

"Aspen! You're all right!" Noelle yelled as she came running towards him. She tackled him to the ground with a huge hug as Aspen wasn't quite ready for the sudden embrace. Noelle took a good look at him, noticing his eye, then immediately turning away from it.

"I'm glad you're safe, Noelle, I've been worried all day." Aspen hugged her back tightly, savoring the feeling as much as he could. He didn't want to let go. He looked at Noelle and Willey. "The general won't stop looking for Noelle. He has this plan, a plan that talks about humans harnessing powers of the Mogoniwais."

"Harnessing our powers?" asked Noelle, "how is he going to do that?"

"I have no clue. For now, all we can do is be safe and stay hidden. We'll have to be on alert from now on," said Aspen.

"I see. I've already talked it over with Noelle. She can stay here with me for as long as she wants. If she stays here, she'll be safe, you have my word," Willey promised.

"And in return, I told Willey that I'd help out with baking for the store and with some chores around the house," Noelle added.

"Oh, I see. I'm sure Willey certainly could use some help around the place." Aspen felt reassured knowing that Noelle could find a home here for the time being. General Ulger wouldn't expect that a Mogoniwai would be hiding right under their noses.

"So, did the general do anything to you? You didn't get hurt did you?"

"Just a few scrapes. It actually could have been a lot worse if my dad didn't step in." *My dad, I completely forgot.* He'd have to tell Noelle that he was being sent away for a while. "Hey, Noelle, I have something to—"

"I'm glad you're alright. I was worried all day that you had gotten hurt." Noelle took a closer look at his face and his swelling eye but chose to smile through it, knowing full well that he wouldn't want her reacting too much to it.

Aspen bit his lip. He had to tell her but couldn't, not wanting to ruin the smile that she wore in front of him.

"That's not all that happened..." said Aspen. "My dad was there. He actually stopped the problem from escalating even further."

"Oh, that's good, right?" Noelle asked with confusion.

"Not so much, I told him the truth about you."

"So, he knows that she's hiding here?" Willey asked. He and Noelle looked at each other with worry.

"He doesn't, I didn't tell him that much. Just the truth about how I have known Noelle for years now." *Just tell her. Just rip it off,* Aspen thought to himself, *like an old Band-aid.*

"Is that really all that bad?" Noelle chimed in.

"It is...he's uhhh...he's thinking about sending me to school, far away from this town, an academy near Cresnough or something," Aspen explained.

Willey looked distraught. "Oh my. Maybe if I go talk to him he might change—"

"He's made up his mind already," Aspen interrupted. "I don't think any amount of convincing will do it any good. He believes that it'll be beneficial for me if I were to be sent to who knows where." Aspen already knew that his decision was resolute. His dad had never enforced something like this before, usually he was more hands off in his life. Also, this case was much different, this time it involved a Mogoniwai. Out of all the moments in his life, he wished that his dad hadn't chosen *this* moment to be a parent.

"Oh, I see..." Willey was at a loss for words. "Are you sure you're alright, Aspen? It's okay to feel—"

"I'm fine. I'm fine, Willey, honestly," Aspen reassured him, being less worried about himself and more worried about one other person and how they were taking the news. He looked in Noelle's direction, whose face was mixed with emotions, changing ever so slightly as the news sunk in.

"What does that mean?" she asked. "Are...a-are you going away forever?"

"No, no, no, of course not," Aspen reassured her. "I'll come back as soon as I can. There's no way I would—no...I could live without you for such a long time."

"You're not forced to go away because of me, right?" The ever-growing mountain of guilt stacked on top of her. Noelle knew all this started because Aspen had been with her. Not only was she making his life more difficult, but now he was being forced to live alone, far away from his home, from his friends and family. All because of her.

Aspen put his hand on her shoulder. "It's not your fault, you didn't do anything wrong. I mean it."

Willey let out a huge sigh. "I only pray that this town will change. Maybe one day they'll be smart and see things like the two of ya."

"One can dream, right? Then we wouldn't have to go through all of this." Aspen chuckled. He hung his head and spoke softly to himself, "One can dream..."

Aspen sprang up, "But when I do come back, we'll resume our plans, we'll go out and find a new home! We'll go somewhere far, far away from here, away from Ulger and away with whatever he's planning. A home for you and me, where we can live freely!"

"I can't wait!" she cheered. Noelle knew he was trying to keep her spirits up, doing her utmost best to mask her dejection. She hated it. But for now, for Aspen's sake, she'd bury these feelings so that he wouldn't worry about her.

"So, what's something that you're looking forward to for our new future home?"

Noelle took a minute to think about it. "Desserts?"

Willey and Aspen looked at each other and burst out laughing, and soon enough, Noelle joined them as well.

"That's definitely a very important aspect of a home," Willey agreed. "I'll have to stop by once in a while to eat them. Maybe you'll make different desserts that even I don't know about."

Noelle was exhilarated. "But your store has so many sweets, Willey, do you think anyone could ever make something you've never seen before?"

"The world is such a big place, Noelle, and you've only seen a fraction of it. I would have no doubt that there would be many things that you haven't tried before. And who knows, maybe one day you'll open up your own bakery, where strangers get to try the desserts *you* bake."

"I can't wait..." Noelle could already picture it in her head. Everyday, she'd meet new people and watch the smile grow on their faces as they took a bite of her homemade desserts. She snapped out of her daydream and looked at Aspen, "What about you? What are you looking forward to in the future?"

He couldn't think of anything in particular. "Well, the only thing that comes to mind is that I can spend even more time with you. That's all I really need."

Noelle felt flushed at how embarrassingly sweet his answer was.

"Well, just because I'll be away from you guys, it doesn't mean that you won't hear from me."

Willey and Noelle didn't know where he was going with this. "What do you mean?" Noelle asked.

"I can write to you and send the letters to Willey's address." Noelle looked quite enthralled with the idea. "At least this way, we'll still be able to keep in contact. I promise I'll write to you whenever I can. No matter how little or how long it is, I'll write to you."

"That's a great idea," complimented Willey. "It will give you something to look forward to. And while Aspen is away, you'll be busy learning how to be the best baker in the world. Time will fly by, and you'll see each other again, before you even know it."

"I'll write to you, too! And while you're away, I'll keep learning. Soon enough my desserts will be so good that your tongue will fall off. Look forward to it!"

Aspen let out a nervous chuckle, "Hopefully that never happens. That sounds like it'll hurt a lot."

The three sat together in silence once the laughter had died down. Though they tried to keep their spirits high, the realization that Aspen would be gone was still looming on their minds. Despite knowing Ulger was on the lookout for her for his nefarious plans, something else bothered her at the moment. It was the fear of being left behind that persisted in Noelle's thoughts. Aspen was leaving, going to a place far, far away from here. He would make new friends, friends that he could openly converse with and laugh with without any repercussions. Perhaps he'd find them to be much better company than she was. Perhaps she'd just become an old memory.

"You won't forget about me?" Noelle softly muttered.

Aspen could see beyond the mask she wore. Past the gentle smile was a quivering lip. Behind the spirited expression were eyes ready to tear up at any minute. Beyond it all, beyond everything, was someone whose heart was about to shatter in a thousand pieces. But she would never tell him that. He held his hand out and stuck his pinky finger towards her, "I'll come back to you."

She smiled to herself. Back when they were kids, their pinkies were about the same size, but now, his finger was much larger than her own. *In the end, we really did keep our promises didn't we?* Aspen ended up becoming brave—brave enough to stand up to his bullies, and even brave enough to stand up to the general and his soldiers. He wasn't the insecure little kid that he was years ago. As for herself, well, Aspen had promised her that he'd make her happy. And ever since meeting him, her life had been abundantly filled with happiness. He taught her how to read and write, took her to a festival, showed her a new way to live life, and most importantly, filled in a void of loneliness that was missing this whole time. A day wasn't enough to list out everything he'd done for her, she'd received the better end of the bargain no doubt. Noelle held out her finger and interlocked her pinky with his, connected together like a wrapped scarf on a cold winter day. It symbolized an unyielding bond, a never-ending vow, a—

"Promise?" asked Noelle. Though she knew that Aspen would try to come back as soon as possible and that he'd write to her as much as he could, the bitter reality was that this could very well be the last time that she'd get to spend time with him for a long while.

"I swear on it." Aspen pulled a book out of his bag and handed it to her.

"The Village Boy and the Snow Princess? Why are you giving this to me?" Noelle asked, as she held the book delicately in her hands.

"Remember the night I left you for the first time, I lent you that book," reminded Aspen. "A temporary parting gift...I promise I'll return for it later. This way you'll know that I'll come back. Just like before, when we were kids, I swear that I'll come back for both of you."

Noelle hugged the book in her arms as if it was a piece of him. It was something much more than a simple children's book, well, to the both of *them* that is. It was a book that represented the start of their relationship together and the past that Aspen held onto dearly. By giving away this book, not only did it give her something to remember him by, but it also showed that he was ready to move forward in life. "I'll guard this book until your safe return."

"I know you will," Aspen grinned.

"Well, I made you something. Are you still hungry?" Noelle tried to change the subject, she didn't want to think about him leaving just yet.

As if on cue, Aspen's stomach started to rumble. "Yeah, starved. I haven't been able to eat dinner yet."

"Just wait until you try the stew Noelle made, it's amazing. It's something I haven't tasted in a while," Willey gushed.

"Stew? That's my favorite! It smells good already." Aspen couldn't wait to sit down, relax, and eat, after the long day he'd had. While he waited at the table, Noelle prepared and set a plate of stew and a side of rice for him.

The stew wasn't steamy and fresh, since she had made it a few hours ago, but it still looked just as tasty. Aspen took one big whiff of it and could already feel his mouth drooling. *It smells strangely familiar.* Noelle was staring intently at him, waiting for his reaction as he scooped up the stew with his spoon. He shoved the stew into his mouth and swallowed. *It can't be.* Aspen took another bite, then another bite, and another bite. *It is.* Without warning, tears began raining down, making little splashes onto the table. The salty tears mixed into the stew, and only then did Aspen realize that he was crying. Though he wiped them away from his face, more tears followed. Aspen started sniffling between words, "S-sorry, I-I don't know why I'm crying."

Noelle stood up from her seat and sat beside him.

Willey looked at him, already knowing full well the cause of his sorrows. He put his hand on Aspen's shoulder. "I'll give you two some time." After disappearing to his room, it was now just the two of them. The room was not as warmly lit, which cast a shadow onto their faces. *Drip. Drip.* The leaky sink faucet dripped droplets of water as the two sat in the cramped dining table. And his right leg became restless, bouncing onto the wood floors, causing them to squeak and break the silence.

Noelle looked concerned. "Was it bad? Did I do something wrong?"

Aspen tried speaking without choking on his words, "No... it's....the best I've ever had." He stared at the bowl again. "I haven't tasted something like this for a long time now...it tastes like how my mom used to make it." He sniffled and took another bite. "W-what's in it?"

Noelle caressed his hair and smiled at him. "I made it with marinated beef, carrots, potatoes, and Willey had some fresh fish, so I added chopped-up fried fish."

"So that's why I never tasted it again. My mom always tried to make me eat fish when I was a kid...I hated fish." Bite after bite, a flood of memories of his mother filled his head like raging waters, breaking through the mental wall he'd built up after all these years. He remembered how she'd caressed his hair when he had a nightmare and how she'd always read to him before bed no matter how tired she was. He missed it. Aspen also remembered his mom's terrible habit of forgetting one item from her grocery list, often causing them to make another trip. He missed those days as well. He could see the glimpses of her smile that comforted him in hard times —it'd been so long since he remembered the shape of it. The more memories that popped up, the more he couldn't stop crying.

Soon enough, the flashbacks subsided. And before realizing it, Aspen had finished the entire bowl of stew. He looked at her with eyes still red, and said, "It's not fair..."

Noelle pulled his head to her chest and embraced him. Aspen's body glowed iridescently in faint pale colors, and hers did as well, both glimmering to the rhythm of his heart. She didn't have the words to describe this feeling but she felt a connection to him on a much deeper level, feeling like they had one body, one soul. Aspen had opened his heart to her, allowing Noelle in, and she did her best to tread lightly. Their souls resonated and merged with one another, along with the light in her body. Soon enough, Aspen's chest glimmered in a bright warm light that illuminated the room that matched her own. With that, the pain of loneliness, the loss of his mother, and the guilt he harbored for not saving her all became abundant and clear.

"I understand, Aspen. You don't have to say a word," Noelle comforted him while holding back her own tears. His emotions became her own. And because of that, she knew that he had been bottling up his feelings all this time until he couldn't hold them any longer.

"Why did the world have to take her away from me? Why are they taking me away from you? I lost my mom, and now I'm losing you, everyone I care about disappears around me," Aspen cried out softly. No longer could he feign a strong mental fortitude. "After all this time, I'm still not strong enough to help you."

"You tried your best, didn't you?"

"I'm so tired of it all. Why is it so hard?" Those closest to him always and eventually disappeared in his life—first his mother, then father, and now Noelle. His nightmares had come to fruition, haunting him in both his sleeping and waking hours. Allowing for a moment of weakness, he took off his mask, revealing his truest feelings. The stew triggered a memory within him, reminding him that the weight of the loss had hurt him more than he realized.

"You had such a long day didn't you? It's okay, you can rest now." Noelle embraced his scared self, his nervous self, the self that needed specifically her, embracing him so tightly as if he'd wither away had she let go.

Aspen sat upright to get a good look at her, caressing her silky white hair, still as beautiful as ever. By his lonesome, he'd relapsed to his scared self at an instant, the self Aspen had strived to rid after all these years. With one taste of the stew, he remembered years of loneliness and dread. But with one glance at Noelle, he was reminded that things had changed—he had changed. Though it seemed grim, Aspen hadn't lost everything just yet. The girl in his sight was still here, not gone from his life. He didn't quite have the courage and strength to face his past, present, and future alone. But with Noelle, he didn't have to. After all these years, she had become his anchor, preventing him from drifting away, the shoulders to lean on when he couldn't stand, and the other half of his heart that made him whole.

"I need you in my life," Aspen stared lovingly into her eyes. "I love you, Noelle."

She stared back into his eyes. His were blue, as blue as the sky, a sky she wanted to get lost in forever. Noelle loved his eyes, she loved his messy black hair, and she loved how Aspen loved her. He could have the other half of her heart, no, he could have the whole thing, her emotions were no longer barred.

"I love you, too."

They slowly leaned closer and closer to each other, their lips getting nearer. Noelle's heart started to skip a beat, her stomach twisting in a knot when they were just a breath away from each other. She could feel the warmth of Aspen's breath— warmth of familiarity, a warmth that made her feel safe, a warmth that burned away desolate thoughts. His lips touched hers. For a moment, her body tingled and mind went blank, as if everyone else in the world had disappeared, leaving just the two of them. The joy within her sparked and bursted into the sky like a grand finale of fireworks. But that moment was fleeting, because as they kissed, those desolate thoughts had returned: *Don't leave me.* Noelle clasped Aspen in her arms tightly as if he was fading away from her grasp.

How I wish I could stay in his warmth forever, Noelle thought. She savored every moment, knowing full well that Aspen would be sent away soon. Her other half would be leaving her to some unknown place, and the void of loneliness that he filled in her life would be empty once again.

FOURTEEN

"Bye, Niko, until next time," Aspen said.

Niko bumped fists with him with a look of dejection. "Until next time, man."

"Do be safe out there and come back when you can," Willey had come to say goodbye to him as well. He handed Aspen a small bag of cookies, "These were specially made."

Aspen took the bag, knowing full well what he meant. *Noelle probably baked these this morning.* He felt a little glum. *I guess this will be the last time in a while that I'll get to eat something she prepared.* Aspen looked at his dad. "I'm ready to leave now."

His father nodded and approached the carriage driver, "Be sure to be extra careful, make sure he gets there safely." The driver gave him a thumbs-up as he checked up on his horses.

There wasn't much that Aspen wanted to say to his dad, since he was the reason for his forced departure in the first place. He took one last look at the town before stepping into the carriage. It had only been two days since his dad first told him that he had to move away. He didn't think he would leave so soon. Aspen didn't even get the chance to see Noelle one last time besides that night. The following days after the decision was made that he would leave, his dad had watched over him like a hawk, making sure he packed and got ready for the move, giving him no chances to escape.

Aspen leaned his head against the door of the carriage once inside and let out a big sigh. Then, without warning, the carriage began to move against the bumpy roads. Aspen peered out of the window of the carriage, watching as he became farther and farther away from town. *All I can do now is hope Noelle stays safely hidden from the general until I return.* He should be out there trying to end whatever Ulger was planning, but he would not get the opportunity for the time being. *Perhaps if Noelle and I just got away from here, somewhere so far Ulger would have to give up, it would be enough.* The leaves outside were starting to fall. The seasons were changing once again, but this time without Noelle by his side.

Aspen couldn't stop thinking about the night he kissed her. *It's not fair. I wish I still got to see her at least one more time after that night.* It was the first time they both finally admitted their true feelings for each other. He sulked a little bit and muttered to himself, "I should have told her sooner."

The trip was just one long bumpy road with nothing to stare at but vast empty fields and dreary skies. After about six hours they finally pull up to the town of Denmar.

The driver called out to Aspen, "Here we are. The Denmar Academy for Boys is just up ahead."

Aspen looked out the window, seeing only unknown places and unknown faces. His intuition was already screaming that he wouldn't like it here. Up ahead was a huge building with a large gate around it. *This must be the school.* Boys of different ages roamed around the yard, all trying to peek into the carriage that passed them by. The carriage stopped.

He got out of the carriage to come face-to-face with a tall man with glasses. "H-hello, I'm—"

"Aspen, I'm sure. I am Principal Oto, and I run The Denmar Academy for Boys. You can address me as Principal Oto. Usually we don't accept students this late...but your father called...about your peculiar case." Principal Oto eyed Aspen from head to toe as if examining him like an animal.

"Take this. Don't lose it. This is your key and room number," he warned, handing him a set of keys. He also handed Aspen a folder filled with papers. "This should be everything that you need to know about classes and such, don't lose that either." Aspen took the folder and keys and put them inside his backpack.

"Should I go take my stuff—"

"No need, we shall have a staff member take them up. You still have some time to make it for one of your classes. Let us make haste." The principal gestured to him to quickly follow along while snapping at the staff member to unload his bags.

Gee, he is super impatient, isn't he? Aspen thought as he hurriedly followed after the principal. "Can we go a bit slo—"

"You'll find that many of the lads here at Denmar Academy are proper gentlemen," Principal Oto cut him off, giving him another quick glance. "I'm sure you'll become one as well. Eventually, that is..."

Aspen made an extra effort to pick up the pace so that he could walk side by side with his new principal. "So, is there—"

Before he could ask his question, Oto suddenly stuck his hand out to the right, nearly striking Aspen across the face. "This way. This is the way. We must go through here."

The two cut through the school courtyard. Aspen looked around, noticing that many of the plants were withered away, benches half broken, and seats graffitied. *I'm guessing there's also no sort of maintenance here.*

Making himself friendly, he waved to a fellow student passing by but was only met with a mean scowl. Aspen sighed, already feeling himself counting the days of when he could finally escape this wretched place.

"Here you are, enter this room," the principal told him. Aspen entered through the large doors and inside was a huge classroom filled with students and a teacher at the front.

"Hello, Mr. Trottel, we have a new student registered here today. This is Aspen." Principal Oto turned to him, "Here you are, try to behave now," and left the classroom.

"Well, Aspen, go ahead and take an empty seat at the front there," Mr. Trottel said.

Aspen took a seat at the front. *I didn't even get a chance to breathe.*

"Well, I will resume the lesson. We will continue where we left off about the Mogoniwais," Mr. Trottel said.

Aspen groaned. *Of course that's what today's lesson is.*

"Most Mogoniwais live in the small country, Granada, a nation that neighbors us. The people there lived in communities such as ours—albeit more rustic and less advanced than us. Typical homes would consist of stone huts to even tents outdoors. Back then, they did not have stoves, or bathhouses, or even light bulbs, and instead dug holes for their toilets and used fire to cook and light their homes. I'd say the only real advantage their country had was that it was enriched with great artifacts and resources that often their merchants would cross over to sell."

"What did they even sell?" Timmy asked. He was proper, prim, and seemed like the studious type as he wrote down every single word that came out of Mr. Trottel's mouth. Too bad he was being spoon-fed lies.

"Good question, Timmy. Well, some of the stuff that they sold were clothes, as they had higher-quality wool or rare gemstones. If there's one thing that demons—I mean Mogoniwais—are good at, it is making high-quality products. Those Mogoniwais would often hoard over their natural resources despite not knowing what to do with them or reaching their full potential. This is where we come in. Officials from Cresnough, Grasalia, and many other towns came to them and sought to help utilize their resources in a more beneficial way. Though, they had accused us of trying to steal them."

"Why would we ever steal from some demons?" Rick hollered. He and his slicked-back hair had his dirty sneakers leaned up onto his desk. Rick sat with much confidence and looked as if he was too good for this school.

"We would never," Mr. Trottel answered. "They misunderstood our intentions. But from that day, relations with them had just gotten progressively worse. It wasn't until the demon merchants near Grasalia were attacked did the hostility and tensions reach its peak and the War of the Demons occurred. Now, can someone tell me, how long did the war last?"

"It lasted about four years," John answered. He was a student with shaggy brown hair who often chose to sit in the back so he could take naps. He combed over his bangs so that he was finally able to see the teacher. "It wasn't until General Ulger or someone wiped them out did it stop...or something like that."

"You are correct, John," Mr. Trottel confirmed. "General Ulger led an assault team that targeted the central homes of the Mogoniwais. He and his team of scientists developed some sort of bomb that, upon detonation, wiped out several large communities, causing their number to diminish drastically. Not that we, as humans, wanted that of course, but it was the only way to get them to stop. And stop they did, as we were finally able to settle for peace and a ceasefire with them."

"Though Mogoniwais are known for their brutish behavior, so initial terms and agreements were very hard to negotiate with them," he added. "Some say that because their minds are not developed enough to learn and understand our human language, it had caused many headaches during negotiations."

"That's not true..." Aspen inadvertently called out.

The teacher eyed him, "Aspen, did you have something to say? What's not true?"

Crap, I didn't mean to open my mouth. The statement the teacher made was so blatantly wrong that his mouth just blurted it out. "Never mind..."

"No, no. You clearly had something to say, please elaborate to the entire class," the teacher called out.

Aspen looked around the classroom, all of the students' eyes were on him now. "Well...I...read somewhere that Mogoniwais can be quite clever. When taught, they are able to understand human speech and learn to write. I mean, they had traveling merchants and such, so they had to have amazing comprehension skills to do trades with our towns, right?"

The teacher burst out in laughter as if he just listened to the most outlandish, ridiculous statement ever. Mr. Trottel held his gut, needing to take a few seconds to regain his composure. "Please tell me you are joking, Aspen. I don't know where you get your sources, but no, that is incorrect. Mogoniwais are not capable of learning how to speak our language, let alone read and write."

Aspen rolled his eyes. *Obviously he has never met a Mogoniwai, let alone fact-checked his own teachings.* The smart thing to do would be to ignore the fallacy of his teachings, but his guffawing and disparaging of the Mogoniwais irked Aspen to his very core. Indirectly, this man was mocking Noelle, and he was not going to stand for this. If Aspen kept allowing this slander and discrimination against the Mogoniwais, people's perception of them would never change. He was going to spread the truth, whether the class believed him or not.

"What are your facts based on? Have you ever met one to make these claims?" Aspen snapped back at the teacher. "Because I know they aren't as stupid as you're portraying them to be."

Mr. Trottel was befuddled, not expecting such a response from the new kid. Pretending to skim through the book he was holding, he cleared his throat. "Books, Aspen. Maybe if you had read them, you would know the answer to your own question. Moving on from this subject now, no more comments." Mr. Trottel quickly turned back to the chalkboard, not wanting to hear another word out of him.

"Demon-lover!" Rick yelled out from the back of the class. Soon enough, like a herd of animals, everyone started chanting.

Aspen felt something hit the back of his head. He turned around to see a clumped-up paper thrown at him. When he straightened out the paper, it read "demon lover" in the most illegible handwriting possible.

"Now, now, class, settle down. You shouldn't punish him because he doesn't know about the subject matter. That's why I'm here, to teach kids like him. Now, pay attention to the board," Mr. Trottel retorted.

Though it seemed to Aspen that he couldn't care less whether the class was mocking or bullying him. It was a punishment he deserved for opening his mouth and calling out the fallacies of Mr. Trottel's teaching. Aspen bobbed his head down, doing his best to keep quiet and lie low for now. It was probably a good idea to not have the entire school hate him within the first hour of being here.

I can't believe I'm saying this, but I think I would rather be in Mr. Gallafo's class instead of this place. Just admitting the very thought made his body shake. *Guess the grass actually isn't greener on the other side.*

The class had finally ended after a grueling hour which seemed to have lasted forever. Aspen wouldn't be able to even recollect what he learned during that lecture; half the time was spent staring at the ceiling, the other mentally banging his head against the wall. As he was exiting, a student behind him bumped his shoulder and then another did the same.

"Sorry, freak," the two sarcastically apologized.

Aspen shook with anger, already building up a case for when he gets called into Principal Oto's office for slamming two kids into the trash can. After being bullied by Gerard for years, he wasn't about to become another punching bag. *Calm down, don't let them get to you. I'm in my third year, so I just need to survive for another two years and then I'll be away from this crappy place. I'll be with Noelle soon.* Just reiterating that thought made him a little calmer; Aspen only needed to hold out until he was legally old enough to leave on his own.

He stepped outside to the courtyard. *Where are the dorms at again?* It was hard to understand where anything was, with the lack of any signs and everything being painted in a monochrome gray. *Oh wait, the folder!* Principal Oto had given him something earlier today, hopefully it was actually something useful. Digging through his backpack, Aspen found it. And luckily enough, the principal had a school map stashed in there.

"This doesn't make any sense at all," Aspen said, holding the map above him. The map hardly had anything marked and had labels that made him more confused than anything. He started wandering in circles, just trying to follow the map, only to be completely lost. It was only until Aspen ditched the map and followed random students did he actually find the dorm building.

He walked up to his dorm and opened it with the key given to him. Aspen flickered the light switch on, though it barely illuminated his side of the room. Inside, there were two beds, two desks, and two closets. The walls were of gray concrete with one barred window right in the middle—to stop students from escaping, Aspen figured. The hard floors were cold to touch when he took off his shoes, cold much like the hearts of the entire student body. He tossed his bag atop his desk. Unsurprising to him, the room was quite fitting for this school.

"I guess I have a roommate." He lay on his bed. It was an exhausting day of sitting through boring lectures and getting lost in the labyrinth that was Denmar Academy.

"You're sitting on my bed," a voice called out from the entrance of the room, startling Aspen.

"Oh, sorry about that," Aspen apologized. He picked up his backpack and sat on the other bed. Extending his hand out he introduced himself, "My name is Aspen, and yours?"

The boy ignored Aspen's hand and went to his desk, "Elliot."

Aspen awkwardly pulled back his hand. "I guess we're roommates. Hopefully we can get along." The boy did not say a word, which was annoying to him. Elliot was a tall, lanky kid with brown hair, his uniform was nice and clean, and hair kept tidy. "So, how long have you been here?" No response again, which, at this point, was not a surprise. He was going to get Elliot to talk to him no matter what. After all, having at least one friend might make this place a bit bearable for the time being.

Aspen tapped him on the shoulder. "So, have you eaten yet? If you want, we can go grab a bite at the cafeteria."

Elliot looked at him. Aspen stood there with a huge grin on his face, which creeped Elliot out as he wasn't used to people staring at him for this long. Elliot dug his head back into the book he was reading and muttered softly, "I ate already."

"Alright then, perhaps next time," Aspen suggested. He walked out of the room and headed for the cafeteria. *Well, at least I got him to respond to me. That's a win in my book for now.*

Aspen walked through the cafeteria doors. Upon entering, it was filled with nothing but the chatter of mindless conversations of hundreds of students and food splattered on the ground. He lined up to go get dinner, feeling quite famished as he feasted on nothing today but the cookies Noelle made.

"Over here!" Rick turned around and yelled. His friends cut the line, standing in front of him. They turned towards Aspen. "Sorry, bud, saving these spots for my friends."

"No problem," Aspen replied. Just then, about six more of his friends also stepped in front, paying no heed to him, and making Aspen last in line once more. *Did you really need to cut me in line when your friend is literally second to last in line?* Though not wanting to start any more trouble on the first day of school, he simply let them be.

"No way! Demon-lover? Is that you?" Brody—one of the friends who cut the line—was now gawking at him with his eyes wide, realizing that the person behind them was the new kid who spoke out in class. Brody had terribly-dyed blonde hair, something that looked like it was done for attention. Brody was the type that needed validation from those around him or else he'd feel like a loser. He started grinning from ear to ear as if Aspen was some kind of circus animal.

He tapped another one of his friend's shoulders. "Hey, hey, hey, this was the weird guy I was talking to you about! The dude that like...loves demons or something." It didn't take long for the group to herd around Aspen, gawking at him with their incoherent questions.

Aspen just brushed them off, not caring to answer any of their questions. Not that he could anyway, as they all shouted and spat out their questions at the same time, making it that much harder to understand them.

I don't blame Elliot for not wanting to talk. I wouldn't either if I had to deal with these guys. Aspen sighed. Today had been nothing but disappointment; surviving here might be much harder than he anticipated.

He eventually made it to the front of the line where the food selection was quite bare, the remaining options left didn't seem too appetizing. The choices left were dried-up fish, a glob of mystery meat, or a stew that looked to be a few days old. He contemplated whether he should go hungry for the night or satiate his appetite, and in the end, Aspen opted for the stew.

He held his tray and scanned the cafeteria for a place to sit. It seemed like everyone had already formed cliques, leaving no empty seats. Aspen felt alone. Luckily, at the far off corner of the cafeteria was a table with an empty seat that no one occupied. He hurried along and placed his tray on the table, just in case someone snatched the seat from him. Aspen stared at the stew and poked at it with his spoon. It looked quite dry, bland, and lukewarm, a far cry of the vibrant, warm, and delectable stew Noelle and his mom both made. Bracing himself, Aspen took a spoonful and shoved it in his mouth.

He made a nauseated face, "It tastes just as it looks." As he scooped up another spoonful, something smacked his hand, causing him to drop bits of mystery stew on his pants. *A ball?* He looked around to find the culprit.

"Demon Lover!" someone at a table across from him yelled out. It was the same group of kids that had cut in front of him at the cafeteria line. Compared to Gerard, these kids weren't the least bit intimidating, Aspen was sure he could take them. The group hurled taunts and made gestures towards him, trying their best to make him tick.

It was an invitation, and Aspen was heavily thinking about accepting it.

Calm down, Aspen, calm down, they're not worth your time. He took in a deep breath and then exhaled. *Good behavior, Aspen, if you lay low, maybe dad will free you from this prison of a school before the two-year mark hits.* He released the balled-up anger that welted up in his fist. They weren't worth his time. Aspen wiped off the clumps of food that dropped on his pants and continued his supper.

The group of friends hollered once more after only a few minutes. Thinking the insults were directed to him, Aspen turned around. But, to his surprise, the group was preying on a new target.

"Hey, look who decided to join us! It's El-Idiot!" Rick mocked. Aspen stared closely at the kid, only to find his new roommate as their next prey. Elliot hunched his shoulders and avoided eye contact with the group, trying to avoid any interaction as he tiptoed into the main cafeteria hall.

I thought he already ate dinner? Aspen wondered.

Holding his tray of food, Elliot was left with the same problem Aspen had earlier, looking for a place to sit. Though he didn't need to look further as one of the bullies, stood up and dragged him over to their table.

"Hey, El-Idiot, why didn't you come sooner? Didn't we tell you to come here at five p.m.?" Brody threatened. Elliot's body trembled as he tried to find any excuse to leave.

The way they were treating Elliot irked Aspen, maybe because he could sympathize with him—after all, he was in his shoes for a good portion of his life. It reminded him of the way Gerard had treated him. Though, this time, there was no Noelle in sight to save poor Elliot.

"El-Idiot, did you do the homework like I told you to?"

"I-I didn't have time to finish, s-sorry, Rick," Elliot responded. The sounds of his feet quickly tapping matched the beating of his heart. "I...I didn't think I'd see you here at this time. I'll do it after I f-finish eating."

"Well, hurry up and eat up so you can finish it!" Rick yelled out. Taking a handful of food, he tried shoving it in Elliot's mouth, "Eat up!" Rick, Brody, and all the other friends hovered over Elliot like a pack of wolves circling a rabbit, laughing at and enjoying his anguish.

Don't get involved, you have to lay low. Aspen swallowed the urge to jump in and help Elliot. He was trying to leave this place as soon as possible, which meant being on his best behavior. Only then would his dad possibly reconsider and let him come back home. Aspen ignored the group and focused on his unappetizing dinner, turning a blind eye to his roommate getting bullied.

Rick keenly stared at Elliot's necklace. "You know, that's a cool-looking necklace, you don't mind if I take it, right?" Around his neck was a chain connected to a small, beautiful green stone.

"N-no, you can't have it, my mom gave it to me, it was a gift," Elliot begged. "I-I'll do your homework for an entire year, just don't take this."

Rick smiled mischievously. "It must be worth a lot of money if you're willing to do all that." He hesitated to weigh his options. "You know what, I want it. Besides, you're doing my homework regardless, so I wouldn't even get anything in return." Rick and his friends started trying to rip the necklace off of his neck.

"No! You can't have it!" Elliot shouted, gripping his necklace like his life depended on it.

Come on, isn't anyone going to do something? Aspen surveyed the crowd of students, who all simply minded their own business. Standing idly by doing nothing gnawed at him like a dog on a bone. He couldn't look away. *Someone, anyone. Just help him out already,* Aspen thought while watching Elliot squirm his way from his bullies.

"Listen here El-Idiot, if you provoke me one more time, you're actually going to regret it," threatened Rick. His breaths were shallow and short along with that his face was bright red like a tomato that was about to burst. "I'm not about to let someone beneath me act this way towards me." As Elliot squirmed to get away, Rick raised his fists, readying to strike him.

Before Rick could pound him, his arm was held back.

"Okay, that's enough," Aspen demanded. Rick turned around, now staring face-to-face with him.

"What do you want, demon-lover? You trying to play hero? You should leave now before you get hurt," Rick warned. He returned his focus to Elliot.

Aspen scooped a clump of nearby stew on someone's plate and smeared it onto the back of Rick's head. "My bad, man."

"You must think you're brave, huh?" Rick turned around and faced Aspen, looking quite visibly riled up.

"I'm not brave, just pissed off," Aspen stood tall, refusing to let Rick intimidate him. He glanced at Elliot, who was cowering in fear, reminding Aspen so much of his younger, more timid, and scared self —the self that hadn't met Noelle yet. Back then, he wished that someone would have stood up to Gerard when he was getting bullied. Of course, Aspen had Niko, but when they were outnumbered or got isolated from each other, even Niko was limited in what he could do to stop him. But things are different now, and Noelle was the one who gave him the skills and courage necessary to force his own change. Being face-to-face with another bully, Aspen didn't feel nervous or terrified, rather, he smiled to himself. *I actually did become a bit braver, didn't I?*

"You gonna smile all day? Or are you prepared to get beat?" Rick roared. Aspen snapped back to reality; right now his focus should be on helping Elliot.

Aspen let out a smirk. "Stop trying to talk big. You're secretly just insecure aren't you?" A revelation had just hit him, whereas Rick's fist still had not. *Perhaps Gerard is like this guy as well. All that bullying, all that bravado, just to hide how insecure he really was on the inside.* Rick's body burned with anger, fumes blowing out of his ears as he wildly swung at him but missed. Aspen had hunted with Noelle in the last four years, where there were plenty of cases when he had to dodge charging wild boars or fend off feral animals. Rick was just like one of those feral animals, except that he was much slower and far more predictable.

Rick threw out his fists like a madman, but Aspen easily dodged them left and right. When he made a wide swing, Aspen simply ducked down, reading him like an open book.

An aura faintly covered Aspen's right fist, though everyone was too busy taking bets on who would go down first to notice. In that moment, he could feel Noelle's presence, as if she was right behind him, giving the confidence he needed to face down his enemies. The magic that she had imbued to him was now coursing through his veins, and collected into his palm. He had never felt this power before, his right fist throbbed at the weight of it. If Aspen were to describe the sensation, it was as if his fist was a cannon, readying itself to explode.

Aspen's eyes widened—*an opening!* He lunged and punched Rick square in the face, unleashing all that mana in one go. This caused Rick to slingshot several feet into the air and then flat to the ground.

He's definitely a lot softer than Gerard, Aspen thought. Rick's friends slowly backed away from Elliot like scared little wolves. They were helpless without their so-called fearsome leader. He stared at his hands in awe, astonished at the development of his powers. *I haven't been able to do that before...*

"What is going on here?" yelled Principal Oto as he rushed into the cafeteria hall.

"That demon-lov—I mean he...errr...punched Rick. We were just minding our own business," Brody accused, pointing at Aspen. The principal eyed only him, as if he were the bully in this scenario.

Aspen rebutted, "That's partly true, but earlier, these guys were bul—"

Principal Oto cut him off, "There are no excuses for fighting within my school. I will let you off with a warning since this is your first day, but I will be contacting your father about this first thing in the morning. Do I make myself clear?"

"But these guys were—"

"I said, do I make myself clear?" he repeated.

Elliot jumped in to Aspen's defense, "But he only got involved because—"

"That is enough!" the principal bellowed to everyone in the cafeteria. "Everyone, head back to your dorm rooms. The next time I see fighting in my school, there will be severe consequences." Rick and his friends stood up and headed back to their rooms without another word, with all the other students following soon after. Before Aspen could leave, Principal Oto grabbed his shoulder, "I hope this is the last I will hear of your bad behavior." Aspen brushed it off, staying silent as he headed back to his room.

"T-THANKS BACK THERE," Elliot said when Aspen returned to their room. "This necklace was given to me by my mom, it's the last thing I have to remember her by."

"You're welcome, Elliot." Aspen chuckled to himself. *We really are alike.*

Elliot fidgeted with his necklace, "Why did you do it, anyway? W-why did you help me?"

Aspen looked at him with an eyebrow raised. "Why wouldn't I help a friend in need?"

"Are...are we friends?"

"Of course we are."

Tears snuck up on Elliot, which made him quickly turn away from Aspen to wipe them. "F-from the very first time I stepped foot in Denmar Academy I'v hated this place." He ran his fingers through the large piles of books and paperwork on his desk that were not his own and threw them to the ground. Papers that had Rick's name on them were scattered to the floor, which Elliot promptly stomped on until the dirt on his shoes covered his name. "No friends, constantly getting bullied, being alone at this stupid school. I mean, it came to a point where I was happiest when I was asleep. I haven't had a...had a friend in a while." Aspen's words made his eyes flicker with a glimmer of hope, because the guy standing in front of him was treating him like he was visible, but more than that, this guy was offering to be his friend.

"I don't know how to be a good friend, you know?"

"You can start by eating with me in the cafeteria," Aspen suggested.

"Yeah," Elliot said, smiling brightly for the first time in a long while, "sure thing."

Aspen sat down at his desk and pulled out some papers and a pen. *It's only been the first day, and there's already so much to tell her.* His yearning for Noelle was beyond immeasurable at the moment; he'd take sitting through Mr. Trottel's lecture for an entire day if it meant seeing her for at least five minutes. Aspen tilted his head, staring blankly at the ceiling. *I'm doing my best, I'll live day by day until we can be with each other once again.* He picked up the pen, recollecting every thought and every moment that happened today. *Just wait for me for a little while longer, but for now...* He started writing.

Dear Noelle...

PART THREE

One Year Later

"Willey, I finished baking the batch of muffins!" Noelle yelled out. She wiped her forehead with the sleeve of her shirt, only to spread more flour on her face. The aroma of freshly baked pastries wafted all throughout the store from all the goods Noelle had baked.

Willey hobbled into the back of the kitchen. "That's great, what about the cookies?"

Noelle stepped to the side with a smug expression, revealing dozens of baked cookies of different varieties. "Done and done."

A smile grew on his face, "To think I used to do this all by myself. I don't think I'd be able to do this without you anymore."

She took her apron off and hung it on the wall. "You don't ever have to." The two went on to taste test some of the batches, which was Noelle's favorite part of baking. They bit into the muffins, still moist and hot from the oven, and didn't even bother containing the squeal and visible delight on their faces.

Willey licked his fingers. "Honestly, I think you're better at baking than I am now. Most of the customers complain that the quality of the cookies aren't as great when I bake them."

"Don't fret, it's because I learned from the best," Noelle consoled him.

Ever since she started living with Willey, Noelle did her best to help out in whichever way she could while still staying hidden from the public eye. It became a routine—she would help bake in the morning before the store opened, and then stay upstairs until closing time. It wasn't all too bad as she occupied her time with reading or picking up new hobbies, such as drawing or trying out new recipes. And often, at the dead of night, Noelle would leave town and go back into the woods that were her former home. It gave her a chance to hike, stretch her legs, and get some fresh air, though she always had to make sure she came back before morning sunrise. Her life seemed much more restrictive now, but it wasn't necessarily a bad thing.

Noelle walked around the aisles of the store, pretending to casually be looking for something, "So, Willey...did any letters come in?" To her disappointment, he frowned and shook his head. It had been one year now since Aspen left, and she hadn't heard from him. He had not sent a single letter.

Noelle marched upstairs and plopped down onto the couch to quietly sulk. "I thought you said you would at least write," she said aloud, imagining Aspen could hear her. Though she enjoyed her time staying with Willey, her life just wasn't the same without Aspen. She missed him. She missed the times where they would go exploring together, she missed when they would hunt and eat together, she missed their late-night conversations. She missed his adorable smile and piercing but gentle blue eyes. Ever since he left, her world was at a standstill.

She went to her room and hugged the stuffed animal that Aspen had won her a year ago at the festival, a habit she had picked up whenever she began to miss him. Noelle grasped the concepts of her powers at quite a young age, especially her sensory powers. The more she missed Aspen, the more her connection to him deepened, often being able to feel his presence. After all, the two of them were connected to each other ever since the day she saved him. Throughout parts of the year, his emotions became so strong that Noelle could perceive them, too. And most times he'd feel troubled, distressed, and downhearted, or a combination of it all. It took full restraint to not rush over in his direction and kick whoever was messing with her Aspen.

"Idiot, Aspen! You promised you'd write back..." Noelle groaned while kicking her feet up in the air.

The day had dragged on yet again, with nothing happening out of the ordinary. She looked outside, the sun was finally setting now. Noelle got up to cook dinner, it was a stew kind of night, Aspen's favorite. She started with frying the fish then marinating and cooking the beef. Next, she chopped up the carrots and potatoes and added them to the pot. *I wonder if he's been eating well these days,* Noelle thought while mixing the ingredients together with a large wooden spoon.

While mixing the stew, she felt a burning sensation from her fingertips. Noelle instinctively jerked her hand away from the wooden spoon, only to feel the burning sensation still linger. It wasn't from the stove. Her body was heating up, feeling the emotions of distress that were burned roughly with a match. These emotions weren't her own.

"Aspen?" she called out. Noelle could feel it, Aspen was in trouble. He needed her.

She rushed to the door and opened it abruptly, only to come face-to-face with Willey, giving him quite the startle.

"What's the hurry, Noelle? Something wrong?"

The burning sensation that she felt faded away. Noelle loosened her grip on the door, "I...felt it even stronger this time. He's in trouble. I must go out and find him!" Willey stepped inside and closed the door, guiding her to the sofa.

"It may still be much too dangerous to go out and find him," Willey said. Noelle had confided with him in the past about her connection with Aspen, and he was probably the second person she trusted the most. Despite him being hundreds of miles away, she could feel his emotions, in which they have been getting progressively worse. Each time, Willey had managed to convince her to stay, but at this moment, Aspen's emotions felt burning hot like raging lava that could not be quelled, burning so deeply into both their souls.

"Y-yeah." Noelle began to calm down. *What was I thinking?* There was no way that she could head over to where Aspen was. For starters, she had no clue where he was nor had the means to reach him. His feelings were affecting her own, which only fueled her impulses and irrationality.

Willey looked at Noelle with discernment, her restlessness had become increasingly evident day by day. And her apprehension had only deepened because of the uncertainty of Aspen's situation and whereabouts.

"Aspen promised me that he would write..." Noelle grumbled, "at this point it just seems like I'm writing to a ghost." She turned to Willey, seeking validation, "I mean...do you...do you think he forgot about me?"

"Of course not!" Willey was quick to quell her doubts. "He loves you. He loves you dearly. There must be some reason as to why he can't."

This of course did not make Noelle feel any better.

Willey sighed. "Are you worried about him?"

"Yeah, I am...I have been getting these intense feelings, feelings of despair and troubledness."

Willey nodded his head, "Must you really need to go look for him?"

Noelle's eyes lit up at the thought of seeing Aspen again. She only needed to check up on him, to see him doing okay. If he was doing fine, perhaps it'd be okay to just hold him tightly and feel the warmth of his breath for a little bit. Five minutes—five minutes was all she was asking for. That would be enough for her to not yearn for him for another year. But her selfish thoughts only brought light to the promise she made with him. To stay hidden and safe was much more torturous than she'd imagined. Noelle didn't want to cause Aspen any more problems.

"I...I want to, I really do! It's just...I promised I'd stay here where it's safe. But Aspen...what if he's in trouble?"

"You know I can't let you leave here to go out for him. Even if I really wanted to let you."

"I know," Noelle frowned, shaking the thought out of her head. "You're right. I should just stay here."

Willey could not bear to see the look of disappointment on her face for the umpteenth time. He opened his doors to her so that she could live a happy life, and at this moment she'd never be happy cooped up here. Noelle was being considerate of everyone's feelings, for so long she had buried her own desires for the sake of others. "You know what? How long has it been? One year now? And Aspen hasn't written back to us at all; you deserve to complain and give him an earful in person. Listen to me, since living with me you have never once complained. You've kept your selfish desires to yourself, all to protect everyone else. You deserve to be a little selfish in life."

"But what about the people who are looking for me?"

"It's been one year of hiding since that incident. The soldiers in this town aren't known for their patience, I'll tell you that much. Heck, I wouldn't even be surprised if they forgot about it by now," Willey assured her.

"But the towns still hate my kind, don't they?"

"They do," Willey said. "I won't lie and say this won't be a dangerous journey. You'll have to keep your wits about you. Keep out of sight, stay hidden, avoid areas that are densely populated. I wouldn't normally suggest you go, but I know that you're resourceful enough to avoid any trouble when a situation arises."

"Is it really alright for me to go to him?"

Willey placed his hand on her shoulder. "You deserve to be happy, Noelle. And I know you won't be happy until you talk to him."

Noelle sprang up and hugged him. "Thank you, Willey! For this, for always watching over me and for all the things you do!" For a brief second, her eyes must have been playing tricks on her, because the man before her became an image of her late father. She always wondered what life would be like if he was still around, but this must be what it would have been like.

"Of course, my dear, you're like a daughter to me," Willey said.

Noelle smiled at the fact that the feelings were mutual.

"Can you promise me one thing, Noelle?" Willey asked.

"What is it?"

"Please, Noelle, please come back safe and sound," Willey said. Memories of his late daughter resurfaced in his mind, which made him immediately regret allowing Noelle to go. He could not bear to lose another child.

"I will," Noelle promised.

"So, how does this work now? Can you sense his whereabouts? I've lived with Mogoniwais before and they often were able to find each other by sensing each other's mana."

Noelle stretched her arms, sat upright and closed her eyes. She needed to concentrate. "Let's put it to the test then."

Noelle had always been able to feel his presence, perhaps if she concentrated hard enough, his feelings would lead her straight to him. Every time she felt Aspen's presence, it was when he displayed intense emotions. So, perhaps under the same conditions, she'd be able to find him the same way. Noelle tried to call upon that troubled feeling she felt not too long ago, thinking that maybe it could serve as a beacon that she could trace back to. Despite concentrating with all her might, her efforts were to no avail.

spen and the demon princess

"I can't do it, I thought that if I recall those troubled emotions again I would be able to follow it back, but it's not working," Noelle exasperatingly proclaimed. They both looked at each other with defeat.

"Well, you did say that you and him are connected by mana, right?" Just then, an idea popped into Willey's head. "Maybe instead of concentrating on Aspen's negative emotions, you should try concentrating on the love you have for one another. Maybe that would work better?"

"I'll try it." Noelle closed her eyes and concentrated once more. *I want to know where you are at, show me Aspen.* From there she started to think about him from when they first met to the many days they'd leisurely spent their childhood together.

Just as that fateful day when she saved him, light sprouted from the living room floor and encircled her. The shutters from the window rattled and the pots and pans that hung from the kitchen wall banged and clanged against each other. Willey nearly stumbled to the ground as the air had pushed him away from Noelle; he could hardly keep his eyes open as the warmth of the light wrapped around her.

Little by little, Aspen's mana formed in her head. *It's working, I just need to remember.* She thought about him some more, their time at the woods, the festival, watching the stars, when they kissed. The veil of light had completely covered her, and from the top, a thin wave of light painlessly stabbed her heart. She thought about the experiences, the dreams that they both strive for, and the love they feel for one another. Until, eventually, she could see it. A single, thin thread, now colored red. The veil of light that enclosed her dissipated and left a visible mana thread that could only be seen by her, sprouting from her heart, leading towards Aspen. It was like a beacon that led her directly to him. "I can feel it! I can see his path! It's about 10—no, maybe even a bit longer—maybe 20 miles before hitting Cresnough," Noelle excitedly shouted, though how long she'd be able to see it was in question. "But it's fading, I don't know how long I'll be able to hold it."

"Well then, I guess you should go as soon as possible then."

"But how would I be able to travel there? It might take days or even weeks on foot," Noelle pointed out.

"I have a buddy who owes me a favor. He can let me borrow a horse and a carriage at any time."

Noelle's eyes lit up. "So you mean..."

Willey nodded. "You can leave soon if you would like." Noelle became enthralled at the fact that she'd finally be able to see Aspen after so long but soon after the feelings turned bittersweet. This trip was not meant to be a reunion but a potential search and rescue if he was in trouble. She swiftly swallowed her cheery elation, treating this now much more seriously. "But you must have someone go with you."

"No problem at all, so does this mean you are coming with me, too?"

"Oh no, I can't possibly leave. I still got to watch over the store."

Noelle was at a loss. "So who's the person that is going to come with me?"

"Niko. I told him to stop by earlier today. I'll have him chaperone you."

"Oh, Niko. Okay..." She would have much rather Willey come along with her. It wasn't that Noelle didn't like Niko, she didn't mind him at all, but they were never really the best of friends. They were more like acquaintances if anything, and that was only because of Aspen.

"Go ahead and pack up what you need for the trip, I'll need to go talk to my friend to get the horse." Willey walked downstairs soon after and locked the doors behind him as he headed outside.

"I have to hurry!" Noelle sprang out of her seat and ran to her room. She grabbed her backpack and packed the essentials—an extra pair of clothes, a hunting knife, matches, and snacks for the journey. Noelle looked around to see if she needed anything else in her room, rummaging through her belongings until pulling out something white and fluffy—Aspen's white scarf. It wasn't a necessity for her journey, but she packed it anyway. He had forgotten to take this with him so she had been caring for it in his stead. This was one of the few rare things that he had held onto, as it reminded him of his late mother and gave him peace of mind when holding it. Aspen would be elated to be reunited with it once again. It had been only a few hours by the time she finished packing, and by then Willey was outside with the horse and carriage. Noelle peeked her head out the window and could see Niko walking down the street, heading towards the store along with Willey. *He really wasn't kidding when he said he could get a horse and carriage quickly.*

"So, what's going on here? Why did you ask me to come later when the store closed?" Niko asked as he entered Willey's living room.

Niko hadn't really spoken to Noelle aside from a few exchanges when he stopped by Willey's place. He was Aspen's best friend but without him here, the two of them really had nothing that brought them together. She never really expected him to be friends with her, as they had not met on the best of terms.

His attention quickly shifted towards Noelle, who stood there donning a fully stuffed backpack. "Okay. So, where does she think she's going?"

Willey rubbed the back of his neck. "Well, she will be going to find Aspen."

Niko was taken aback. "Aspen? What do you mean? Isn't he somewhere far away? H-how would you even know where he is?"

"We're connected to each other," Noelle pointed out. "We have a thread connecting to each other that could lead me to him."

"What kind of Mogoniwai magic mumbo jumbo is that?" shouted Niko. He began turning around to look at all sides, "You have trackers now? Do you have that stuff on me?"

Noelle looked unamused, "No I don't have it on everyone! The only reason I can see Aspen's thread is because he has a portion of my mana."

Niko turned to Willey, "You can't seriously be on board with this, Willey? She's safer in this place, right? Isn't staying put what we promised Aspen? What about Ulger? Isn't he looking for her?"

"Well...we're all worried about him. He hasn't communicated with us ever since he left that day. It's strange isn't it? Aspen wouldn't be the type to do something like this, especially after promising Noelle that he would write." Niko stood silent and averted his eyes. "And also the general is away from the town at the moment. If there was a time to go, it'd be now. Noelle could feel that Aspen was in trouble. I, too, fear that something may have happened to him."

"He's been feeling troubled for a while now, and even more so recently." She twiddled her thumbs, "The sensation gets stronger with each passing day."

Niko opened his mouth but no words came out. "You know, I'm not even going to question all this mystic stuff that you can do and just accept it." He shook his head, clearly against her proposed adventure, and rubbed his eyes. "Okay. Okay, so when are you two heading out?"

Noelle and Willey exchanged a knowing look. "You mean...when are *we* heading out?" Noelle corrected, pointing to him.

"Did you just say *we*?" Niko picked up his jaw that had promptly dropped, and scoffed in disbelief. Willey gave him a big smile. "There's no way I am heading out there to who knows where. And another, my dad isn't going to let me just leave town without a moment's notice! Why don't you go, Willey?"

"I can't go. I'm getting too old for these spontaneous trips, and plus, I have the store to watch over. Don't worry, I've already told your father that you are working on an important delivery from one of my largest clients. And he already said okay," Willey assured. "And besides, Noelle can't travel on her own. If you drive then she can stay hidden in the carriage. We promised Aspen that we'd keep her safe, right?"

"But I...you can't expect...it's dangerous and..." The two looked at him with eyes beaming with delight, there was no way of talking himself out of this. "Okay, fine. But we are only going to check on him real quick, and I mean it. Really quick. Then we are heading straight back," Niko argued.

Noelle nodded her head and cheered, "Okay, I promise. Just real quick and we head back. That's all we need, really." The trio headed downstairs after an agreement was made.

Willey surveyed outside for any onlookers. Once the coast was clear, Noelle quickly hopped into the back of the carriage and closed the curtains. Willey and Niko loaded the carriage with supplies while she waited inside, hiding from public view.

"I packed enough food to last you guys the entire trip. Be careful, you two. Towns very much hate Mogoniwais, so if you get caught, they won't hesitate to hurt you. Don't talk to anyone, don't trust anyone, especially the soldiers that you may pass by. Just lie low and be safe out there and everything'll be just fine," Willey said. "And follow the Nine Leaves route, it's quicker and less often traveled because not many know of it. And—"

"Hey, what's with the carriage, Willey!" a voice shouted out, startling everyone. It was one of the town's wandering soldiers. The soldier headed towards them. His name was Jerry Mcclain, a novice soldier who was just about average in every aspect aside from his ludicrous amount of loyalty towards General Ulger.

The two looked at each other in unison, hoping the other would come up with an excuse. Willey cleared his throat, "Oh, yes...well...I am...I mean...Niko is here helping deliver some packages for me."

"Oh, a package?" The soldier pulled on the curtains to take a peek at what was inside the carriage.

Noelle laid deathly still and covered her mouth, hoping to not make a single sound. She only hoped that the thumping of her own heartbeat wasn't so loud and obnoxious. *He's going to see me, the whole town's going to go after me before I reach Aspen.* Her mind imagined flashes of pitchforks and torches and angry faces. If she got caught now, she'd take the reins of the horse and storm out of here before they even realized. Noelle readied herself, preparing for the worst.

Niko swung the curtain back before the soldier could pull it away completely. "Sorry, only personnel are allowed to look at the packages that are sent."

A bead of sweat formed on Niko's brow as the soldier clicked his tongue and shot him a suspicious look. The soldier eyed the curtains with one eye wide open. Niko smiled, hoping to mask his guilt and ease his suspicions.

The soldier chuckled. "You are a postal worker's son, after all. Always taking it seriously." He pulled out his watch and looked at the time. "Well, I have somewhere to be, you be safe now, okay?"

The three of them let out a huge sigh of relief once the soldier was gone and disappeared from their line of sight.

"Alright, you two should go now before you draw more attention," Willey whispered.

Noelle popped her head out ever so slightly. "Goodbye, Willey. Thanks again for letting me do this."

He gently patted her head. "Just come back safe and sound, okay?"

"I promise." The horse started to gallop and the distance between them grew.

Niko sat in the driver's seat, guiding the horse outside the town gates. "I'm relying on you to tell me where to go, you can still see it, right?" he whispered to the back of the carriage where Noelle was lying.

"Yeah, I can still see it...so, how long until we get there?"

"Wha...what do you mean? Shouldn't you know?" Niko yelled out.

"I'm kidding, I'm kidding, just trying to liven up the journey,"

Noelle chuckled. "It's been so long since I got to step out of town when it's not pitch black."

"Yeah, yeah, whatever."

"So, when are we getting there?" she asked again. Niko hissed at her, with Noelle laughing to herself. "The trip will take about six hours from here," Noelle finally revealed, "but five hours if we really book it."

"Okay, okay. Hey, by the way, maybe you should avoid telling him about the missing letters," Niko said.

"Why? Is there a reason why I shouldn't? If he hasn't been writing to us after promising, I have to give him a piece of my—"

"He...he must have had his reasons why he didn't," Niko interrupted her. "Aspen cared a-about you. Of course he'd write if he could. We shouldn't stress him out anymore than he probably is already. Just as much as this trip is to calm your nerves, it's also to alleviate his as well. What good would it do if we do nothing but get angry when we see him."

"Oh, okay I won't..."

"I just don't want him to feel bad, as his friend. I'm sure he has his hands tied." Niko bobbed his head to the carriage, "You promise?"

Noelle's pinky finger popped out of the curtains, "I promise."

He turned his head. "What's that?"

"A pinky promise. Surely you know what those are," she said, her finger was still waving in the air. "It's a promi—"

"Yeah, yeah, I know what a pinky promise is." Niko quickly crossed fingers with hers and then continued driving.

Noelle sat comfortably in the back of the carriage. It didn't matter if Aspen hadn't written to her; she was willing to let that go. Niko was right, he must have had his reasons. All that was on her mind right now, all that mattered, was that she was going to finally see him again. Whatever trouble he was in, she'd come in and save him, no matter who stood in their way.

The ride felt like it was moving at a turtle's pace. Her body trembled with excitement and dread. It took a lot of restraint for Noelle to not dash out of the carriage and sprint the whole way there. She kept chanting the same phrase over and over again in her head. *I'm coming, Aspen! We'll see each other soon! I'm coming to save you!* She did so not only to keep her emotions at bay, but she thought that maybe by doing so, it would bring her to him quicker. *I'm coming Aspen, just you wait!*

CHAPTER

FIFTEEN

The thread connecting Noelle to Aspen was becoming shorter and shorter. She and Niko were getting close. Noelle peeked outside of the carriage window, where a gust of wind blew onto her face, giving her quite the chill.

"Are you alright? Are you cold?" asked Noelle, realizing that Niko had been riding outside the entire way.

Niko turned his head, "You don't have to worry about me. I don't really get cold easily, and I layered up." He turned his attention back to the barren, straight road. "So, how were you...you know... able to live on your own for all that time?"

"It wasn't easy at first," Noelle said. "There were times when it was cold, times when food was scarce, times when human soldiers came into my part of the woods. It was all trial and error throughout the years. Perhaps it was a combination of skill and luck, or maybe my parents had been watching over me from above, that I'm still here today."

"And if you were sick?" Niko asked.

"Those times were the hardest, especially since I was alone."

"How come you don't seek out any other Mogoniwais?"

"I wouldn't have a single clue as to how."

"Any relatives at all?"

"Not that I know of."

Niko continued on with questions to pass the time, and every time Noelle answered earnestly. He blurted out, "Do you miss your parents?"

"There's not a day where I don't."

"I'm...I'm sorry about that." His lips curled as he gripped the reins tighter. Niko knew that Noelle was a good person, and now knew that she lived a hard life. For a good person who had lived a hard life, that she was still able to smile was rare. It wasn't fair that the world had taken so much from her, he could see why Aspen wanted to help her so much. A part of him wished he had not asked her so many questions as it made it harder for him to root against her.

The sun had set after a while, and was soon replaced with a blanket of stars and the shine of the moon. Noelle brought out Aspen's scarf and wrapped it around her neck. It was a familiar warmth with Aspen's fleeting scent that still lingered on it.

"Hey, Noelle," Niko's voice whispered up front.

Noelle poked her head through the curtains, "Yeah?" The roads were quiet, the only sound that could be heard were the gallops of the horse's feet and the sound of the wheel turning as it hit the ground. She looked at him, Noelle could tell he was hesitant to speak.

"Don't you think it's better if you and Aspen stopped being in contact with each other? I have nothing against you, really...but Aspen will keep putting himself in danger to protect you at all costs, without any regard for his own life. The truth of the matter is that you two being with each other is just no good. It's just not something the world can accept right now."

Noelle clutched the curtain tighter, hanging her head low. There it was again. Another voice among thousands that screamed she and Aspen shouldn't be together. "It's not possible, not anymore. We fell into each other's lives, deep into a hole we don't want to climb out of. I can't live without him, and I know he feels the same way."

"Right, but perhaps...it's time you both climb out of it," Niko responded, not uttering another word.

Noelle retreated back into the carriage, his words echoed in the back of her mind. She was being selfish. For the sake of love, the right choice would be to leave, this certainly was the best way to protect him. The morality of it all made her question which was the right choice, but by now it was all too late.

"Hey, Noelle, I think we're here."

Noelle peeked outside again to see the rusty gates of a large school building. The thread towards Aspen was close, the infinite rope that connected the two together was now finite. She was finally here. Though her excitement was still immense, sprinkles of doubt and guilt persisted. They stepped outside, now in front of the school gates—this was the only thing separating them from Aspen.

"We don't want to cause too much of a commotion, so let's leave the horse outside here and just find a way to sneak inside," Niko suggested. "And wear this, you'll need a disguise. Not only is this place anti-Mogoniwai, but this is also a boy's academy." The two of them hopped off the carriage, and hid it from plain view.

Noelle tied her hair and wore a cap that hid her long hair. She wore gloves to hide her hands and a mask to cover a majority of her face. And lastly a robe with a hood that completely hid her horns.

The gates were huge, but climbing over it to the other side was an easy feat for Noelle. Niko, on the other hand, was quite the opposite. Noelle offered him a helping hand, but his stubbornness wouldn't let him take it. Time was of the essence, and they weren't going anywhere if it meant him getting over the gate on his own. Only after landing on his butt a dozen times did he accept Noelle's help to climb over the gate.

Niko breathed heavily. "Okay, where to now?"

She looked at the thread; it seemed like he was outside. "Follow me."

Noelle led the way for the search. *Aspen is close. I'll be able to see him after all this time. I wonder how excited he'll be. Only a few buildings and walls now separate me and my loved one.* Traversing through the corridors and buildings made her frown at the sad state of this school, as one could tell that there was a time when this place brimmed with beauty. The brick walls that used to shine bright red were discolored and graffitied, the courtyard that used to house beds of flowers were now replaced with dead grass and weeds, benches that were once used between classmates to share a good time were now wobbly and broken. "This place looks quite run down compared to Grasalia," Noelle mumbled to herself as they crossed through the schoolyard. Even though Grasalia is not the nicest place, the stark contrast between the two is clear. "Even my cave felt warmer than this place."

She could feel the other students' stares beneath the large hood. Though it may be due to the way she was dressed, it still felt uninviting, as if having her hood on wouldn't have made a difference. A much different atmosphere than the Grasalian townspeople, where warmth was replaced with cold animosity and depression.

"Hey, you! Come over here," a student said, pointing at Noelle. "Hey, are you shy or something?"

She pulled down her hood even lower. Covering up from head to toe probably makes her stand out amongst the sea of students. But it was better than baring her full demon self to the public. Who knows what they'd say or do.

Another student chimed in, "Looks kinda shady, why're you here?"

Please just leave us alone, Noelle hoped, avoiding eye contact with the passing students.

Niko quickly stepped in front of her. "Sorry...my brother. He has... uh...a condition. It's quite...contagious, so you don't want to come any closer."

The two friends looked at each other and backed away. "Gross, man, don't come into our school with that shit."

"Sorry, we have some urgent matters to attend to," the student lied, worried about catching her fake disease. The two students quickly left.

"Nice save," Noelle thanked Niko.

"Thanks."

"But I don't have a disease! That makes me sound gross."

"Yeah, yeah I know. It was the only thing I could think of, so cut me some slack."

The two continued following the thread, avoiding large crowds and busy corridors. And it was not too long until the other end of the thread was but a short distance away. Noelle looked up and across from her, she finally saw him. Her heart was beating rapidly, bursting with joy that the time of their reunion had finally arrived. It was Aspen, live and in person. He was outside laughing with another person, seemingly enjoying himself.

He doesn't look troubled at all, Noelle thought. From where she stood, Aspen was all smiles with his new best friend. The feelings of jealousy and betrayal replaced the excitement within her. He was not in any danger, far from it from her point of view. Her fear had come into fruition, she had been replaced after all by this lanky new man. *Was Aspen too busy to at least write to me once because he made new friends here? Did he just up and forget about me?*

From a distance, they could see Aspen's chest glow before wrapping his arms to cover up. He awkwardly excused himself from his friend, and looked for a place to hide until his glowing chest had ceased. Noelle pulled her hood down to hide her face.

Aspen looked around, and said aloud, "Why is it happening now?" He stumbled towards a secluded space until his eyes locked onto two figures in the dark, one male and one covered up entirely. He froze in his tracks. *It couldn't be,* Aspen thought, walking towards them. His jaw dropped. It was Niko! A great smile grew on his face at the sight of his best friend but turned upside down when he realized that there was someone beside him, the one fully covered up, could only be one person. He rushed over with a flushed fury of emotions.

"Aspen," the hooded figure silently called out.

"Noelle," he responded back.

Aspen grabbed her shoulders with his two hands, checking to see if his dreams had actually manifested. She was real. Noelle was here before him in the flesh. For so long his heart longed for her, to be able to see her. The scent of familiarity, the warmth of her being brought about gentle memories of their past, but then reality settled in. He curled his fingers, still gripping her shoulders, Aspen suddenly grew furious, *Why are they here right now?* He pulled them over before they could utter any words, grabbing their arms and leading them to a secluded groundskeeper's shed.

"What's going on here?" Aspen demanded. Noelle's hood came down along with her cap, revealing her red skin and white hair.

"I...I..." Noelle tried to speak up but no words came. The anger on his face spoke volumes already. *Does Aspen not want to see me anymore? Is that why he never wrote back?* She could only conclude that it was a mistake coming here after all.

"Noelle wanted to see you," Niko tried to explain. "She was worried about you."

"What made you think bringing her to a school that hates Mogo-niwais was a good idea?" Aspen exclaimed, halfway toning down his voice before becoming too loud. Niko didn't respond. He turned back to her, "Don't you know how dangerous being here is for you? You were much safer with Willey!"

"G-go a little easier on her, man," said Niko.

"I...I thought you were in trouble. We haven't heard from you in over a year. I just wanted to see you...because I missed you," Noelle couldn't look him in the eyes as she spoke. This was not how she envisioned their reunion.

"What are you even talking about?" Aspen asked, dumbfounded, he tilted his head and took a brief pause. "I wrote to you. I wrote to you *every day*! It's you who hasn't even bothered to write back! You didn't even bother answering my question..." He took her hand, and said, "Listen, I missed you, too, each and every day. But how can you be this naive to come here! You should have known how bad of an idea this was!"

Noelle yanked her hand from his grip, tears welling up in her eyes. "Liar! You know what? Fine! Have fun with your new life and your new friends!" She rushed out of the shed before he could see her cry. It was a bad idea to come here after all. Aspen should have written to her, saying he was having the time of his life here, it would have at least saved her the trouble of worrying about him day in and day out. *Was it so wrong to just want to talk for five minutes?* She always thought it didn't matter if the world wanted to separate the two of them, but it did matter if Aspen didn't feel the same way. Noelle stormed off, not knowing where she was going, but she didn't care, as long as it was anywhere but here.

ASPEN DROPPED to the ground with his back against the wall. *Why did she have to come now of all times? I told her about how dangerous it is. They hate Mogoniwais here even more so than back home.* He hung his head lower, "My dad is coming to visit tomorrow, Niko. Everything has to go perfectly. I was going to make a plea to come back home earlier...but now everything...turned out so wrong." Once he calmed down, the feeling of regret kicked in. His emotions and the initial shock got the better of him, spouting words he hadn't meant. Even though specifically telling her to just wait a little longer in his letters, even though it was he who had not been getting a response, he still felt guilty. If time were to repeat himself, Aspen would have simply embraced Noelle like he wished for so long rather than yell at her. He glanced over to his friend, who knelt beside him. Niko seemed pretty regretful, perhaps realizing it was a bad idea to bring Noelle here.

"I should go out and look for her," Aspen said.

"Don't worry, I'll check up on her." Niko could not bear to stare at the regret his friend wore, feeling that he was partly to blame. "This was supposed to be a short trip but we can't leave things like this.

Why don't you give her some space tonight? Noelle and I can camp outside of the school grounds, hidden safely from everyone, and then when the coast is clear, you guys can talk it out."

"Noelle's probably mad at me," Aspen frowned. He ruffled his hair, leaving it in a disheveled mess, and then buried his face in his knees. "She probably doesn't want to talk to me."

"You guys are too obsessed with each other to stay mad for too long," Niko stood up, "I'll go find her, you just stay put." He opened the door and rushed outside, but not before quietly mumbling a few words to himself.

Aspen barely heard the words he muttered before leaving. *What was Niko hiding?* He was worried about Noelle; more than anything, he wanted to join in finding her. The problem though was that the school does room checks every night, and he had already been reprimanded for hiking through the woods at night a couple weeks ago. If he was missing one more night, well, the chances of him getting into trouble were pretty high. This would not be good, especially if he wanted to appeal to his father to let him leave now. *I should hurry before it hits curfew. Niko said he would take care of it. I can trust him.*

Niko frantically roamed around the schoolyard trying to find Noelle. He knew she was a smart girl, and the smart thing to do would be to go back to the carriage, staying far away from the school. He reached the outer part of the gate, looked up and groaned. Niko stood far back, preparing to sprint, thinking that the momentum from a running start would help propel him up over. Niko made a dash towards it, managing to climb halfway to the top, but ultimately lost his grip and fell back to the ground. "Stupid tall gate, who are they even trying to keep in? It's not like these people are wild animals." Niko looked around for anything that could help him climb over the gate.

"Wait a minute, the shed! There's bound to be something useful there." Niko rushed back to the shed, shuffling through all the drawers in hopes something would be useful to him.

"I've got it!" Niko exclaimed, holding out some rope. He tied a bowline knot and ran back to the gate.

Niko threw the rope onto one of the gate spikes and scaled up using his body weight to hold him up. Though out of breath, this strategy pushed him over to the top. "Okay, just need to go down slo-" but before finishing his thought, he lost his grip, plummeting straight to the ground. His back was screaming in pain but he quickly shook it off. He promised Aspen he'd make sure Noelle was okay, and that's what mattered for now. Niko ran back to where they hid the horse and carriage.

"Gone!" he blurted out loud, "The horse is gone!" Before panic setted in, Niko considered the possible scenarios that could explain the horse's disappearance, "either A) the horse escaped on its own, B) Noelle took the horse and ran off, or C) someone kidnapped Noelle and stole the horse." He prayed that it was not C. Not too far from him were horse prints and beside it, footprints. "Are these Noelle's footprints?" He followed the trail, hoping, praying to himself, that they were hers.

The footprints went off trail and deeper into the woods. At a certain point, he heard water splashing and a girl's voice.

"You must be thirsty after this long trip," Noelle said while brushing the horse's mane.

Niko breathed a deep sigh of relief at the sight of them. "Noelle," he called out, startling her.

Noelle turned to him, already in a fighter's stance, but dropped her fists when she realized who it was. "Oh, it's just you, I heard some noises but I guess it was from you after all."

He took a minute to catch his breath. "He didn't mean it back there...Aspen...he missed you, too."

"Well, it didn't seem like it." Noelle sulked. "Why was he so mad at me? It's his fault in the first place for not even sending me a message. No, 'Hey, I'm doing okay,' not even a simple 'Hello.'"

"Noelle...about that. I have a confession to make..." He had to tell her, he decided. It was the right thing to do. Niko raised his head to meet hers, only to see her visibly terrified face, a face he had never seen her make. Something—no, *someone* was behind him. Niko turned around only to be met with a syringe stabbed into his neck. He stumbled on his feet, struggling to stand up straight. His eyes weighed heavily, "What...is going...on?" Niko felt tired, as if his body was shutting down on him.

"No-oelle...run..." He was laid flat onto the ground, no longer able to fight his growing fatigue. And before realizing it, he fell unconscious.

Noelle watched in horror as Niko fell to the ground. "What did you do to him?" she shouted angrily.

"Oh, he is just taking a little nap. I didn't want him interrupting our conversation." The moon's light reflected onto the medals adorned on the man's military jacket as he emerged from the shadows. "Where are my manners? You can call me General Ulger." His ever-growing devilish smile sent a chill down Noelle's spine, a chill colder than any winter night she'd ever experienced.

General Ulger? Is this the same man Aspen warned me about? Noelle attempted to recollect. "I don't care what your name is! Just leave now before I decide to hurt you!" Anger filled her blood; she was not scared of him in the slightest. She'd faced larger foes before, another human would be no match for her.

"How rude of you. I guess your parents never taught you manners, did they?" General Ulger laughed uncontrollably. "After all this time, I finally found you! Who knows how long it's been since I'd last found one."

"You were looking for me?" Noelle still held the horse's reins, thinking that it might be possible for her to escape. She glanced down at Niko's unconscious body, lying beside General Ulger. Noelle let go of the reins. *If I leave without Niko, who knows what will happen to him.*

"Why yes, yes I was, my dear."

rushing towards him. "I'll kill you!" *This man is unforgivable.* Tears rolled down her cheeks. *After all he...he...*

Noelle poured her whole weight into her right fist and curved it to his temple. He anticipated this, simply sidestepping to dodge her attack. She tumbled to the ground, losing footing after her wide swing.

"What's that? Is that all you got? Your ancestors are going to weep in their graves," he taunted.

Rage overtook her senses. Noelle sprang up and charged again. Each punch she threw was guided by anger rather than reason, and because of that, none of her hits landed on its mark. General Ulger managed to catch one of her closed fists by the palm of his own, ensnaring her like a snake would a mouse.

"It's time you learn some respect!" he shouted. With all his might, he struck her in the gut, a blow that would bring most men to their knees. But not Noelle.

She quickly kicked his chest away, escaping his grasp, and propelled herself to the ground. Noelle grabbed the earth, pissed that he had gotten the better of her.

"You're tougher than I thought," the general commended.

"You're about to see how tough I can get." Noelle rushed in his direction once more.

"This again?" He looked unamused. General Ulger readied himself, preparing to take on whatever punch was thrown his way.

But rather than thrusting a punch, Noelle emptied her palm, throwing dirt in his eyes.

"What in the—" His eyes burned as dust scratched his corneas. Now, it was the general's turn to have his blood boil with anger.

Though Noelle did not stop there; while he was quickly rubbing his eyes, she once again poured her whole weight onto her right fist. This time, however, she hit her mark, the satisfying gush of blood flowing in the air as she pounded his face with her fist.

"Oh, you shouldn't have done that," the general warned. Before she had the chance to react, General Ulger grabbed her by the neck and slammed her to the ground. Her body shook as it made contact with the earth.

"It's time for you to take a little nap." Digging out from his bag, he pulled out a new syringe, the same kind that had caused Niko to lie unconscious.

Noelle tried to stand but her body failed her.

"Don't worry, I'll wake you up when you get there," laughed General Ulger. He plunged the syringe into her neck until the contents were empty.

The white scarf that Noelle wore unraveled, dropping to the ground. She struggled to fight back the effects, but it had overpowered her. With her body feeling heavy and legs like gelatin, she could not move at all. It was as if she had gone sleepless for several nights. Noelle slowly succumbed to it, slipping into unconsciousness.

"A...A-Aspen..." Noelle weakly called out before being held in General Ulger's arms. With her fleeting consciousness, the last thing Noelle saw was a glimpse of the general peering down at her, his wry, devilish grin elongated across his face and teeth gleaming in the moonlight.

CHAPTER

SIXTEEN

Aspen stared blankly at the ceiling of his dorm room; he'd just woken up, still feeling quite restless. He'd had a difficult time sleeping, Noelle had been on his mind the entire night. Even after sleeping their interaction off, the regret he felt was immeasurable. *I was too harsh on her, why didn't I listen to her before yelling?* Aspen angrily threw his pillow on the floor.

"What's got you so upset this early in the morning?" Elliot yawned while rubbing his eyes.

"S-sorry, I just...I made someone close to me mad at me."

"Mad at you? So? I probably get mad at you every other week. Like now for instance, for waking me up so early."

"This is different," Aspen snapped. "I made this person really upset with me. I hurt her."

Elliot shifted his body to sit upright, he could tell that it really weighed on Aspen. "Well, you seem to be really close to this person if you're that upset about it. What did you even do?"

"I yelled at her," he muttered quietly.

"Look, maybe I'm not the best person to ask on account that you're my only friend at this school and I'm a loner...but people who are close to each other fight sometimes. After that happens, all you have to do is apologize like crazy." Elliot stood up and opened his closet to get his uniform.

"You're right." Aspen cheered up a little bit, "I'll apologize the next time I see her." *Next time for sure, I'll apologize and apologize some more. Even if she doesn't accept my apology, I'll beg for forgiveness.*

"So, who's this girl that's mad at you?" Elliot asked, changing clothes.

"Noelle," Aspen said, "I've told you about her."

"Yeah, you have, countless times in fact. I would love to meet her if she swings by again. To finally meet the famous Noelle that you spoke of...countless times."

Though, Aspen knew his request to meet her might not turn out to be what Elliot expected. Mogoniwais were hated here with a passion. He glanced at him, wondering if that was the same for all the students. "Hey, Elliot, do you hate Mogoniwais?"

Elliot turned around and gave Aspen a confused look. "What?"

"Do you hate Mogoniwais?" he repeated.

"Why are you asking this all of a sudden?"

"I'm just curious. This entire year, you've never really talked about them."

Elliot took a minute to think about it. "Well, I don't really have an opinion about them since I've never met one before."

"Do you hate them?"

"Nah, not really, I guess."

"Why not? Don't you think that they are scary?" Aspen pushed on, thinking that for sure he'd be the type to hate them only on account of all the scary fables surrounding them.

"They are scary. But it's not like humans aren't either. I'm probably just as scared of Mogoniwais as I am of people. I mean, I haven't met a Mogoniwai that bullied me relentlessly for several years, so there's that."

"Yeah, you're right." Aspen smiled. *Maybe it would be alright to introduce him to Noelle, they'd probably get along perfectly.*

230

Elliot threw Aspen's uniform at him, changing the subject, "Hurry up and get dressed already. You're meeting your dad today, right?"

Aspen jumped out of bed. "Right!" He put on his uniform and headed to the restroom to get ready for the day.

Aspen stood outside the school gates looking out for his father's carriage. The weather was a bit gloomy, and the wind was extra chilly this morning. He regretted not layering up, or at least wearing something a bit warmer. It was in these moments Aspen wished he had not forgotten his scarf. He wrapped his arms around his body to combat the shivers. *I wonder if they camped out all night in this cold?* This made Aspen worry whether or not his friends had frozen to death from the harsh Denmar winters.

"Maybe I should find her right now after all," Aspen contemplated, despite not having a clue where Niko and Noelle were. *They couldn't have gone too far.* Aspen began heading towards the woods on the off chance that he'd find them, until he heard the *clip-cloppity* sounds of horse hooves. *Darn it, I guess it'll have to wait.*

Aspen straightened out his uniform, trying to look as proper as can be as the carriage came closer. He had to be on his best behavior with his father. Then, maybe there would be a chance that he could go back home. The driver stopped the horse in front of the school gates and out stepped his father.

"Hey, Dad," Aspen greeted. The greeting didn't really roll off his tongue, he hadn't spoken to him since he forcibly sent him here.

"Hello..." his father greeted him. Aspen could see this was awkward for his dad as it was for himself. "Have...you been well?"

"So-so, I guess." The two were silent. "Are you hungry?" Aspen asked, attempting to fill the silence.

Aspen's father grabbed his stomach, just now remembering that he hadn't eaten. "Yeah, I guess I could go for a bite."

Aspen guided his father to the school cafeteria while showing him around bits of the school, though there wasn't much to show. "So...this is the cafeteria, where everyone eats and...stuff." The two lined up to go get food, both deciding on getting scrambled eggs, bacon, and bread—the safest options. Then, they scoured the area for an open spot to sit.

"Aspen! Over here!" a voice called out. Aspen spotted a familiar tall, lanky guy waving at him. It was Elliot. Luckily for him, he had saved them a few seats.

"I see you found a new friend here," his dad said, taking his seat.

"Yeah, Dad, I'd like you to meet my roommate and friend, Elliot."

Elliot stuck out his hand, "Hi, Mr. Chase, nice to meet you. Aspen here really helped me out this past year. If it wasn't for him, I don't know what I would have done."

Ben let out a slight smile. "Nice to meet you, Elliot, I hope you continue being good friends with my son." He shook his hand so firmly, Elliot's arm wiggled like a wet noodle.

"So, how did you two meet?" his father asked, stuffing some scrambled eggs in his mouth.

"Well..." Aspen wasn't sure what he should tell his dad. *Should I tell him that we just met in class or that we met when I got in trouble for getting into a fight with his bully?*

Before he could answer, Elliot chimed in. "I was getting bullied, sir. If it wasn't for Aspen, I'd probably still be getting bullied to this day. Ever since, he's been a good friend to me."

Aspen's dad looked at his son and ruffled up his hair. "Good on you. Your mom raised you right, after all."

The compliment astonished Aspen, it had probably been the first nice thing his father had said to him in a while. *Maybe if he keeps being in this good mood, I'll get to leave after all.* So far, things were looking up.

Aspen was glad that Elliot was here, conversations between the three of them seemed to run seamlessly. There was a sense of normalcy within the conversation.

They put away their dishes and threw away their trash as they headed out the door. They had already exchanged hellos and had breakfast together, but he wasn't really sure how long his father was planning to stay. Aspen rubbed his neck as the nerves kicked in. He had to make a plea to leave this school before his dad left or else he'd be stuck here for another year, another year apart from Noelle.

"Aspen?" his father shook his shoulder. "You alright?" This gave Aspen a little startle.

"Could you repeat that?"

"I said you're probably enjoying the school life here, right?" repeated his father.

Aspen twiddled his thumbs, "I..." If there was ever a time to bring it up, it should be now, before he lost the nerve to do so. "I...um...I actually wanted to talk to you about that."

His dad raised his eyebrows. "What did you want to talk about?"

"I..." *Say it Aspen, there's no point in dillydallying now.* Aspen raised his head and looked his father straight in the eye, "I want to go back home."

His dad had a disappointed look on his face. Elliot looked at the two of them, not knowing what was going on.

Aspen's dad shook his head and sighed, "I thought you were finally moving past this...past her."

"Her?" Elliot whispered quietly. Now that he thought about it, Aspen had always been vague as to why he was sent here. Elliot didn't know whether he should silently slip away or stay. Though, it was getting too interesting to leave now, so he stayed put.

"Dad...my feelings for her won't change from just a short passage of time. A year, two, even a decade can pass, but my love for her is sure enough that for as long as I live, it will never wither. You can only keep me here for so long. When I'm an adult, I can leave here on my own and be with her. And I just...I just want you to give me your blessing."

"Like I told you before, Aspen, she is a demon. You know there is no future with her," Aspen's dad scolded. Though he did so quietly, so no other students nearby could hear. "Staying here, I was hoping you would forget about her."

Elliot's jaw dropped as he blurted out, "Demon? Did you just say demon?" Their conversation this morning played back in his head. "You met a demon girl? I thought there were none left. Scratch that, you loved one?" Elliot quickly covered his mouth, as this was the wrong moment to blurt out his inner thoughts. He stared back at Aspen. After a year, Elliot thought he'd know him pretty well, but little did he know that his friend was holding such a big secret.

"If there is no future with her, Dad, regardless, that's the future I'll choose," Aspen answered. The two stood in front of each other, without batting an eye, both resolved and grounded by their decision.

"Aspen! Noelle, she's—!" a voice yelled out. All three of them turned to see a distressed Niko, with dirt all over his face. He looked like quite the mess, a far cry from his usual self.

"Niko? Is that you? What are you doing here?" Ben asked.

Niko ignored his question and focused only on Aspen. "She's in trouble, we were attacked last night." He handed him a white scarf.

Aspen took the scarf from him. *Noelle was holding this for me.* "W-what happened, Niko? W-where is she?"

"I-it was General Ulger. I was unconscious before even realizing it—he ambushed us. I was knocked out before I had the chance to react. I have no doubt that he kidnapped her."

"General Ulger? Why would he be involved in all this?" Aspen's dad asked.

Aspen couldn't form any words, nor was he hearing what anyone was saying. Fear had overridden his senses. *Noelle.* He gasped in short breaths, feeling as if someone was strangling his very neck. *Noelle.* It didn't take long for the rest of his body to shut down, causing him to stumble to the ground.

Why did I yell at her? The guilt weighed on him like a long-casted shadow. *If I didn't yell at her, maybe she wouldn't have run off. Maybe she would have been safe in my arms at this very moment.* He hated himself for yelling at her. He hated himself for not just simply embracing her. It was his fault that she was kidnapped. *Ulger probably...he's going to use her to steal her powers...he's going...he's going to kill her.*

Niko called his name several times, but there was no response. He grabbed him by the collar, "Aspen!" No response again. Niko swung and struck him in the face. "You said you would protect her, right? Snap out of it! We don't have the time!"

Aspen's right cheek felt numb, sore from where Niko struck him, but it was what he needed at the moment. *He's right, I just have to have faith that she's still alright.* Aspen couldn't break down right now, he needed hope. *She's waiting for me to come get her.* He turned to Niko, asking, "So, where do we even get started? How do we find her?"

Niko's eyes lit up—he had an idea. "Your mana! Noelle was somehow able to figure out your location with her mana. She mentioned that by channeling the inner emotions and experiences she shared with you, some thread popped up. One that only she could see that led her straight to you. You guys are connected...so maybe you can do the same!"

"It's worth a shot. Come on, let's go, we don't have time to waste." Before he had a chance to leave, someone grabbed his arm. Aspen turned around to see that it was his father. Given Noelle's sudden disappearance, he had completely forgotten about him.

"It's too dangerous for you to go, Aspen," his father warned. "The general is someone you don't want to mess with."

"I have to go, Dad, she needs my help! Ulger is trying to use her to harness her powers! She's in danger!" Aspen pleaded.

"Harness her power? What nonsense are you talking about? You're not strong enough to face him!" Ben yelled.

"I can handle him just fine!" Aspen yanked his arm out of his grasp. A visible aura enveloped his arm, giving him that extra strength. Niko and Elliot's jaws dropped.

"Y-your arm!" His father was taken aback by this.

"I'll help Aspen. Maybe we can talk it over with the general and we can settle it one way or the other," Niko offered.

"I mean he works for the government, right? There's no way what he's doing is legal," Elliot said.

"You think you can just strut on in and ask him nicely to give her back?" Ben asked. "He's not like that. He does whatever he wants and doesn't listen to anyone, and especially he won't listen to some kids who are in way over their heads."

Noelle's power coursed through his arm, Aspen could feel his strength vitalizing and raging through his veins. "I CAN TAKE CARE OF MYSELF!" He threw a punch and struck at a nearby tree like an ax, causing it to topple over.

"Did you know he can do that?" Elliot whispered.

"Not at all..." Niko responded.

"Oh okay. So, what? You don't need your family anymore?" Ben asked. "You don't need your dad anymore, is that it?"

"I never said that!" Aspen grumbled. "Why can't I go to her? Do you really think I'm still the scared little kid from years ago?"

"No, I don't think that," Ben answered.

"Is it because I'm not strong enough?"

"It's...it's not because you're not strong enough."

"So, what? Do you hate Mogoniwais that much? Is that it? Is it because Noelle is a Mogoniwai?"

"I don't hate her because she's a...a Mogoniwai anymore."

"Then why, Dad? Please just tell me one good reason why," Aspen pleaded, frustrated tears building up. "You've never opened up to me in your life, you never bothered to ask me how my day was, never told me why you hated Mogoniwais. You...you never talked about how you felt when mom was gone! For once, just tell me the truth, just tell me the fucking truth already."

"I can't let you go," Ben covered his face as he shook his head.

"Why?"

"Because..." Aspen's dad couldn't look him in the eyes.

"Because why, Dad?" he asked again.

"Because you're the only family I have left," his father finally admitted. Water splashed to the ground as he revealed his crying face. "When you fell down those cliffs and when you got involved with that girl—do you know how scared I was? I lost your mother, I can't lose you, too."

Elliot jumped in. "We'll make sure that he's—"

Niko quickly threw his arms around Elliot's shoulders and covered his mouth, whispering, "Let them talk, we shouldn't butt in. They need to talk it out themselves. It's been years coming."

"I understand that you're worried about me," Aspen reassured. "I truly do. But I'm all that she has, too. Noelle needs me. He's going to...he's going to kill her. I promised her that she'd never be alone, from now on, for as long as I'm here. I'm begging you to let me keep my promise, I'll accept any punishment afterwards." Aspen looked his dad in the eyes. "You have to let me go."

"Alone..." Ben mumbled. A single word that resonated with Aspen's father, evoking a feeling that was all too familiar, bringing forth memories of his late wife once more. For what seemed like his entire life, an anchor manifested from the guilt he harbored for not being there for his wife, an anchor that was tied to his leg, dragging him deeper and deeper into the icy dark depths of the ocean. Despite the years, the anchor did not weigh any less than the day she died. When Ben tried to open his eyes, all he could see was darkness, all he could *feel* was darkness. A punishment for leaving her all alone. If he could turn back time, there was nothing that would stop him from being with his ill wife. During her final moments, Maya's lungs could not draw in enough oxygen and eventually gave out, according to the doctors.

"It was easier to blame the demons," Ben admitted. He swallowed the truth that he refused to see for the first time, and it tasted as bitter as the alcohol he had consumed through the years.

"I know it wasn't...it wasn't their fault," his voice quivered. He clenched his teeth and dug his nails into the palm of his fists, to feel the piercing pain of it. "Part of me just wished that those demons caused it all, maybe they used some magic on her, maybe they...they cast some sort of curse." His eyes flared up, "That it wasn't just some unfortunate, inevitable occurrence." Ben shook his head, "That the world wasn't this cruel!" This would at least justify his anger towards them, but of course he knew that this was unlikely.

"I of all people should know how you're feeling." He looked his son in the eyes, wondering if he would turn into a drunkard coward like himself. There was no doubt in his mind that Aspen had taken after him—that is, except for his baby blue eyes that he had gotten from his mother.

"Okay." Aspen's father let go of his son's arm, and he gave in, "You can go to her." Whether he kept his son locked away or let him go, it would be painful either way. At least this way, Aspen had a chance to prevent the pain of losing the love of his life, a pain that would not heal no matter how many years passed.

"But I am coming with you," he added. "It's still a parent's job to keep their child safe. Just...give me a minute," Ben excused himself as he walked off. No matter how much regret and self-pity Ben threw at himself, nothing would change, it wouldn't bring back Maya. But Aspen was still here, pleading with him about wanting to save the girl he cares most about. Here, there was something that Aspen's father could do. "Maya," he tilted his face to the sky, "I couldn't be there for you and I don't think I will ever move past the regret. But for now, until I join you in those heavenly blue skies, I'll need to move forward. I'm still alive and breathing now, I can still be here for Aspen. I still need to be. Our son needs me now. I'm going to move forward now, okay?" Ben felt a gentle breeze that seemed to push him towards his son. He smiled, as if receiving the validation that he needed, and returned back to the group. "Ready to go?"

"Yeah," Aspen smiled. For the first time in a while, the two raised their heads and met each other's gaze.

"Now that we've got that settled, let's go back to the horse and carriage," Niko hurriedly told them. The three started heading back to the carriage, on their way to save Noelle.

"Wait, I want to come with you," Elliot abruptly chimed in.

"Elliot, it's too dangerous." Aspen was glad his friend wanted to help but he couldn't allow him to potentially put himself in danger for his sake, especially for someone he didn't know. "You don't have to involve yourself in—"

"It's my choice!" Elliot yelled out. "I didn't ask you to help me with the bullies, but you did anyway." He pressed his finger on Aspen's chest, "You made me get involved by making me your friend. As a friend, why wouldn't I help you after all the times you have helped me?" He wasn't slouched or ducking his head down like usual, Elliot planted his feet firmly on the ground. "In times like these, shouldn't you be asking your friends for help?"

He wasn't the same scared kid that he had met a year ago. Without realizing it, Elliot had changed right before his very eyes. Aspen smiled to himself. *Elliot isn't going to back down now, huh?* Aspen walked over to him, put his hand on his shoulder, and asked, "Can you help me out?"

"Gladly."

"Oh, by the way, I'm Niko, Aspen's best friend from back in his hometown," Niko butted in.

"Hi, I'm Elliot. Aspen's...uh...best friend at this school." In different, less dire circumstances, they'd be arguing about who was the better friend to Aspen, but time was of the essence, and there was no time for trivial arguments.

And so, instead of three, it was now the four of them heading over to the carriage to save Noelle.

"Okay, so run it by me again. Did Noelle tell you how she found me? Like some sort of magic or ability she did?" asked Aspen.

Niko shrugged, "She found your location by tracking down your mana and recollecting your past experiences and emotions. I figured you would know the rest."

"Oh, okay...I guess I'll give it a shot." Aspen barely had any control of his magical strength, nor had he ever thought to use his powers in a varied way like tracking Noelle's location. He sat on the ground, closed his eyes, and took a deep breath.

It had only been a couple seconds until someone coughed, completely ruining his concentration. Aspen opened one eye to see his dad, Niko, and Elliot staring intently at him. "Can you guys turn around or something? I can't concentrate knowing that everyone is staring at me."

"Oh, yeah, sure," Niko muttered.

"My bad," Elliot apologized. "I didn't want to miss the magic mumbo jumbo."

Aspen resumed his concentration.

Okay, Aspen, focus. Show me where she is, I want to see Noelle. Aspen took a deep breath as he tried reliving his memories with her, thinking far back to when Noelle saved him on his birthday. *Remember all the good times you had with her.* He thought about their time in the woods, where he'd teach her from morning to noon and then they'd hunt for lunch. He thought about the festival and the excitement and joy they felt as they played games and talked endlessly for hours. *Please, please work.* He thought about when they would stargaze at night and just talked about whatever came to mind until their mouths were too tired to move. Aspen's chest glowed faintly, as his heart was filled with memories of Noelle. *I think I can feel it, show me her, I want to see her. Show me Noelle!* Despite his efforts, nothing happened, and establishing a connection with her was futile.

"It's not working," Aspen lamented.

"Try again, man, you have to try focusing again," Niko urged on.

Aspen closed his eyes and concentrated once more. But just as before, nothing happened. He slammed his fists on the ground in frustration. "Why isn't it working? Why can't I find her?" Aspen's woe started to pile. *What if General Ulger harmed her? Maybe he had already—* He shook that idea out of his head; he needed to be hopeful.

"Maybe we can just try and search for her?" Elliot suggested.

"I don't think that'd be the best idea. It's been several hours since he abducted her. Who knows where he is hiding her," Niko said.

Aspen couldn't give up here, closing his eyes once more. *Noelle, if you can hear me, I need your help. I'm not talented or strong enough to do what you can do, please tell me where you are.* He clasped his hands together, begging for something to work. *I'm sorry for yelling at you last night. I swear you can give me an earful when I see you again and I'll gladly take it. Just give me a sign.* He dug his fingernails into his hands so hard they bled. *Don't let me be too late. Don't leave me just yet.* Aspen sunk his head low, and nothing happened again.

Aspen's father put his hand on his son's shoulder. "We'll find her, son, even if it takes all night. We'll find her." Aspen didn't respond.

"Well, let's get on the carriage, it's better to move around and look for her instead of standing here," Elliot suggested.

With no ideas left, Niko and the others agreed. Aspen's dad took the driver's seat, while Niko and Elliot sat inside the carriage. Aspen, feeling defeated, walked towards the carriage. But before stepping inside, he felt a jolt of electricity tingle throughout his body and froze in place. His heart slowly beat to a rhythm that wasn't his own, but a beat that he was quite familiar with.

"Noelle? Was that you?" He looked around the woods in all directions, looking for another sign. His dad and friends bobbed their heads out of the carriage and watched.

"Where are you, Noelle?" Aspen screamed out. Her inexplicable presence grew stronger and stronger. "I'm right here, Noelle!" he yelled. Waves of light emerged from the ground, and with it a fleeting memory of when he first met Noelle appeared in his head. This sense of warmth was all too familiar with him.

"Aspen!" his father rushed to his aid and tried to claw his way towards his son, but the light propelled him away.

Aspen could only hear the lulling sound of birds chirping from within. The magical aura spun faster, until it was hard to see his father and his friends. The light had completely covered him, sealing him off from the world.

And then, darting through the woods, he felt it. It zoomed through the trees and from up above the mini magical dome, it struck him dead center in the heart. Aspen looked down to see a single thread. A single thread of mana that attached itself to his heart, faintly he could feel Noelle's heart as it slowly beat. The magical walls that had enclosed him slowly peeled away, like a budding flower that had just bloomed. It felt like his mana was traveling back and forth from him to Noelle, like how veins take blood back to the heart. He clutched his chest, feeling her warmth as if she was right beside him. Noelle was calling out to him.

"What's the matter?" Niko asked.

"She's alive...s-she's alive," Aspen cried with relief; there was still hope. "It's Noelle! She heard my call. I can see it! I can see it now! We can find her now! We can save her!"

Niko almost jumped out of the carriage. "You did it! Can you see how far she is?"

Aspen concentrated on Noelle's location. "It's not too far from what I can tell, but she's moving."

"General Ulger shouldn't be too far."

"I don't really understand what's going on or how Aspen's communicating with her, but since we know where she is, let's all head out now," Elliot said. Without wasting another minute, they all jumped in the carriage and followed the thread.

"Over there, follow that route," Aspen pointed out to his father.

"Hmm, that direction leads us back into town," his father said as he guided the horse per Aspen's direction. He looked back to his son, "Let's go save her."

Niko put his arm around Aspen's shoulders, "We'll teach him not to mess with us."

Elliot popped up from behind, "Let's get the son of a bitch."

Aspen smiled, "We're coming, Noelle, just hold out a little longer."

SEVENTEEN

I t had been a few hours since they all pursued the other end of the thread. Ulger's pace was slowing down, while they were steering towards them like crazed maniacs, it would not be long until they caught up to them.

"So, what's the game plan?" asked Elliot.

Aspen and Niko looked at each other, waiting for the other to respond.

"You're the idea guy! I don't have a plan," exclaimed Aspen.

"You're the one who's trying to chase after her, why don't you have a plan?" scoffed Niko.

"Great...so, I guess we're just going to wing it then," groaned Elliot. "Just in case my lanky appearance fooled you guys, I am definitely not the best fighter. I'm basically like a moving punching bag."

"You guys aren't going to do any fighting," affirmed Aspen. "There's no way I would put you guys in danger for my sake."

"It's not for your sake. It's for Noelle's sake," corrected Niko. "I...I want to help her."

"Honestly, I've never even met her, but I'm here to help because I owe it to Aspen," Elliot jumped in.

"Well, we should think of a plan while we're still chasing after him," Aspen suggested. He called out to his dad, "Is there anything important that we need to know about General Ulger?"

His dad took a minute to think. "When I knew him during the war, he was always a ruthless fighter, with no hesitation to kill whoever stands in his way." Elliot gulped, feeling the tension in his body slowly rise. Aspen's dad continued on, "He's an arrogant man, and obsessive, to the point that he gets fixated on one thing and that one thing only. Other than that, I wouldn't know anything more about him. We didn't see eye to eye often."

"Maybe we can use his arrogance and hyperfixation to our advantage," Niko said.

"Okay, let's make this simple. We go in and sneak into wherever General Ulger is taking her. One of us will distract him from a distance—like telling him that we told public officials and they are on their way, or getting him to ramble on about his plan—while the others snag Noelle. We have the last guy stay on the carriage. Once we grab her, we all jump in and leave as soon as we can. No overcomplications, just simple and straight to the point."

"Sounds like a good enough plan for the most part," Niko agreed.

"I'm in as well," Elliot chimed in. "So...who's going to be the one to distract that guy?"

"I'll do it," volunteered Aspen and Niko simultaneously.

"What do you mean you'll do it? It's because of me Noelle is in trouble, I have to do it," Aspen declared.

"You're too emotional when it comes to these types of things. You need someone level- headed, and you're not in the slightest," Niko argued back.

"Enough, boys!" Aspen's dad called out from the driver's seat. "I will be the one to distract him. There's no way I can leave you all to the most dangerous part of this plan. Since I'm mayor, he'll at least be threatened by what I have to say. My words hold more weight after all." Everyone agreed without another word.

"Okay, that settles that. This means that my dad will distract him while Niko and I take Noelle away from him. Elliot will be waiting outside at the carriage ready to leave when we have her," Aspen confirmed.

"Sounds like we're all set now," Elliot said.

"How much longer are we from them? Are we close?" asked Niko.

The thin red thread that connected Aspen and Noelle didn't seem to be moving any further; it wouldn't be long until they closed the distance from each other. "General Ulger stopped moving. It looks like wherever he was going, he made it there." He peeked his head out to his dad. "You'll want to keep going straight, when you reach the fork in the road, go left and follow it."

"Sounds good." Aspen's dad set his eyes back onto the road. "It seems this route leads back to Grasalia."

Everyone stayed silent for the duration of the trip. The looming thoughts of failure only deepened their anxieties and hushed their mouths.

Elliot in particular was the most tense out of the group; his entire body moved with so much anxiety that he was worried that it'd shake the carriage. He crossed his arms to hide it from the others, not wanting anyone to worry about him. Elliot had talked pretty big throughout this trip, but deep down, this was one of the most nerve-wracking things he'd ever done on a whim.

"It's over there, Dad, in that cave," Aspen pointed.

"Have you and Noelle ever explored this cave before? You and her lived in caves, right?" asked Niko.

"You lived in what now?" Aspen's father asked, though was ignored.

"No, not this one..." Aspen gulped, "I've never even noticed that this cave was ever here." The thread was flickering now; it seemed like it could disappear at any second. He had a bad feeling about this. As they got a little closer, Aspen's dad made sure to stop the carriage well away from the cave so that the general wouldn't hear them coming.

The cave was on a grassy plain on the side of a mountain, and near its entrance was a horse and an empty carriage, presumably belonging to General Ulger.

"Who knew I'd actually be back here in Grasalia so soon. Too bad it was under these circumstances," Aspen quietly said. He peered down the mountain that overlooked the woods and his hometown. And over in that cave, she was right there, waiting for him. "I'm coming, Noelle."

"Stay hidden over here, Elliot. When you see us come out, drive the carriage and pick us up. Don't even stop," Niko instructed.

"You got it," Elliot exclaimed.

Aspen's dad placed his hand on his son's shoulder. "Whatever you do, stay hidden and stay safe. If something bad starts to happen between me and General Ulger, forget about me and prioritize her. You got it?"

"I..." Aspen was a little hesitant to accept. "I understand, Dad." He abruptly turned back and gave his dad a hug. "Thank you. For everything. I just want you to know that I don't ha—"

Aspen's father cut him off, "You don't have to say another word." His dad hugged him, a hug that was long overdue. "I'm sorry it took me this long to start acting like a father."

"Hey, Niko I forgot..." Elliot grabbed his shoulder, "just in case I don't make it out of here I wanted to ask, will you be my friend, too?"

Niko gave him a shove, "Really? You're gonna joke around now? At this very moment?"

"Ouch. I mean, it was partly a joke, and partly serious." Elliot rubbed his shoulder, "I'm awkward when it comes to serious moments like these."

Aspen jumped and wrapped his arms around the two of them, bringing them closer. "I have a feeling that you two will be the best of friends. Thank you for coming with me. I wouldn't be able to save her without you guys."

"Of course," Elliot said.

"I swear you have me meet the weirdest people and get me into the worst situations," scoffed Niko. "But...anytime, man, just say the word and I'll be there."

"Come on, boys, we have a person to save," Ben reminded. "We can celebrate together once this is all over—*with* Noelle."

Aspen smiled at the sound of that, "Alright, let's go get her."

The three snuck into the cave, making sure that they didn't make a single sound. It was getting darker the deeper they ventured to the heart of these seemingly endless tunnels, so dark that Aspen's father had to light a torch that was stashed inside of the wagon. By this point, Aspen was used to venturing through unknown and unexplored caves, though this would be the first time doing so without Noelle's guidance. Luckily, the thread that connected him to her was still transparent, making navigating through the cave's twists and turns that much easier.

It wasn't until they heard voices echoing straight ahead did the group stand to a halt. Aspen recognized those voices—the general's and Noelle's. He steadily followed the direction of her voice. As Noelle's voice became more audible, Aspen's spirits were reinvigorated. *Just a little longer, Noelle, we're here to save you.*

At the very edge of the cave, they could see a light. The three crept closer until the sounds of a loud buzzing noise filled the cavern. *What is that noise?* Aspen wondered, taking a peek inside. General Ulger paced around the room, seemingly mesmerized by something. It was only when he took a closer look did Aspen's posture change almost instantly, Noelle was bound and tied up to some mechanism twice his size. Anger almost overtook him as he nearly stormed into the room to save her. Had Niko not grabbed and yanked him to the ground, he'd be in the cavern, ruining their element of surprise. His friend silently scowled at him; words weren't even needed for Aspen to understand what he said.

Don't let your emotions get to you, Aspen, stick to the plan. He nodded to Niko, vowing to keep his emotions in check. *We need to wait for the opportune time to strike.* Aspen scanned the room; it was quite cavernous and full of places to hide behind. While General

Ulger was distracted, they could slowly creep closer to Noelle, hide behind cover, and free her.

Aspen stared at the contraption that Noelle was strapped to, beams of light were protruding in and out of it, looking like it was going to burst at any minute. General Ulger kept staring at it, enthralled by the light like a summertime moth. This wasn't the usual prim and proper general that he had come to know. His attire was wrinkled, hair disheveled, he kept muttering to himself, and looked unhinged. And there was Noelle, who was conscious and looking very much pissed.

It's now or never, Niko thought. He gestured to Aspen and his father to get into position. As Ben was about to head inside to distract the general, Noelle and Ulger began to argue. They all hesitated and kept their ears to the ground, curious as to what General Ulger was planning to do with her and the bomb that seemed it would detonate at any second.

NOELLE COULDN'T BREAK free from her shackles no matter how hard she tried. The last thing she remembered was being confronted by General Ulger, and then she had suddenly woken up bound in the back of a strange carriage. Without explanation, he dragged her inside this cave, hooked her up and placed her next to a metal object that she could sense was holding an extraordinary amount of mana. She looked up and locked eyes with General Ulger's crazed face. "You took my people's mana by force, didn't you? There's no way they would willingly give it to you."

"You're such a clever girl, aren't you?" General Ulger sarcastically pointed out. "I was in awe of what your kind can do. Your powers and abilities—if all of your kind banded together, there's no doubt you could have placed humanity on its knees. Which is why I had to strike first." He kneeled down towards her and continued on, "The first time I killed a Mogoniwai, the blood spilt out of their bodies. It was glistening bright red." General Ulger smiled, "It was a glorious sight. I just had to have it. During the war, I would take a few Mogoniwais for...my experiments. Eventually, I got one of them to break, and with the help of a demon speak expert, I was told I, too, could attain such power."

"You're crazy!" Noelle listened on, trying to bide for more time. Noelle knew Aspen was on his way here, she heard him call for her. He was close. Although the general was rigid and serious most times, he became the complete opposite when talking about Mogoniwais. She could use this to her advantage in the meantime.

"Normally, the Mogoniwais can transfer their mana to others by touching the person, but I found a loophole. If I'm careful and draw the right amount of blood, I can inject it into myself! But just even an ounce off could mean poison to the body!" General Ulger boasted.

"You can transfer our powers that way?"

"Oh, no no. That's not the only requirement. The transfer of mana also requires emotion. And where do emotions typically lie?" He pointed directly towards her chest. "It's the heart... Of course, I don't have an emotional connection with any filthy demons, but I found another way." The general licked his lips. "*Consuming* the heart works just as well."

Noelle trembled, her eyes now wide with terror. This man was a nightmare incarnate; if he were to shed his skin, it would show nothing but a pure essence of evil with a pair of eyes. Part of her didn't want Aspen to come rescue her, worried of what this man might do to him. "Y-you're a monster."

"What actually defines a monster in this world? To you, I probably seem like a monster, but to the outside world, to us humans, your race are the monsters," General Ulger asserted. "We humans are afraid of those we cannot control and those that make us powerless. I mean, who wouldn't be afraid of a walking firearm? No longer will we have to cower in fear, no longer will humans have to fear being subjugated by the demons!" he screamed.

"What have the Mogoniwais ever done to your people? Your kind were the ones who started the war!" Noelle bellowed. "You attacked us first! My people were peaceful folks until you humans invaded our lands, stole our treasures, and killed us in cold blood! Even then, with your sick, cruel methods I've read that you killed mothers, the elderly, even children, all because they were Mogoniwai! Why?

"Well, it's not *what* they have done to us, but what they *can do* to us! Who knows when your race will crawl out of whatever caves they're hiding in and attack us!" Ulger argued back.

"But why my parents? They had done no wrong! All they...all they wanted to do was live peacefully and yet...and yet..." She could not bear to imagine the pain this man had put her parents through.

"Your parents? Why would I care if they did no wrong? I couldn't care less," Ulger scoffed. "It could have been anyone of your kind that day—all you guys look the same—they just happened to be the unfortunate ones."

"I'll stop you..." Noelle said.

"Sure, sure," The general turned his back to her, "Enough with this nonsense, there's still much to prepare before it's too late." He gazed upon the bomb, becoming mesmerized by its light once again. "To think I have finally found it. The next step of human evolution."

"Sorry to intrude General Ulger, sir, but the compatibility rate is near a one hundred percent match. This one will do, she may be the key to finishing it," Jack Bellard informed. "Brilliant, Bellard!" the general celebrated. "Hunting countless Mogoniwais, seeing failure after failure, just hoping each one we caught would be compatible. Here it finally is. Our work is finally completed."

"W-what is this thing?" Noelle asked, looking at the machine. It didn't seem like the conventional weapon—like rifles or dynamite—that you'd see in books.

"I call it a mana bomb—akin to the explosions you can produce out of your hands but grander—and I couldn't have made this without your race's powers. It's made of mana that I have collected from your kind. It would have been selfish of me to keep this gift to myself. Eventually, I was able to discover how to contain and disperse the mana on a larger scale," the general explained. "Bombs are in development in many nations, but this here is probably the deadliest when it comes to effectiveness and range. It'll wipe out the weak and from the ashes will arise the strong survivors."

"Disperse the mana? How is this bomb going to do that? It looks like it's going to—"

"Explode? Why, yes, that's the point. It will soon have enough power to reach from Cresnough all the way to Grasalia."

"Sir, General Ulger, sir..." Jack pleaded. "I just wanted to remind you that you promised you w-wouldn't detonate it until I'm safely far, far away from here. I created what you asked... can we halt it for maybe a day or two, just until I'm out of the way?"

Noelle could feel mana leak out of the bomb, already sensing the destructive force behind it just by her proximity to it. She screamed out, "You have to stop this! Not everyone is going to survive. Most are going to burn up and die from the raw mana output! Hundreds of thousands could die!"

"S-she's right, sir. A small amount could destroy a town. If it exploded entirely, the aftereffects could be even more catastrophic. Look, mana compatibility is not guaranteed for every individual— especially for me—maybe we should test this hypothesis some more. Let me just do a few more tests," Jack suggested.

"Tests?" General Ulger asked. "Are you saying after years of research, after years of experimenting, you suddenly lose confidence? What...have you been lying to me this entire time?"

"No, sir...I mean, in theory the mana will pass through our bodies and will combine with and merge with our own DNA ,then it would be sound. B-but not all bodies will be able to have a perfect match with it, and if they don't match, their bodies will burn from the inside out and...and...I need to get away. I...I can die!"

"I don't want to wait any longer," Ulger responded. "I guess we'll either see you in the new world or on the other side."

"Ulger! This is nonsense!" Noelle screamed. She turned to Jack,

"You're going to kill everyone, humans alike! Think of everyone in town, you have to stop this now!"

Jack Bellard gulped as his arms trembled in fear. The man before him scared him shitless, but the aftereffects of his own creation scared him even more. "S-she's right. I don't want any part of this anymore. I...I'm a scientist, not a mass killer! I'm not going to risk human lives just for this experiment. I...I'm shutting this down and letting everyone know what you have done all these years. I h-have to protect myse– I mean the people in town!"

Ulger casually walked towards Jack, who stood still with the color of his face now pale white. "Let's not be hasty, Jack. Okay, you have been my trusted scientist after all these years and have given me everything I have ever asked. Let's stop this, okay? Only after more tests will we start again."

"Y-you mean it?" Bellard adjusted his glasses, crooked from his body's constant shaking.

Ulger placed the palm of his hand on Bellard's chest. Heat started to emit from his palm until it burned into a magnificent light color, "No."

"S-sir?" Bellard asked, already aware of his impending demise. Where Ulger had touched, a burning sensation built up.

BOOM!

A burst of fire blew through his chest, leaving a hole where his heart should be. His body slumped and dropped to the ground, like a heavy sack of potatoes. Jack Bellard, the scientist, was no more.

General Ulger brushed away his warning. He slowly began to chuckle until it eventually turned into loud, hysterical laughter. "I will let evolution choose who lives and who dies. Though most will die, whoever lives shall be reborn again as the next evolution of humanity! Can you imagine it? Humans being able to heal each other from death and having superhuman strength that can topple the mightiest soldiers, the possibilities of what we can do will be endless! No other creature or nation would be able to defeat us with this kind of power!"

~

ASPEN AND EVERYONE's jaws all dropped after hearing General Ulger's nefarious plan. He was about to detonate a weapon made of mana, that could potentially wipe out everyone within its vicinity, for the slim chance of creating an army of pseudo-Mogoniwais with magical powers. Something much larger was going on than they anticipated —it wasn't just Noelle that they had to save, but the entire town, too.

"One of us has to go back and warn the town about this," Aspen whispered. Though he was going to save Noelle no matter what, thoughts of their failure loomed over his head. But if they didn't end up saving her, if they ended up failing, someone should at least warn the town before it's too late. A bead of sweat rolled down the side of his furrowed brow.

"I'll go back and warn everyone, you two go and save Noelle," Niko suggested.

Aspen shook his head. "They'll never believe you, especially something as crazy as this. I mean, the general is planning to blow up the country and turn everyone into Mogoniwai hybrids. No way the entire town would listen to a kid saying this." He looked at his dad, "You're the mayor. It has to be you." Before his father could speak, Aspen could already tell that he was against this idea.

Aspen's dad shook his head. "Aspen, there's no way I can let you two stay here and try to handle the general. Do you know how dangerous this situation is?"

"I do," Aspen said. "But out of the three of us, the town would most likely believe you. I know that you're worried about me, but it's the only way. Trust me, Dad. I can save Noelle."

"But who's going to save you?" Aspen's father paused at the fork in the road, debating whether he should travel towards the path to the town or his son. After his wife's death, he was negligent, and after Aspen's fall, he watched him every chance he had. His mind told him to stay on the path to his son. But looking into his son's eyes, he thought otherwise. There was a gleam in his eyes that showed a determination and mental fortitude that he had never seen before. "How did you grow up so strong without me realizing it? Okay...I...I'll trust you." Aspen's father started heading out, but before he did so, he whispered in his son's ear, "Please, whatever you do, come back safe and sound."

"I will," Aspen nodded.

"I'll distract the general, and you go get Noelle out of here," Aspen whispered to Niko. Now that his dad was gone, there had been a change of plans.

"No way, let me do it. You'll let your emotions get the better of you," Niko refuted.

"This is no time to be arguing about who does what right now. I'm going to distract him and get Noelle safe," Aspen repeated himself. Niko bit his tongue and complied—Aspen was right, time was of the essence. They looked back at the general and Noelle, waiting for the opportune time to strike.

"So, why do you need me here? Why didn't you just kill me?" Noelle asked, still buying time for Aspen.

"Because I never could find the right Mogoniwai to charge my bomb. Every time they'd all just burn up and die," General Ulger grinned from ear to ear. He grabbed one of the many collars that connected to the bomb and wrapped it around her neck. "That is... until you! Be satisfied that you'll play a part in human evolution before you perish!"

The collar hummed and glowed as Noelle tried to desperately shake it off. She felt weaker by the second. This collar was draining her of her mana and feeding it to this bomb. Her eyes filled to the brim with tears. *Is this how things are going to end?* Noelle regretted leaving Willey's home where she was safe, she regretted getting into a fight with Aspen, she regretted running away from him. *Don't save me Aspen, it's worse than I realized. You have to get as far away from here as possible.* Noelle hoped for the first time that he would not come find her, hoping that he would just turn around and leave. She could not bear to be the reason for his suffering any longer, she had ruined his life enough as it is. Despite Noelle not wanting to see him in person, she still wished she had a picture of him right now. If she was going to die here, she at least wanted to see a glimpse of him one last time, Noelle would have been content with just that.

"Aspen!" Noelle cried out with tears rolling down her cheeks.

He clenched his fists, no longer could he idly watch Noelle suffer, it was too much for him to bear. Aspen leaped out into the room without a moment's hesitation. "Get your hands off her! Now!"

Noelle formed a rueful smile at the sight of him, happy that she was able to see him one last time. But that only meant he was going to put himself in danger against this monster, and not to mention, he was now currently in the same room with a ticking time bomb.

General Ulger turned to him, and the two stared down at each other like fated enemies. "Well, well, well, what took you so long?" He let out a mischievous smile. "Nice you could finally join us... Aspen."

EIGHTEEN

"Sorry I was late, Noelle, but I'm here now. We're going home," Aspen reassured her. "Let's go home, okay?"

"I'd..." Noelle quietly nodded, "I'd like that."

His palms began to sweat as he focused his attention back on General Ulger. One punch from him last time had brought Aspen to his knees. *Just distract him long enough until Niko grabs Noelle, and run as fast as you can.*

General Ulger cracked his knuckles, unfazed by Aspen's sudden appearance. "Well, here you are, like a mouse sneaking their way into a lion's den. This time, though, I'll make it so you'll never be a thorn in my side again. You should have stayed in whatever hole you crawled out from. There's nowhere to scurry off to now. No one will save you."

Aspen scanned the room, his eyes darting from one part of the cave to the other. "This is your last chance now, give up and free Noelle or...or else."

General Ulger laughed in his face. "You're talking to the next step of human evolution, you're just a small little rat, what can you even do?"

Yeah, I didn't think I sounded too convincing either, Aspen thought. He rushed behind a pillar of rocks to hide, using the dimly lit cave to his advantage.

Noelle tried breaking her hands free, but she didn't have the energy to do so. The collar had drained her mana like a parasite. All she could do now was watch helplessly.

"Still hiding are we?" boasted General Ulger, his hands lit up. He extended his palm towards Aspen's hiding place. A ball of fire formed from his palms.

Great, he has fireballs now. No one told me he could create fire balls, Aspen grumbled.

"Let's see how long you'll be able to survive this," the general yelled. He thrust his fists forward, sending a concussive fire blast towards him. *Boom! Boom!* Upon impact, rocks exploded into debris, leaving nothing but a smoke of dust behind.

"You missed! I guess magic doesn't matter if you can't aim!" Aspen taunted from a different location. Truthfully, despite his demeanor, he was sweating, having barely escaped the explosion. Aspen wiped the sweat off his forehead. "I'm over here!" he yelled, making a dash towards the opposite side of Noelle and the bomb.

General Ulger's brow furrowed as he gritted his teeth. "Why don't you stop hiding and fight me like a man?"

"No, I'd rather fight like a coward and win!" Aspen snapped back.

"Impudent little brat!" The general ran towards the direction of his voice, stepping away from Noelle, and charged up his mana to hurl another fireball at Aspen.

"General Ulger is chasing after him, now's my chance." Niko saw the opening that Aspen was providing him and tip-toed towards Noelle's direction. He lightly tapped her shoulder, to her astonishment.

"I'll get you out of here," whispered Niko. He could feel the heat

257

radiating from the bomb when he tried to rip off the rope that bound Noelle. With all his might, he tried to unravel them but to no avail, "This thing is tougher than it looks." Niko scanned the area for the sharpest jagged rock and used it to help free her. Slowly but surely, the rope started to tear. The sounds of the explosions became much more frequent off to the side. "J-just break off already," and with one final burst he managed to saw it off, finally freeing Noelle.

"Much appreciated, Niko," Noelle thanked as she yanked the collar off. She looked towards Aspen's direction, her head still spun while her mana slowly recovered.

Niko grabbed her hand, "Stop, you're in no condition to help right now. You should escape while you still can."

"No." Noelle brushed him off, "I won't run away while he's still out there." As much as she would have liked to rest a little longer, Aspen needed her right now. *I won't let this happen again. I wasn't strong enough to save my parents, but now at this moment...I am strong! I won't lose another person I love to this man!*

ASPEN TOOK a minute to catch his breath, even if taking a short break could result in his death. Though, at this point, his legs hardly had the strength to move. He'd been dodging explosion after explosion, and it wouldn't be long until he was cornered. Aspen didn't have any means to counterattack, not with the general throwing balls of fire at him from thin air. Before forming his next thought, another fireball was thrown his way. Aspen jumped back up and darted to the other side, but ended up tripping on his own two feet due to his legs failing him. The explosion sent him flying, where the general immediately pinned him to the ground.

"I got you," General Ulger said with a smug look on his face.

Aspen could feel the heat radiating from the general's hands. He struggled to get free, but General Ulger had a good hold on him. Aspen closed his eyes, bracing himself for the inevitable pain.

"Get your filthy hands off him!" Noelle screamed, super-charging her fists with mana. She landed a clean hit onto General Ulger's face, which sent him tumbling in the air until he hit the ground.

"Are you alright?" Noelle asked, extending her hand to help Aspen up.

Aspen grabbed her hand and stood up. "Noelle, I...I'm..." Now that he was standing face-to-face with her, he wasn't sure how he should apologize.

"It's okay, Aspen," Noelle said. General Ulger groaned nearby as he began to shake off Noelle's attack. "Besides, we have another problem that we have to deal with first."

"You managed to sneak one on me," General Ulger was rubbing his head. "Let's see you try that again."

"So, Noelle, do we have a plan?" Aspen asked.

She cracked her knuckles. "Just treat it like our typical hunting days. You still remember, don't you?" While hunting when they were young, Noelle would usually be the one to draw attention to the animal while Aspen sniped from afar. She had always been fearless and free while he was more careful and scared of confrontation. Together, they made up for each other's weaknesses; this was their tag team dynamic.

Aspen smiled, "Of course." He ran away from her and disappeared within the cave.

General Ulger looked disappointed. "Aspen, Aspen...you're gonna let a girl fight your battles for you while you hide?" Noelle lunged at him, but he dodged her with ease. "You're gonna have to do better than that." Before he could react, a jagged rock struck his mouth. He touched it. General Ulger clenched his fists in anger once noticing the blood from the cut on his lip. "How long are you going to keep hiding?"

"Who says that I'm hiding? Come find me if you can," Aspen mocked. He used the darkness to his advantage—all that time spent playing in caves with Noelle was about to pay off. He tossed the rock lightly in the air and caught it, Aspen didn't have his bow and arrow with him, so these rocks would have to do.

"Come out and fight me, you rat!" General Ulger yelled. He tuned everything out for a few seconds, trying to only listen to Aspen's footsteps as he darted and zipped around him.

"I got you now!" Ulger yelled, charging towards him. Though he didn't get far, as Noelle took this opportunity to strike. General Ulger held his throbbing cheek and muttered under his breath, "Pesky, little demon."

As Noelle went in for another strike, General Ulger avoided it by sidestepping in the other direction. He then grabbed her by the wrists and with full force punched her in the gut, making her gasp for air. Ulger held her by the neck and lifted her off the ground. She repeatedly kicked at him, but he did not waver.

"Noelle, I'm coming!" Aspen yelled, leaving his hiding spot to come to her aid.

"Predictable," said General Ulger with a sinister smile. "I knew that you couldn't resist coming to her. And so now..." With Aspen finally out of hiding and within close proximity, General Ulger threw Noelle off to the side to swing a roundhouse punch at him. Though it didn't stop there, as he pulled Aspen by his hair and struck him once more in the face. And then another for good measure.

Aspen spat out blood.

General Ulger grabbed Aspen, who was hunched over, and threw him towards an unsuspecting Noelle. The two collided, knocking each other to the ground.

"Ouch," groaned Noelle.

"Sorry," Aspen apologized. "Are you okay?"

"I'll be fine."

"It is only delaying the inevitable, you have no way of stopping me! I am the man who led the armies against the Mogoniwais and won! I will bring humanity into the next phase of evolution!" boasted General Ulger.

Niko, who was waiting for an opportune time to strike, rushed towards General Ulger during his rant, though he was easily caught in a chokehold. Niko gasped for air, trying to break free.

"Like I said, inevitable," General Ulger continued, throwing him across the cave like a ragdoll. He looked at Aspen and Noelle, who were slowly standing back up, "I just need to finish off this problem first." He collected all the mana to his palms, forming it so large that it covered his entire body.

Noelle reacted quickly, extended her palms forward, and coated it under a layer of mana, a last-ditch effort to try to block it. A trail of light shot out like a cannon as he fired it in their direction. The beam collided onto her palms. Noelle planted her feet firmly to the ground, though still feeling herself get pushed back.

General Ulger exerted even more force, pressing down on her further. "Humanity is and will always be the apex predator!" he yelled out, moving forward step-by-step.

Noelle gritted her teeth; she could feel herself losing ground. *I can't hold out much longer. I can't...I'm not strong enough, I...* Just then, she felt a warm, gentle touch on her back. Noelle turned around to see Aspen right behind her.

"You're not alone, Noelle! I'm right here with you!" Without meaning to, Aspen's mana radiated onto his fingertips. He was still not quite in control of his powers, merely standing behind her as a pillar of support, though inadvertently he transferred mana into her, rejuvenating Noelle.

This warm, familiar presence put her at ease; not only did his mana give her strength, but his words as well. *For all the suffering he caused to Aspen, to my parents, to all Mogoniwais everywhere!* Noelle took a step forward. *Even if I have to use every last drop of mana in my body!* One foot forward after the other. *Even if my body breaks!* General Ulger was slowly getting pushed back. *I'll win!*

"I'm finishing this!" she screamed out. Energy burst from her as her body sparkled like stars in a night sky. With one final spurt, Noelle pushed forward, reflecting the beam back towards the general. General Ulger screamed in agony as he became engulfed by his own attack.

"Is...is it over?" Noelle asked, panting heavily. She collapsed to the floor in exhaustion, her legs felt like jelly.

Aspen let her rest against him. He looked over to see a plume of smoke coming from General Ulger's body as he laid on the ground unconscious.

"Yeah, I think it's over now," Aspen smiled, holding onto her.

"Good." The fight had taken a lot out of her. After today, she promised herself she'd sleep for all of next week.

"Nobody moves or I blow his brains out!" a voice demanded.

Their faces went white upon hearing that voice. It was a voice that was again, all too familiar. Aspen turned around to see Gerard holding a gun towards Elliot's head.

"I...I'm sorry Aspen. I couldn't..." Elliot apologized. Guilt and disappointment filled his heart as he closed his eyes in shame. "I'm sorry, I was only in the way after all."

Gerard glanced over to see his unconscious father lying on the ground, which only fueled his anger. "You're gonna pay for this, Aspen!"

A bead of sweat rolled down Aspen's cheek. Noelle was in no way able to move right now, and there was no way he could reach Gerard before he fired his gun.

Niko slowly raised himself up upon hearing the commotion, "Gerard...calm down."

Gerard turned to him. "Shut your mouth, Niko, or else I'll shoot!" He aimed his gun towards them, his finger fidgeting against the trigger.

"Gerard...you don't have to do this," Aspen stuck out his arm, gesturing to him to calm down.

"I said don't move!" Gerard's eyes darted back to Aspen.

Bang!

He discharged his gun prematurely, barely missing Aspen's head. Aspen's blood froze on the spot as he felt the air of the bullet.

Gerard pointed the gun at him once more, while holding Elliot by the throat, "You three against the wall over there right now! If you move, I'll shoot him, and then I'll shoot you!"

Aspen noticed Gerard's hands trembling; he was scared. He helped Noelle up and went up against the wall along with Niko. It was better to comply for now, as who knew what Gerard might do in his current state of mind.

"You. Come with me," Gerard ordered Elliot, holding him by the back of his neck.

Elliot trembled, his mind and body remembering how it felt to be at the whim of another. The two headed over to the unconscious general.

"Father? Father, are you okay?" Gerard asked, waking him up. General Ulger groaned as he slowly gained consciousness. Gerard tucked the gun in his pants and extended his hand out to help his father up, but was immediately swatted away. As General Ulger turned to him, Gerard gasped in shock, though he held it in for the most part.

"I don't need your help getting up. Who do you think I am?" snapped his father. Gerard flinched and recoiled upon instinct. Ulger chose to show mercy, and instead hobbled towards the bomb, breathing harder and struggling to walk in a straight line. Aspen's jaw dropped at the sight of him—his face was disfigured to the point that he was unrecognizable. As if nothing else mattered in the room, General Ulger took his time to marvel at the time bomb. "You are just about to be complete, finally no more nuisances. The flames of humanity will be ignited."

"What should we do now?" Niko whispered to Aspen.

Aspen bit his lip, not a single answer popped up in his head. With Noelle too fatigued to do anything and Gerard keeping Elliot hostage, their hands were tied. The group couldn't even head towards General Ulger, not with his son standing right between them. They didn't have any options.

Gerard walked over to them. "Once a loser, always a loser, Aspen."

"What's your problem with me, Gerard? What did I ever do to you?" asked Aspen.

"What did you ever do to me?" repeated Gerard. "You jumped in front of me when some wild boar came towards me years ago. I didn't forget. You, who was weaker and smaller than me, thought you could protect me. As if I needed you to protect me! Do you know how embarrassing it is to have someone beneath you try to protect you?" He repeatedly stamped his feet to the ground, imagining it was Aspen's face. "Remember to know your place," Gerard said, pointing to himself. "I am the apex predator!"

It took Aspen a minute to remember until it clicked. "G-Gerard... that was years ago...when we were kids. All this time, you targeted me just because of that?" He hadn't recalled that day with the boar because it seemed so negligible at the time. *Gerard and his dad are indeed related, they both have a screw loose in their heads!*

"Just looking at your face pisses me off," Gerard shone a mischievous smile towards him, "but I won't have to see it for much longer." He set his backpack on the ground and pulled something out of it.

"Gerard, what are you going to do with that?" Niko asked, a bit of apprehension in his voice. They all stared at what he was waving in the air—explosives.

"I think you already know what's going to happen to the lot of you." Gerard smirked, "I could always let that bomb over there burn you alive. But honestly, I don't want to lose the chance of killing you myself."

"Gerard, don't you realize how bad this situation is? Your dad wants to essentially blow up the town and everything nearby. You can still help us stop this," Niko pleaded with him.

Gerard made a face as if he was entertaining the idea but immediately stuck his tongue out. "The only thing that will happen is that that bomb will clean out the weak. It's not like we need people like that anyway. People like you, Aspen. And besides, those that are strong, like me, will be fine. Plus, I'll become even stronger, and no one will ever look down on me again!"

Aspen shook his head, realizing that there was no point in reasoning with him. Perhaps it was due to the environment Gerard grew up in, or the way his father never showed him an ounce of affection; whatever it was, he was too far gone. *I need to do something, who knows what his dad is doing with that weapon right now. I'll have to strike at the first moment he's distracted.*

Elliot had remained silent and abiding throughout this whole ordeal, cursing at himself for his cowardice. He knew he had to do something, but his body would not listen; fear had forced him to stay put. "I was supposed to be helping them, it wasn't supposed to turn out this way. I was going to be useful for once, for my friend." He hung his head in shame, realizing that he hadn't changed at all this past year. Elliot had always strived to be brave like Aspen, but in the end, it all turned out the same. Looking over his shoulder, Gerard was laughing like a maniac, dismissing him completely. He was just like the people who bullied him in the past. Elliot clenched his fists and gritted his teeth, "Aspen wouldn't let this happen to himself. If there was ever a moment to be brave, it would be now."

Gerard continued on. "You know, despite how much I hate your guts and every fiber of your being, I guess I should thank you. Because you and that demon over there met each other, my dad's plan finally came into fruition. He told me about it a few months ago and said she was the missing piece that he needed. And here you are, hand delivering her to us." Gerard pulled out a match, "There is a new world order coming, too bad you won't be here to see it." He stuffed the gun into his clothes and struck the match, the little bright flame burned brightly in the cave. Just as Gerard was about to light the explosives, Elliot screamed, startling him. *Smack!* Elliot head-butted Gerard with the back of his head, causing him to drop everything.

"Why, you little–" Gerard reached for his gun when Elliot tackled him to the ground.

"I'm not going to let you bully my friends! Not ever again!" Elliot yelled as he wrestled to keep the gun away from him.

"Get the hell off me!" Gerard repeatedly punched him on the side of the head until Elliot let go. He pulled out his gun and sat atop of him. "For your sake, let's hope I miss."

"Stop! He has nothing to do with this!" Aspen took off in a sprint with Niko running alongside him.

Gerard aimed his gun, but Elliot fought back, pushing it away. As the struggle continued, Gerard quickly overpowered him, pushing the barrel to his head. Elliot shut his eyes, not wanting to see his final moments. Elliot made a half-hearted smile, accepting that his end was perhaps not so bad, he was brave for once—at least for a little bit—and after all, it was for his friend.

"What are you smiling at? Freak." Gerard licked his lips as his finger was about ready to pull the trigger.

Thwack!

Aspen kicked the gun out of his hand, the bullet ricocheting in the opposite direction.

Bang!

Niko then punched Gerard in the face with all his might, knocking him out.

Aspen put his hand on Elliot's shoulder,."You were brave ou–"

"The explosive!" Niko yelled. "The explosives are lit!" Everyone had been so preoccupied with Gerard that no one had realized that the fuse had been accidentally lit.

What do I do now? Aspen panicked. It was going to detonate and kill everyone here in a matter of seconds. He grabbed the explosives and sprinted in the opposite direction, hoping to throw it far away before it detonated. *I gotta–oof.* Aspen tripped on a rock, falling flat on the ground and dropping the dynamite a foot in front of him. Sparks nearly reached the end of the cord.

No! Aspen watched helplessly, desperately trying to claw for it.

Noelle jumped right in front of him with haste.

"Noelle…" Aspen muttered in confusion. "Have to r-run…"

Aspen's desperation rose, he began pumping his own mana onto Noelle. Slowly but surely, the color came back into her face with her heart now beating normally. Aspen breathed a huge sigh of relief.

Though his relief was cut short as a hand emerged from the dust and smoke, grabbing Noelle by the collar and dragging her away. Aspen dove through the smoke to chase after the culprit, only to be met with a punch to the face by General Ulger. He recoiled in pain as the general took off with her.

"If you want something done, you always have to do it yourself. Everyone is useless, every single one of them," General Ulger muttered under his breath. He brought Noelle back to the site of the bomb. "I just need to pull the trigger," he stared at Noelle, "and you're the trigger." General Ulger put another collar around her neck and gathered some of her blood onto his fingertips.

"The bomb has already collected enough power, all I need now is the blood of a demon to initiate the start sequence." He poured the droplets he gathered into the bomb, where it began to resonate with Noelle's blood. The buzzing intensified as the bomb shone brightly, mimicking that of a full moon in a clear night sky. General Ulger took a minute to marvel at its intensity, "I've done it..." He thrust his hands in the air. "I've done it! It's finally done!"

Noelle slowly regained consciousness, though her vision was still hazy and ears still rang like crazy. *What's going on? Who's dragging me?* She tried to push off her captor, but her arms would not budge. She tried to summon her mana to force him back, but it too had failed. She was completely at the mercy of the general.

"What the hell are you doing?" Aspen charged towards General Ulger, who had tuned out everything, too mesmerized by the bomb's light. Aspen tackled him to the ground and swung his body to face him. Aspen then struck the general twice in the face and shook his hand in pain. *Punching his face is like punching a rock.* It was at that moment where he channeled his mana towards his fists, until it burned brightly, just as Noelle had done in the past. He ignored the pain and went in for a third punch, this time the pain on his hand subsided. Unfortunately, however, the third punch was enough to snap General Ulger out of his dreamy state, and once he did, he kicked Aspen off him, causing Aspen to stumble to the ground.

General Ulger pointed to Noelle. "You can't hide behind her anymore." He touched his jaw and spat out blood. "So, is the rat going to run away and hide within the crevices of this cave again?"

Aspen glared at him. "No one's running away anymore." He was angry—angry that this man had put his friends in danger, angry that he had disrupted his peaceful day-to-day life, and most importantly, angry that this man had hurt Noelle. Aspen didn't want to hide now, he wanted the satisfaction of punching General Ulger in the face, multiple times. The mana that circulated about his body gave him a confidence boost, increasing his strength to levels he had never reached before in the past. "I'm going to make it so you'll never harm Noelle ever again! You'll never even breathe the same air as her!"

The general swung his arm, aiming to hit him in his blind spot. Aspen noticed just in time and dodged. With his wide swing, the general was left defenseless, and Aspen struck him in the gut with a magically-endowed punch, almost making Ulger falter. *He's getting slower, more predictable. He must be getting tired,* Aspen thought as he watched the general pant heavily. *He's been expending his mana this entire time, even General Ulger should have a limit.* Aspen felt determined. *I could win.* Uncharacteristically, it was the general this time recklessly charging towards Aspen, throwing haymakers in random directions.

Aspen backed away, dodging each of his punches in quick succession. He saw an opening between each swing, and punched the general in the chest, then another to the gut. A trail of light followed Aspen's fists in an afterglow, like a long ribbon flowing in the air. Blow for blow, he did not let up, striking with enough force to send a normal human flying. When the general tried to strike back, Aspen would side step and punch him in the face, putting all of his weight into it. Blood spurted out from General Ulger's charred nose as he stumbled backward. He touched it and saw the vivid red color of blood on his fingers, which only made him go into a frenzy and come at Aspen once more.

Aspen couldn't help but recollect that fateful day where he had almost died. Back then, he had shut his eyes and lay helplessly, waiting until the moment the wolves tore his body to shreds. This was when Noelle jumped in and saved his life. But not this time. This time, his feet were planted firmly on the ground. This time, he was going to be the one to save Noelle's life. He wasn't going anywhere. "Come at me!" Aspen shouted his invitation to General Ulger. *Whatever it is, I will not run. I'll take it head on.* The general pulled out a knife at the last minute, putting his all into one final attack. Aspen didn't falter; rather, he took a step forward and shifted his body. His hand became heavy, redirecting all his mana towards it for one final attack of his own. The two locked eyes with each other, though Aspen still held his fists tightly for the right moment. Ulger's knife began to slice through Aspen's shirt, almost slashing his bare skin. *POW!* But that was when Aspen uppercut him square in the jaw, sending General Ulger flying to the ground.

"This ends now." Spotting the knife the general dropped, Aspen picked it up with murderous intent and headed towards him.

"I give up, I give up," General Ulger pleaded as he curled up in a ball, groaning in pain. Aspen hesitated and stopped in his tracks. "I know when I've lost. I lost, okay? Have mercy."

Aspen raised his eyebrow. "And the bomb?"

"I'll stop the bomb, I swear I will," General Ulger promised.

Aspen glared at him. This man had caused Noelle so much pain. Gripping it tighter, the knife shook within his fist. *The world would be better off without someone like him around.* Aspen wanted to inflict more pain—the price for making Noelle suffer could only be paid upon the general's death. He stared at Ulger's neck, and imagined himself running the knife through it. Aspen bellowed, "Why should I let you go? After what you made Noelle go through, I should—"

"I'll leave you alone. I promise. I swear, you have my word," General Ulger pleaded once more. "I have a...a journal, I can tell the people the truth about the Mogoniwais. Yes! I'll tell them I was the one who had attacked the merchants that started the war. That they really did not strike first, it was us. And I did this all because I wanted their treasures, their powers. You and her...you want to live together peacefully, right? I can make that happen."

Aspen couldn't let go of his anger, part of him wanted to exact twice the pain that he delivered onto Noelle, but the other part of him just wanted to move on. Spreading the truth and providing sanctuary for Mogoniwais outweighed his vendetta. One day, the two of them would be able to coexist peacefully with everyone else. One day, Noelle wouldn't be judged for her appearance. And that day would start now. Aspen dropped the knife to the ground. "You better keep your end of the bargain. You'll make sure Noelle will be able to live life as normally as everyone else." Aspen still harbored a rage that could not be quelled but let it go for her sake. Despite who he really was on the inside, the general was still a powerful and respected man who everyone listened to within the town. If there was someone who could enforce peace, it would, unfortunately, be the man before him. "And you will leave her alone forever. I better not even see you breathe the same air as her," Aspen demanded as he turned his back on him to check on Noelle.

"What a fool! I can't believe the naivety of the youths these days! Never turn your back on the enemy!"

Aspen quickly turned his head to see the general sprinting towards him with a smile on his face. He tried to defend himself but his body couldn't react fast enough for the surprise attack. The general grabbed onto Aspen's wrists, effectively keeping him in place.

Aspen tried to wriggle free from his grasp, but the hold on him was too great. The general had more strength in him than he let on. Aspen stared at the general's disfigured, unrecognizable face. His charred and burned face only made his scowls even more terrifying.

"I should have killed you when I had the chance years ago," Ulger said. He pulled out the last of his pack of syringes from his pocket and plunged the tip of the needle into Aspen's neck. Aspen quickly swatted it away and tried to fight him off, but the numbing effects of the syringe had already taken effect.

Aspen panicked. His eyes now weighed heavier as the drowsiness in his body settled in. Aspen closed his eyes unintentionally, but then opened them immediately. It was much too dangerous to even shut his eyes for even a few seconds. *If I fall asleep, it's over. I have to fight it for everyone's sake!* Though the temptation to fall into a deep slumber grew with each passing second. His eyes flickered back and forth from complete darkness to the general's devilish grin.

"You can't fight the effects. Just give up and fall into darkness," General Ulger slowly wrapped each of his fingers around Aspen's neck. The volume of his laughter rose once knowing that he had won. "Before you lose consciousness forever, I just want you to know that you have lost. You will die a spineless loser. Once I'm done with you and the bomb finally detonates, and if by chance the demon girl lives through it all, I'm going to kill her." He leaned over to his ears and whispered, "And I'm going to enjoy it."

A jolt of energy coursed throughout Aspen's body. He promised Noelle that she wouldn't be alone anymore; he couldn't fail here. With the last ounce of strength he had, Aspen fought back. Mana coursed through his body, his veins glowed faintly, but enough for the naked eye to see. *We're supposed to move away together and live happily ever after, right? I made a promise to you, Noelle, that I'd make you happy.* He channeled his mana towards fighting off the effects of the drug and forced himself awake. The inner mechanism of his mana clicked in his head, mastering his inner emotions that powered his magical abilities.

Aspen grabbed hold of Ulger's arms.

"M-my mana...is slowly draining from...my body?" Ulger stammered, suddenly feeling weaker by the second.

Aspen squeezed onto his wrists, as he stole mana from Ulger's body. A glowing, pulsating hue flowed from the general into him, replenishing the strength he had lost.

I won't give up until it comes true. I'll see to it until the very end! A flow of mana reinvigorated his body; he felt it run through his arms, his chest, and down to his very toes until it cleansed his body of the effects of the drug. Aspen tilted his head back, braced for impact, and headbutted Ulger in the forehead with such force that the general stumbled to the ground. Aspen stood up. Immediately, he backed away to create more space between the two, only to lose balance and stumble to the ground as well, still slightly under the effects of whatever drug he had been injected with.

The general screamed in pain as his severely burned face had bled profusely. Fueled by anger and desperation, he picked up his knife once more and rushed towards Aspen one final time.

He's not going to stop is he? Aspen's breathing became slow. *No matter what I do, he won't stay down.* Aspen placed his palms to the ground to prop himself up until he felt something from behind him. He grabbed hold of it, only to realize that it was Gerard's discarded pistol. Ulger pointed the knife towards Aspen's heart, resembling a savage monster with a murderous gleam in his eyes.

"You're too far gone." Aspen closed his eyes and opened them again with a pistol in hand, pointing directly towards General Ulger.

BANG!

BANG!

He shot him twice in the chest, stopping the general in his tracks. Ulger dropped the knife and fell to the ground. He quickly cast aside the gun, already knowing that the fight was over. "T-there was no other way, ri—" mid sentence Aspen dropped to his knees and covered his mouth, forcing his vomit to not come out. Despite wanting to kill him earlier, the act of actually doing so made him sick to his stomach. His head spun in a frenzy as his mind kept screaming "murderer" over and over. Aspen had to do this because Richard Ulger would not stop, because he would not just simply stay down, despite telling himself this, the guilt weighed just the same. "Why didn't you just give up! Why! Why didn't you just give up!" Aspen screamed in agony "You gave me no other choice!" Whether killing him was the right call or not, his hands would forever be stained with Ulger's blood. His hands trembled from this feeling and would not stop; it was the first time he had killed a human being. He hobbled past the general and headed towards Noelle. There wasn't time to wallow in that now; they weren't in the clear just yet.

"It's too late," the general coughed out blood as he laid helplessly on the ground. "The bomb started its countdown to detonation from the very moment we had begun our fight."

Aspen stopped. "I'll find a way."

"The bomb has more than enough mana at this point. It will detonate soon. You won't be able to save her." The general's breathing became more labored.

"How do I save her?" Aspen yelled out.

General Ulger became glassy-eyed, seeing nothing but the gates of death's doors. "You can't. The bomb has already reached a point of no return. That demon has already used up every bit of mana, no one can stop it now...you ruined my dream, so I ruined yours. At least, in my defeat, she goes down with me..." He shut his eyes with a smile on his face, "I win."

"Tell me how to stop this! Tell me how to save her! Tell me how to save her now!" Aspen yelled at the top of his lungs. But it was already too late, as he was now demanding answers from a corpse. He screamed in rage.

Aspen hobbled over to his friend's unconscious bodies, frantically shaking them until they woke up. Time was running out.

"Wake up, there's no time to be passed out right now!" Aspen yelled at the two of them. Niko grumbled as he awoke.

"What's happening?" Niko asked, finally opening his eyes.

"The bomb is going to blow! And we need a plan! Now!" Aspen yelled so loud that Elliot had woken up as well.

Niko looked over to his side and saw the general's lifeless body on the ground. "What happened to the gener—"

"There's no time for that now. The bomb, Niko. The bomb," Aspen repeated.

"R-right...okay," Niko stood up with Aspen's help. The last thing he remembered was Gerard and the explosion.

Elliot steadily got to his feet. "Are we dead?" His entire body ached in pain, so much more painful than what his bullies had inflicted onto him over the years in school. He passed by Gerard's lifeless body—Gerard was the closest to his own explosives and took the full brunt of the blast—looking at his charred and messed-up body made him shiver. Elliot joined the two of them as they headed towards Noelle and the impending time bomb that was ready to detonate.

Aspen held Noelle's hand as he went to check up on her. Her breathing was faint but her heartbeat was still beating steadily. He let out a little sigh of relief.

"She's fine for now," Aspen confirmed to his friends. Though, now the three of them had to solve the biggest issue, which was stopping the bomb while saving Noelle.

"Did the general say anything about the bomb? Anything that we could use at all?" Niko asked.

Aspen repeated General Ulger's final words. "He said we're too late. The bomb will blow at any moment now. Nothing we do now can stop its detonation." Both Niko and Elliot mirrored each other's forlorn expression.

"Do you think he's lying?" Elliot asked the others.

"He could be," Niko said. "What about Noelle? Could she do something? Maybe she can—"

"Look at her, she's in no state to do anything." Noelle was battered and broken; she had gashes in several areas of her body that were oozing blood, swelling on her arms and legs, and was grimacing in pain. Aspen knew how selfless she was; somehow Noelle would figure out a way out of this, even if it meant sacrificing herself. "I can't expose her to any more harm than what she's already experienced."

"I mean, you're the idea guy, right? Do you have any plans?" Eliot asked, directing his question to Niko.

"I...I...I don't have anything." Niko desperately tried to come up with something, anything, but his mind was at a complete blank. With heavy disappointment, he turned to his friends, "I-I'm sorry guys."

"It's okay," Aspen reassured Niko. "Listen, you guys have to get out of here. I'll think of a way to save Noelle and the town. It'll be alright."

"No, we're not going to leave you here alone!" Elliot snapped at Aspen. "You're...you're the first friend I've ever had. There's no way I can leave you."

"I promised that I would help you save Noelle," Niko said. "I was wrong about her! About you guys! You guys...you guys deserve a happily ever after, too." Even he recognized now that Noelle had gone through so much in her life, that she was owed some sort of happiness after suffering for so long. She was the one who most deserved it. "I'm not leaving here without her."

"Thanks, everyone." Aspen looked at Niko and Elliot, "It's not every day you have someone willing to go the distance for you. And I have two of them. You're the best of friends a guy could ever have."

"Of course," Niko said. "We'll think of something, we always do."

Aspen stared at the bomb and stuck out his hand to feel the air around it. The mana from his fingertips materialized to a visible hue of blue which had been absorbed by the bomb as quickly as it appeared, stealing it from his body. As he snatched his hand away from it, the light from his mana vanished as well. His heart pounded fast—faster than it had ever been before as he came to realization. *It's the only way, isn't it?* Aspen quickly glanced at Noelle, and that alone was enough to solidify his resolve, shattering his mask of despair. His heart was going to be broken into a thousand pieces one way or the other, at least here, he was in control of how.

"I think I know how to save everyone. I can save Noelle."

CHAPTER

TWENTY

"Are you sure that whatever you got planned is going to work out?" asked Niko.

"Not really, but it's a hunch," Aspen said. *This plan is going to work. It has to work.* He ripped the collar off of Noelle's neck. The bomb whizzed ferociously like an angry swarm of bees. And then, without hesitation, Aspen placed his bare hands one by one onto the bomb.

"What are you doing?" Elliot yelled.

"Are you crazy?! You're going to burn yourself!" Niko screamed. He was about to yank Aspen away from it until he realized that his hands were perfectly fine.

"It's okay, trust me on this," Aspen said. "Do you trust me?"

Niko and Elliot looked at him, realizing that Aspen was clearly dead set on going forward with whatever he had planned. The two nodded to each other; for now, all they could do is put their faith in him.

"I do," Elliot confirmed as his heart beat with apprehension.

"Okay, we'll trust you," Niko said. His arms trembled and shook with anxiety, all their lives depended on Aspen. "Please, please work.

It's all I'll ever ask in life, just let us all make it out of here in one piece," Niko prayed aloud. He held his breath and shut his eyes, scared of what would come next.

Aspen closed his eyes and focused. *If this thing can siphon the mana off of Noelle, maybe just maybe...I can do the opposite.* It felt just like Noelle's. They both had the same mana running through their veins, so they were able to give and take mana from each other, which meant he could do the same with the bomb. It was a gamble, but Aspen banked his hopes on that connection. The veins in his body glowed and flickered as he siphoned off the mana like a battery and absorbed it into his own. "Come on!" he yelled, his body now burning all over, but that didn't stop him. The whizzing sound of the bomb slowly lulled and Aspen pulled his hands away, now out of breath.

"It worked! You did it!" cheered Niko.

"No...It's..." Aspen huffed, "It's not enough." Soon enough, the whizzing returned; draining a small portion of the bomb's mana was not enough to quell it. "I'd only been able to take a portion of its mana."

"So, what can we do now?" Elliot asked.

He let out a disheartening chuckle. Aspen sat himself down so Noelle could sleep in his arms, and so that he could get a good look at her. "The first time I met Noelle, she saved my life by allowing me to siphon some of her mana. It brought me back from the dead and runs through my veins as we speak. Because this bomb absorbed her mana, I think I can do it. I'll drain the bomb, absorbing its mana into my own body. I can't drain it completely, but I think I can absorb just enough to reduce the blast radius and save everyone in town."

"W-what do you mean?" Niko asked with a looming sense of dread. "Then that means...that..."

"It's okay, don't worry about me," Aspen weakly smiled. "Just take Noelle and run. You three need to leave. It's the only option we have. Go on."

"Aspen, we...we can't leave you here alone, I won't let you!" Niko shouted, kneeling down before his friend. He couldn't accept it. "There must be some way out of this, there has to be!" Niko had known him for the majority of their childhood. He refused to accept it. "W-we still have time." They had played together, they had fought with each other, and they had laughed together. They were supposed to have a friendship that withstood the test of time. "Damn it." It wasn't supposed to end like this, not this soon.

Elliot froze in place as reality settled in. Aspen was his first friend —actually, his only friend—and now he was going to lose him. He punched the ground with vexation until his knuckles colored bright red. "I couldn't even...I..." All Elliot wanted was to help his friend the one time he needed him the most, but in the end, he failed.

The bomb whirled and buzzed louder than before, almost deafening everyone. It was nearly time. Aspen turned to Elliot. "Thank you for being my friend back at school. Days were a lot more fun with a friend, right?" He let out a short chuckle. "When I'm gone, make sure you stick up for yourself. Don't be afraid. You're one of the bravest people that I know—today proved that. Always remember... you're a friend any person would be lucky to have."

Elliot started choking up, and he couldn't control the tears any longer. They rolled down his face, like rain on a stormy night. He swallowed Aspen's departing message to him, tasting so bittersweet that Elliot could hardly form his own words from his mouth. "You changed my life, I'm glad I got to meet you."

Aspen closed his eyes and then turned to Niko. "Niko, thank you for being my friend after all these years..."

"Stop talking as if it's the last time you're going to see us! I can still think of a—" Aspen gently placed his hand on his shoulder that silenced his dear friend.

Aspen continued on. "No matter what, you always had my best interest at heart. From sticking by my side when my mom passed and when Gerard bullied me, you stuck by me. Through thick and thin, you've always been there for me. I only wish I could have returned the favor. Thank you."

Niko wiped the tears on the sleeve of his shirt. "You returned it, Aspen. Damn it, it's not even up for debate." Tears flowed down his face like raging waters through a destroyed dam. "I w-was the lucky one. I—"

Before Niko could say another word, the walls of the cave began to rumble with such a tremor that it was difficult to keep balance. Mana from the bomb shot out and ricocheted off the walls, causing them to cave in. Noelle slowly regained consciousness, awakening from the thunderous noise.

Noelle wearily opened her eyes, though her vision was still fuzzy. She tried lifting up her arm but had no energy whatsoever to do so. *What's going on? Where am I?* As her vision became a little bit clearer, she surveyed her surroundings. *That's right, we're in a cave, there was an explosive...and I tried to shield it from everyone. Did it work?* Noelle looked around and spotted Niko and another boy their age. And then she looked up and managed to form a weak smile— Aspen was right there, holding her in his arms. *If this is a dream, please don't let me wake up just yet, let me just lay here for just a while.* Noelle couldn't understand the conversation as tears ran down their faces, their mouths were moving but she couldn't hear a thing. Her ears were still ringing. Before she could ask any questions, she suddenly found herself being taken away from Aspen's warm embrace and into Niko's arms. *Where are you taking me?* Noelle desperately tried to reach out towards him. *I want to stay here...with... with...*

And finally, Aspen turned to her, happy that she had finally opened her eyes and that he was able to give her one last departing message. "Noelle, I don't even know how to begin. We've been through so much, haven't we?" He wiped off a speck of dirt on her cheek. "Before I met you, I was scared, insecure and alone, but that all changed. Day by day, I became a little more daring, a little more brave. I found my courage. And it was you. It was always you."

The cave walls were crumbling, shaking so tumultuously that their bodies would not stay still, but she didn't care. *What are you saying, Aspen? I can't hear you.* Noelle hopelessly tried to listen to his words, but the ringing in her ears didn't allow her to hear them.

Aspen smiled at her, "Everyday was so much fun whenever I was with you, some days I could hardly sleep because I was too excited to see you again. You made the bleak skies bluer, the sun feel warmer, and made me wish that time stood still so that I could be with you always." He ran his fingers through her beautiful silky white hair for the last time. His chest began to gleam brighter, illuminating the area around them. Aspen continued on, "Thank you for saving my life that day. Thank you for making me stew. Thank you for going to the festival with me. Thank you for every little thing you do. I feel like I could say thank you to you a hundred—no, a million times over —and it wouldn't be enough."

Within the muffled sounds, she could already feel it. The world was trying to separate the two of them yet again. Noelle mustered enough strength to reach out to him. *I want to stay with you. It was always just the two of us, even if the world is against us, we can take it head on. I don't care about anything else. I just want you.*

Aspen grabbed her hand and gently pressed it against his cheek. "Please don't cry when I'm gone, you have new friends who will watch over you now." The light in his heart was dazzling, a manifes- tation of how much he loved Noelle. He gently pulled her head close and kissed her on the lips. Though it was only for a few seconds, that kiss gave them visions of the future. A future of struggle, a future where they eventually find their way, a future where they had kids and even grandkids, a future of them growing old with each other until the end of time.

A future...

A future that was now nothing but a beautiful, idyllic dream—as it no longer existed.

With their foreheads still pressed onto each other, he whispered. "If you ever feel alone, look up to the stars, because that's where I'll be watching over you. I love you, I'll always love you...from then...to now...until all of eternity. Forever and always. I'm sorry, Noelle, but

I'll have to leave now. Maybe..." Tears trickled down his cheek as he tenderly pushed her away from him. "Maybe it's better if you don't wait for me anymore, okay?"

In that one moment, the ringing in her ears had ceased. She could hear him clearly as if the world was lulled just so that she could hear his voice one last time. She could feel the light in his heart start to dim, her connection to him slowly severing. Noelle tried to escape out of Niko's grasp, but couldn't muster enough strength to do so. *Aspen's crying, he needs me! Let go of me! I have to stay here with Aspen, I don't want to leave him alone.* She cursed her weakened state, and pleaded to the world to just let her stay with him.

The cave roof was collapsing in on itself—if they were going to leave, it would have to be now. Aspen looked Niko in the eyes, mouthing the words to leave. Niko bit his lip; he knew what he had to do. He swallowed the regret dwelling inside him and resolved his faltering heart, looking now towards the exit. He dragged Elliot's arm up, signaling for him to follow.

Noelle's throat tightened as she gasped for air, bursting into more and more tears as the distance between her and Aspen became greater. She became frantic, doing whatever it took to reach his side once more, but Niko held onto her tightly. "I can't leave! Aspen's still back there!" She screamed, "He's going to be alone! I can't leave him alone!" Niko gritted his teeth to hold back the tears; her words pained him with a wound so great it would probably never heal. He continued forward, closing his heart once and for all so that he wouldn't go back for his friend. Whereas Noelle's heart broke into a million irreparable pieces as Aspen disappeared from her view, his fleeting smile was replaced with nothing but darkness.

ASPEN CLOSED his eyes as he watched Noelle disappear from sight, the pain in his chest began to hurt far more than any other part of his body. Rocks from the ceiling tumbled to the ground, closing off the exit. He gazed at the bomb, whose light continued to brighten even the deepest part of the cave. "How could something so beautiful be so unsightly at the same time?" The bomb expanded like a balloon getting ready to burst. Once more he placed his hands on the bomb, draining it of its mana. His body began flickering in a blue glow as he tried to contain the blast radius. "I hope they were able to get far away from this place by now."

Aspen took a deep breath and exhaled, staring into oblivion, waiting until the gates of death finally opened up for him. Aside from Gerard and General Ulger's lifeless bodies in this cave, he was alone now. "It's for the best, it's the only way to save her."

His body began to burn up as if he was sunbathing on the surface of the sun, but that didn't stop him. Everyone's lives were on his shoulders, and the thoughts of his friends and family allowed him to persevere through the excruciating pain. Aspen grunted, talking to himself although he was alone. Doing so gave him comfort and also kept his mind off of what's to come. "I'm sorry, Dad. I couldn't keep my promise to you in the end after all. Please keep living on for my sake." He and his father had finally started to get along with each other after all these years, only to have it be short-lived. "I'm glad I was born as your son." In his final moments, Aspen regretted that he didn't make a better attempt to open up to his father a lot sooner, perhaps he would have understood back then after all. "And thank you for being my dad."

"Willey...I wish I could have eaten your freshly baked cookies one last time," he muttered. The aroma of melted chocolatey goodness filled his mind the more he thought about it. "Thanks again for helping me keep Noelle safe. For that, I can't thank you enough."

"We had a lot of good times, didn't we, Niko?" Aspen chuckled a bit as he reminisced about all the trouble the two of them got involved in growing up. "Through thick and thin, you were there for me. For the good times, and the bad, I knew I could always count on you for help. You saved me more times than you probably realized. Thank you for being my best friend."

And then, he started thinking about Elliot. "You always saw me as this brave and fearless guy. You don't know how much that meant to me. It made me feel like I changed after all. I'm glad we became friends at school. I'm going to regret that our friendship didn't last as long as I had hoped. Thank you for believing in me."

"And Noelle...Noelle, I..." Aspen muttered. He had thought about everyone and saved her for last. There was so much to be said, with so little time. The bomb was going to blow at any minute, but he wanted Noelle to be the last thing on his mind before his demise. "Before you stormed into my life, I hated the woods so much. But now, it has become my home away from home. I'm going to miss us talking for hours on end, eating together until we no longer could, and watching the stars every night. I'm going to miss your white hair that glistens under the starlight. I'll miss the way you perk up when you eat chocolate. I'll miss the way you call my name out and—" Aspen went silent. He didn't want to sink completely into sadness in his final moments.

The mana he absorbed was burning him from the inside, but Aspen refused to stop, draining every last drop of the bomb his body could contain. He cleared his throat and continued on, "I won't be here much longer to watch over you. So, don't get into too much trouble. You can't eat too many sweets, it's bad for your health. Try to control your temper, you sometimes can get combative when things don't go your way. There are times where talking things out can lead to a better outcome. Also, be wary of who you meet—I won't be able to judge whether they are nice or not, not everyone's as nice as I am. Who knows, maybe you'll find someone who loves—" Aspen hesitated. He didn't even want to think of Noelle loving another person. Though it was a selfish thought, it was the one thing he couldn't readily accept right now. Aspen had held it in for as long as he could but now that everyone was gone and he was alone, a tear rolled down his cheek, and then another, and then many more until it broke into a stream.

"I wish I could've stayed with you longer!" Aspen cried out, the pain of his heart was too much to bear, hurting much more than being burned alive. "More than anything, I wanted to spend my entire life with you! I wanted to live with you! I wanted to protect you! Cook and eat with you like we had in those careless summers of when we were children and much, much more!" He swallowed his regret. "I wanted to...to grow old with you..." Aspen sniffled, "and continue loving you until the end of time..."

"I'm sorry I couldn't keep our promise," Aspen apologized. He made a promise that he'd be there for her so that she would forget the definition of loneliness. Despite how strong and brave she was, Noelle was always scared to be alone. "I'm sorry I couldn't be with you to the very end," Aspen apologized once more. Despite all that regret, the one regret that he didn't hold was coming here to save Noelle. If all circumstances were the same, and he had to choose to exchange his life for hers, he'd do it again in a heartbeat.

"I'm sorry..." Aspen mumbled. The red thread that connected him to Noelle was severed, no longer could he feel her presence. The space around him was tightly enclosed now, making it harder for Aspen to breathe. He closed his eyes and thought of Noelle. In his final moments, he wanted her to be the last thing that he saw. Aspen envisioned her smile and etched that picture of her into his heart and soul, "...and thank you."

"I hope you will find happiness one day," he said, his breathing heavy. "To the stars and back..." His body became a permanent glowing hue of blue, no longer could his body hold any more mana. "I will love you...forever and always, my dear...my dearest...sweet..." Aspen softly mumbled with a smile on his face, "Noelle."

The bomb exploded into thousands of pieces, engulfing Aspen and everything inside its vicinity with a brilliant bright white light.

Leaving not a trace of the cave in sight.

CHAPTER
TWENTY-ONE

Noelle steadily opened her eyes as she woke up, feeling the soft ground beneath her. *Where am I?* She was lying on a bed. Noelle sat upright, only to feel a pain in her chest. Clutching onto it, she still writhed in pain. *Sniff Sniff.* With her nose tilted up, a sweet scent waltzed into the room. *Sniff Sniff.* The creamy rich aroma of sugar and cocoa filled the air, which immediately invigorated her, being a smell she was quite familiar with. Noelle knew that she was back at Willey's home. Out the window, it appeared to be nearly dusk. She sat there motionless, blinking slowly until it dawned on her.

"Aspen!" Noelle shouted, immediately jumping out of bed. She fell to the ground, not realizing how much pain her body was in. Her fall had made a loud thud that could be heard from across the hall.

Willey rushed into the room immediately, "You're finally awake, Noelle!" He was smiling through his apprehensiveness, as if trying to decide how to react.

Niko poked his head into the room. "We were getting worried about you. You were out. We eventually had to have a doctor come check up on you, but he had said that you were fine."

Elliot joined in as well, not wanting to be left out. "Hi, Noelle, well, you probably don't know me, do you?"

"How...how long was I out?" Noelle asked, rubbing her head.

"You've been out for nearly three days now. We were starting to get worried that you would never wake up," Niko answered.

"But now that you're awake, it's such a relief off everyone's shoulders. Everyone here was all worried, you know?" Willey added.

"I was asleep for three days!" Noelle's jaw dropped. "The general?" she yelled out looking around the room. "Where is he?" Her memory was still hazy, having only a short recollection of the events that proceeded after she shielded everyone from Gerard's dynamite.

Niko gestured to her to calm down. "It's okay. You won't ever have to worry about him. Not ever again. You're safe...we're all safe now."

Noelle felt a sudden weight lifted off her shoulders upon hearing his words. The threat that stood between her and Aspen was finally gone. *We're all safe,* Noelle's thoughts echoed, *so that means surely...* She breathed a sigh of relief, becoming happy for the first time in a while.

"So, where's Aspen? Is he back at his house? Don't tell me he's still asleep? I swear he always has a hard time getting up," Noelle asked. She scanned the room but didn't spot him anywhere. "Where...where is he?" repeating once more, this time with a hint of anxiousness in the tone of her voice. Noelle looked at everyone, their heads hanging low, trying to avoid eye contact with her. Her heart skipped a beat. "I-is...is he okay?"

The three of them looked at each other, not sure how to tell her the news. Willey put his hand on her shoulder, "I'm very sorry, Noe—"

"No...this can't be true. It's...not true," Noelle refused to believe it. Her heart plummeted like a stone down a never-ending chasm. She had known that Aspen had stayed behind and sacrificed himself, but deep down still held on to hope that he would still be fine. "I...I j-just saw him the other day. We were arguing with each other but it wasn't like I was going to stay mad at him forever." The image of Aspen weakly smiling at her as Niko carried her out of the cave now lingered in her mind. "I didn't even get to apologize..."

"I...I don't know how to tell you this," Niko lamented, treading carefully on his next few words. "Aspen stayed behind, he...he stayed behind to save the entire town. He's the reason we're alive today. He saved all our lives."

"No...No...No," Noelle covered her ears and shook her head, refusing to listen. "No, no, no, no, no, it can't be true." Tears streamed down her cheeks. "He can't be...he..." She turned to look at each and every person in the room. "W-we were supposed to move away together...s-somewhere away from here." Noelle had a hard time breathing, as if someone had stolen all the oxygen from her lungs. "We w-were going to l-live together...w-we were..." Noelle choked on her words. She couldn't see anyone at this point. Her vision was blurry from the tears in her eyes that rained down her face.

Willey pulled Noelle closer to him and hugged her, and teared up alongside her. "I know Noelle, I know. I'm so sorry. I'm so, so sorry."

Noelle buried her face on Willey's shoulder, drenching his sleeve with enough tears to fill a lake. "I...I promised him. I...p-promised him that I w-would make him stew again." The pain dug deep into her heart, it was only once where she felt a pain as pernicious as this. The last time she felt this was when she lost her family. "H-he promised that he'd come back, it's not fair, it's not fair..."

Niko and Elliot broke down as well, no longer could they keep up their defenses. "I'm sorry, Noelle, it's all my fault. I wasn't there when he needed me, I failed him," Niko sobbed. "If it wasn't for me, he'd still be alive today."

"It's my fault, too. I was just in the way. If I wasn't there, maybe things would have been different," Elliot cried out, still blaming himself for being caught. "If I had been more careful, maybe things would have turned out differently."

"No, you kids did nothing wrong, nothing wrong at all," Willey reassured them. "I encouraged you two to go find him. All the blame..." he took a big sigh, "all the blame should fall on me." More than anything, Willey wished he could retract what he had done. Had he not allowed Noelle to look for Aspen, she would have been safe and hidden from the general, and Aspen would still be alive.

Noelle cried and cried, and cried some more. Crying had become an involuntary function, just as how a lung breathes or a heart beats, her tears continued to fall without meaning to. Time passed and thirty minutes turned to an hour and one hour turned to five. Time didn't matter anymore. For when Noelle found out that Aspen died, her world stood still. He had been the sun that kept her world spinning, but now that he was gone, all that was left was a desolate, cold wasteland.

Eventually, she cried herself to sleep.

NOELLE HAD AWOKEN ONCE MORE. A day had passed, or perhaps it had already reached a second. Her face was puffy and eyes red and dry from all the crying. Noelle gently stepped out of bed, her strength returning. In the corner of the bedroom were Niko and Elliot loosely wrapped in a blanket, sleeping on the ground. She tiptoed over to them without making a single noise, and rewrapped them with the blanket.

She stepped out of the room and opened the window to feel the cold air, wanting a distraction to feel something else for a change, anything else would do at this point. Noelle tried one last time to search for his mana, hoping he was still out there, but found nothing. "He's really gone, isn't he?"

"Noelle, how...how are you feeling?" Niko asked, now awake, with Elliot by his side.

Noelle turned around to look at him. "I...I feel like a part of me is gone, like it died along with Aspen. I don't know how to go on anymore." She slowly sank to the ground and buried her head in her knees. "It's my fault that he's gone, he's dead because of me. If I would have stayed away from him, he—"

"That's not true at all, Noelle. Not in the slightest," Niko interrupted. He sat on the floor in front of her. "Back at the cave, he told you about how much you meant to him."

Noelle bobbed her head up. "He did?"

Niko shined a slight smile. "Yeah...he did. He mentioned how he treasured every single minute with you. Staying away from him would probably have hurt him a lot. You meant the world to him, you know?"

Elliot sat on the ground as well. "Back at school, he always talked about a girl he was crazy about. You. In fact, I couldn't get him to be quiet. If he was able to, he would have talked for hours about how great you are."

"So, don't ever blame yourself for what happened. You didn't do a single thing wrong. I already know that Aspen wouldn't want you to wallow in depression forever, he'd want you to look forward. He'd want you to raise your head high and be happy," Niko said.

"What if I don't know how to be happy anymore?" Noelle asked.

"We're still here," Niko said, Elliot nodding in affirmation. "We can grieve together, we can remember Aspen together, we'll keep his memory alive. No matter what, Elliot, Willey, and I will be there to help you along the way, until one day you can find happiness once again."

Noelle wiped the tears that were welling up in her eyes and hugged the two of them, "Thank you."

"That's what friends are for," reminded Niko as they hugged her back.

Willey walked into the living room from downstairs, surprised that everyone was already awake. He turned to Noelle, "You should keep your strength up, let me make us some breakfast."

Noelle's stomach grumbled, realizing that she hadn't eaten in days. "I..." she hesitated. The lingering guilt gnawed at her, she didn't want to eat. She just wanted to curl up in a ball forever. But to ease the worry of her friends, Noelle hesitantly nodded her head.

"Great, I'll start cooking," Willey hopped to the kitchen.

"I'll help out," Elliot volunteered, joining Willey while Niko stayed behind to keep Noelle company.

Within an hour, the whole table was bountiful with eggs, bread, muffins, and bacon. Everyone sat at the table and started eating. Noelle scooped up a good portion of eggs and consumed them as if it was going to be her last meal. She couldn't feel the warmth of the eggs when it touched her tongue, or taste the sweet flavor of the muffins as it melted in her mouth, nor did the crispy texture of the bacon give her any delight. Bite after bite, Noelle tried to appreciate the effort Willey had taken to prepare this breakfast, but to her, it did not spark any sort of joy. *The food doesn't taste right, not when you're not here.*

Knock! Knock! A loud banging on the door downstairs could be heard by everyone at the table. Willey went down to go check. *Who could that be this early?* Noelle thought. Within a few minutes, he came back with an imposing figure behind him, someone she had never met before, which instantly put her on guard. *Who is this person? Am I in danger once again?*

"Sorry...to interrupt...you guys," the man said. His eyes grew wide once he locked eyes with Noelle. She slowly stood up from her chair, preparing for her escape if needed.

"I guess this is the first time you've met Noelle, right, Ben?" Willey asked.

"Yeah, it is," Ben replied. He walked over to Noelle and awkwardly extended his hand to her. "Pardon, I didn't mean to stare. N-nice to meet you."

Noelle looked at the man, and the more she stared, the more he seemed familiar, but couldn't figure out why. She shook his hand. "Nice to meet you as well. My name is Noelle. So...who exactly are you, if I may ask?"

"Oh, that's right, introductions, introductions are in order,"

Willey said. He turned to her, "Noelle, this is Aspen's father. It was him in fact that warned the entire town of General Ulger's weapon and his entire plan on that day it happened. Had it been another person, people probably would not pay any heed to it. But when the normally stern-faced, serious mayor frantically storms through the town warning about a weapon that will kill tens of thousands, people'll listen."

"S-sorry, I should have introduced myself earlier," Aspen's father apologized.

Noelle gasped as it finally dawned on her. She instantly kneeled before him, lowering her head with her forehead touching the ground. "I...I'm so-sorry.." Noelle apologized. *No amount of apologizing would ever be enough for forgiveness. Because of me...He's...*It was as if someone had forcibly ripped her heart out when she found out Aspen had died, she couldn't even imagine what his father was going through. "Aspen risked his life to save me...and...and in the end, he exchanged his own life to let me live." Noelle clutched her chest, holding her heart in place to prevent it from shattering again. "If you need someone to blame...if you need someone to direct your anger towards...it should be me. A-Aspen shouldn't have died. It should have been me instead of him."

Aspen's father didn't move as her words echoed in his ears. Without even realizing, a few of his tears snuck up on him and dropped to the ground. This was all too familiar to him. After quickly composing himself, he looked her straight in the eye. "Noelle, I don't ever want you to think like that again." He suddenly saw himself in Noelle. For many years, Aspen's father wished that he had been the one to die instead of his wife. He ended up closing himself off from everyone and lived each day with no purpose, awaiting the day that he would take his last breath. But now Ben had a new purpose— although his son was gone, he still had a chance to make one of Aspen's dreams come true. "He loved you, loved you so much that he went behind my back, and even argued back at me for the first time." Noelle looked guilty. "It's okay. He gets that from me. When it comes to the woman we love, we'll do anything to make her happy." She looked up and smiled a bit. "I can tell you loved him just as much, didn't you?"

"I loved him!" Noelle declared without hesitation. "I loved him... more than anyone in this whole world..."

Aspen's father chuckled a bit and then broke into a short laughter. Laughing at both her sudden outburst and how foolish his misguided anger towards the Mogoniwais were after all these years. And he had his son to thank. Though it was so late, he finally heard what his son was trying to tell him. Aspen's father marveled at Noelle, whose presence glistened and sparkled along with everyone else's. "How could I have treated dem—I mean Mogoniwais—like monsters? I'm sorry for being so foolish and..." He placed his hand on top of her head. "From the bottom of my heart, I want to thank you for loving my son."

This took Noelle by surprise. "I'm the one who's grateful to have met your son. If it wasn't for him, I would still be all alone. It was only because of him that I was able to meet these people here. People I can call friends."

Aspen's father nodded. "Well, the town will be having a memorial service for my son. It would mean a lot if you were to come along. I know that's what Aspen would have wanted."

Noelle pointed to herself. "Can someone like me show up?"

"Oh, that's right. You don't know yet, do you?" Elliot said.

"Know what?"

"Everyone knows what Aspen did," Elliot said. "He did it. He saved tens of thousands of lives that day. Most in town feel indebted to him and want to honor his wish. Aspen was the bravest amongst us all, he died a hero."

"He was the bravest of us all..." she repeated. "So, what was his wish?"

"Of giving you a place to call home."

At that, Noelle felt quite bittersweet.

Niko chimed in. "News of what happened also went widespread

throughout the country. With Aspen's father's influence, we helped uncover the story to the public. They found all sorts of evidence of Mogoniwai abuse from General Ulger's home. As a result, places have talked of enacting laws to further enforce the treaty with the Mogoniwais."

"Ben here worked day and night for the past three days, talking to other town mayors and high ranking senators, spreading the truth about the Mogoniwais and the war," Willey added.

Noelle covered her mouth. "I don't know what to say. Why did you go to great lengths for someone you've never met before?"

Aspen's father rubbed the back of his neck, avoiding contact with everyone. "It was my son's last wish. He wanted you to have a home, a place where you wouldn't be judged and could belong somewhere." He raised his head and looked her straight in the eyes. "I wasn't there for my son, and I failed as a father. I can't even apologize to him anymore. Right now, all I can do now is make it up to him by making his wish come true. And I'm going to do my damndest to give you the happy life I couldn't give to him."

"I don't know how I'll ever repay you."

"You don't owe me. You don't owe me a thing at all," he reassured her.

"Well, at least let me cook for you. Aspen told me my stew tastes amazing," Noelle compromised.

"Stew? Sure, I'd like that. It was both mine and my son's favorite, after all," Aspen's father sadly smiled. "So, about what I mentioned earlier, will you attend the memorial service? I understand if you still feel afraid to be out and about in public."

"I think everyone in town would love to have you there. The ill will people harbored is gone...well, for most of them, that is," Niko said.

"And plus, we'll be here. We can be with you every step of the way and make sure no one messes with you," Elliot promised.

"The choice is yours, Noelle," Willey said.

Noelle didn't have to think very hard to make a choice. "I'm going, whether the town wants me there or not. It's for Aspen," she announced without batting an eye.

Aspen's father smiled. "I'm glad to hear it, it will be held a few days from now." He stood up and started heading for the door. "Well, I better leave. I still have a lot to do now."

"What are you doing?" Noelle asked.

"I'm creating a new safe haven for Mogoniwais here in this town. From my blind hate, I initially wanted zones to separate us from them entirely. I changed that, because of you and my son. Right now, all I want is a place where they can be safe, a place where humans and Mogoniwais can finally coexist, a place that they can finally call home. Well, take care now. See you soon."

A place where humans and Mogoniwais coexist. Noelle smiled through the pain, as it was their shared dream that came into fruition too late.

Niko turned to Elliot. "Come on, we should head out as well. You promised that you'd help out with deliveries."

"Okay, okay," Elliot groaned. "See you soon, Noelle."

"I'll come visit again," Niko said, waving goodbye.

With Aspen's father going back to work, Elliot and Niko working on deliveries, and Willey downstairs at the shop, everyone in the room had left. Leaving Noelle all by herself.

Noelle silently waddled to her room and sat in front of a mirror that was placed on top of her desk, staring at her reflection. She tried to form a smile but could not find the muscles to form it. In the reflection was her, and only her, and that's how it will be for the rest of her life.

"W-why...why couldn't you let me go with you?" Noelle stammered.

Now that everyone was gone, her lips quivered. Now that she was alone, the tears rained down her cheeks. She watched her reflection cry out, revealing her true emotions. Noelle covered her face, not being able to bear looking at it anymore.

Don't cry, Noelle.

"Aspen?" Noelle immediately looked up, now seeing Aspen in the reflection of the mirror. Her mind began to play tricks on her, taunting her with her own memories.

"How can I not cry when you're not here anymore?"

Don't cry, Noelle. In the reflection, Aspen wrapped his arms around Noelle from behind.

She reached for his hand, but could feel nothing but her own skin. Her fingers wrapped into a fist, "What's the point of wrapping your arms around me if I can't feel your warmth?"

It's going to be okay, Noelle. Aspen's reflection gently smiled at her.

Noelle covered her face once more, not wanting to look at what she lost. Her body now shaking. "S-stop it."

It's going to be okay, Noelle.

"No, it's not."

It's going to be okay, Noelle.

"It will never be okay," now slightly raising her voice.

You'll find happiness, Noelle.

"Just leave me alone!" Noelle swatted the mirror across her room, hearing it shatter upon hitting the floor. "Oh no, Aspen, what have I done?"

She quickly picked up the pieces and put them back together on the floor. This time, his reflection did not return. It was only of herself, with tears still rolling down her face. "I-I didn't mean it...just come back one more time, Aspen."

It was still just a distorted image of her face through the fragmented mirror.

"Please."

No response.

Noelle curled up in bed, and pulled the blanket over herself. It had been a long day—a day that, despite the setting sun, didn't seem to have an end in sight.

"How am I supposed to find happiness?" Noelle closed her eyes in hopes that underneath the blanket of the moon and the stars, Aspen would be watching over her from up above.

TWENTY-TWO

I t had been a total of one week since the incident. For the first time ever, Noelle stepped out of the store front with Elliot and Niko by her side. In fact, it was the first time since then that she made herself be presentable.

A gust of wind blew through the group. She wrapped the white scarf that Aspen had given her around her neck. They were all dressed in black today. Noelle covered herself from head to toe, even wearing a large sun hat so that she didn't draw too much attention.

"What's in the box?" Noelle asked Niko. He had been clutching a medium-sized box with him this morning and had not said a word about it.

"Yeah, he wouldn't even let me take a peek at it," Elliot remarked.

Niko held onto it tighter. "It's...it's for Aspen's memorial service."

"Okay, so what's in it?" Noelle asked, even more intrigued.

"I...can't show you...not yet, at least," Niko replied, refusing any further questions on the matter.

"So, are you settling in well?" Elliot asked Noelle.

"Willey offered me a place to stay and a job. I'll be working at the bakery when I'm ready to. He even mentioned that I might be able to inherit it one day once he retires."

"That's awesome," Elliot said. Niko walked in the middle of the two, not uttering a single word. Noelle noticed that something was still on his mind, as did Elliot. He nudged him by the shoulder. "Are you sure you're okay, man? You're being strangely quiet."

"Y-yeah, I'll be fine...I'm fine, I swear," Niko reassured. They continued walking.

Noelle's body swayed from side to side as she walked through the town's streets, still nervous deep down that her sudden appearance would cause a commotion. Though whatever happened, she was going to go to the memorial service no matter what. No one cared more about Aspen than her, so she must attend. As the group walked towards the service, Noelle could see a few onlookers stop and stare at her. But that was all that it amounted to—staring. Staring was something she could handle.

Noelle people-watched around the crowded road. Mostly everyone minded their own business, not caring that a demon was walking among them. *Maybe people don't mind after all.* They eventually ran into Aspen's father who was on his way to the service as well.

"You three are a bit early," Ben said.

"Yeah, we all decided to head over in the morning to avoid the —" Elliot took a brief pause, marveling at the figures standing behind Ben. "And who are these people?" Two little white-haired children popped out their heads, with their mother holding each of their shoulders so that they did not wander off. The three seemed timid and scared, which was not surprising as they were among humans in an unknown territory.

"Mogoniwais, similar to Noelle, who have lost their homes and nowhere to go," Ben answered. "I found them while I was coming back from a conference in Cresnough."

Noelle covered her mouth as she shyly walked a few steps

towards them. She stared at their glistening white hair, stared at their cherry-red faces, stared at their pointed ears that wiggled with curiosity. Noelle stopped herself from coming any closer. Despite belonging to the same race, she had no clue how to react to them as it had been nearly a decade since last seeing her kind. Noelle extended her hand, wanting to reach out to them. *My people. Others like me, I can't...I can't believe it.* She quickly pulled it back, fidgeting with her hands and retreated back to her friends as panic settled in. *What if I can't speak the language well enough? How do I even interact with another Mogoniwai? What if they think I abandoned my people in favor of the humans? What am I supposed to do?*

"Pri...Pri'cess...No...elle?'' one of the children asked. He looked at his brother, and for the first time since coming here, formed the largest grin. The two young brothers rushed over to Noelle, escaping from their mother's grasp and latched onto her, knocking the large sun hat off her head.

"Pri'cess Noelle! Pri'cess Noelle!" the kids cheered once more.

Had this been a wild animal, she would have swatted or clawed it away from her. But Noelle raised her hands before her survival instincts kicked in, not sure of what to do at the moment. The boys ignored any formalities and jumped around her as if she was family. "Princess?"

"A nickname of yours that has spread to Mogoniwais and humans alike," the mother answered in their native tongue. "My name is Alabasta. And these are my sons, Ale and Aba."

"Asa Iee mo trysa de ko?" Ale asked.

"Is it true that I beat the bad guy?" Noelle mumbled before switching to Mogoniwai speak. She ruffled their hair, "If you mean Ulger, then yes, I did beat him. No one has to worry about him again."

"S-safe? Aba mo lo safe?" Aba, the younger of the two asked.

"What do you think they are saying?" Elliot asked.

"Shush, don't ruin the moment, man," Niko scolded and pulled him aside.

Instinctively, she brought the two children close to her and hugged them so tight their bodies could no longer tremble. Looking at them, Noelle saw a bit of her past self at that moment. The self that did not have a home, the self that felt unease and in danger all the time—something that she did not want others of her kind to experience. She failed in stopping Ulger from killing those she held dearly. But at least these children will have a mother. At long last, Mogoniwais can be with their loved ones without worry of being torn apart. "Of course you are. You're safe now."

"Sorry about my kids," the mother apologized on their behalf, still speaking in their language. "They were just so excited to meet you ever since your story became widely known to everyone. How you lived alone all these years, and found love with a human, and defeated the man who tormented our people."

"Everyone knows?" Noelle wondered.

"Yes. In fact, they found it inspiring," Alabasta continued in Mogoniwai speak. "It was because of you that we came out of hiding and found the courage to accept this man's gesture of having this town become our home. It was all because of you, did our people realize it."

"Realize what?"

"Realize that humans and Mogoniwais can once again coexist after all."

Ben scooped up both boys and put them atop each of his shoulders, "Thank you again for putting your trust in us."

"I should be the one thanking you for giving us a home again," Alabasta said, switching back to human language.

"Wait a minute, you can speak our language?" Niko exclaimed in disbelief.

Alabasta put both arms on her hips, "Of course. I've been living here for decades now. Sooner or later, it was inevitable for me to pick it up. My boys on the other hand...they need some work."

"Can...show...us around?" Ale made his best attempt to speak the language.

Noelle grabbed their pinky fingers with her own, "I'll show you around. I promise. I will show you all the tasty things this town has, starting with Willey's candy shop of course."

Sitting on the top of Ben's right shoulder was Aba, "Here...is good? No sad?"

"For as long as I'm here, I promise you'll never be sad. It'll be filled with smiles and laughter everyday," she spoke, now comfortable answering in her mother tongue. *It wasn't all for naught, Aspen.* As she said those words, Noelle was reminded of her happiest days. Glimpses of Aspen and his smile, his laugh, and his hand firmly holding onto hers played back from her memories.

"Excuse me, Mayor Chase, I'm back. I can take them from here," Arthur interrupted.

"Oh, thank you." Ben turned towards Alabasta, "Arthur here is one of my trusted office assistants. He'll show you to your temporary lodgings and keep company until I get back from the funeral."

Alabasta made a bow towards him, "Thank you for everything you have done for my family. And...I'm sorry about what happened to your son. May he be reincarnated into a beautiful soul."

"I appreciate the thoughtful words," Ben thanked her.

She then turned towards Noelle and gave her a hug, "I'm sorry for you as well, child. I wish I could have met the man that gave us Mogoniwais a home here."

Noelle reciprocated, "I wish you all could have met him, too." Arthur led the Mogoniwai family in the opposite direction, leaving Noelle and the rest of the group.

Sniff Sniff. Elliot wiped a few tears, "That was beautiful." He looked at everyone, "What? Am I the only one who thought that?"

Niko put his free arm around his shoulders, "It was."

"Let's get going to the burial grounds," Elliot suggested, "before I cry on this street even more."

"Well, since we're all headed the same direction, why don't we go there together?" Ben suggested. Though not too long on their way to the service, an older lady called out to him, something the people in town would have hesitated to do had it been the man of a few weeks ago. Lately, Mayor Ben Chase had not worn the sour scowl he used to wear for many years, and he even began cracking a smile and a laugh, making him more approachable once again.

"Ben, dear, could you help me hang this sign here in the shop real quick? My back has been acting up in the morning," she asked.

"Sure thing, Maggie. I have a little bit of time." He turned to Noelle and everyone else. "Sorry, you guys will have to go on first," and headed inside the shop.

And so, they brushed through the crowd with eyes piercing at them and teeth nearly at their necks the farther they went. Her outfit wasn't enough to hide her burning red skin. A hand pierced through from deep within the crowd and grabbed onto Noelle's wrist, startling her. She turned around and locked eyes to an old man, who relentlessly shouted obscenities.

"Go back to where you came from, demon! We don't appreciate your kind around here!" the old man yelled at the top of his lungs. It was Jeremy. "You don't belong here!" The huge scene attracted the attention of people nearby.

At that moment, Noelle felt like retreating, she could feel the eyes of the crowd of people on her now. *I guess it was stupid to think everyone would change their minds about me. If only Mogoniwais could turn themselves invisible.*

"She deserves to be here just as much as you do!" Elliot yelled.

"Be quiet, kid, you don't even know how dangerous they are! You ever fight in a war with them. If not, then sit the hell down!" Jeremy yelled back.

"Obviously you don't know crap at all!" Niko jumped in. Soon enough the crowds of people intervened, the streets filled with rage as they vocalized their opinions. The crowds were split between the older generation, who still harbored hatred towards the Mogoniwais, and the younger generation, who seemed to be defending Noelle.

The more the arguing persisted, the angrier she became. *This isn't right,* Noelle thought. *This day was meant to mourn for Aspen. It isn't time to be fighting among each other. I'm not going to let them make this day about their senseless hatred.* Noelle ran out of patience as she faced the crowd behind her. "Enough! You can insult me or talk about how terrible I am on a different day! Not today, not now of all days! This day is to mourn for Aspen!"

"Why are you even here! You don't belong here! You monster!" yelled Jeremy.

Elliot was going to speak out but she stopped him. "I'm here for Aspen," Noelle proclaimed. "Do I not get the right to mourn for him? He was the man who saved my life, in more ways than one. When I was a kid, my parents were killed, and I grew up alone in the woods, fighting every day to survive. It wasn't until I met Aspen that I finally felt like I wasn't going to be alone in this cold world. I was content if he was with me, I was finally happy. I loved him. I loved him with all my heart! Am I not allowed to feel sorrow or compassion because of my red skin or white hair? Am I not allowed to mourn for him like everyone else? Answer me that!" The crowd grew silent immediately.

"What is going on here?" Aspen's father asked as he rushed back outside after hearing the commotion. Though, he could already grasp the situation once he saw Noelle confronting the crowd. He marched forward and stood up front so all could see. "Let me say this one more time—the xenophobic behavior of this town ends now! The people had been misled to believe that Mogoniwais were the monsters. They are not monsters any more than we are. What right do we humans have to call Mogoniwais monsters when we launch an attack against them? We killed children and mothers and are now ostracizing this girl because of our misguided fear. My son tried to tell me this but I was ignorant. And that ignorance is the reason why I have to bury him today! Please let us end this senseless violence. Today, we strive to be better—we must be better. And if anyone has any objections to that, say it now to my face."

A little girl navigated her way through the crowd and stood right in front of Noelle. Though she seemed familiar, Noelle couldn't quite put her finger on who she was. The little girl was facing the ground, watching her feet make little shuffles until she finally built up the courage to look up and pull out a stuffed cat from behind her back. "You're that girl from the festival!" Noelle realized.

"You gave me my kitty, I don't think you're a scary monster," the little girl reassured her. She gave Noelle a hug. "Don't listen to the mean people."

"Thank you, that means a lot." Noelle hugged her back. "I won't let these people scare me anymore." The girl's words were enough to validate her place here, washing away any doubts with a ray of sunshine. The little girl ran back to her parents soon after.

Jeremy disappeared and wandered off into the crowd, opting not to escalate the scene any further, grumbling that it wasn't worth his time. Everyone else followed suit and went off on their separate ways. The turmoil and clamor that filled the street was hushed as quickly as it started.

"Are you okay, Noelle? They didn't hurt you, did they?" Ben asked.

"No, I'm fine. They wouldn't be able to hurt me if they tried," Noelle spoke with confidence. "And...thank you for what you did, for standing up for me."

"Don't even mention it. And I believe you on that note," chuckled Aspen's father, "Jeremy's lucky I stopped him. Wouldn't want him to piss himself like he did in the war." He gestured everyone towards the direction of the burial grounds. "Alright, well, hopefully without any more interruption, let us be on our way."

Noelle had a feeling this would happen sooner or later; these people had hated Mogoniwais for decades now—and even more so about nine years ago when the war transpired—changing their beliefs wouldn't happen overnight. Though the little girl did give her hope that perhaps the people could in fact change one day.

Within ten minutes, they all arrived at the graveyard without any more interruption. Noelle could breathe a little easier now and hoped that the rest of the day would proceed without any other surprises.

Before they walked through the steel gates, Niko stopped Noelle prematurely. "I h-have something I need to tell you," he eyed Elliot as he spoke. "Preferably alone."

"Sure..." a confused Elliot responded, having not a clue of what his secret message was, "I'll meet you guys inside." Elliot and Aspen's father walked in, leaving the two of them behind.

"So what was it that you needed to tell me?" asked Noelle.

Niko averted his gaze. "I...I'm sorry."

"Why would you have to be sorry?"

"I'm the reason that Aspen is not with us today. It's...it's all my fault."

Noelle wasn't following along. "Of course it's not your fau—"

"It is!" Niko interrupted. He couldn't even raise his head to make eye contact with Noelle as the guilt weighed too heavily on him. "It is..." He brought out the box that he had clutched tightly since early this morning and handed it to her.

Noelle took the box. "Why are you giving this to me?"

Niko picked at his nails and twiddled his fingers, attempting to preoccupy himself so that he didn't have to look at her. "Because, Noelle...it is actually yours."

Noelle was now brimming with curiosity as she lifted the lid of the box and peered inside. To her astonishment, it was filled with envelopes. She dug her hand in the box. *There must be hundreds of letters inside...*

"Aspen *did* write to you. He wrote to you often...sometimes he'd even send you multiple letters in one week," Niko admitted.

Noelle grabbed a couple of letters and looked at the address, and sure enough, the letters were addressed to Willey. She lifted the letter and took a look at the sender; she'd recognized that messy handwriting anywhere—it belonged to Aspen. "I...I don't understand." She looked at Niko in confusion. "W-why do you have these?" Niko still couldn't look her in the eyes. He stood there motionless, not knowing what to say next. Noelle held the box with one hand and with her free hand gave him a shake on the shoulder. "Answer me, Niko! Why do you have these?" He slowly raised his head until they met each other's gaze. *I didn't even notice the heavy bags under his eyes this morning, it looks like he hadn't slept a wink,* Noelle thought after getting a closer look at him.

"I...I thought I was doing the right thing as his friend. Whenever he would send letters to you, I would stash them away. I never delivered them. I'm sorry, Noelle. I'm...I'm sorry." Niko's voice cracked, "I thought I was protecting him. I realize how wrong I was...how terribly, utterly wrong."

"Protecting him...from me?" Noelle asked. For just a moment, her heart throbbed with betrayal. Anger had taken over her, as she grabbed Niko by the collar of his shirt, hoisting him in the air, almost punching him in the face had she not been holding onto the box of letters. "So, all this time, you have been stealing our letters? How, Niko? How could you do this?"

"No...I...it wasn't like that, I just..." Niko stammered. "Back then, I thought that if he stayed near you, he'd get hurt." The guilt gnawed at him like a hungry dog on a bone. "If you had received all of his letters, then you wouldn't have gone after him. He would still be safe in school, and you'd be safe in Willey's house, no one would have gotten hurt, no one would have..." he tearfully muttered. As soon as she let go of his shirt, Niko dropped to the ground and buried his face in his hands. "I killed him. I killed my best friend."

Looking at Niko, she couldn't help but see herself in him. She, too, put the blame of his death on herself. Noelle knelt to the ground and put her hand on his shoulder. "It's not your fault." Niko's intentions hadn't been entirely malicious, and she knew that. Though she was upset by what he had done, Noelle knew the right thing to do for now is to let it go.

Niko looked up with tears rolling down his cheeks. "Why aren't you mad at me? I'm the reason that he's not here today! Yell at me! Curse at me! Hit me! Hit me already, will you?"

"You did it because you cared about him so much, right?" Noelle asked, trying to cheer him up. She wiped some of his tears off his cheek, "I don't blame you for what happened. You didn't kill him, Niko. I know that much is certain. Hatred towards my kind killed him. The general's thirst for power killed him. Besides, Aspen wouldn't want you to blame yourself for the rest of your life."

"I don't know if I'll ever be able to forgive myself," Niko said as he clutched his chest. "How could I go on living with this regret? I'll never be able to apologize to him."

Noelle hugged him. "I'm still here, and so are Elliot and Willey, and even Aspen's father. We can rely on one another when we're at our lowest, because that's what friends are for. Isn't that right?"

"I don't think I'll ever be able to get rid of this regret, not ever. But...I'll try to live on with it," Niko said while trying to calm himself. "T-thank you, Noelle...for forgiving me when I don't deserve it." Niko's face was puffy and his eyes red as he stood back up again. "Should we join the others?"

"You go on ahead first, I just need a minute to myself," Noelle told him as she went through the box of letters.

"R-right then...I'll see you there, okay?" He walked off through the steel gates, leaving Noelle alone with the box.

"He sure did write a lot," Noelle muttered to herself. Looking through the box, she noticed a peculiar envelope that was much larger than the rest. Noelle set the box down beside her, ripped open the envelope from the top, and started reading the letter.

Dear Noelle,

I hope you haven't gotten tired of my letters just yet. I haven't received a single letter, perhaps the faculty are throwing all mine away because they hate me or maybe something happened on your side. Whatever the reason, I'll still write to you, no matter what. School is terrible, just as usual, but I think the food is even worse. Once I get out of here, you have to make your beef stew again. I've been craving it so much, you have no idea. I hope you haven't been eating too many sweets. It's bad for your health, you know.

"He's the one that eats too many sweets, not me..." Noelle scoffed.

Lately, I've been sleeping in class. I try my hardest to stay awake but the teachers are just so boring.

She let out a small chuckle, "This is why you do poorly on your tests."

My father is going to visit me here in school in two months—maybe this will be my chance to convince him to let me come back home early. I know it's been a while, but I feel like we'll be able to be together soon. And then I'll take you away to a brand new world, a world much happier than you've ever experienced. So, because of that, I have something for you inside.

"Something inside?" Noelle hadn't even realized that he had stashed a small gift inside the envelope. She reached in and grabbed it. Upon realizing what it was, Noelle couldn't help but cover her mouth.

You'll have to be alone for just a little longer, and then I promise we will spend the rest of our lives together. I want you to stay with me till the end of the world. The stars have guided me to the lost you, and now you're found. We're found. I only hope that it will continue to shine a light just a tad bit longer, until we're in each other's arms again. It's a little crude, but I made it in school.

Noelle pulled out the round metal object and held it above her head. She could see the metal polishes Aspen had done by hand on the white and red painted surfaces. Taking a closer look was a date etched inside. It was Aspen's birthday, or also known as the date the two had met.

It's a ring. When you wear it, you always are reminded of how much I love you. I would have waited, but I just wanted to give it to you soonest.

She sniffled.

More than anything, I want you to be happy, Noelle. For that is my only wish in life, and that's all I'll ever ask for. If I know that you're happy, then nothing can make this smile on my face disappear. Nothing at all.

Even if I'm somewhere far, far away, promise me that you'll have enough happiness for the both of us. Okay?

"Okay..." Noelle softly whispered.

You don't have to answer now, but when I get back, Noelle...

She held the letter with trembling fingers, no longer able to shield away her crestfallen visage. Noelle read the last line of the letter over and over again, imagining how the words would sound in his voice:

Would you marry me?

Willey was heading into the memorial service in which he spotted Noelle at the front gate. "Hey, Noelle, what are you doing out —" but before finishing his sentence, he rushed over and knelt down towards her.

The tears came without warning and splashed onto the letter like drops of rain. "I p-promised that I'd b-be happy for Aspen's sake." No matter how hard Noelle tried to hold them in, the tears wouldn't stop flowing.

Willey put his arm on her shoulder. "It's okay, Noelle, just let it all out. Life can be beautiful and kind, but it is also quite cruel." Having experienced the pain of losing a loved one, he was well aware of how fortune and happiness and misfortune and sadness came and went as it pleased. "It's one of the worst feelings in the world, isn't it?"

"W-what is?" Noelle asked.

He patted her shoulder and looked up at the sky. "Meeting the right person at the wrong time."

"I-it is..."

Noelle continued to cry, feeling as if her body was completely expunged of water and resorted to using the blood that ran through her veins. For each tear that dropped, was also a small part of her soul that dropped down to the ground with it. *On another day, I promise I'll be happy for your sake, Aspen, and I'll live my life with my head raised high. I'll live a life filled with enough joy for the two of us. For you, who gave me another chance at life...I won't waste it. But not today.*

Just for today, let me have this moment of weakness. Noelle slipped the ring on her finger. *I don't care how long it will take. You're clumsy, so maybe we'll bump into each other, or maybe the stars will guide us to each other once more. I'll wait and wait and wait and wait for you again, until even a whole lifetime passes. I'll keep waiting and hoping that in the next lifetime, we'll meet...and eventually embrace once more.*

ABOUT THE AUTHOR

Alexander Chau is an emerging author who recently found his passion for crafting and writing stories. When Alexander is not writing, he is often traveling the world, watching movies, or cafe hopping. If you enjoyed Aspen and the Demon Princess, feel free to follow him as there will be many more stories to come.

www.ingramcontent.com/pod-product-compliance
Lightning Source LLC
Chambersburg PA
CBHW050739230626
47052CB00004BA/710